A CAINE & FERRARO MYSTERY ROMANCE

CHASING CAINE

JANET OPPEDISANO

Chasing Caine

ISBN Digital: 978-1-7778856-3-2
ISBN Paperback: 978-1-7778856-2-5

For everyone who believes
love is worth chasing

FREE NOVELLA

To instantly receive the free romantic suspense novella *The Phoenix Heist*, with cameos by Samantha and Antonio and introducing the Reynolds Recoveries heist crew, claim your copy at

https://janetoppedisano.com/ThePhoenixHeist

CHAPTER 1
ANTONIO

AUGUST 28, Pompeii Archaeological Park, Naples, Italy.
One day before the end of Burning Caine*...*

My phone was fortunate I was in the crowded laboratory building. Had I been alone, I would have smashed it against the wall, stomped on it, and called it the pezzo di merda it was.

"No luck?" My cousin Mario appeared at the door of the office I was using for my calls and leaned against the frame, casually folding his arms. Tall and muscular with dark hair and our grandmother's cheekbones, we were often told we looked eerily similar. He wore navy slacks and a primrose pink collared shirt under his lab jacket.

And he was too calm about the situation.

I'd arrived in Napoli three days ago and had spent most of my waking hours in Pompeii. Meeting the team my father and Mario had hired for my conservation project, inspecting the newly excavated Casa di Marte where we would work, and reacquainting myself with the city.

In July, I would have called this the perfect way to spend

the next four months. I would have been ecstatic about my father and cousin planning all this behind my back. And a critical piece of equipment missing from yesterday's delivery would have been little more than an inconvenience. I wouldn't have spent two hours on the phone trying to get a replacement. A delay would have extended my stay in this amazing city, a problem I'd gladly accept.

But in August, I met Samantha Caine and everything changed. My life was at home in Michigan with her, not here in Italia. How could I win her back from so far away?

I dropped the phone to the desk and dragged my hands through my hair. "Marone, none at all. I've been trying to pull every string attached to the Ferraro name, to no avail. A college in Paris has one, but they can't release it for a month. The best option was Delaware, who could do a week and a half."

"Roma?"

"Niente!" I picked the phone up again, just to wake the screen. On it, a photo of a newspaper clipping, of Samantha and me dancing together at a charity gala. She'd blushed through our dances, voice trembling, heart pounding as strong as mine. I could still smell her, remember the feel of her in my arms last Friday night at my parents' house.

But then she found the Chagall in their private gallery and realized I'd been lying to her almost since the day we met. We'd gone from such a high to such a low. To her never wanting to see me again.

Mario moved soundlessly, withdrawing the phone from my grip before I realized he'd crossed the room. "Stop staring at her photo. She doesn't have that modulator or gas or whatever—"

"You have not listened to a word I've said since I arrived." I snatched the phone from him, placing it facedown so Samantha couldn't look at me. "You were supposed to read my dissertation before we started. It's a specific lens for the laser, used to focus the—"

"That's more like my Antonio!" His irritating lip twitched and he flicked a hand toward the phone. "Stop your ridiculous pining for this woman. She turned you down—"

"Did not."

"—and we're going out to La Fiamma tonight. I have a few candidates to introduce you to." He bit his bottom lip and did a horrific version of the Cabbage Patch.

"I don't need another woman." My hand crept across the desk to rest on the phone, as though it brought me closer to her. I hadn't texted her since I left the States on Tuesday, praying she'd get in touch. My only response was three days of silence. Enough time had passed. I should call her again. "I can't give up on her, Mario. She's the one."

He sat on the edge of the desk and shook his head. "How did you get so stubborn?"

"Do you remember I told you about a girl from college—"

"You've told me about a *lot* of women, Antonio. College, graduate school, Italia, America, Francia—"

I shoved him off the desk and he laughed at me, practically inviting me to hit him. "Roman Art Girl. Do you remember me speaking of her?"

"Sì, this one, I do." He threw his hands wide as he said to the ceiling, "The magical creature who shares all your interests and passions. She who is as beautiful as the sunrise, whose voice—"

"Stop," I said, tossing a pen at him and trying not to laugh.

He grinned at me and sat back down on the edge of the desk.

"This—" I turned my phone over and woke the lock screen. "—is her."

He flipped the phone back down. "This is an obsession."

"No, Mario. Literally. It's her. And she's all those things, plus so much more. She's perfect for me." I let out a long sigh. She was so much more than I'd dreamed of all those years since we first met in college. There had to be something I could do to fix this rift between us.

A knock came at the open door.

Dr. Bianca Capasso stood there, fists shoved deep into the pockets of her lab coat. She was in her mid-thirties, average height and build, with shoulder-length light brown hair. Her glasses dangled on a beaded chain over her Park employee lanyard. "Ciao, Dr. Ferraro. Any word on the missing part?"

Her eyes flicked from Mario to me, to the desk and back up again. It would be a long four months working with her if she couldn't get her nerves under control.

I stood and slipped my phone into my pocket. "The delivery company is looking. If they can't find it within the next week, they'll deliver one from Delaware."

"You had an inventory list, didn't you?" she asked. "Who signed for the rest of it?"

"Océane." I shrugged.

Bianca frowned at the Parisian microbiologist's name— she shouldn't have been signing for deliveries. Unlike Mario and Bianca, who worked at the Pompeii Archaeological Park full-time, Océane was a PhD student, only joining us for the duration of my project. But she was cocky, and it hadn't surprised me.

"Is there any work we can do while we wait?" she asked, still hovering in the doorway.

"I want to say yes, but if the lens is more than a couple of weeks late, we'll end up stopping again. Perhaps we tell everyone they have a week off, then we can regroup?"

She nodded, muttering, "So strange."

"Strange?" Mario asked.

Bianca's lips tightened and she focused on Mario. "Did you hear about the pigment pots?"

The Park was the most-visited archaeological site in the world. Within its borders, it held an immense treasure of historic significance, including dozens of tiny terracotta pots filled with pigments of various colors. From the smallest, the size of an olive, up to the larger ones more akin to lemons, they normally sat nestled in foam-lined drawers in storage at the laboratory.

Mario and I looked at each other and shook our heads.

"Three of them have gone missing." She jostled her fingers around in her big pockets, as though she fiddled with something. Always anxious, this one. "First the lens for your laser, now these pots. Perhaps a curse has finally arrived for us."

Mario laughed. "Curses only strike the robbers who steal antiquities, not those of us who preserve and study them, Bianca. Everyone knows that."

Still, it was a strange coincidence.

A smile tugged at my lips. What would Samantha do if she were here? The night of the gala, she exposed a stolen painting at the charity auction. She was focused. Determined. Utterly brilliant. If she were here, she'd leap into action and begin an investigation. Perhaps that's what I should do.

Sì, that would be something I could text her about. Surely she wouldn't ignore me with information like that. What would I send her? In my head, I could imagine my fingers on my keyboard, *Ciao, bella. You won't believe what happened here. I tracked down—*

"Dr. Ferraro?"

I snapped my eyes up to Bianca, whose brows furrowed. I'd missed something. "Scusi. I was thinking about the lens and other options."

Mario nudged me. He likely guessed I was covering.

"I was saying... there's a mosaic in one of the other rooms in the Casa di Marte. It needs to be extracted and brought into the lab for some repairs. Did you... want to help me with that?"

I'd almost booked a flight to Michigan three times already since my arrival. Torn up my father's contract with the Park and just left. But my family name came with obligations. A broken heart didn't absolve me of my duty.

Working on the mosaic with Bianca would be the type of distraction I should jump at. But it was not what I wanted: To finish this project in Napoli and get back home. It was the only way I could follow through on my promise to Samantha that I would spend all the time in the world regaining her trust.

"Grazie, Bianca. It's a good offer, but I think I'll focus on tweaking the work schedule. If I can figure out how to shave a week or two off, we can finish when we were originally supposed to."

The only other choice was to track down the missing lens or find another one available somewhere, which was proving more difficult than expected. Letting fate derail this project was not an option.

Because I had to return to the States and win my woman back.

CHAPTER 2
SAMANTHA

As the captain announced our flight time remaining until Rome, the plane gave a bounce. I gripped the armrest and breathed through the turbulence.

It was five in the morning at home in Brenton, Michigan and I'd slept for maybe three hours in the last forty-eight.

Yesterday, I'd completed a spontaneous tour of my favorite places in New York City. That visit was supposed to sort my brain out and remind me that I was better off without Antonio Ferraro in my life. But it only jumbled things up further. I realized I didn't want to let him go, despite the secret he'd kept from me.

Now here I was on my way to Italy. Half the cells in my body were screaming for sleep, the other half were spinning around with such energy that my leg hadn't stopped twitching for two hours.

What was I going to say to Antonio when I got to his cousin's place? *Hi, sorry I was such a stubborn jerk* or *Surprise! I forgive you.*

Or maybe I could just be honest and tell him how much I

missed him. Missed his arms around me, his lips on mine, the way he called me 'bella.' Missed his bad jokes and his laughter and his never-ending questions.

I unfolded the letter he wrote before he left town, still clutched in my right hand, all rumpled and torn from when I'd first read it. Not like there was any need to look at it. I'd memorized everything Antonio had written. His apology for lying about the Chagall. Telling me he wanted a future for us.

The head of the woman next to me lolled to the side, then snapped up. She blinked at me rapidly, like I was responsible for waking her, and she jutted her chin toward the aisle.

I undid my seat belt and stepped out to let her pass, her stale breath overwhelming me. Tucking my nose against my shoulder, I inhaled the scent of my motorcycle jacket. What I needed was a fast ride down a long rural road. That would've been smarter than flying to New York, let alone to Italy.

No, Sam, it wouldn't have.

A young couple a few rows behind us caught my attention before I sat back down. He had dark hair and bronzed skin; she was blond with porcelain skin and freckles. Her head on his shoulder.

The last time I'd made this flight, I'd landed in Rome and driven to the town of Amelia. The idea was to help my boyfriend finish packing, ship his stuff off to Michigan, and we'd fly back together. A surprise. He was supposed to be excited.

An itch pricked at the back of my eyes, and I slipped into my seat, letting my head fall into my hands.

Vincenzo had lied the whole time. He hadn't packed a damn thing. Had a shiny new job and hadn't bothered to tell me. Didn't want to hurt me, he'd said. He just floated along, hoping I'd eventually tire of waiting and end things so he didn't have to.

I was so naïve back then. The delay with his passport. His visa. The job offer in Detroit he claimed fell through. His sick mother.

All lies.

Antonio had only told me one lie, but it was a big one. No, it was a small one that snowballed.

I'd brought a burned painting purportedly by Marc Chagall to him for authentication—for an insurance claim I was adjusting—and he knew from the get-go it was a fake. Instead of telling me, he pretended to go through all the steps of cleaning and testing it, dragging the process out for weeks. If he'd told me the truth that he knew where the real Chagall was on day one, I would have denied the claim and been done with it.

But then no one would have figured out that the house fire that destroyed the painting was arson, nor that it was covering up a murder. I wouldn't have made up with my estranged best friend. I wouldn't have fallen for the most remarkable man I'd ever met.

A hand brushed my arm, and a soft male voice said, "Stai bene? Are you alright?"

"I'm fine."

A flight attendant knelt next to me. "It's just a few bumps. Nothing to worry about."

Nodding, I straightened to give him a weak smile. Turbulence wasn't what had my stomach churning.

He patted my hand as my seat mate returned.

She was tall and slender, dressed in a navy suit that traveled surprisingly well. She carried a small Chanel bag under her arm and didn't seem the type who normally flew coach.

I stood again to let her by and cast a glance back at the couple. He was awake and turned to kiss her head. She cracked her eyes open and yawned. He smiled and they looked at each other in *that* way.

The way Antonio looked at me Friday night at his parents' house. Before I discovered the truth about the Chagall—that his parents owned the real one, purchased in a private sale, legal, but strictly confidential.

My gut twisted at the memory. I had to stop focusing on that and make this right. People made mistakes and deserved forgiveness. Both of us fell into that camp.

But what if he'd already moved on? Maybe I should email him first. I pulled out my phone as I sat, which opened on the email I'd been reading before takeoff, from Elliot Skinner, my old boss in the FBI Art Crimes Team.

My seat mate, who'd freshened her breath while she was gone, smiled at me. "Work or pleasure?"

Good question.

Elliot was arriving in Rome soon. Before I left New York, he'd emailed me about how I could help his team investigate an art smuggling ring. I'd wanted to be in the FBI since I was twelve. Had been for a short time, before I ran away from it. I could just stop in Rome, abandon the next leg to Naples, and not make a fool of myself falling at Antonio's feet.

But less than a week after I'd told Antonio I never wanted to see him again, the harsh truth had slammed into me. I wanted *him* more than anything.

"Vacation in Naples," I said. I was tired of running. Of the pain in my fingertips every time the possibility of being hurt came up. Of the gnawing in my stomach at the thought of Antonio being with anyone else.

To be with him, I'd have to stay in Brenton. To rejoin the FBI, I'd have to leave it.

Was what I had with Antonio enough to give up my dream? Or was he just another Vincenzo? Nothing more than pretty words and promises?

I was going to be sick.

"Will you be there long?" she asked.

Ten days would get me back home in time with a little buffer before my sister's next chemo. "Week and a half. You?"

"I'm headed to Rome for work."

"What do you do?"

"Tech security. Pretty boring stuff."

"No way," I chuckled. "I've got the market cornered on that. I'm an insurance adjuster."

She feigned a grimace and held out a hand. "Scarlett."

I shook her hand. "Sam. Good to meet you."

"You had a stranglehold on that piece of paper when we got on the flight." She gestured to Antonio's letter. "I'm guessing you're not just on vacation?"

"Perceptive." I loosened my grip but didn't tuck it away.

"Was it a fight with a man?"

Normally, my response would be to tell her to get lost. It was none of her business. But I was so tired. "Pretty much."

"Flying away from him or to him?" Scarlett flagged down a flight attendant and made a drinking gesture.

"Tech security *and* amateur psychiatrist?"

"Precisely." She smiled at the attendant who handed her a bottle of water. "Security's about trust, Sam. So are relationships."

I gave a long sigh. Antonio had broken my trust. No different from Vincenzo. Except after I left Amelia all those years ago, Vin hadn't bothered calling to explain, apologize, or make things better. We were just done.

Antonio? He'd called, texted, emailed so many times. His sister even told me how sorry he was. My family was happy he was gone, but I really wasn't. "To him."

"And the letter's..." She took a sip from her water. "An apology he sent you?"

I stared at the letter. This woman was reading me too easily.

"And you're pretty sure you want to forgive him, but something's holding you back." She gestured to my left hand. "I'm guessing whatever's on that phone?"

My gaze flicked from one to the other. Antonio versus the FBI. Boyfriend versus career. The possibility of a future and a family versus my childhood dream. I was a brave woman. I could stand up to my fears. "I need a nap."

"I've got a feeling that things are going to work out for you. No man who writes actual letters could resist a woman who flies across the Atlantic to make up with him."

"I hope so." I chuckled and slipped my phone back into the inside pocket of my jacket. Of course my choice was Antonio. Over the years, I'd worked on several art cases with Elliot. Most were insurance-based, plus a few investigations and provenance proofs.

And not a single one provided the same rush as being with Antonio. None of them made me want to slow down and stop running for more than a few days.

But if I was completely honest with myself, what I really wanted, deep down inside, was to have both.

CHAPTER 3
ANTONIO

THE BAREST HINT of chocolate danced over my tongue from the espresso. Coffee was always better at Mario's villa than anywhere else on the planet. Even at my condo, I hadn't come close this perfection.

It was Saturday morning—one week after my fight with Samantha.

I sat at the bistro table on the patio outside Mario's kitchen. Shadows danced around me as the sun fought with the grape vines covering the pergola. My head ached from the night before, having drank too much and stayed out too late. I flipped mindlessly from app to app on my phone.

As threatened, Mario had introduced me to several beautiful women at La Fiamma. But they all lacked something.

They were not Samantha.

A text popped up from my sister. *Papa was so proud! Fix it, stupid!*

A second message appeared with a link to YouTube.

"Good morning," came a cheery, distinctly feminine and English voice from the kitchen. I peered in through the open patio doors to see a woman in a short dress. Her red hair hung limp and she wore no makeup, looking rather washed out.

I gestured vaguely, no idea what her name was.

"Where's the... Nevermind, I found it!"

Most of me wanted to ignore Sofia's text, but it also piqued my curiosity. I tapped the link. The video was dated two days ago and its title read, 'FBI Press Conference: Public's help wanted in Lansing murder.' What was this?

The Brenton Police Chief introduced the press conference from a lectern, then handed it off to a tall Black woman with buzz-cut hair in a police uniform. Behind them, a blue curtain hung with the Brenton Police Department emblem and a large-screen television.

Officer Janelle Williams said, "Good morning. We are here to provide an update on the death of Robert Scott, who died in a fire at his residence on—"

The camera pulled back to show a line of people behind the officer, including... Samantha? I skipped ahead and ahead and ahead. What was Papa proud of? What was Samantha doing in the press conference?

The strange woman from the kitchen eased into a seat at the table with me, sighing as she took her first sip from the cup she'd poured for herself. "Antonio, right?"

Continuing to skip the video forward, I nodded absently to the woman, watching as the officer was replaced by a man with dark brown skin in a black suit. FBI Special Agent Elliot Skinner. I continued skipping forward while he spoke and images flashed on the television behind him. But when he looked to Samantha, who stepped out of the line and to the front, I slowed to regular speed.

She scanned the crowd, that same squared posture and

blush on her cheeks as the day in college I first spoke to her. "There was a particular painting that suffered serious damage in the fire covered by Foster Mutual. Through close work with the team from Ferraro's Fine Art Restoration and Conservation, we were able to identify that the painting was a forgery. The trail of evidence brought us to the eventual discovery of the arson. I can't say more than that, as it's an ongoing investigation. Direct any further questions to Special Agent Skinner or Officer Williams."

She gave a tight smile, the FBI agent nodded back at her, and she resumed her spot in the line behind him.

Next to Nathan Miller.

My hand gravitated toward my discolored cheek, to where Miller had punched me last Saturday night, before he whisked Samantha away from me.

He touched her back and leaned close, whispering something to her.

I shut the video off and dropped the phone to the table.

"That the one you were talking about all night?" asked the woman next to me, gesturing at my phone.

"Who are you?" I snapped, more irritated with seeing Nathan Miller touch Samantha than anything else.

"Bellissima!" called Mario from the kitchen. "There you are! Why did you leave the bed?"

"Needed coffee." She held up her cup. Of course. The woman Mario brought home from the club.

Mario joined us at the table on the patio, kissing her on the cheek as he sat. "Surely you have enough time for another round?"

"I wish." She—whatever her name was—bit her lip and gave him a regret-filled once-over. "But I need to go."

"My heart..." Mario pulled his chair closer to hers, running a finger up her arm, his voice oozing like warmed syrup. "It's breaking."

"Mine, too, but we'll get over it." She took a sip, then turned to me. "Where's Cindy? She told me she was going home with you."

I shook my head, the movement rattling about painfully. "Who's Cindy?"

She placed the cup on the table and stood. "Five foot six, brown hair, blue dress, all over you last night?"

Last night was still a blur, but no one was all over me nor did I bring anyone home. Scanning my memory for the women I'd met, I finally recalled her. "Sì, I remember. All we did was talk. She told me I was boring."

"You are." Mario laughed, standing with the woman and walking her to the door.

Perhaps showing Cindy photos of Samantha a dozen times was not what Mario had hoped I'd do, but I didn't care.

I turned the YouTube video on, backing up to when Samantha took the front. Everyone looked at her—the FBI agent, the female police officer, and Nathan Miller—in a way that seemed more familiar than professional courtesy.

"Five women, Antonio!" Mario said as he returned to the patio. "And you left them all at the club! You're going to ruin my reputation." He sat and pulled at my phone to see. "What's this?"

"Just watch." As it played again, my heart swelled. Samantha thanked our company. That must have been what Sofia referenced, what made Papa proud—her passion for solving art crimes, her knowledge of art history.

Mario asked, "Is that about the burned painting you worked on before you came here?"

"This—" I restarted and pointed at the screen. "—is my Samantha."

"That's her?" Mario's nose wrinkled. "Cindy was prettier."

My smile fell and I smacked him. "Listen to her words. So clever, so confident."

"Who's the handsome one she's smiling at on the end?"

I pointed to my cheek.

"That's the one she left you for?"

"She didn't leave me." I restarted her portion of the video once more and sighed. "I could fly home this afternoon—"

"Who's the one at the start?" Mario pulled the video back to the FBI agent.

"He's with the Art Crimes Division, they said." Was he involved because of the Chagall copy?

"Looks like he knows her."

"It does."

"You'd almost think," said Mario, leaving the table for the kitchen. "That she belongs up there with them."

I paused on her confident gaze at the start of the video, before the blush had started, before she spoke, and took a screenshot. My new lock screen image.

"That reminds me..." Mario returned to the patio with his own coffee. "Someone from the Carabinieri will be stopping by today."

"Why?"

"Bianca filed a report on the missing pigment pots." He shrugged. "They came by the lab yesterday after we left. She mentioned the missing lens, and they're going to look into that, too."

This was good news. Perhaps they could speed up the process. "I should fly to Delaware and help hurry whatever they're doing. That way, if the shipping company can't find the missing lens, I could still guarantee the project doesn't start too late."

Mario took a sip, eyebrow raising. "You don't find that strange?"

"That a branch of the Italian police would look more closely at anything with the Ferraro name on it?" I cocked my eyebrow back at him.

"Could your Uncle Giovanni be involved? Or Cristian?"

"Why would they bother with those pots? Or my equipment?"

He set his coffee down and clasped his hands. "Because that's what they do, is it not?"

I let out a long sigh. Memories of blood, tears, and anger flooding me. Despite the years I spent with my uncle and cousin, I only knew the portions of their business they'd let me see—primarily money-laundering and extortion—but I'd always suspected they trafficked in looted antiquities. "Possible."

"And knowing that..." He tapped my phone screen and shook his head at the photo. "Do you think a woman that at home at a police press conference—who appears to know not only the officer in charge, but the FBI agent—would be the right one for you?"

I started the video again. She scanned the crowd, the intelligence sparkling in her eyes. Was it my imagination, or was there pain? A pinch in the corners of her eyes when she said my company's name? Did she feel regret for what happened between us? Did she miss me even a fraction as much as I missed her?

"Mario..." I paused the video and looked him dead on. "There's not a doubt in my heart."

CHAPTER 4
ANTONIO

After the headache faded, I took an easel and fresh canvas to the terrace atop Mario's villa. His home was built on a hill, providing a stunning view in all directions. I could see Capri to the west, Vesuvio and Napoli to the north. The olive grove nearby, the bay, the boats, the red and pink potted flowers by the ancient green railing.

Painting usually calmed me and inspiration was all around. Yet I was frozen, the palette and brushes taunting me, rather than inviting me. Samantha was all I could think about. I'd watched the press conference at least a dozen times before Mario threatened to take my phone.

The confident, professional woman in the video was such a change from the one in my office last Monday. The disdain in her eyes that day had torn through me.

Had it only been five days since she told me her heart was as broken as mine? That her heart wept as mine did? The next day, I'd boarded a flight to Napoli, crushed under the weight of time. Four and a half months working in Pompeii, at my father's behest, and only after that could I return to the States and see Samantha again.

If she would see me. If she was still in Brenton and not half-way across the country chasing storms and fraudsters.

A car motor sounded three stories below on the small side street running alongside the villa. A car door slammed shut, then the gate to the courtyard creaked open.

"Buongiorno, bellissima," came Mario's voice.

Was his friend from last night back already?

"Is Antonio here?" said a female voice in English.

My chest tightened. My brain was so fixated on Samantha, I was hearing her voice.

"Antonio?" Mario scoffed, in his Italian accent so thick, even I recognized it. "He doesn't see the pretty tourists. But I do. I'm Mario, his far sexier cousin."

I picked up a tube of titanium white and put some on the palette. Perhaps I'd start with clouds. Mix with a blue, but which one? Or a green? Or I could paint the sea, like Capri, like Samantha's pale sea-green eyes.

Why had I lied to her? Because my father told me to keep his ownership of the real Chagall a secret, and I was not man enough to stand up to him.

'Work with the insurance adjuster,' he'd said. 'Find out who created the forgery, but don't tell her the truth.'

The logical parts of my brain told me it was not Papa's fault. And yet, I could barely speak with him on the phone. I'd lost her because of his demand for family loyalty.

"Un momento," said Mario. "I know this face. You are his Samantha?"

"I hope so."

My heart bounded into my throat, and I bolted to the terrace railing to look down. It was not my imagination.

It was Samantha.

She was here.

I raced to the stairs at the back of the terrace, knocking the table and my materials to the ground. What was she doing here? I charged through the door into the upper floor and recklessly took the flights two and three steps at a time.

At the bottom, I halted, sucking in steadying breaths and folding my arms to conceal their tremble. As I breathed, Mario continued talking.

"He has been very boring."

He had told me too many times to stop speaking about Samantha. I couldn't help myself. She was all I wanted. She was everything. My heart crashed against my chest. I could do this. I could face her.

Walking across the large terracotta tiles of the entryway, I stopped before crossing the threshold. "Mario, leave her alone."

He grinned and winked at her before heading inside.

She was as breathtaking as always, in jeans and a tank top, wearing her leather jacket and motorcycle boots. Why was she dressed like this? It must have been stifling under the late summer Neapolitan sun. Her caramel-colored hair was confined to a long braid and dark circles clung under her eyes.

A lump lodged in my throat. "What are you doing here?"

Her jaw was tense, just as it had been the last time I saw her. "You remember when you asked what I'd do if I knew I would die the next day? And you told me how sad my answer was?"

The lump in my throat grew larger, accompanied by a pit

in my stomach. She'd told me she would fly to New York City and spend the time alone. Why was she asking this? "Sì."

Her chin was up, voice defiant. "I had to prove you wrong, prove I was right about everything. I was better off by myself, without you."

The pit in my stomach widened. If she didn't want to be with me, why come all this way? I'd gotten my hopes up too high in the States, when I was carrying the time bomb inside of me that ruined it all. "So, you come here to break my heart all over again?"

"You gave me fourteen hours. So, I got on my bike Friday morning, drove to Detroit, and caught the first plane to New York. I did everything I told you I would." Her words were sharp, every syllable an attack. "I walked across the Brooklyn Bridge, went to the top of the Empire State Building, ate pizza in Times Square, and went to the Cloisters. And it was peaceful and beautiful, exactly like I said it would be."

This was not a second chance. This was pushing the knife in deeper and twisting it. I sighed and hung my head, turning back into the villa. She was acting petty, something I'd never expected from her. I'd beaten myself up enough times over what I'd done. There was no need to hear it from her.

"But." Her voice broke, freezing me in place. "All I could think about was that you weren't there with me. Holding my hand, making me laugh, asking me a million questions."

I turned to face her, unable to uncross my arms. Her eyes glistened. Those captivating eyes I saw in my dreams every night. Was this a second chance?

"The whole thing took twelve hours." She flashed her watch at me. "I had two left, Antonio. Then Sofia sent me your address. I went back to the airport and paid a ridiculous amount of money to get on a plane to come here. Because I want to spend those two hours with you. I don't want to be anywhere else in the world, unless you're there with me."

My arms dropped as her tears began. When I saw her in my dreams, she reminded me I wanted a woman who would choose to spend her last hours with me. But Samantha never talked this much, especially about her feelings. If I were awake and this was really her, she would just be staring at me, as though hoping her words would appear magically in my brain.

And yet, her tears flowed freely. "I want you to forgive me for being so stubborn that I couldn't forgive you. I couldn't believe someone as miraculous as you would want me. I was scared to fall for you, but now, I'm terrified I've lost you. I don't care if you tell me to get back on a plane after those two hours are up, I just want to be with you right now."

Dream or not, it didn't matter. I would accept it for one night, hold her and wake alone in the morning. I hurried to her side and took her hand in mine. Touching her again, the strong yet soft hand, sent goosebumps up my arms and legs.

"I don't want your heart to weep anymore," she choked out.

I lifted the hand to my lips and kissed it gently. Her leather jacket creaked, its scent mixing with the citrus aroma I knew as hers. "You have come back to me. What can my heart do now but sing with joy?"

"I want this to work, Antonio. More than anything I've ever wanted."

"But how?" I pressed my forehead to hers and wiped her tears with my thumbs. "You'll be gone three months after I get home."

She dropped her backpack and slid her arms around me. "I

started looking at apartment websites when I was at the airport."

I took in a shaky breath, the pit in my stomach closing in an instant, a vibrating energy building where the hole had been. "You're staying in Brenton? To be with me?"

As she nodded, I pulled her closer, holding her tight. She nestled her face against my neck and I pressed my cheek to hers. This was where I was meant to be. With my arms around her.

"Again, I'm a lucky man." I leaned back to look at her, brushing my knuckles along her cheek, blinking away the tears clouding my vision. My chest swelled and everything faded away beyond this wonderful woman. Words I'd felt for so long tumbled out. "Oh, Samantha, I love you."

She squeezed her eyes shut and bowed her head. This was more like her. Quiet when the words were important.

I put a hand under her chin, tilting her face up, afraid of her answer. "Do you love me?"

"I don't know." Her voice quavered. "But I do know this is the first time I've ever run toward something that could hurt so much."

She was not ready. But she was here. She was making plans to stay in Brenton. To be with me when I finished this project.

I would give her all the time she needed. "I swear, on my life, I'll never hurt you again."

Taking her face in my hands, I poured every ounce of tenderness and devotion in my heart into the most perfect kiss. A kiss which showed her I loved her. Told her I wanted forever with her. She pulled herself closer to me, our bodies fitting together perfectly. The sorrow of the last week faded, replaced by the burning desire we'd shared on the beach.

"There is only one problem left, bella." I grinned as I picked her up and she wrapped her legs around me. "I need far more than two hours to make love to you properly."

She kissed me again and laughed as she brushed away her tears. "I have a week and a half. Is that enough?"

"That's not much time. We must get started right away."

I sealed my mouth to hers and carried her inside, ready for my ten-day campaign to win her back for good.

CHAPTER 5
SAMANTHA

ANTONIO LED me into an expansive corner bedroom on the third floor, windows open to the bay on one side and a private balcony on another. As he closed the windows, drawing their white linen curtains, I stepped onto the balcony to see the view.

Being in Italy, let alone Naples, had barely registered on the drive from the airport. All I could think about was Antonio and what I was going to say.

But I did it. I told him everything—even more than I'd planned.

Now I could marvel over where I stood. The semi-circular Bay of Naples cut into the bustling city, with its rolling hills, the still-active volcano, and a million cultural treasures. With the villa built so high up, I could see down the rocky shore of the Sorrento Peninsula, maybe even to the island of Capri, but I couldn't tell for sure. The spicy scent of the nearby olive grove was strong on the gentle breeze.

I gripped the warm metal railing and breathed deeply. I'd said everything I needed to say. He was happy. I was happy.

I was, right? Then why were my fingertips still aching with pins and needles?

Music began in the room, soft, sensual.

Rubbing my fingers on the railing helped, but the knot in my stomach tightened. Thousands of dollars on airfare for two hours with Dr. Antonio Ferraro. Art conservator. Flirt. Rich, brilliant, and gorgeous. What was I thinking?

The air grew thick behind me, and his hands slid around my waist. His familiar scent of amber and vanilla replaced the olive grove as he pulled me close and kissed my neck.

"Would you like to stay out here and enjoy the view?" The sound jostled inside me, vibrating through every cell as his lips crept up to my earlobe.

I turned to face him and wrapped my arms around his neck, flexing my fingers to get the feeling back. The last time I'd seen him, I'd broken his heart and pushed him away. After he'd violated my trust.

Now, I'd flown five thousand miles on a whim to be with this man. To be in this moment. And he welcomed me without hesitation.

"No," I whispered.

He released his hold and took my hands, walking backward to lead me into the room, like I was a skittish animal that might bolt if he moved too fast. He paused to close the balcony doors and their curtains. We passed a cream upholstered couch and his dark-wood desk, stopping next to the enormous bed with its cherrywood frame and light blue sheets.

He slid off my leather jacket, fingers brushing my upper arms, along their length, to my forearms. When the jacket fell to the floor, he pulled my hands to his lips. Goosebumps crept up my arms and across my chest as I gazed into his big brown eyes. Those eyes I hadn't been able to put out of my mind since the night we met and he'd cheered me up after a horrible week.

I clenched his hands. This was the right choice. The only choice.

"You have no idea how happy you've made me." He placed my arms around his neck and slid his around me. His solid build surrounded me, a surprising comfort. "I've waited so long for you, Samantha."

Someone who dated a different woman every month—a stable of women who called themselves the Calendar Club—wasn't exactly waiting for anyone.

"I know this look." He shook his head and leaned in, touching his lips to mine gently. "I've been searching for the right woman, not playing around, remember?"

I knew this. That's why I changed my mind and flew to Naples. But still, the gravity of this choice felt like a boulder crushing my lungs.

"No more running." He pulled the hem of my tank top from my pants and slipped his fingers underneath, easing it off. His large hands moved up either side of my body, a tingle trailing in their wake. Along my rib cage. Across my bra.

My arms lifted for him to remove it.

"Be here with me, bella."

I moistened my lips as he threw my shirt over his shoulder.

He ran a thumb along the fabric of my bra and deftly popped the hook at my back. The fabric released and I looked down. I'd shaped my body for rock climbing, self-defense, and a career in the FBI. It wasn't curvy like the women in the Calendar Club, the type of women Antonio normally dated.

He pulled the bra off and I wrapped my arms around my front. What was wrong with me? The last time we'd almost made love, I'd been nervous, but nothing like this. Hell, I'd been the one who planned it.

A deep rumble sounded in his chest as he unfolded my arms and took my breasts in his hands. A cascade of energy began flowing out from my core. Need. Hunger. Desire.

He kissed the mounds which formed when he squeezed them, and my inner muscles clenched.

"Perfetto," he growled, his breath shallow.

I blinked slowly, the devilish smirk on his perfect lips and the growing bulge pressing against me making it clear. He liked what he saw. A lot.

"Your body is the most magnificent thing I've ever seen." He pulled me against him, the skin of my chest touching his for the first time. He was warm and smooth, solid and even more overwhelming half naked than fully clothed.

We kissed again, falling into a bubble like the one we shared at the charity gala, everything else a blur outside of his body and mine. Had it only been two weeks since that night?

The boulder shifted, some of the weight falling away, and my breasts heaved, swelling against his pecs. This was going to be more than just two hours of heaven.

"I—I'm wearing more clothes than you." I separated from him, hesitant, and sat on the bed. It was thick with a luxurious pillow top. I'd sleep well in this bed. Although from the look of him and the way I was feeling, I probably wouldn't sleep much.

I lifted one boot to the opposite knee, but before I could unlace it, he placed it between his legs, undoing the laces for me. As I leaned back on my elbows, his eyes locked on mine, full of that same innuendo as when he'd opened the cornetto box for me at his office four weeks ago. He'd been thinking about undressing me since that day, hadn't he?

One boot, two boots. He let them fall to the floor, a gentle thud accompanying each, then he took care of my socks.

"I think we're even now." He came to the edge of the bed and placed one knee next to me, leaning in close.

"Not yet." I bit my bottom lip to stop it from trembling. Antonio was a man who joked his way through everything. A little play would hopefully be what he liked. "You're only wearing one layer."

He straightened with a smirk and inched down the lounge pants to show me bare skin underneath. He knelt on the floor between my legs and placed his hands under my knees, pulling me to its edge. My arms gave out and I fell to the bed with the sudden movement. We both laughed, carving off a sliver more of my anxiety.

I lifted on one elbow, but he kissed my abdomen, his tongue tracing my navel. I lay back, sipping slow breaths to calm myself, but my nerve endings were already on fire. He undid my jeans, pulled them over my ass and off, holding them as he straightened. He stepped away, raking his eyes over my near-naked body.

"Now we're even." He held my pants while he stared at me, not moving one muscle of his awe-inspiring body.

Fighting off the idea of ripping the pants off him and slamming him into the bed, I drank him in. He stood just over six feet, broad shoulders and chest, perfectly sculpted torso and arms. Chiseled cheekbones and sharp jaw, constantly smirking lips, and those eyes I couldn't help but get lost in. Deep brown with flecks of gold that danced in the right light.

And then there was the dark wavy hair, just long enough on top to run my fingers through. I would have been happy to stare at him for two hours.

I crawled backward on the bed, hoping he would pounce. Maybe just staring for two hours would be a bad idea. "What now?"

He shook his head slowly, exhaling through pursed lips. "So beautiful." He let my pants fall to the floor and covered his heart.

The feeling had returned to my fingers, but they continued to tremble. I was a grown woman. I'd had sex plenty of times. Just not with someone like him. Someone with whom it mattered on a deeper level. It wasn't just going to be sex.

I lay down and bridged, sliding my underwear off while he watched, then sat up. My heart was beating so fast, I could barely control my movements. I threw the underwear toward the spot the rest of my clothes had fallen, but he snatched them out of the air. With a wink, he held them to his nose and inhaled before tossing them over his shoulder.

Oh, god. All the little muscles inside me clenched again, as well as several of the larger ones. I removed the tie on my hair and loosened the braid, running my fingers through until it was all free. His gaze traversed my body, his cheeks flushing and cock tenting his pants.

"Now the only thing left..." He eased his lounge pants down, revealing a patch of dark hair, gradually sliding the pants along his swollen length. Once his cock was free, he let the pants fall to the floor and stepped out of them, stroking himself slowly. "...is to decide which part of you should I taste first?"

I sucked in a shaky, excited breath at the sight of him—and the realization of what was finally about to happen. "Whichever part you want."

"Perhaps I should start with your forehead…" He put a knee on the bed, then the other. It angled under his greater weight and he crept closer. "…and work my way down?"

"That sounds good."

"Or…" Jesus, he was moving so slowly. "…start from the bottom?"

I swallowed hard, difficult with so little moisture in my mouth. When I headed toward him, he grinned and stopped, shaking his head.

"Make me a promise, bella." He could have asked me to steal the Mona Lisa at that moment, and I likely would have agreed.

"Anything."

As he reached me, I kneeled flush against him, our bodies touching—chests, legs, groins—sending a thousand jolts through me.

"If this is a dream, promise not to wake me." He ran a hand through my hair, settling it behind my neck, and inhaled deeply. "I've always thought you smelled of Napoli. Like citrus on a summer breeze. The air could be playing tricks on me."

"The air here smells more like olives."

He frowned at me, and I laughed at his feigned irritation.

My arms wrapped around his back, tracing the shape of the muscles lining his spine. "Only if you promise not to wake me, either."

CHAPTER 6
ANTONIO

SHE TILTED her face up to mine, and I kissed her. Soft lips and eager tongue. Our mouths paused on each other as we moaned together and she pressed herself against me harder.

I broke from the kiss, unable to speak above a low rumble. "Where did we leave off?"

Her brows furrowed. "At the beach?" She smiled, easing into the moment, and lay back on the bed. Knees up, her hands slid along the sheets to her head. "I was here."

Her body was long. Lean. A body worthy of being commemorated in marble. She clenched her thighs, rubbing them against each other, building my need for her heat.

My cock, full and ready, begged to show her how much she meant to me. "How would you feel if you traveled all this way and saw nothing beside this room?"

"Not going to happen. You promised me a tour of Pompeii." Biting her lip, she sat up to grab me.

But I nudged her back down again. "You said you'd rather go with a friend than me."

"Tomorrow." She narrowed her eyes playfully. "Maybe we'll be friends by then."

I grinned and crawled to her feet. Picking one up, I kissed each of her toes. "So I must work hard at becoming your frien—"

A knock came at the door and my heart jumped. Samantha's face snapped toward the noise, but I dragged my tongue up the side of her calf and her attention returned to me.

"Ignore it, bella." I pressed kisses along her shin, up to her knee, doing my best to follow my own advice.

The knock came again, more insistent, accompanied by Mario's voice. "Antonio?"

I held my lips against the base of her thigh, imagining my hands around Mario's throat. Our moment was ruined. Again.

"Antonio, I need you out here." The knock came harder.

Samantha was as tense as she normally was. "I think you should answer that."

I crawled up her body, hovering over her as the knock came again. "Don't go anywhere."

"Hurry," she said, a twinkle in her eye. "Your two hours are ticking down."

With a quick kiss, I slid from the bed, pulled my lounge pants back on, and stalked to the door. I whipped it open only wide enough for my face and gave Mario my lowest growl. "What?"

He shrugged, palms up in apology. "I thought you would have been sweet-talking her for at least a few minutes before you—"

"Enough! What's so important?"

"The officer's downstairs."

"Tell them to wait." I pushed back from the door and began to close it, but Mario inserted his foot.

"The officer won't wait—" He gestured toward the door, likely aiming for the bed. "—*that* long."

I turned to look at her, lying with a sheet pulled up strategically on the bed. She'd rolled over to her side, head propped up, emphasizing her narrow waist and gentle hips. Marone, that woman was gorgeous.

"He said he has a few questions," said Mario. "No more than half an hour."

Samantha bit down on her lip, her jaw quivering as she suppressed a yawn. We'd both sleep well tonight. Eventually.

I turned back to my infuriating cousin with a curt nod. "Fine, I'll be right down."

He stifled a laugh. "To the kitchen?"

"Sì, to the kitchen." I shoved him before closing the door.

"Everything alright?" asked Samantha. "Is this bad timing?"

"I have something to deal with." I crossed to my dresser and pulled out a T-shirt and some lounge shorts. "Put these on. Go out and enjoy the view."

She sat up and accepted the clothes, pulling only the T-shirt on. It was an old cotton band shirt from some friends, washed so many times it was the softest thing I owned. Navy blue with gold lettering across it.

"You look beautiful in that."

Her eyes reached for the sky, as they so often did. "How long will you be?"

"I'm hoping for five minutes, but more likely twenty or

thirty." I put a knee on the edge of the bed and pulled her face to mine for one more lingering kiss. My blood traveled lower and I eased away. "Keep the timer on your watch paused. I want every second I can get."

She blinked slowly. "I'll be waiting."

I'D PULLED a white polo shirt over top the dark gray lounge pants, as formal as I would be at this moment. A matter of hours ago, I'd sat outside with Mario, thinking how lucky I was that the Carabinieri would be investigating. Now? I couldn't get him out of here fast enough. The woman of my dreams was waiting for me in bed, and I had to answer questions for an investigation that wasn't nearly as high of a priority to me as it was yesterday.

As I entered the kitchen, Mario sat at the dining table with the young officer, a man with dark hair and eyes, a whisper of a beard on his chin. He wore the light blue summer uniform with a white belt across his chest, peak cap on the table. Each had a coffee in front of him.

"Dr. Antonio Ferraro." I thrust my hand out to shake. "I trust this won't take long?"

"Carabiniere Fredo De Rosa." He stood and took my hand. "And no, it won't."

I joined them at the table and Mario pointed to his coffee, offering one to me, but I shook my head. "What can I do for you?"

The officer flipped open the notepad in front of him and clicked his pen. "I spoke with an archaeologist at the Pompeii Archaeological Park yesterday who explained that three pigment pot relics had been stolen. She also advised me that a highly valuable piece of equipment vanished at the same time."

"Not really," I said. "I wouldn't call it *highly valuable,* nor did it vanish. It went missing in transport and the shipping company is trying to track it down."

He nodded, making some notes. "The precise value? Street value, perhaps?"

I shrugged, looking at Mario, who did the same. "That information would be on record at the lab. I don't have it here."

Mario said, "Neither do I."

De Rosa continued. "We just got word that one of the pots—with a blue pigment in it—was recovered in Rome only hours ago."

"Really? Only one? Were they split up for transport?" Or perhaps the theft was by more than one party? No, that would be too coincidental.

"Good question." De Rosa made another note. "You're familiar with how things move secretly around the country?"

What kind of question was that? Was this about my Uncle Giovanni or my cousin Cristian? "I'm familiar with mathematics. Three pots were stolen and one was recovered. That means there are still two left, so they were not togeth—"

He raised a hand to cut me off. "No offense intended. We need to cover all angles."

"You think someone from the lab took the pots?" Mario asked.

"My first assumption was that someone simply misplaced them. Small items like that are easy to lose, even if there's a good inventory system. It made more sense. But with the discovery in Rome—that changes things." He gestured toward Mario and then me with his pen. "They were last accounted for on Thursday. Can you two give me a summary of your activities since that day?"

We reviewed for him, a boring list consisting primarily of work, food, and sleep. Visits to the Casa di Marte, time in the lab. Our chaotic visit to the club. Breakfast. He took notes as we spoke, interrupting only for clarification on minor points and contact information for the woman Mario had brought home—which Mario didn't have.

"I interviewed everyone at the lab yesterday." Skimming his pages, De Rosa nodded to himself. "That just leaves Océane Monet and Thomas Grange for me to speak with."

"They may be out of town," I said. "With the lens—the missing equipment—delayed, I told them to take a week to explore. They're both from outside Italia, so I thought they might enjoy their extra time."

The officer's head cocked. "When did you tell them that?"

"Yesterday."

De Rosa was slow to return to his notebook.

So slow I could almost hear the dominoes falling in his brain. If either Océane or Thomas were behind the theft of the pigment pots, they would have had ample time to get to Roma. "You said one of the pots was recovered. Was it just the pot? Or was there a courier or..."

"Another interesting question." Now he made several notes while Mario and I glanced at each other.

Mario said, "Neither of them would—"

De Rosa held up a hand. "Grazie mille, gentlemen. I'll be in touch if I have more questions."

"And my missing lens? Are you going to pursue that?"

This was supposed to be the benefit of the police investigating. It would hurry the shipping company in their search.

"Nothing I can do if it's simply a delayed shipment." De Rosa flipped open his notebook and clicked his pen. "Unless you think the delivery company may have stolen it? Or it was actually delivered to the Park but vanished before you could verify? Perhaps it's more valuable than you were suggesting?"

No. I wanted to speed up its delivery so I could finish the project in Pompeii sooner and get back to Samantha. But she was in Naples now. And we'd postponed the project because the piece was missing.

A smile broke deep inside me, warming my chest. The missing lens was now a blessing. I had time to spend with Samantha before I started work.

Mario began, "It would be helpful if you could—"

I cut him off. "You're right. I'll call the delivery company again and apply pressure."

De Rosa took a sip of his coffee and stood, nodding to us both. "If there's anything else you think of, I work at the office attached to the Park. You can contact me there."

We saw him to the door, shook hands, and he left.

I turned to Mario. "Why would Bianca tell him the lens was valuable and imply someone stole it?"

"You know her." He took a sip of the coffee he'd brought with him, a faint scowl on his lips. "So dramatic all the time."

"And other than the question about knowing how things were transported, not even an implication about my family."

"That was surprising," said Mario. "I expected that was why he was here."

We walked from the front door to the base of the stairs. What a turn the day had taken.

"Part of me wants to call Cristian to find out if they're involved. But—"

Mario rolled his eyes theatrically. "But I'm guessing you have a naked—or close to it—woman upstairs who should be your priority?"

Lightness surged through my chest and I let out a small laugh. "I can't believe she's here."

"Go tell her that instead of me."

Any concern over my visit with Carabiniere De Rosa faded as I climbed the stairs, replaced by the prospect of hours with Samantha. I knocked quietly when I arrived at my room and opened the door.

She was still in the bed, on her side. But under the sheets, facing away. And she didn't move when I came in. No doubt sleep had overcome her. A nap was likely a good idea to ensure she was prepared for everything I had in store.

I stripped off my shirt and pants, sliding in next to her. Not stopping until my cock pressed against... against the shorts I'd given her.

"Bella," I whispered in her ear, wrapping an arm around her waist, snaking my hand up to cup one breast. "I'm back."

She didn't move, other than the gentle rise and fall of her breathing.

"Samantha?" I said, a little louder.

Nothing.

I pushed up to look down on her face, at the dark circles under her eyes. She was so peaceful, so calm. So unlike the intense woman I knew.

If she'd been sleeping even half as poorly as I had since we broke up, she must have been exhausted, let alone from the cross-Atlantic flight. Much of my body told me to wake her and prove my love, but my brain knew better. Proving my love was letting her sleep. Wrapping my arms around her and just being next to her would have to be enough until she woke.

I lay my head on the pillow behind her and nestled close. I'd waited eleven years for this woman. I could wait a few hours more.

CHAPTER 7
SAMANTHA

I STEPPED TENTATIVELY into the kitchen on the main floor, *Walk of Shame* written all over me, despite not having actually taken that walk. I'd woken up with Antonio's arm around me and snuck out of bed before he woke up in search of coffee. The T-shirt he gave me yesterday fell to my thighs and I'd had to tighten the drawstring of the lounge shorts within an inch of their life.

For how large the villa was, the kitchen was relatively simple. Terracotta floor tiles, an L-shaped wooden counter over white cupboards, open shelves with dishes above. The ancient black stove and marble sink contrasted with a stainless dishwasher and refrigerator. At the end of the counter, open doors led to a pergola-covered garden with a bistro table and metal chairs.

As if this weren't awkward enough, Antonio's cousin was at a rough-hewn dining table next to the garden doors, having breakfast. I made a quick turn before he saw me.

"Samantha! Come va, bellissima!" His voice was loud and full of joy. So much for going unnoticed. Did he know what happened the night before? When had Antonio come back from whatever he'd needed to take care of?

When I turned, Mario was right there, grabbing me by the shoulders and giving me two enthusiastic cheek kisses.

"Come! Sit! Would you like cappuccino?" He walked to the counter before I responded, shooting a wink over his shoulder. "I hear it's your preference." When he spoke English, his accent was far thicker than Antonio's and his words were stilted.

I sank into a chair diagonal to Mario's seat, glancing out at the table in the garden. "I speak Italian, if that's easier for you."

"No, no." He waved the offer away. "I need to practice English for the tourists." He sat, placing the cappuccino and a cornetto in front of me.

Two of my favorites. "How'd you know?"

He took a sip from his small espresso cup, leaning back in the chair. "My cousin tells me everything, so I know a lot about you. I pray, now that you're here, he'll speak of something else?" He gave an exaggerated eye roll.

I savored the cappuccino. With hints of chocolate and honey, it was easily the most delicious coffee I'd ever had. A breeze drifted in through the garden doors, and I inhaled the scent of the sea and the olive grove nearby, some sort of flowers mingling with it.

"You are quite pretty, you know, even in his clothes. He tells me you're intelligent as well."

"Um, thanks." I turned around, hoping to see Antonio appear so he could rescue me from the awkwardness of the moment.

"You work for an insurance company, sì?" He bit into his pastry, still smiling. Maybe I was the only one feeling awkward.

I took a deep breath. If I was going to stay with them for a week and a half, I'd have to talk to his cousin eventually. This was probably a good time to try. "Yeah, that's how we met. He repaired a painting for one of my clients."

"I told him he should do something different. Restoration is all old men, I said." He winked. "Looks like I'm wrong!" His gaze rose at the sound of footsteps behind me.

Antonio's muscular arms slid around my shoulders, and he kissed my neck. "Mario, leave my girlfriend alone." His deep voice vibrated inside me, suffusing me with a warmth that soothed my nerves.

Girlfriend. We were already back to that. Despite the disappointment he likely felt over last night.

I smiled after him as he crossed to the counter with the espresso maker.

"Look at that smile." Mario nudged my leg with his. "Antonio, I think this one likes you! Perhaps she's not as intelligent as you said?"

"Quiet, Mario."

I chuckled and picked up the cornetto, splitting it in half, a rich, dark brown filling oozing out. "Mmm, chocolate hazelnut."

"Antonio used to prefer lemon custard." Mario raised an eyebrow at me and took another sip. "But this is all he eats now."

"Samantha has good taste."

Mario nudged my leg again. "Except in men!"

Shaking his head with a grin, Antonio sat, placing his coffee on the table. He moved his chair closer to mine and took one of my hands, intertwining our fingers. Butterflies swirled around my stomach. Maybe he wasn't upset over last night after all.

I took another sip of the cappuccino, barely able to look at the sexy man next to me. "I think I have pretty good taste."

Antonio lifted our hands to his mouth and kissed the back of mine, smiling. "Sì, you taste marvelous." He winked at me, and I spluttered, almost spitting out my drink.

Mario rocked back, laughing. This was going to be an exceptionally long ten days. He clapped his hands together. "Not to spoil the mood, but when are we leaving?"

"We?" I looked from him to Antonio.

"Samantha and I need to do some shopping first." Antonio took a bite of his pastry.

"I hate shopping."

He looked me up and down, pursing his lips. "We're going to Pompeii today. You can't wear your jeans and motorcycle boots, nor can you wear my clothes."

I opened my mouth to protest, but stopped. He had me there. Thursday evening, I'd thrown one change of clothes and my passport into a backpack for an overnight visit to New York City. Then I'd gotten it in my head to fly to Naples with only that backpack. Southern Italy was scorching in summer, so I needed lighter clothes and walking shoes.

"Bella, we can pick up enough for today in Sorrento and head to the Park after that. Tomorrow, we can spend the day shopping in Napoli. Sound good?"

"Don't you have to work tomorrow?"

He squeezed my hand, leaning over to kiss my cheek.

Mario said, "Some of the equipment has not been delivered yet."

My head snapped toward him. "Really?"

Antonio made a low rumbling noise, but was smiling by the time I turned back to him. "My goal upon arriving had been to hurry the project along so I could see you again. And now with this missing equipment, we don't expect to start for at least another week." He nudged my shoulder with his and waggled his eyebrows. "But here you are, and I'm available to do your bidding."

My heart sank into my stomach. Memories of Vincenzo flooded over me. Waiting for him to join me in the States. A string of postponements and *one more month* promises catching in my throat. I couldn't go through that again. "That means you'll be delayed coming back to Michigan?"

"Worry about that later, bella." He brushed light fingers across my cheek, voice soft. "Today, we worry about essentials and Pompeii. Tomorrow, shopping in Napoli. After that, who knows? But trust me—we will have a wonderful holiday together."

"I mentioned I hate shopping, right?"

He took another sip of his coffee and looked at Mario. Eyebrows rose, lips twitched, and they nodded. They communicated in some unspoken cousin language and ended with a shared smile.

Looking from one to the other, their two faces disturbingly similar, I asked, "What?"

"Nothing," said Antonio. "You and I'll go to Sorrento, do what we need, and come back here. Mario will join us for the trip to Pompeii."

I squeezed his hand. "Join us?"

"You're in luck, Samantha!" Mario winked at me.

"Stop winking at my girlfriend, or we shall have words."

Antonio chuckled, releasing my fingers and sliding his hand onto my bare thigh, under the shorts.

Pompeii slipped lower on my priority list as the heat pooled in my core.

Antonio said, "Mario's an archaeologist at Pompeii and sometimes gives tours on the weekends. I know the site well, but he's a better guide."

Mario leaned closer to the table, speaking in a whisper. "And I'll be his boss while he's here."

Antonio nudged him with a foot, while continuing to rub the inside of my leg, creeping higher with each stroke. "You will act as a consultant and learn from me, cugino."

I put a hand to my lips to hide my hitching breaths.

"And reporting back to the Board!" retorted Mario.

"But I'll be—" Antonio's hand made it as far as my underwear.

"Okay!" I shot out of my seat and stepped away from his temptations. Number one on my bucket list was a couple hours away and it would take hours to see the site. The stubborn throbbing between my thighs would not help with that. "When do we leave?"

They furrowed their brows at each other.

Antonio held his small cup to me. "Let me finish this. Then we can shower and go?"

"Okay, I'll shower first."

He shook his head. "Not what I meant."

Mario grinned at me, likely at the blush I could feel sneaking up my cheeks.

"But it's what *I* meant." I turned and hurried toward the staircase, which wound up around a small central elevator.

"You're right, she's shy," said Mario.

A cup hit the table and a chair slid across the floor. Antonio said, "Can we take your scooter? I'll leave you my—"

By the time I was halfway to the third floor, I couldn't hear more of their conversation.

The bathroom next to Antonio's room was tiled, like the rest of the villa. It had a deep malachite green floor, the tiles stretching up the bottom half of the walls. White tiles covered the counter, where my tiny toiletries bag lay open.

I stared at myself in the mirror, at my slumped shoulders, and ran my palms over the edge of the sink. Antonio was over-whelming all on his own, but this was like dealing with two of him. I wanted to be here more than anything, but the longer I sat with them, the twitchier my muscles got.

Flying all this way was stupid. Seeing him again, kissing him, holding him—it had all been wonderful, but I was practi-cally back to day one, nervous just looking at him. What if we finally had sex and he decided I wasn't what he wanted? What if he'd made his conquest and was done with me? What if the flight really only earned me two hours and a trip to Pompeii?

We barely knew each other.

"That's why you're here," I said to my reflection. This was the only way to find out if making big changes was worth it or not. And he'd called me girlfriend again. That meant some-thing, right?

There was a knock at the door and Antonio's voice came through it, "Do you need your back washed, bella?"

I nodded to my reflection and stepped to the door, cracking it open. "Shower's pretty small."

He gave me a quick peck on the forehead and whispered, "I need very little room. I prefer tight, confined spaces with you." He tugged on my shirt until my grin broke free. He didn't barge his way in or demand anything, just tried his charm. I was a sucker for his charm, no matter how hard I tried to fight it.

"I suppose an extra pair of hands will hurry things along." I opened the door, and he came in. There was plenty of room, but he locked the door and closed the distance between us.

"I should warn you, Samantha. My intention is rarely to hurry anything along." He looked at the small array of items I'd brought with me. "Is this all you have?"

Shrugging, I said, "I only planned for one night in New York."

He pursed his perfect lips and placed his hands on his hips. "No makeup? You didn't even bring shampoo?"

"Hotels have their own shampoos."

He leaned closer, inhaling deeply from my neck. "That scent is just you? I assumed it was perfume."

I placed a shaky hand on his chest. "I'm sorry about yesterday."

His lips pressed right below my ear. "About what? Flying all the way here and giving me the best surprise of my life?"

"Falling asleep."

"For the record..." He eased back, slowly, sweeping his nose along my jaw as he moved. "That was the best sleep I've had in a long time."

"But it wasn't... you know."

He leaned down to meet my downcast eyes, the raised eyebrow and sure smile confirming he genuinely wasn't upset. "We still have nine days left."

My gaze rose to follow his as he straightened. "How long will you be here?"

He smirked and ran his hands along the sides of my head,

combing them through my hair. "Until you're clean enough to pass my inspection."

"I meant Naples. Because of the equipment problem."

His arms fell around me, and he pulled my body to his. "Assuming we can start within the next two weeks, it should be just after New Year's."

"More than four months." My thumb stroked the lower edge of his chest, up and down over the ridge at the bottom of his pectoral.

"Be here for now, Samantha. Worry about that later." His mouth gravitated toward mine.

Later. How many laters would there end up being? "I do want to see Pompeii, you know."

He leaned back. "You want me to *only* wash your back?"

No. I wanted him rubbing my thigh again. Kissing his way up my leg. Wanted to wrap myself in his strong arms and never move. But we had to leave if we were going to pick up clothes and make it to Pompeii with enough time. Not that we'd be able to see the whole Park; the excavated portions covered over a hundred acres and I was going with two employees. We'd have access to just about everything, even areas not open to the public.

Antonio inclined his head so he could give me a semi-grave look. "You think too much. Have I ever told you that?"

Try to enjoy the moment, Sam. My hand traveled to the back of his neck. "You told me I was too serious."

"I'm very serious as well."

"Hardly." Hand around his neck, I urged his mouth toward mine.

We didn't kiss, but his tongue flicked out to touch my lips.

"I'm serious about wanting to get naked in the shower with you."

I slid my other hand to his ass, pulling myself against him. "If we do that, we won't leave at all today, will we?"

"Probably not." His hardness pressed against my hip, and my resolve faded. Fortunately, he had some resolve left. "Be quick and I'll shower after you. But you are not escaping me tonight."

CHAPTER 8
ANTONIO

OUR FIRST TWENTY-FOUR hours hadn't gone according to plan. Samantha fell asleep while I spoke with the police. Mario told her about the missing equipment—although he didn't mention the pigment pots, so she kept her focus on me instead of leaping into investigator mode.

And then she chose Pompeii over me.

All the same, watching Samantha discover the Park made me fall for her even harder. I got to witness another of her faces: the giddy little girl, breathless, hand covering her mouth in excitement. I'd spent a great deal of time among the ruins over the years, so I could focus on her while Mario guided us.

He gestured over a short metal gate into one of the houses. It was little more than a rectangular space surrounded by crumbling walls which varied from four to eight feet high, depending on how much survived. Gravel, moss, and weeds covered what was once a floor.

To the uninitiated, most houses in Pompeii were nothing more than that. Many tourists restricted their visits to those with the best frescoes and mosaics, but Mario knew every square inch. "The large stone in the floor, with the heavy ring in it was used—"

Samantha leaned over the gate, snapping a photo with her phone. "To store ice underneath to keep things cold."

I held the chuckle at bay as best I could. It had been four hours so far, and this scene had replayed itself at least a dozen times. Possibly two dozen. Mario would begin explaining, and Samantha would complete the lesson for him. While she'd never been there, it was clear she'd read a great deal about the ancient city.

"Why am I here?" Mario's hands flew up in my direction as she continued to speak about which mountains the snow could be collected from, the terracotta tiles in the cellar below the stone, and how important cold wine was to the elite of the city.

She stopped taking photos and smiled politely at him. "Because you're a great guide?"

"Sì, you are." I took her hand as we began walking again, Mario on her opposite side. "But you should take some lessons from Samantha on what's interesting here."

She squeezed my hand lightly and frowned. "When do we get to the real highlight?"

I smirked at her, knowing what she meant, but teasing anyway. "We've already seen the Villa of Mysteries, is that it?"

"No, cugino," said Mario. "She means the Lupanar."

Samantha laughed, rolling her eyes. "The brothel?"

"That's what most people want to see." He winked at her and I let go of her hand to smack the side of his head.

"Marone, I told you to stop winking at her."

She shook her head. "You two are way too alike. How did that happen when you lived so far apart?"

We rounded a corner onto Via di Nola, once a main artery of the city, heading to the building she wanted to see most. The roadway was only six feet across, made of gray basaltic lava stones. The sidewalk rose on either side, with large stones edging it and a surface of finely crushed gravel. At the cross street before the Casa di Marte, three wide blocks jutted up from the road, like an ancient crosswalk.

I took her hand again and lifted it to my lips. Being there with Samantha, my Roman Art Girl—among all the history I'd spent a lifetime studying and she'd spent a lifetime wanting to visit—was like a dream.

Her eyes continued to scan the ruins as I spoke.

"My parents moved us to Roma when I was five. My mother's family is from Napoli, so we were here often. Mario and I were born a few months apart, so we spent a lot of time together on those visits."

Mario nudged her. "He wanted to be with the cool cousin."

"Back to Michigan for undergraduate, and then when I was in Roma for my master's, I visited frequently."

Mario nodded, his gaze dropping to the stones at his feet, silent. Four long years which saw many changes for me. A great deal for the best, others not. I stayed with him each time I was in Napoli, sometimes for school, some as an escape from what my life became. Mario had always been there for me, had always been one of my closest friends. He'd seen me through the worst of everything.

"When I was studying for my doctorate in Delaware, I was back here many times for research. All told, we've lived together for—what would you say, Mario?"

"Too long."

Samantha nudged Mario and my heart warmed to see her becoming more comfortable with him. Granted, Samantha even looking at him was an improvement over how awkward they'd seemed together in the kitchen this morning.

"Two or three years? Perhaps more?" I suggested.

His eyes rose from the stones at our feet, and he pointed to the entry on our left. "We have arrived. Casa di Marte."

The front was indistinguishable from the buildings on either side of it. They were not free-standing and independent, but more a continuous rambling structure, broken only at the cross-streets and alleyways. The walls facing the road were seven to eight feet high, small gray stones wedged together and reinforced at the entries with thin red brick.

The Casa di Marte had three entrances. One on an alley to its left, one through fallen walls on its right, and a space which opened onto the street. The last was excavated decades ago, the standard short gate blocking tourists from entering.

Samantha had dragged me behind her at most of the significant stops, but here she was going in near-blind. It was an active research and conservation area, blocked off to the public, so the photos we'd looked at on the train from Sorrento were all she knew.

My heart galloped at the prospect of showing her my project. Every time I'd visited since I arrived on Tuesday, I'd glared around the space, angry at it for tearing me away from her. But now, I had her hand in mine, and she would love this.

I put an arm out to stop Mario from going in first. "I want to take her to the room alone. Give us fifteen minutes?"

"Only fifteen?" He waggled his eyebrows, while she rolled her eyes so dramatically I couldn't do anything but laugh.

I opened the gate to let her through, ushering her across

the earthen floor of the ancient storage room. "To stabilize the edges of the city's excavation, they've been clearing new areas at the perimeter. This space was exposed generations ago, but when they inched back the dirt and rock, they found the garden walls and then the Mars and Venus fresco. Its condition was so good, they finished unearthing the entire building, calling it Casa di Marte, or the House of Mars."

She frowned and raised an eyebrow.

"Scusa, bella, I know I don't have to translate."

We continued through an open doorway, exposed at the back of the storage room, leading us into what was once a garden. Newly excavated, it was only a dirt surface. But the paleobotanists had found it a treasure trove, taking casts of the root systems preserved after the volcanic eruption nearly two millennia ago. They planned to identify—and perhaps someday reproduce—the garden's original layout.

Low, painted walls surrounded the garden, and columns of various heights stood sentry at its corners and midpoints. Before the city's destruction, the area would have been open to the sky, an oasis for the owners alone.

I hurried her along as she tried to stop and inspect the images of flowers and vines decorating the first walls. She had to see the special frescoes before anything else.

From the garden, we passed into the atrium, where the temporary roof structure began. Few ceiling and upper floors remained within Pompeii, so tall scaffolding was erected to hold sheets of corrugated metal high above. It would protect the precious walls until we had them stabilized and prepared for the elements.

Finally, we passed into the triclinium, the formal dining room which my team would work on for the next four months. It was only fifteen feet wide and long, but the completeness of the paintings was as breathtaking as the woman beside me.

The main decorative frescoes through most of the Casa di Marte alternated in ochre and crimson, with top and bottom borders in blacks and whites. But this room was more artistic, more a showcase of the family's limited wealth, with Pompeian Fourth Style panels designed to look like dozens of paintings embedded in the wall. Images resembling alcoves lined the top, containing well-dressed men and women, with marbled panels along the bottom to evoke the designs of Ancient Ptolemaic Egypt. Intricate frames surrounded each piece.

Dust from hiding beneath a layer of ash for almost two thousand years washed the colors out, but when we finished with the room, the frescoes would shine.

She let go of my hand and walked closer to the wall on the right. Seven feet of plaster remained. Above that, the decorated wall hadn't survived, revealing the stone structure behind it. What had it looked like before Vesuvio claimed it?

On the wall, Mars, the Roman god of war, stood naked, save for a red cloak. To his left, the pale Venus, goddess of love, with an orange fabric draped around her lower half. To his right, their son, Cupid, held Mars's spear and shield. There were other elements to the fresco and many cracks and missing pieces, but it was in remarkable condition, the reds and golds the most vibrant.

"Wow," she breathed.

I gestured to the northern wall, which was in the worst state, only five feet of plaster covering the wall, one foot of stone extending above it. The latrine behind was visible over the wall. "Cupid on the hunt. From what remains, they suspect this was originally very similar to one—"

"From the House of the Deer in Herculaneum."

Her memory for artwork was astounding. All I could do was chuckle. "Good thing Mario's not here to see you finish my explanations, as well."

She turned around to me with the same beaming smile she'd sported most of the day, even when we were shopping for the single pair of shorts, shirt, and shoes she agreed to pick up in Sorrento. She moved to the western wall. "And the last one. Perseus presenting the Medusa's head to Minerva."

"If it were my decision, I would have called this Casa di Minerva." The background was pale blue sky with white clouds, a smudge of green trees behind them. The pegasus off to the side, and mighty Perseus with his winged feet holding the monster's head up to the goddess.

Minerva was the glory of this domus and no one could tell me any differently. A faded orchid-pink stola pooled at her waist and draped to the floor, the flowing dress a marked contrast to her plumed helmet and golden spear. A large crack ran between the two figures, and the plaster of the wall only extended a foot above their heads. But she was magnificent.

"Perseus is the big hero. Why not after him?" Samantha stood two feet from the ancient fresco, hand outstretched, seemingly battling her desire to touch it. A braid confined her hair, the shorts revealed her long toned legs, and the fitted T-shirt skimmed her subtle curves. She stole my breath away, doing nothing more than standing still.

"Minerva was the Roman goddess of wisdom and strategic warfare, among other things. She was tall, strong, and fierce." I crossed the distance to my Samantha, wrapping my arms around her waist, resting my head on her shoulder. The scent of my soap on her skin was not enough to overpower the faint scent of citrus. "And beautiful. Every day I came here, I looked at her and all I saw was you."

She wrapped her arms over my forearms, pressing her cheek against mine.

"I would look at Perseus, offering this gift to the goddess who helped him slay the monster. I would think how my memories of you from college helped me get through many difficult times. And over the last month, getting to know you has helped me push past even more."

She turned around in my arms, brow furrowed. Perhaps this was too soon after we'd made up. Only one day. But it had been a day of tremendous intimacy, despite its premature end. And now, we had enough privacy that she would listen and hear me.

"In my heart, this room is you. If we must be apart for the next four months—"

She placed a finger on my mouth, shaking her head slightly. Jaw clenched, she swallowed hard.

I leaned down and pressed my lips to hers. Not only would I be restoring a fresco that reminded me of her—repairing the crack between Minerva and her hero—but I now had this memory to hold on to, as well.

"That all you could do with fifteen minutes?" said Mario as he stepped in behind us.

The kiss ended and we separated, but the shared smile lingered.

"Samantha," continued Mario, "which part's your favorite?"

Casting a shy smile at me, she said, "Perseus."

"Really? Not Mars?" He raised a fist as if in triumph. "The great god of war?"

She joined him in front of the building's namesake, truly taking the fresco in. Her gaze swept side to side, absorbing the entirety of the wall. Her head paused in the survey, staring at one of the side panels.

I came even with her. I knew this face she wore.

This was not the giddy girl, the tender girlfriend, nor the shy woman. This was her face from the auction, when she studied the stolen painting only she recognized.

I touched her arm and spoke slowly. "Samantha?"

Her eyes narrowed, and she stepped directly in front of one frame, with a crack which entered its top corner, expanding into a gash a foot wide. "Can you bring up those photos you showed me on the train?"

"What's going on?" asked Mario.

Pulling out my phone, I scrolled through the pictures. "Something not good, if the look on her face is what I think it is."

Samantha kept her gaze forward, holding out a hand.

"Cazzo!" I swore under my breath when I reviewed the correct photo. I handed the phone to her. The missing pigments would not be what stole her attention from me. It would be this.

Her eyes flicked to my phone and she passed it to Mario. "This panel had a pair of yellow flowers on it when those pictures were taken. Now it's just a thin layer of plaster covering the structural wall."

There were many sections of the painted wall which had cracked or the plaster was missing, not having survived the eruption or the excavation. But she was right; the bare stone in this frame had been covered with a fresco earlier this week.

Mario looked at my phone, then at the wall. "You saw that picture one time on the train, not even one of the primary frescoes, and you immediately recognize it at the site. How did you do that?"

"Her mind is a mysterious thing." I grinned at her, but she didn't react, too focused on the wall.

"Fourteen by ten inches, roughly." She pulled out her phone and snapped a photo of the missing section before tucking the phone away again. "The outline's jagged, but there are tool marks."

Mario hummed. "I wonder if it's related to the pigm—"

I nudged him, my glare intentional. *Don't tell her*, I beamed into his brain. If she knew the pigment pots were also missing, there was no chance I could keep her attention away from it.

As Mario spoke, he watched me for any sign he was going astray. "The restoration team probably removed it to do some tests."

"He's right." I took her hand and squeezed it, bringing her focus away from the wall. "Someone probably took it back to the lab."

"And I don't suppose they're in on Sundays?" she asked.

"No, bella."

She nodded slowly, fingers tapping her lips. "When were your pictures taken?"

"Wednesday."

"And the last time you were here?"

"Friday afternoon."

"Were the flowers still here then?"

"I was here to check on Minerva and the scaffolding, so I could have easily missed it." It was only Sunday. Someone had removed a portion of this wall since Wednesday. And I'd been too distracted on Friday to narrow our timeframe.

"We need to report this." She dropped my hand and pulled out her phone again, finger hovering over the numbers. "I don't have anyone to call over here."

Mario handed my phone back to me. "I'm sure it's in the laboratory. No one would have stolen it."

Samantha whipped around to scowl at him. "You're kidding, right? You're an archaeologist working in one of the world's most significant historical sites, in a country with the world's biggest cultural heritage crime problem, and you're *sure* no one would have stolen it?"

Mario looked from her to me, his usual charm fading under her intense glare.

"I have two words for you: Civita Giuliana." She counted on her fingers for emphasis, sliding her phone into her bag. "Looters digging tunnels around the site, less than a mile outside this Park's border, destroying ancient walls and relics, searching for things to sell. Who knows how many artifacts they stole or destroyed before the Carabinieri caught them. What makes you think Pompeii itself is immune to that?"

He shrugged, practically wilting under her gaze. "Better security?"

"How many tourists are stopped every year trying to smuggle items out of here?"

Mario opened his mouth to respond, but she continued speaking over him.

"Because I guarantee you, there are far more who don't get caught. Just look at—"

"Samantha." I touched her arm, which fell from where she was pointing at my cousin.

She snapped out of her moment and looked at me, the tension in her muscles and jaw releasing. A blush crept up her cheeks. "But, you're right. It's probably at the lab."

"Antonio told me you were passionate about cultural heritage crimes, but…" Mario flailed his arms, searching for words. Finding none in English or Italian, he blew out a deep breath and smiled at her. She had won him over in that instant.

"Never lose your fire, bella." I stepped closer and kissed her temple. "And we'll check with the lab when they're open."

The Casa di Marte was not reserved for my team alone, but I would've expected the courtesy of someone alerting me or Mario if part of the wall was scheduled to be removed. I had a bad feeling Samantha was correct. If she was, there was not a great deal to be done, other than to report it to the authorities.

But that would have to wait for us to speak with the conservation officers in the laboratory. Which would also have to wait until after the surprises I had waiting for Samantha at the villa.

"Okay, boys." She gave a tight-lipped smile and intertwined her fingers with mine, finally ready to learn something. "Why don't you tell me more about Casa di Minerva?"

CHAPTER 9
SAMANTHA

We rounded the corner, climbing the gently inclined side street to Mario's villa. The road was narrow, a concrete barrier on one side, a white stone wall on the other. Olive trees surrounded by long grasses and weeds dotted the space opposite Mario's. A few houses in red or white stucco stood nearby, but none as tall or built as high up to obscure his amazing view.

We'd walked back from the train after our full day at Pompeii, and I was looking forward to getting off my feet. The hastily purchased shoes weren't as good a choice as I'd hoped.

"At least fifteen times," laughed Antonio.

I tugged his hand and shot him a disapproving glance, which accomplished exactly what I expected. Nothing.

"Seriously?" asked Mario.

"Sì, she turned me down at least fifteen times."

I shook my head. "I'm sure it was only two or three."

"Two or three times the night we met, bella!"

"Okay, okay." I put out my free hand in surrender. "Can we be serious for a moment?"

"Not usually." Mario nudged me with an elbow.

"Antonio, we're going back tomorrow, right? To talk to the people at the lab?" I couldn't just let this go. This was my opportunity to have both of the things I wanted: Antonio plus working an art crime. If I could accomplish something with this missing fresco, maybe I could turn it into a counter-offer for Elliot Skinner, my former boss at the FBI.

Antonio grimaced briefly as he pushed open the gate to the small stone courtyard with its seating area and decorative plants. "Mario will have to take care of that. We are—"

The front door flew open.

"Antonio!" A young woman came barreling toward us, early twenties with the same olive skin and dark hair as the two men. Antonio dropped my hand and reached out to catch her when she jumped into a hug. Who the—

"Chiara! It's so good to see you!" He hugged her tight and put her down a moment later, gesturing to me. "This is my Samantha. And Samantha, this is my little cousin, Chiara."

She squealed and grabbed me in a hug. She was shorter than me by at least six inches, but there was enough enthusiasm in the embrace to make up for it. "I can't wait to see what you think!"

Unlike her two male cousins, Chiara's accent wasn't Italian. It was Bostonian.

"Think about what?" I asked.

"I may have gone overboard." Chiara slipped a credit card out of her pocket and handed it to Antonio. He winked at me and grabbed my hand, towing me inside. The other two followed us, whispering.

I peeked at them over my shoulder as we hurried through the foyer. "What's going on?"

Antonio tore up the two flights of tiled steps that wound around the elevator to the third floor landing and continued to his bedroom. Pausing with a hand on the door, he pulled me to him and kissed my temple. "I have a surprise."

I liked surprises about as much as I liked shopping.

Mario and Chiara arrived as Antonio opened the door for me, ushering me in with a broad smile.

The bed was covered in shopping bags. Stand-up boutique-style shopping bags. Which hadn't been there when we left.

Antonio stood behind me, hands on my shoulders, and kissed my neck. "What do you think?"

"About what?" I stared at the bags, a knot twisting in my stomach. Luxury brands, Italian brands I wasn't familiar with, small bags, large bags. Covering the entire bed. My breath grew more rapid, feet stuck to the floor halfway between the door and the bed. I wasn't as stupid as I must have sounded. It was obvious what this was.

He released my shoulders and walked around me, lifting a lightweight summer dress out of one bag. Holding it in front of himself, he swept it back and forth to show the elegant drape of the fabric. Deep blue with pink and yellow abstract flowers.

His smile faltered when I didn't respond. "You said you hated shopping, bella."

I cast a glance behind me. Mario and Chiara stood in the doorway, eyebrows raised and excited smiles plastered on their faces. Expectant. He'd told Mario in the morning he was going to leave him something, and Chiara had given him a credit card when we arrived. Surely it wasn't all for me.

Stepping tentatively toward the bed, I peeked into a few

bags, not daring to touch anything. Flowers and lace and silk. Leather. He hadn't done this. He couldn't have. "What's all this?"

His normally confident, buoyant voice was strained. It was slight, but it cracked. "You needed clothes. I thought I could save you some time. Chiara spent the day—"

"I'm only here a week and a half. Two pairs of shorts and a handful of T-shirts. Not..." Moving the bags in front, my breath caught. "Versace? Prada? I don't need this stuff."

How much was I going to owe him? The last-minute tickets to Naples had cost an arm and a leg. I didn't need to spend a small fortune on clothing, too.

He looked past me, and the door closed. He spoke slowly. Quietly. "They're gifts. From me to you."

I stared at the bags. "Gifts?"

"Sì. I booked a night at a hotel in Capri tomorrow, instead of shopping." He stepped closer to me, placing the dress on top of the bags. "You... you said you hated shopping."

I met his eyes, his brows turning down. "You don't have to buy my affections, Antonio."

"That's not what I—You don't like this?"

"It makes me really uncomfortable."

He took my hand, nodding several times and flexing his jaw. "We can... allora... we can take it all back. Is that what you want?"

I returned to mentally cataloging the bags, trying to guess what was in each of them. "We're going to Capri tomorrow?"

Sliding his hand out of mine, he reached into a bag and withdrew a black, wide-brimmed sun hat. He kissed my forehead and placed the hat on my head, its floppy brim blocking out half the room. "Sì, to explore and visit a beach and some restaurants."

"That's why we can't go back to the lab tomorrow?" I dragged the hat from my head and threw it on the bed.

"Mario can take care of it." He reached into another bag and withdrew a white string bikini.

My style was one-piece racing suits or a racer back with boy shorts. Something I could do laps or go scuba diving in. Not little triangles of fabric which would expose me if I turned around too quickly. And not a little costume for a trip, which would prevent me from tracking down what happened to the flower fresco. I snatched the tiny bathing suit from him, shaking it. "I'm not a dress-up doll."

"Alright." He stepped away and pulled his phone out of a pocket. He forced a tight smile, but the still-flexed jaw told the real story. "I'll reschedule the trip to Capri and we can go to the Park tomorrow. Then we can visit Napoli to return everything and buy what you want."

I put my hand on his phone before he finished dialing. "Why did you do this?"

He stared at my hand on his phone, but didn't move it. "I already told you."

"But it's so much money."

He shrugged and turned toward the bags, slipping his phone into his pocket. Picking up a Versace bag with its Medusa emblem, he stretched out his jaw. "I told Chiara how little you brought and that you needed enough for ten days. That was it. It was a brief phone call while you were in the shower. She bought more than I expected." He shook his head and passed the bag to me.

Running a hand through his hair, he settled it at the back

of his neck as he continued, "Pretend for a moment I'm Perseus, presenting the head of the Medusa to Minerva."

His eyes stayed locked on mine, crinkled at their corners. I recognized this side of him, the rare nervous side. We'd only made up yesterday. He'd gone too far too quickly, and he knew it.

"Bella." He picked up another bag and handed it to me. I looked inside this one and saw more floral fabric. Another dress? And another bag. Sandals. "Pretend you're in a movie."

I held three bags by their straps, and he handed me two more. Lingerie and another dress.

"Pretend you're on a spontaneous trip to Napoli with your sexy Latin lover." His brows remained drawn, but a hint of a smirk appeared.

As he piled three more bags on top of the ones I already held, I cracked a smile. "Well, that one's kind of true."

"Samantha, you're unlike any woman I've ever dated." He placed the hat back on my head.

I intentionally frowned, looking up at the floppy brim and turning it into an eye roll.

"I'm accustomed to women who want me for my money."

"You know that's not what I want."

"I do." He paused, tilting his head. "It's harder to accept than you may think."

I dropped the bags. Hopefully, there wasn't anything fragile. Stepping over them, I flipped the hat off and threaded my fingers into the short hair at the nape of his neck. Pulling closer, my lips met his, and we pressed together. Eyes closed, I inhaled his fresh vanilla scent and slid my tongue along his. Why would he try to buy me when I'd already flown to Naples to be with him? Maybe I was overreacting.

He broke from the kiss, but held my waist tight against him. His breathing had picked up, and his lids hung low. A shiver ran the length of me, my heart thundering in concert with his and the ache beginning between my thighs.

"Per favore, bella. Say you'll accept my gifts."

"But it's too much mon—"

His mouth pressed against mine before I could say another word. He leaned away from me, the familiar smirk back in place. "Say it."

"Antonio, I can't—"

He kissed me again, and we both laughed through it. It was a weak kiss, meant only to shut me up. When the kiss ended this time, he doubled down and raised the eyebrow to emphasize the smirk.

Feigning irritation, I said, "You're just going to keep—"

When he came in for another kiss, I avoided his mouth. He tried again and I spun out of his grasp, but he kept enough of a hold on me to throw me onto the middle of the bed, where he'd removed the bags. Reaching into another one, he pulled out something small, black, and lacy.

I gasped. "What is that! Did your cousin seriously buy me underwear?" And where was the cotton?

"Underwear?" He winked at me and threw it over his shoulder, crawling over top of me. "Bella, it's lingerie. Something for your sexy Latin lover to appreciate."

I inched my way up the bed away from him, moving bags as I went. They were all around us, like a cocoon. "They're still outside the door, right?"

"Perhaps." He withdrew a pink silk slip from a bag. Pausing in his slow pursuit of me, he ran it across my arm, the gentlest caress. "You'd look stunning in this."

Faint voices at the door. Mario and Chiara *were* still right there.

Settling himself over me, hips between my thighs, he popped the button of my shorts, and his mouth found my neck. One hand slid down the front of my underwear, cupping my sex.

There was nowhere to go other than to push him away. Not what I wanted, but his cousins were listening. I twisted my hips and pulled my neck away from him. "Should we do this later?"

His head snapped up, facing the door. "Privacy, you two!"

Chiara's voice sounded from the other side of the door. "Is she going to keep everything? There was a white dress I really liked."

"It's yours!" I hollered, and Antonio gaped at me playfully.

"Perfetto!" called Mario. "Can we go for gelato now?"

"Get lost, Mario!" Antonio yelled.

Two quick raps on the door, followed by silence.

"Now where were we, bella?" He bit my bottom lip, his fingers pulling my underwear aside to trace the edge of my opening.

I arched my back, tugging at his shirt. "Pretty close to there, I think."

"I love you for who you are, not the clothes you wear." There was that word again. "But I want you to know how beautiful you are."

He withdrew the hand from my shorts and I whimpered.

Sitting up, he pulled his shirt over his head, allowing me to take in his remarkable body. His broad shoulders were the first thing I noticed about him beyond his gorgeous face and sharp jawline, but his hipbones were my favorite. I traced a finger along one, which poked up from the waistband of his shorts.

When I reached for the button at his waist, he smacked my hand away with a grin. He pulled his phone out and streamed some music through the speaker, then tossed the phone onto the bedside table.

"Samantha, you flew all the way here to tell me you wanted to be with me. You could have called."

I froze. This conversation was leaving me dizzy from all the curveballs.

"That was something you did for me."

He still had the look of lust on his face and the bulge in his shorts made it clear where our bodies were headed, but his emotions threw me for a loop. But that was him, wasn't it? Always more emotional than me. It hadn't taken long to figure that out.

"Now I want to do this for you. If this is going to work between us, you'll have to accept I have money and I'll want to spend it on you."

"Okay." Words stated. Moving on. Time to take care of the pulsing between my thighs. I hauled my T-shirt off, but his eyes stayed above my jawline.

"We're going to Capri tomorrow and you'll keep everything, sì?"

I shimmied my legs out from underneath him and sat up on my knees so I was eye-to-eye with him. "Depends on what *everything* actually is. Is there jewelry?"

He gestured around the bed, to all the bags surrounding us. "You said you want me for me. This is part of me."

My turn to play. I lifted one leg to plant next to him, grabbed his shoulders, and swung my weight toward him, pivoting us as I rose. The move flung him to the bed, eyes wide, and my leg followed so I straddled him. "If I say yes to all of it, will you stop talking?"

He rocked his head back in laughter. "Marone, bella! I do! I promise."

"Then yes, I'll keep it all. Whatever it all is."

He sat up, checking in several bags around us.

"Ah ha!" he exclaimed, pulling out a box of condoms. "This was a specific request."

Squeezing my eyes shut, I shook my head. "Seriously? You had your twenty-something female cousin buy that for us?"

"The other thing you need to promise is that you'll relax a little. Spontaneous vacation with your sexy Latin lover, remember?" He kissed me quickly, waggling his eyebrows.

"I might need help with that."

"Just as well..." Playful Antonio vanished, transforming into Hungry Antonio. He grabbed my waist, the two of us crashing into the hollow between all the bags, and he hauled my shorts and underwear off. "It's my specialty."

His mouth traveled back up my body, more breath and teeth than there'd been yesterday. Somehow my bra and his clothes were off by the time he reached my mouth. He drove a hand into my hair and leaned in to kiss me, his moans setting me on fire.

I pulled his hand from the side of my head, intertwining our fingers. Telling him the truth when I arrived had been the scariest thing I'd done my entire life. Where did it leave us? With him spending too much money on me, taking me to Capri instead going back to the lab, and with his return to Michigan delayed at least two weeks.

This wasn't what I planned.

He lifted on an elbow to look at me. "You're shaking."

I squeezed his hand, trying to ground myself. Sex. I could do sex. Push the rest of it aside.

"Is this not what you want?"

"That's not it." It was everything I wanted, but that was the problem. What happened when we finished? Was that the end? "I'm terrified."

His body grew a different type of rigid. "Of me?"

"Of…" Those big brown eyes. I could keep telling them the truth instead of running or hiding. "Us."

"Us," he whispered, leaning back in to run his teeth along my jaw. "This is something to celebrate, not fear."

How long had it been since I'd done that?

"First…" His hand sank between my legs, and one finger dipped inside me. "I remember you liked this."

"Yeah, I do." My hips rolled against his grasp, the small inner muscles firing all together. I gasped as he added a second finger, working them in and out, exploring inside me. "But it's not what I want."

His lips brushed my ear as his thumb found my clit, the fingers continuing to move. "You want me inside of you? Filling you?"

I nodded furiously, clamping my eyes shut, breaths coming in rapid spurts. "I want to learn to celebrate. *With you.*"

He chuckled low in his throat and the fingers left me so he could pull a condom from the box. "Open your eyes, bella. Look at me."

I did as he said, following his movements as he rolled the condom onto his cock. My body screamed for it. *Just let there be more after that.*

As he finished with the condom, my eyes latched onto a small scar I hadn't noticed yesterday. On the inside of his hipbone, below where the waistband of his shorts had hung. Small and puckered. Round at one end, extending straight for an inch. *Ignore it, Sam.* But I reached for it. I should focus on what was going on. "What's this?"

CHAPTER 10
ANTONIO

Samantha paused, blinking at the scar on my groin.

"Another part of me." I wove my fingers with hers again and pushed her back against the bed. "But not the part I want to focus on at this moment."

It was far more than a physical scar. An eternal reminder of the horrible mistakes I'd made in my life. Of my days with Uncle Giovanni and my cousin Cristian. But my goal was to win her over. Remind her I was worthy of her. And that story was not one to be told yet.

I lowered my mouth to hers and she moved on from the scar with me.

My tip played against her, and her leg wrapped around my back again. It was finally time for us to be together. I slid inside hesitantly, and our kiss paused as we sighed in unison. Her walls stretched around me and she squeezed tight.

I pushed hilt deep, joining myself with her, and stilled. The lightness surging from my chest through my entire body was unlike anything I'd felt before.

She was mine. Samantha Caine—the woman I'd held in my heart for so long—was mine. And I was hers.

"Oh my god," she whispered with a smile, her breath coming in a shuddering torrent. She clenched my hand, and it was clear, no matter how difficult the words were for her, this was far more than just any physical action.

I pulled back, almost withdrawing completely, then filled her again. Our eyes locked and the world vanished, leaving us with only our connection. I held each stroke deep inside her, lost in the moment's magnitude.

She used her leg to meet my hips, pulling me in faster, the pressure and delight building rapidly after our day-long delay. Our pace quickened and soon I was driving into her so hard she gasped over and over. I didn't want it to end. Ever.

"Right there." She dug her nails into my hand and my back. "Don't stop."

I raised my face enough to watch her beauty, the layer of sweat beading across her forehead. She grabbed my neck and pulled my mouth to hers as I felt her release approaching.

When her tongue froze and she tensed, I let go. Let go of the guilt, the regret, the fear none of this was real. Blank slate. She may be guilty of running and hiding from how she felt, but she was here with me trying to make this work.

She groaned and threw her head back with a silent wail of climax, the nails digging into my neck triggering my eruption inside her. All the pain and sorrow of the last week left, granting space for love. For happiness. For Samantha.

I flagged against her as we finished, pressing her into the soft bed, my head resting next to hers. Cheek to cheek, my heart thundered against hers, trying to match its rhythm. Her leg and arm slid off me, limp, knocking a few bags to the floor.

Our intertwined fingers, though, remained together.

"Us," she whispered, and kissed my neck. It was the most beautiful sound in all the world. Her walls were down, if just for a moment, and I snuck into that private space in her heart.

"I love you, Samantha." Lifting on a forearm to take my weight off her, I kissed her again. Running a hand along her side, feeling the curve of her narrow waist, I wanted more.

Regretfully, I had to pull out.

"Stay. Please."

I paused long enough to caress her cheek and smile at her. "Un momento." I left her and the bed, disposed of the condom, then returned. I lay next to her, dragging a finger and my eyes across her breasts, down the curve of her hip, and back up to her torso. Soft, gentle curves over hard muscle.

"Thank you, bella."

"For what?" She took my hand and kissed the fingers, then put them back on her chest. Much better than when she hid her body from me.

"For giving me a second chance."

She rolled onto her side and propped her head up, matching me. The post-sex glow and the calm suited her. Even more gorgeous than she'd been an hour ago. And she was still naked. Gloriously naked.

"I'm not ready to talk about it yet." She traced a finger along the arm supporting my head.

My jaw clenched. Another thing she was not ready for.

I had to respect that.

While trying my hardest to change her mind.

CHAPTER II
ANTONIO

THE SUN STREAMED through our hotel suite's patio doors, surrounding Samantha with radiance. She rose and fell, slowing once the climax had rolled through both of us. Her breasts heaved and she let out a long exhale as her head drooped forward. Strands of hair stuck to the slick layer covering her glorious face and chest, the little pink slip clinging to her curves.

Our room sat high on the cliffs of southeastern Capri, looking down over the Faraglioni rock formations far below. The night before, we shared a romantic dinner at sunset on our private balcony, as the sun dipped into the ocean. This morning, we woke in each other's arms and made love. Called for breakfast. Made love again.

She stroked my chest, still straddling me as I softened. Scrunching her nose, she said, "Sorry about that."

I wrapped an arm around her waist to sit up and kissed her gently. Her fingers raked through my hair and down my back, sending jolts through my happily exhausted body. There was no getting enough of this woman.

She slid a leg off me, breaking our contact. I crossed the room to the mirror and inspected the red marks on my chest, eyeing her in the reflection. She'd snuck into a silk negligee while I was guiding room service out to the balcony with our breakfast, which was surely cold by now.

"Don't worry, bella, I don't think it will bruise." I prodded where she had dug her fingers into my flesh and pretended to wince. "Much."

"I'm so sorry!"

I crossed to the bed and nudged her, eliciting a yelp of laughter as she fell back onto the tangle of sheets.

"I'm teasing. You're not the only tough one in this relationship, you know."

She shook her head and cleared the hair covering her face. As she sat up, she smoothed a hand over the slip. "Good surprise?"

"The best. I had no idea you packed it."

The corner of her mouth lifted as she sat up. "Chiara has good taste."

"Speaking of things which taste good." I raised an eyebrow, rewarded by her widened eyes, and I extended a hand to her. "Breakfast?"

She frowned at me, flicking her eyes down my body. "You should put some clothes on if we're going to eat outside."

I considered heading for the patio doors anyway to see her reaction but thought it smarter to retrieve a pair of shorts from my suitcase. "Probably."

She got off the bed and came closer, rubbing a hand along my back while I dressed. "So, we did the Blue Grotto, the funicular, and Anacapri yesterday. What's the schedule for today?"

I turned and wrapped my arms around her. "Shopping, beach, lunch, and back to Sorrento this afternoon."

"Ugh, you and your shopping." She rolled her eyes and spun out of my grasp, plucking a robe from a nearby chair and heading toward the food.

I grabbed her hand, pulling her back to me. "I promise not to buy anything for you."

She smirked, running her fingers over the deep red marks on my chest. "How generous of you."

"Intentionally not generous, you mean."

She turned to the balcony, a playful sway to her hips which I'd never seen from her before. My plan was working. Her nerves around me were calming and she was growing more confident in herself. I'd found it remarkable, from the first night we truly met, how in control she seemed with everything but her heart. Being near me had once made her apprehensive, sweaty palms and all. A woman as strong and fiery as her, nervous to look at me, scared to touch me. Before she left Napoli, she'd have to be comfortable enough to carry us through four months apart.

"However, if I buy something for myself and it happens to fall into your bag, I can't be held responsible."

She shot a disapproving glare over her shoulder. "Do I need to put a restraining device on you?"

I held my wrists together toward her, waggling my eyebrows. "If you insist, bella."

" Grazie, Mario." I hung up the phone and headed to our table at the beach club restaurant. The exposed beams of the roof were covered in raffia, providing shade to the few dozen tables on the patio. Our table was at the edge, with an unobstructed view of the cliffs rising above us and the sea below.

Samantha wore a long flowered periwinkle wrap dress over her small white bikini. Her wide-brimmed hat sat on the table next to her, and her eyes were fixed on the Faraglioni, the tremendous sea stacks jutting out of the water. Mezzo, the shortest, with the hole at its base, stood over two hundred and fifty feet, while Stella and Fuori stood another hundred feet taller.

Her long caramel-colored hair hung in loose waves, dancing in the gentle breeze. She took in the view, her soft smile telling me she'd found at least some measure of serenity. Surrounded by the sounds of water splashing on the rocks below the restaurant's deck, the buzz of voices in a variety of languages, and the scents of grilled seafood, we were in paradise. I'd been there several times before, but with her, it was different. Wonderful.

When I reached the table, I took her hand and kissed it. Her gaze turned to meet mine and the contented smile grew. Four days ago, I thought I'd lost her, but here she was with me. The love of my life.

"What did he say?" Her brain never stopped. It was likely still on the missing fresco from Pompeii, and she no doubt meant Mario.

"That we've opaid the bill and may go down to the beach now. Our sun beds are reserved."

She nudged my leg with her foot and frowned at me before putting her hat back on. "You know what I meant." She stood and picked up her tan handbag with its asymmetrical F-shaped frame. The way she'd been tossing the bag about put into question how much she actually accepted my spending money on her. Like a tiny passive aggression.

"And our towels are being taken down right now."

Small pleasure craft motored around the edges of the large natural pool formed by the island's shore and the sea stacks. The beach club was built into the side of the cliffs, and the lounge chairs and sun beds sat on concrete slabs among the carved rocks. We walked to the stairs leading down to the most private space available on the outcropping.

"Come on," she said, taking my hand as we climbed down the steps. Her hat was so wide it tickled my ear when she leaned close to me. "What did Mario say about the missing fresco? Did he find any details?"

"Nothing yesterday and nothing so far today. He checked the tracking software, paperwork, areas in the lab where it may have been, and no sign of it. He also spoke with everyone who would have worked on it or authorized work on it, and no one knows."

"Has he called the authorities?"

"Not yet."

A young man in a beach club uniform smiled as we neared our sun beds, laying the towels and a small bottle of sunscreen on a table between them. He'd flattened the beds for lazing in the sun and positioned a blue umbrella behind them, which we could tilt for shade. We were closest to the cliffs, down a few steps and somewhat isolated from the others.

"Due Sangrie, per favore." I slipped a bill from my pocket and shook his hand with it.

"Sì, signore." He gave a curt nod and was off to get our drinks.

Samantha stood with fists on her hips, eyebrow raised. "Why not?"

I pulled my shirt off and folded it on top of my bed. "There are still two of the conservators he's not spoken to. Bianca was out sick and Océane—from my team—took a trip when we were delayed."

"A trip where?"

I shrugged. I was not actually her boss and there was no work to be done, so I hadn't asked.

"So we're going to see them tomorrow?"

"Sì, bella, Bianca tomorrow. Océane if she's back."

"Good. I've been thinking about this non-stop."

"Hopefully not while we were making love," I teased.

She feigned a glower, but didn't miss a beat. "Still, if they knew something about it, they would've logged it somewhere, right?"

"Give me your things. I'll take them to our locker." I held out a hand, waiting, but she didn't move her fists. "Do you think worrying about it right now will fix anything?"

Grumbling under her breath, she undid the ties at her waist. The dress floated off her shoulders, and she folded it on top of my shirt.

"Wow." My eyes scanned the length of her lithe figure and long legs. Seeing her in the small bikini—in public, knowing I was the only man whose hands would touch the skin underneath—sent a spark through my body.

Her frown deepened. "That was eloquent."

Chuckling at her insistence on remaining irritated about the fresco, I leaned closer, pulling the brim of her enormous hat down on either side of our faces, creating a private space. "I want to rip that bathing suit off you with my teeth."

Her eyebrows shot up. Perhaps it was a trick of the light under the hat, but it appeared she was blushing. "That was better."

"If we were alone, I would ravish every square inch of your exquisite body."

She chuckled at that line. Was it nerves? Insecurity? Regardless, chuckles were not my goal.

I dropped the pitch of my voice. "And I would bury myself in you so deeply—"

She sucked in air and her eyes widened. There. That was my goal.

Returning to playful, I smirked. "—that you would relax for a moment." I kissed her on the nose and released the hat as she smacked me. Picking up the dress, my shirt, and her handbag, my gaze traveled the length of her again. She was stunning beyond words. "Now lie down. I'll be right back."

"Yes, sir." She winked at me and sat, staring up at the sun and letting her eyes slide closed.

After locking our items up, I returned to find her lying on her stomach on the sun bed. A glass of sangria sat on the concrete at her head, with a straw long enough she barely had to move.

"You need some sunscreen, you pale thing."

Her shoulders heaved with laughter and she craned her head around. "I'm guessing you don't use any?"

"Of course not." I waved the silly question off. "Look at me. I was born for this sunshine."

"I put some on before we left the hotel." She lay her head back down. "What if the conservator who claims to be out sick isn't really sick? What if she's the guilty party? You sure Mario shouldn't report it or track her down?"

I knelt next to her, bringing my face to her level. "Tomorrow."

She rolled onto her side, and I brushed my hand along her narrow waist. She worked hard to suppress a laugh. "You going to say something about burials again?"

"You liked that?"

"I think you're ridiculous."

"You tell me this a lot." I pulled on her hip so she lay on her front, and I retrieved the lotion. As I rubbed it into her skin, she sighed, a little more of her tension releasing.

"We're going swimming, right?"

"If you would like, sì." I kneaded her shoulders, eliciting a low moan. The sound brought me back to all the hours we'd spent tangled in each other's bodies the last few days. My hands trailed lower, along her toned muscle, under the top edge of her bikini bottoms.

"Watch those hands, Ferraro. We're in public, you know."

I pulled on the bow holding her bikini top together at the middle of her back. She started to roll over to knock my hand away, but as the string released, she flopped down.

"Stop that." She reached for the strings, to retie them, but I pushed her hands back onto the sun bed.

"Let me take care of you, bella." I leaned down and planted a kiss on her neck before applying more sunscreen. I rubbed it into her sides, brushing my fingers along the curve of her breasts.

The muscles in her hips and ass tensed as she let out a small moan. "Christ, Antonio, that's no way to get me to relax."

"But you still need lotion on your legs."

"You put one hand down there thinking you're going to

put lotion on the insides of my thighs, and I swear I won't stop talking about that damn fresco."

"Perhaps you should have another sip of your sangria."

She raised her head to glare at me, but the corner of her mouth wouldn't stay down. "Just hang out with me."

I stood, moving the table from between our sun beds, and pushed them together. "Is this the part—" I stretched out on my bed, next to her. "—where we get to know each better?"

She tied the back of her suit and rolled onto her side. Her brows drew down as she touched my cheek, rubbing a gentle thumb along the faint outline of the bruise. It was fading, but still visible.

Her friend Nathan Miller had a stronger right hook than I'd expected from such a pretty man. But that was in the past, no matter how he looked at her. She was with me and I had one more week to convince her I was worth waiting for.

She blinked slowly, jaw flexing as though she wanted to say something. Words were much easier for me than for her, particularly the emotional ones. This was something else I had to convince her of—that she could trust me completely.

"You want to know why I lied about the Chagall?"

Her hand paused, and she took a deep breath. "Yeah." The word was quiet, but it held significant weight. She was ready to talk.

I turned my face to kiss her palm and nuzzled into it, placing my hand over it. "You understand how much I regret that?"

She nodded, grasping my hand, taking it in hers to lay them next to her.

"When you first told me what painting you were dealing with, I was afraid my father was involved in the fraud."

Her head snapped back. "What? Does he usually—"

"No, no," I interjected. That sounded more damning than intended. "He's... how can I explain it... almost as passionate as you are about art crimes."

"So, why would you think he was involved?"

I shrugged, not ready to share the full story. No matter how much I wanted her in my life, and how much I knew the truth was important, each detail had to come in its own time. But I could give her most of the truth. "A very good question. 'Panic' is the only word I can come up with."

"Panic? Mr. Confident?" She frowned, no idea the effect she had on me.

I squeezed her hand, smirking. "That morning in Brenton a few weeks ago, I'd had a coffee date with the most amazing woman in the world—"

She rolled her eyes so dramatically she almost fell over.

"—and she put me off my game. Just like every time I saw her."

"Oh my god." She feigned exasperation, but the blush crept up her cheeks, giving her away. Perhaps the nerves were still affecting her.

I moved to the edge of my sun bed. I couldn't be any closer to her unless I was on hers. "Once I'd confirmed my parents owned the original, I spoke with my father about it. We were afraid our family might be implicated in the fraud and decided I would help get to the bottom of it."

"Did you hear what happened? We had a press conference about it."

My chest swelled with pride. "Sofia told me. I forced Mario to watch five times."

She spluttered, releasing my hand to cover her mouth. "You did not!"

"How do you think he recognized you when you arrived?"

"I only spoke for like two seconds!"

I tugged at her waist until she moved to the edge of her sun bed. Our faces were separated by only a foot, but I dropped my voice to a whisper. "Thirty-three seconds, to be exact. And you thanked my company. That meant so much to my father to be involved in catching them."

"They're still on the run, though." Fire flashed behind her eyes. If she were in the States, she would likely be searching for David and Olivia Scott, the mother and son responsible for the Chagall forgery and attempted insurance fraud. She'd focused on them the same way she wanted to search for the flowers fresco.

I nodded.

"If we had a do-over, would you change anything?" she asked.

"That depends. Do I know everything I know now?"

She placed her hand in mine again, holding it against her chest. "Sure."

"Then it's an easy answer. I would tell you the truth, and then insist we work together to prove the fraud. And somehow I would ensure you still figured out the arson and murder." I rubbed at the curve of her breast with my thumb. "And I would have gone a little slower in pursuing you."

She laughed, leaning her head back. "You were a bit pushy."

"And I wouldn't have believed you when you told me you were dating Nathan Miller."

She winced. "Yeah, that was stupid."

"Avoiding me was stupid."

She clutched my hand against her. "Nah, I doubt I would have passed your three-date test under normal circumstances."

It was teasing, laughing, but I stilled and squeezed her hand. The air grew heavy around us, the waves crashing on the beach and the chatter of the crowd faded into the background. I released her hand to run my fingers through her silky hair and caress her cheek.

"Samantha, if I've been unclear about this, please hear me now." My heart pounded against my rib cage. Did I even have the words to explain how I felt? Something more than cheap and easy words like love and forever? And how many words could I use before they scared her away? "I never needed three dates with you. I knew you were the one for me the morning we went to Russo's for coffee. Every moment afterward just confirmed it. The letter I wrote to you before I left town was real. I want to build a future with you. With only you."

She stared at me, no response forthcoming. But she didn't run, frown, or roll her eyes, as she normally did when the emotions grew difficult. Instead, she leaned forward to kiss me. It was tender, a kiss we hadn't shared before. There was no sex, desperation, or need behind it.

And there was no joke to temper her feelings.

No, she was telling me she loved me, even if she couldn't say it. She wanted a future with me as well.

As our mouths separated, she smiled sweetly, and a fullness spread through my chest. I could have leapt from the sun bed and told everyone there that the most miraculous woman in the world was in love with me.

Instead of pushing her too hard, I winked. "Shall we go swimming now?"

She sat up and double-knotted her bikini, a mischievous grin spreading across her face. "Race you to the far end of the swimming area."

Before the words 'What do I get if I win?' could form on my lips, she was sprinting to the water's edge. I chased after her, sure I wouldn't win anyway.

CHAPTER 12

ANTONIO

WE PROCEEDED through the Pompeii laboratory, directly to where Bianca worked. She'd been out sick while Samantha and I were in Capri, and Samantha was dying to speak with her before we headed to meet with the Carabinieri. Had we been there under other circumstances, Samantha no doubt would have stopped me every five feet to ask questions about the lab. But today, she was laser-focused.

Various worktables crowded with tools lined the walls of the room, while larger tables took up the center. Bianca sat facing a computer in the back. Only one other restorer was in the room, at a table with a mosaic tile—perhaps two feet square—surrounded by solvents, cotton swabs, and a dust extractor.

"Buongiorno, Bianca," I said as Samantha and I arrived next to her, causing her to look up from her monitor.

Bianca ripped off her glasses, letting them fall to her chest from her beaded chain. Smoothing out the stray hairs she'd disturbed from her ponytail, she smiled at me. "Dr. Ferraro, good morning."

"This is my associate, Samantha Caine."

The two women nodded to each other and shook hands. Samantha had reluctantly agreed to go shopping with me in Capri before we left. She'd purchased short white pants and a cornflower blue cap-sleeved blouse, which she wore. Today was casual-professional, sporting her visitor's badge and her luxurious hair trapped in a low bun.

True to my word, I'd bought nothing for her. Except for the one gift I snuck while she was not watching. Hopefully, I'd have an opportunity—and the courage—to give it to her before she left. It was mostly for me, though. She couldn't deny me a selfish gift.

"How are you feeling?" asked Samantha.

Bianca continued fussing with her hair, smoothing her lab coat, and running her palm over her leg. I smiled politely, familiar with this response. We met while we were both working on our PhDs, when I'd been spending more time in Pompeii than in the States. Mario liked to say she was nervous, but she always reacted to me this way.

"Good. How are you?"

"We were told you were off sick the last two days?"

"Oh, no. My sister broke her wrist on the weekend and I had to help her get settled."

Samantha nodded. "Are you aware a piece of the wall painting was removed from Casa di Marte?"

"Yes." Bianca focused on Samantha but hesitated over her words each time she flicked her eyes back to me. "Mario was asking about it."

"Did you authorize or request it?"

Bianca shook her head, tucking a strand of loose hair behind her ear. "I checked the inventory this morning. I had this mosaic—" She pointed to the piece the other restorer was working on, likely the one she'd asked for my help with. "—removed from the fountain in the atrium, which I'll—Sorry, but who are you, exactly?"

"I'm—"

I put up a hand. "She's working with me."

"Excuse me," came a man's voice from behind us.

Samantha and I turned to see Thomas, one of the men on my team, approaching. Tall and lean, seven years my senior, he worked for the British Museum in London. He spoke with a crisp accent and knew little Italian, so we'd agreed English would be our primary language.

He gave Samantha a once-over. My first instinct was to grab her hand, drape my arm around her, or step between them. However, she'd been clear she wished to be seen as a professional at the lab, not my girlfriend. She'd earn their respect on her own.

I gestured from her to Thomas. "Samantha, I would like you to meet—"

"Thomas Grange," she interjected.

He tilted his head and held out a hand to shake. Their hands lingered, his smarmy English smile growing. "Sam Caine?"

"It's been too long!" She finally unlocked her hand from his and turned to me. "I worked for Thomas a lifetime ago at the British Museum."

She what? How did this pretty man, who was looking at my girlfriend with too much appreciation, share a history with her I knew nothing about?

"Smartest intern I've ever had. Revamped several of our security models." He continued smiling at her, gaze drifting from her eyes to her lips. What did he mean by *had*? "She helped plan a display on trafficking and smuggling of art and artifacts."

"You working here now?" she asked.

"I'm on Dr. Ferraro's team restoring a new excavation. I can show you around, if you'd like?"

I stiffened, attempting not to clench my jaw too tightly. "I've already given her a tour."

All three of them looked at me, brows furrowed. My words must have been harsher than intended.

"So..." Thomas ran his knuckles along his stubbled jaw, his eyes drifting back to Samantha. "Just here to explore or a security audit perhaps?"

She hummed. "Good question. When Dr. Ferraro was showing me the Casa di Marte, we noticed a piece of the wall painting had been removed. We wanted to speak with a few people to check if it was intentional. You know, before reporting it."

Bianca swallowed audibly. "You think someone stole it?"

I shrugged. "I was hoping to find it in the lab."

"Mario spoke with me yesterday." Thomas smiled at Samantha again. "That's why you're here?"

She grinned, saying nothing more.

"And why are you here today, Thomas?" Perhaps he was our guilty party. "You should enjoy this like a holiday."

"I can't pass up the chance to see the other work going on here just because our project's been delayed." His smiling eyes turned to Bianca for a moment, then returned to Samantha. "There's a lot of beautiful things in this city."

I shoved a hand in my pocket and balled it into a fist while Samantha continued her pleasantness. Did she realize he was flirting with her? Had she ever even noticed me flirting with her? And I'd been far more obvious than this fool.

"I know! I was in Capri the last two days. It was gorgeous! There were some—" She tilted her head toward me, the corner of her mouth lifting. "—burial sites—"

I bit my lower lip to stifle a laugh. Perhaps she did realize he was flirting.

"—that I particularly enjoyed."

Bianca fumbled with something in her pocket. "There are other places I can recommend if you enjoy that."

"I'm good, thanks, although I'd love to see what you're doing with that mosaic after we visit..." Samantha paused, pointing at me. "Are we going to the Carabinieri office directly?"

"Mario should be here in about twenty minutes or so to take us, but no one's spoken with Océane yet. Should we wait for her first?"

"Good point." She tapped her fingers against her lips in that way she did when she was debating. "But she's only here for this project, so if she was involved with a legitimate request to remove the wall segment, someone else would know."

"Another good point, bel—" Not calling Samantha *bella* felt as though something were off in my world. It rolled off my tongue more easily than her name.

Her eyebrow twitched at my near-slip. "We should wait outside. Catch Mario when he gets here."

Thomas smirked. "Same old Sam."

"What does that mean?" I said. The furrowed brows hit me again and the other restorer looked up. That had been snappy. Oddio, I had to get control of that.

He continued smiling, tucking his hands in his pockets as

he rocked back on his heels. "I hired her to work on cataloging items in the Ancient Greek collection at the British Museum. First intern I had who knew the language."

I looked at her askance, and she shrugged one shoulder. She knew Ancient Greek? It would apparently take a great deal of time to get to know everything about this woman.

"We purchased a krater at auction and she was investigating its provenance. Said something didn't sit well with her, despite the collections team being happy with it."

"Let me guess," I said, finally smiling again, at my clever girlfriend. "Stolen?"

"Looted, actually." He stopped rocking and inclined his head toward her. "I'd rather hoped to see your resume cross my desk after you graduated. Or anyone's desk at the museum. On to bigger and better things?"

"Dr. Ferraro," said Bianca. Not a whisper, but quietly, as Samantha continued catching up with Thomas.

I dragged my eyes away from them. "Sì?"

She switched to Italian, pointing at her monitor, which showed an image of the Mars wall in the Casa di Marte. "One of the paleobotanists took this photo Saturday morning."

The flower fresco was still there. "We were there early Sunday afternoon. So that's our timeframe." I kept my voice low. "And the pigment pots were last seen Thursday?"

"Sì."

"Did you hear the Carabinieri recovered one Saturday morning?"

Her eyes widened. "Only one?"

"So there are still two floating about somewhere."

Did that mean anything? The photo told us that the fresco was still on the wall when the pot was recovered in Roma, so they weren't removed at the same time. Could the same person be behind two separate thefts? Or was it more likely two separate people? I touched Bianca's arm and smiled in thanks.

I should talk this over with Samantha. No more secrets. But given her obsession with the fresco, my earlier visions of her diving into an investigation almost seemed an underestimation.

Samantha laughed suddenly, loudly, swatting a hand in Thomas's direction. My attention snapped to his stupid smile.

Bianca whispered, "I think your security consultant has made a friend."

"I'm heading up the volcano tomorrow," he was saying. "Any chance you'd like to—"

"She's busy. With security things." I didn't care that I growled at him that time. I was being ridiculous, not to mention selfish, but I had to get her away from him. "Andiamo, Samantha. We'll track down my cousin, then come back to see Bianca's work on the mosaic and the rest of the lab later."

I ushered her out after she shook Thomas's hand again. I had to conjure a good reason to remove him from the project.

ONCE WE WERE outside the lab, Samantha grimaced. "Was I that obvious?"

"Scusi?"

She walked with her thumbs tucked into the pockets of her skinny little Capri pants, the lightweight blouse fluttering over her curves as she moved. She remained a foot away from me, a spring in her step. "Bianca! Avoiding your gaze, playing with her hair, giggling nervously. Oh my god, I'm embarrassed for my former self!"

"You were adorable." I closed the distance as we walked.

She nudged me with a hip once I was too close. "Do you think she's adorable?"

I pulled her closest hand out of her pocket and interlaced our fingers. My heart continued thrumming. Thomas was too old for her. He lived in London. She was with me. But the words came out anyway. "Thomas certainly thought you were."

She dropped her hand from mine, wrinkling her nose. "What's with you? I was kidding."

Good question. Watching them laugh and share a past I knew nothing about had lit a fire in my belly, burning all the way up my throat. I ran a hand through my hair and withdrew my phone from my pocket. "Mario should be here soon."

I hit his number, but Samantha placed a finger on my phone to end the call. She stepped in front of me, forcing me to stop. She stood there, blinking at me, waiting. Perhaps I was lucky words were so difficult for her. It would save the chastisement I deserved.

"You don't like Thomas, do you? Do you guys have a past or something?" She didn't understand what was going on. She was blind to him.

"No, do you?"

"Do I what?"

"Have a past *or something* with him?" The flame had been growing progressively hotter since the two of them smiled at each other the first time.

Her brow drew down and her lip curled.

I squeezed my eyes shut and clenched my jaw. "I'm sorry. That's none of my business." My hand headed toward my hair, but she snatched it before it was all the way up.

"Alright." She glanced around and snuck a kiss to the back of my hand before releasing it. "Now call Mario. Let's get this thing reported."

Alright? Was it that simple? I could apologize and she would leave it at that? Our relationship was so new, so fragile and raw. It hadn't even been two weeks since she told me she never wanted to see me again.

But she came back to me. Said all the words I'd dreamt of and more. She'd made love with me, laughed with me, traveled with me. And I'd throw it away for what? For petty jealousy?

"Who's the one thinking too much now?" She nudged my shoulder and smiled.

The fire shifted inside me, her forgiveness propelling it from a fit of jealousy to furious desire.

I stuffed the phone into my pocket and pulled her into an embrace. Holding her tightly, I pressed my cheek against hers, wanting her soft skin against mine. Her warm touch, her even temperament. If only I could wrap her in my arms and never let her go.

"You alright, Antonio?" she asked hesitantly.

"I've never been better." Leaning back, I took in her beautiful face. "Are you sure you want to stay here? We could return to the villa?"

"Hardly. I want a tour of the lab, then we're going to the archaeology museum." She frowned, pushing out of my arms. "And no PDAs so close to the office."

I reached for her, the desire to express my emotions fully overwhelming me. "I need to make love to you right now."

She stepped back with a grin. "I think you have the words need and want confused."

When I followed her, she chuckled, placing a hand on my chest to hold me at bay. "Relax. Isn't that what you keep telling me?"

I balled my fists on my hips, unable to control my breath or my smirk. Women rarely said no to me. Until her. She said no all the time, while still saying yes so much more.

Hand still on my chest, her head swiveled around, evaluating our surroundings. Would she kiss me if no one was looking, as she'd kissed my hand? Biting her lower lip, she winked at me.

She strolled toward the nearest building, the flirtatious sway to her hips. I was hot on her surprisingly slow-for-Samantha heels. Instead of heading to the door, she took a detour around the side into the small alley between it and the next building.

Leaning against the stone wall once we were near the back, she beckoned with a finger. "Vieni qui, bello."

Moistening her lips, she was the sexiest thing I'd ever seen. I pressed my body against hers, into her softness, grasping her hands and pinning them beside her head. My mouth approached hers, but I stayed out of reach. "Shall I make love to you right here?"

She tested my grip, as she always did. The rough exterior of the building would tear at her skin if she tried to pull her hands down, but I'd release her in a blink if she wanted me to. "I was thinking a little make-out session. You know, to tide you over until later."

"An appetizer?" I rubbed the growing bulge in my pants

across the front of hers, wanting the appetizer, the main course, and dessert. Not to mention seconds.

Eyes widening, she let out a little gasp. "Where did that come from?"

I ran my tongue along her top lip. "I wonder."

Her tongue darted out to encourage mine into her mouth, and I happily obliged. She moaned as I kissed her, bowing her body away from the wall, eliminating the space between us. Releasing one of her hands—which dug into my hair—I pulled her blouse out of her pants and reached underneath. Splaying my fingers across her abdomen, I skimmed the bottom of her bra with a thumb.

"Lacy," I whispered, pulling away enough to look down her top. Robin's egg blue with white lace. "When did you get that?"

"When you snuck off to *not* buy me something in Capri."

I leaned in to nuzzle her neck through my grin. "Would you be angry if I did buy you something?"

She groaned, rubbing her foot up my calf. "Stop talking."

"You know this is a poorly thought out plan?"

Her hips pushed against me, her breath coming in shorter bursts. "Yeah, I was coming to that conclusion. Maybe we should stop."

"Perhaps." I raked my teeth along her earlobe and she whimpered.

She was such a strong woman and when she made a noise like that, it ricocheted through my body. She wouldn't allow anyone else to hear that sound from her. That was for me alone.

The world dropped away, and it was just the two of us. We kissed again, our mouths growing frantic. I bracketed her supporting leg with mine, and she rolled her hips, creating the friction for both of us. Her leg rubbing my calf rose to latch around my ass.

"You should have worn a dress."

"We should stop." She continued moving against me, the sensation decimating my common sense. It *was* a stupid idea, but felt so good. "You could get in trouble if someone catches us."

"There you are!"

Both our heads snapped to the sound of the voice. Mario strode toward us, unconcerned with what he was interrupting.

"I was looking all over for you! I went to see Bianca, but she said you just left with some security consultant?"

We both scowled at him, and Samantha's leg dropped.

He shook his head. "You should have found somewhere more private. Ask me next time. I know the best places for making out around here."

I let go of Samantha's hand and kissed her cheek, my erection flagging. "Grazie, bella."

"Grazie yourself." She inspected the back of her hand, which bore an imprint from the wall.

"Come, you two lovebirds, we need to speak with the Carabinieri about the missing fresco. Then I hear I'm giving a tour of the laboratory and the archaeology museum?"

As I began walking toward my trouble-making cousin, Samantha smacked my ass. I turned to narrow my eyes at her. "You just wait until we get home, Caine."

She winked at me, unable to contain the smirk gracing her lovely face. "I think we should stay out all day and tour the city. Maybe come home so late we collapse in bed asleep. Mario, do you have a tour long enough for that?"

"To exhaust Antonio so much he couldn't make love to you? I doubt that."

Her jaw dropped, and it was my turn to wink at her.

She caught up with us and nudged his shoulder. "You're supposed to help me harass him."

We walked out of the small alley together, laughing despite my frustration. My fingers slipped into her palm, but she pulled her hand away. Back to the professional.

Mario looked from our hands to each of us in turn. "What are you two playing at?"

"I'm the security consultant." She undid the bun which I'd ruined when I pressed her against the wall and deftly twisted it up. Her eyes slid closed as she worked.

"Scusi?" Mario watched her hands moving in her hair. He stared too intently, and his eyes followed her neck, falling below her collarbone. I shoved him but admired the way her back arched as she pulled at the glorious strands, confining them.

Mario shoved me back, pointing at my hair. I ran my fingers through it a few times to smooth out the mess Samantha had made.

"Long story." She finished a fresh bun, not seeming to notice either of us ogling her. Her pace quickened to its normal stride. "Just go with it for now. It's easier than explaining."

CHAPTER 13

ANTONIO

THE PARK WAS JUST as busy on Wednesday as it had been for our visit Sunday, but the further Samantha, Mario, and I strayed from the core and primary attractions, the fewer people we had to navigate.

"Why do the Carabinieri want to meet us at the site?" Samantha asked Mario. "Shouldn't we go to their office?"

He shook his head. "The officer I spoke with said they wanted to take photographs and would need our guidance."

I folded our clasped hands behind her back, pulling in closer to whisper in her ear. "And then we head to the villa so I can get the rest of that appetizer you promised me."

She nudged me away with her hip. "We're going to the—"

"Dr. Ferraro!" came an excited voice from behind us. We all turned to see a man in his mid-twenties, with light brown hair and dark eyes. Roughly my height, dressed in slim khaki shorts and a mint-green polo shirt.

"Ciao, Umberto." I smiled as he hurried to catch up with us.

Umberto Longhi was another member of my team, a

student from my alma mater in Roma. Just as I had, he was studying for his master's in Architecture Restoration. He was one of the first Mario had questioned while Samantha and I were out of town.

I gestured to her to introduce them. "This is S—"

"I'm so glad I ran into you!" Umberto put his hands on his hips and exhaled sharply—as though the hurry were an effort for him—ignoring the introduction. "Is there any word on the late equipment?"

"Not yet," said Mario.

Despite my speaking in English—a language everyone on my team spoke—he continued in rapid Italian. Umberto's eyes stayed on me, barely even glancing at Samantha. "My girl-friend's getting antsy about it. Eva landed a job at Riccardo Emanuele's gallery and thinks our whole project here's going to be canceled if the lens doesn't come, so we'll have to go home to Rome early."

Samantha slid her fingers out of my grip and clasped her hands behind her back. After the surprise of her knowing Thomas, I'd told her about each member of the team working with me, so she switched to the professional. She bit back a chuckle, likely at how rapidly Umberto spoke. Umberto reminded me of Samantha's protégé at Foster Mutual Insurance, Lucy Chapman. Full of energy, fast-talker, and shared more about his life than even I would have been comfortable sharing of my own.

"They won't cancel it," I said.

"Thank heavens!" Umberto's eyes went wide, and he exaggerated another exhale. "I mean, it's such an honor to work with you. I really couldn't bear losing out on this opportunity."

I gestured in our original direction, inviting him to proceed toward the Casa. "Mario spoke to you about the missing segment of the wall painting?"

"He did, yes. It won't be canceled for that either, will it?"

I laughed as we continued down the road, the four of us descending to the roadway so Umberto could walk next to me. "Don't worry. I'm confident we'll start within a few weeks. If the delivery company can't find the missing lens, I have a few leads on others to replace it."

"It's probably good timing all around," Samantha said. "The initial investigation would have halted your work anyway, I expect."

"Perhaps," Mario said. "It's also possible today will be the only day they consider it."

"You think?" In her mind, the theft of the flower fresco was the most important crime in the country.

Mario attempted to temper her reaction. "It will be difficult to track anything—"

"Dr. Ferraro, I was meaning to ask about your master's thesis." Umberto spoke over their conversation, preventing my participation. "What you wrote about the environmental challenges the wall paintings face in Pompeii really changed the direction of my studies..."

He continued talking, while Mario reached around Samantha's back to nudge me. I looked over only long enough to see him mouth, 'Big fan.'

"Did I tell you my girlfriend worked at your family conservation studio in Rome for a few months? Before I got this offer?"

I nodded. Perhaps Mario was correct. "Sì, you mentioned that."

"She's hoping to work for them after—"

We turned the corner, off of Via di Nola, into the alley along the side of the building. Voices carried over the crumbling walls. I put up a hand and looked at Samantha. We all paused. Even Umberto stopped his chatter. English voices and laughter.

"The Carabinieri?" Samantha asked, but she would have known better. The voices were too young and not Italian. There were signs in multiple languages to keep tourists out. Was it the thieves back for more? Surely not in the middle of the day.

I shook my head and we charged in through the atrium door on the western wall.

A group of young people, early twenties at the most, sitting on the garden ledge, eating chips and drinking Chinotto. Sitting on an unpreserved, freshly excavated wall! They smiled as we entered, but my fists clenched, wanting to wrap themselves around one of these interlopers' necks.

"Get off the wall!" I yelled, eliciting a small yelp from Umberto. "What do you think this is? A public park for your little picnic?"

The intruders all shot up, looking at each other, spilling food and drink.

All except one, who raised his bottle to us in salute. "Who are you, the police?" He spoke with a slight accent. New York, perhaps?

"No," Samantha said, her pitch low and tone commanding. "But they're on their way."

"Calm down," said the sitting young man. "We aren't damaging anything."

"Yes, you are," said Umberto in impeccable English,

raising his voice as he stepped next to me. "This is a sensitive area. Sitting on that wall can cause pieces to break off. The paintings here haven't been preserved yet. They're fragile."

The punk dumped his chips on the ground as he stood, gaze lingering on Umberto before shifting to me, egging us on. "This place sucks anyway."

The group traipsed out together, dumping more chips and soda as they left. Flipping fingers to the four of us.

Umberto rushed to the garden wall, collecting flakes of black fresco which had fallen to the ground where the group sat. "This is why there's a barrier," he mumbled.

Mario knelt next to him, helping.

I slid close to Samantha. "You don't think someone like them would be behind the theft? Perhaps it was simple vandalism?"

It was a reasonable question. They'd damaged the garden walls without realizing it, but she shook her head and beckoned me to follow to the Mars room.

Once there, she pointed to the edge around where the fresco had been for almost two thousand years. "There are smooth cut marks. The flowers were removed with a professional tool. Intentionally. People like them are more likely to chip something off an edge or pry up some mosaic tiles with their keys."

"True."

We turned as Umberto and Mario joined us.

She gestured to the Mars wall, where the flowers had once been. "Umberto, Mario told us you hadn't heard anything about the missing section of the wall painting?"

He shook his head, moving closer to the wall with a soft, almost reverent look.

She continued, "No one mentioned anything at the lab about removing it for some additional tests or conservation? Maybe checking something with the pigments?"

"No, I—" He spun on his heel and pointed at me. "Wait, I forgot! I was giving my girlfriend a tour yesterday afternoon and, since she's an artist, she wanted to see the pigment pots in the lab."

No, no, no. I had to change the subject. But to what? "Where did you say she worked?"

He paused for half a breath only, and said, "We found some were missing. She wasn't happy."

Mario nodded. "Sì, Bianca told us on Friday."

Marone. I could almost hear the cogs grinding in Samantha's brain. Why hadn't I told Mario to keep his mouth shut?

"Missing pigment pots?" Her gaze lingered for a moment on Umberto, then shifted to me. She blinked several times while Umberto said something to Mario. But all I heard was Samantha's flat tone of disappointment. "You didn't mention that."

"I didn't think it was important."

Mario mumbled, "Important enough for the Carabinieri to come by on the weekend."

Her head turned slowly to Mario. "That's why you interrupted us?"

He grimaced. "I *am* sorry about that."

"So…" She stepped closer to the wall. "On Friday, you two find out that a special piece of equipment is missing and some pigments were taken from the lab. Saturday, the police talk to you. Sunday, you discover a fresco's been stolen from your worksite. Does that sum it up?"

Umberto asked Mario, "You heard about the pigments Friday?"

"I need to talk to Bianca again." Samantha frowned. "To someone who'll tell me the whole truth."

I placed a hand on her arm. "Bell—"

When she turned her frown on me, I mirrored it. This was not just professional Samantha, it was professional and irritated Samantha. Pet names and displays of affection were not an option.

"Fine," I huffed, releasing my hand and not caring to hide my frustration from her. "*Ms. Caine*, the Carabinieri are meeting us here in literally five minutes. You don't need to speak with Bianca. That's *their* job. That's why they were asking about the pigment pots and the missing lens on Saturday."

Her jaw flexed several times, her eyes narrowed. There was the silence again. Always with the staring, this woman. I could shake her and yell, 'Let your feelings out!' but it wouldn't make any difference.

Particularly with Umberto there.

Why was she always so restrained in public? What was she trying to prove? And why did she care so much about this?

"I should go," Umberto whispered to Mario.

"Probably wise," Mario responded, more a stage whisper, and they retreated from the room, toward the garden.

"Somebody stole this from you." She jabbed a finger at the blank spot of the wall, as though Pompeii belonged to me. "This is *your* project and you don't care."

"Of course I care." I stepped closer and put a hand on her hip. "But I care more about being here with you. I know you feel strongly about this, and I don't want to detract from that, but…"

But what? She was reacting exactly the way I knew she would. I should have been proud, like I was at the auction. Like when I showed her the first proof the Chagall had been a fake or when I watched her in the press conference.

It was selfish, but part of me wanted to distract her from the thefts so she'd focus on me. On us. We only had so much time before she'd return to the States, and I wanted every ounce of her to myself.

I let out a sigh. Letting things go was not Samantha's style, unless it was her decision. But perhaps a little understanding would help smooth things over.

"My Lara Croft." I cupped her cheek with my free hand. On our first date—or business meeting, if you asked her— she'd explained what her video game hero meant to her. "Protecting the treasures of the world from thieves and charlatans."

"Bianca knows more than she told us and I want those details." Her face softened despite the serious words. Honesty and truth were the two most important qualities to her. I hadn't been completely honest with her and now she thought Bianca hadn't either. "And no amount of Ferraro charm is going to change that."

"Are you sure?" I kissed the tip of her nose, already knowing the answer. "My charm seemed to work when we slipped behind the lab."

An almost-smile crept across her face. "I'm being serious."

I let out a small laugh. "I would never accuse you of anything but, Ms. Caine."

CHAPTER 14
SAMANTHA

THE OFFICER LOOKED twelve years old. Maybe thirteen. Obviously, he was much older than that to be a member of the Carabinieri—sporting the white belt across his blue-clad chest and the flaming grenade insignia on his peak cap—but the rounded features, barely-there stubble, and blush just added to the youthful appearance.

"And who discovered that the segment of the wall was missing?" he said, pen hovering over his notebook.

"That would be Ms. Caine." Antonio gestured to me. At least he didn't huff that time. Respecting my professional boundaries hadn't been a problem at the lab, but once we were out at the Casa, it had become a challenge.

Or maybe that was because he'd been trying to hide the mysterious disappearance of the pigment pots from me.

Fortunately, he'd recovered most of his senses before the officers arrived and agreed to visit Bianca before we went to the museum.

I shook my head. "It was all of us. We were looking at

photos on the train and noticed they didn't match what was on the wall when we got here Sunday afternoon."

The officer nodded. "Can I see the photos?"

Antonio showed the pictures on his phone and forwarded them as requested.

The officer questioning us, Carabiniere Fredo De Rosa, raised an eyebrow. "And you discovered this after our discussion about the pigment pots Saturday?"

Mario said, "We did."

Another officer took photographs with a large camera, an over-sized light attached to the top.

"My notes don't indicate what colors were taken."

Mario looked at Antonio and me. "Colors?"

"Do the stolen pigments match the stolen piece of the wall?" De Rosa focused on his notebook, jotting down information. "Is it possible the events are linked? Maybe the thief enjoys the yellow color of the flower petals?"

The twelve-year-old vanished, his eyes sharpening. That was an excellent question. Two thefts from areas which should have been limited to Park staff. Mario had spoken to almost everyone about the wall segment, but this would change the questions.

Why wouldn't Bianca have told me about the pigments when we spoke earlier? Was I wrong about her fidgeting? Was it actually guilt instead of nerves around Antonio? She'd been working at the Park for years, had access to the computer systems, would have known when people would be in the Casa, and was 'off sick' for two days after the theft.

Or was she hiding it for Antonio? Since he seemed to be hiding it from me. Although, Mario didn't seem to realize

Antonio was keeping secrets, and it was unlikely Bianca was in on something Mario wasn't.

De Rosa continued, "I know the one recovered in Rome Saturday morning was blue, but what colors were the other two?"

Recovered? More things Antonio didn't tell me. "Did you catch someone with it?"

"You'll have to speak with the laboratory staff about that," said Antonio. There it was again. The irritation and impatience. He hadn't cut me off, but put up a barrier between my question and the officer's potential answer.

He hadn't once brushed me off like that while I was investigating the Chagall—even though he'd kept the truth from me the entire time—or the stolen painting at the auction. He'd seemed impressed. Told me he was proud of me.

But now?

Despite his frustration at my wanting to be seen as something more than 'Dr. Ferraro's girlfriend,' he seemed to understand this was important to me. So what was with his attitude?

"We're going to speak with Bianca before going to the museum," I said. Antonio and I had a week left together. Plenty of time for touring, romancing, and following a few obvious leads, even if an official investigation was also in progress.

Antonio exhaled slowly and smiled at me, tight-lipped. "Of course."

"And your name was..." De Rosa flipped pages in his small notebook while the other carabiniere scrolled through photos on the camera. "Dr. Antonio... Ferraro?"

"Sì, I'm in charge of the conservation project which will start here soon."

"Ferraro..." De Rosa inserted a finger to bookmark the page with our names and flipped to a fresh sheet. "You were the last one to see it here?"

Antonio frowned. "No, someone from the lab took photos on Saturday morning. I was here Friday, then Sunday when we noticed the fresco was missing."

The carabiniere nodded thoughtfully, making a few more notes. "Who took the photos?"

Mario said, "I don't know."

"I was asking Dr. Ferraro." De Rosa smiled pointedly at Mario. "It's his project, after all. He should know everything going on here, shouldn't he?"

"The project has not started yet." Mario's jaw clenched, a look I'd seen from Antonio several times before. "And no, he won't be keeping track of everyone who comes in and out of this space, especially considering there's no security to the north of the building. Just fields."

De Rosa's features seemed to age another few years as he said to Antonio, "Your accent is Roman. I was stationed in Rome before I transferred here. It occurred to me after we spoke on Saturday that I know a few Ferraros."

Antonio's face darkened. People recognizing his family should have made him happy or proud, shouldn't it? "My father's brother, Andrea, runs the Ferraro Fine Art Restoration and Conservation studio in Roma."

De Rosa nodded thoughtfully. "Yes, I'm familiar with the company."

That was practically the same thing Nathan had said to Antonio, the first night my big brother stand-in almost got into a fight with him. 'Familiar with your family' had been Nathan's line. Then he'd implied a connection between Antonio's family and some sort of illegal activities. But he was making wild leaps with that information. Wasn't he?

"I didn't ask you the other day... How long have you been in the country, Dr. Ferraro?" The carabiniere's tone was casual, but the questions were coming faster and faster. The note-taking looked more like an act than actual notes.

"I arrived last Tuesday."

"And when was the last time you were in Italy prior to last Tuesday?"

Antonio's shoulders heaved with a deep breath, looking at Mario as he exhaled. "Eighteen months? Two years?"

Mario shrugged. "Between those."

The non-note-taking pen gestured between the two cousins. "You two are living together. How do you know each other?"

Mario nodded. "Cousins."

"But you're not a Ferraro?" De Rosa didn't bother flipping through his notebook to check the names. Mario was a De Luca, from Antonio's mother's side. If the officer recognized the Ferraro name from the start, he'd remember Mario wasn't in the same family.

"No," said Mario.

"And what about that bruise around your eye?" De Rosa gestured to Antonio's cheek with his pen. "How'd you get that?"

Also Nathan. The night Antonio and I split up, Nathan had come to my rescue. I'd only called him to drive me home, but he'd taken the opportunity to show Antonio what he thought of him.

Antonio's face squirreled up. "What does that have to do with anything?"

"The easiest explanation is usually the right one. A man who has full run of the space, able to cordon it off from the public, knows the comings and goings, able to hide away a piece of equipment to delay official progress..." De Rosa waved the pen around as he spoke, as though conducting an invisible symphony of implication. "Not only with the knowledge of how to conserve a fresco once it's gone, but access to facilities in Rome to do just that. And perhaps also pigments to help the process, not to mention..."

The carabiniere slowed, letting the tip of the pen rest in Antonio's direction before continuing. "Contacts who know how to move such a piece along?"

Before Antonio got it in his head to punch the man, which he appeared to be on the verge of, I piped up. "He was with me when the fresco was taken. The entire time."

"Really?" De Rosa looked me up and down, then did the same with Antonio.

I knew that appraising look. We weren't standing next to each other, not in physical contact at all. Professional mode wasn't what the moment needed. I closed the distance between Antonio and me, slipping my hand around his waist, resting it on his opposite hip, while he did the same around my shoulders.

Warmth spread through me, nudging out the frustration. Antonio wasn't being punchy because of me—it was about De Rosa. Something must have happened between them on Saturday.

"Really." When I looked up at Antonio and smiled at him, his tension visibly eased. "I arrived in Naples Saturday just after noon, and we haven't been apart since then. We were in Capri Monday and Tuesday, if it becomes relevant."

De Rosa flipped to the spot in his notebook he'd book-marked with a finger and tapped the pen on it. "So... Ms. Caine? American tourist, you say, yet your Italian is flawless. If you've never been here before, how did you identify the missing fresco, despite two men who work here failing to notice?"

"She has a remarkable—" began Antonio.

"I'm speaking to her, please," said De Rosa.

I shrugged. "I have an eye for certain things. Not quite photographic, but close. Dr. Ferraro showed me photos of the wall on our way here, and I recognized the real thing didn't match, but needed to see the photograph again to know why."

"You have your documentation?"

I let go of Antonio and opened my small crossbody bag to produce my passport for him.

He held it open, comparing my face to the photograph, made some more notes, then skimmed the pages. "Only one stamp?" He passed it back to me, some of the youthfulness reappearing in his face.

"I haven't traveled outside the United States since I got this one." The passport was six years old. And he was right, it needed more stamps. I slid my arm back around Antonio, who hadn't let go of me. Deep inside, I sighed. Maybe more Italian stamps.

The officer with the camera motioned to De Rosa, and they stepped away from us to discuss the images.

Mario whispered, "Do they really think you'd steal from the Park?"

Antonio shot him a look, one of the cousin looks, where the two shared unspoken words. "He's doing his job."

"A little zealously," I said under my breath. "But at least he sounds like he'll do something about it."

More of the tension left him, and he squeezed my shoulder. "Which means I get your focus back on me?"

"After—"

Before I could finish, Carabiniere De Rosa and his partner returned. "Thank you for your cooperation. You're free to go."

The three of us left through the atrium door and made our way back to Via di Nola. Antonio ran his hand from my shoulder down my arm and raised an eyebrow. "As I was saying... I get you back after we speak with Bianca?"

I wanted to find the missing fresco for him. We worked so well together at the auction last month, when we proved one of the paintings had been stolen. And despite its foregone conclusion, we worked well together on the burned Chagall copy. Why didn't he want to do this with me? Sure, it wasn't touristy stuff and it couldn't be done from the comfort of a bedroom, but wasn't our goal to get to know each other better? Mario said Antonio told him art crimes were important to me, but did he think it was just a fun little side hobby? Didn't he realize just how important it was?

No, maybe not. There was so much I hadn't told him yet.

I said, "We'll speak to Bianca, go to the museum, then go—"

He nestled his face against the side of my head as we walked, lips brushing my ear, hot breath and voice quiet enough for me alone. "Back to bed?"

That depended on what Bianca had to say. What if it was an intentional omission? What if there was something suspicious? Something else missing she hadn't mentioned. Something else Antonio knew but hadn't told me.

Carabiniere De Rosa all but accused him of stealing the pots and fresco already.

Was that just a suspicious nature or was there something else behind it?

Had Nathan been right about Antonio all along?

CHAPTER 15

SAMANTHA

THE VAST SCALE model of the Pompeii site spread out across the center of the room. The model provided a unique perspective of the city, showing how the excavations stood over a century ago. Each wall was hand-painted to match how it had looked when unearthed. Many of the walls had deteriorated at the actual site since the model was completed, so it was an even more remarkable example of the city's original grandeur.

Couples, families, and individuals moved through the space, taking cursory glances at it, but it was most popular with the children. It was difficult to absorb the enormity of Pompeii any other way.

A drawing of the city hung on the wall opposite us, frescoes stood in the room next to us, and statuary lay beyond. The National Archaeological Museum should have been a highlight of my visit. Three hours ago, I'd been excited to come.

But all I saw was Carabiniere De Rosa quizzing Antonio.

Mario revealing they already knew about the missing pigments.

And Bianca. What did she have to say for herself? A shoulder shrug and 'I didn't think they were related.'

Unbelievable. Just as useless as Antonio's 'I didn't think it was important.' How could a missing fresco and the missing pigment pots—both under the control of the Pompeii conservators and vanishing in the same week—*not* be related?

And the worst part? I had nowhere else to go. No other clues to follow. No links, no people, nothing to do. Whoever took all those things was probably going to get away with it.

"I was thinking," said Mario. "When Samantha leaves you for me, perhaps you could pick up Umberto?"

Antonio laughed. The two of them had been back to their normal joking selves the moment we left the lab, as though the interview at the site hadn't even happened. "I don't think his girlfriend would be happy about that."

"Or maybe she would!"

They continued giggling like schoolgirls, probably waggling eyebrows or winking at each other. The laughter died faster than it likely would have if I'd joined in—if my arms weren't crossed and I wasn't staring daggers at the model. I was being a piss-poor tourist.

Antonio and I had only known each other for four-and-a-half weeks. Hard to imagine it was so short at times, but it was clear in a moment like this. On the way to the museum, he'd told me *again* that the investigation wasn't my job, tried explaining the role of the Carabinieri to me like I didn't know, and attempted to distract me by suggesting we could hike the Amalfi Coast.

The last one caught my attention. If he hadn't been an ass about the investigation, it probably would have worked.

"I'll see if I can get you access to the archives." Mario patted Antonio on the back and whispered something to him.

Antonio slid his arm around my waist and kissed my temple. "Penny for your thoughts?"

Relationships took time to build. That didn't happen overnight. *Let him in. Stop pushing him away.* "The site's so easy to get into. The thief could be anyone."

"Sì, this is true."

"Someone who figured they'd target a room that hadn't been conserved yet. Maybe the wall paintings would be loose, damaged, easy to remove."

"Mm-hmm."

"And even in that state, incredibly valuable. Maybe more so because of it. But once you finished your conservation work, some of the cracks would be repaired, it would be stabilized, and better adhered."

"You seem to take this personally." His voice was soft, not an accusation or a recrimination like his earlier comments. And worse yet, he was right. I'd come here to focus on him and me together, not to go running off after stolen antiquities.

"Why didn't you tell me about the pigments?"

"Because we're on vacation."

I blew out a long breath and leaned my head against him. *Just tell him the truth, Sam. You want to have it all. Him and your art crime investigations.* But I couldn't. The world didn't work that way. If I wanted to join Elliot at the FBI, I'd have to leave Antonio. It wasn't fair. "Just an insurance adjuster, right?"

"I don't think you're *just* anything, bella." He squeezed

my waist. "Unless you include *just* brilliant or *just* beautiful or perhaps—"

My hand snaked out of my folded arms to smack his chest. Ridiculous. Although I loved how he always started with my brain. What man had ever did that? Who would have taken me to this museum and had intelligent discussions on the pieces and their history?

Only one. Vincenzo. But I couldn't think about him anymore.

I was there with the man I wanted to be with. The one I'd flown half-way across the world to beg his forgiveness. And I was throwing all that away because I was angry I didn't get to carry out an investigation I really had no right to follow?

"Excusa me?" said a woman on Antonio's other side, well-freckled with auburn hair and porcelain skin. An obvious English-speaker attempting Italian. "Photo, per favore?"

"Certainly." Antonio separated from me and the woman's posture immediately relaxed, no doubt from hearing English. He took the offered phone, capturing a few pictures of the woman and her young daughter. The girl was older than my niece, maybe six or seven years old. Antonio knelt in front of her. "Are you enjoying the museum?"

She nodded, her red pigtails bouncing.

"What's your favorite part so far?"

Her hand flung out toward the model of the city.

Antonio nodded. "Like a giant doll house, sì?"

"I don't have any dolls small enough."

"Have you been to the real Pompeii yet?" He wanted kids. I knew that. But seeing him interact with the little girl—the way her eyes fixed on him like she was instinctively comfortable around him—made my breath catch in my throat. What kind of father would he be? He was so emotional. Would he be patient or quick to anger? Tender?

The mother put a hand on the little girl's shoulder. "That's tomorrow."

Antonio stood and returned the phone. "Be sure to take her to the small theater. Sit her up high in the stands, then walk down to the stage so she can hear you speaking clearly. No need to yell. The acoustics are remarkable and she'll be amazed."

The woman nodded, smiling. "Thank you so much."

She ushered her daughter away, who waved over her shoulder as they left to view the frescoes in the next room.

After he returned the wave, I slid my hand into his.

I chewed on my bottom lip and scrubbed across my face with my free hand. Family was important to him. But Nathan had concerns about his family. So did Carabiniere De Rosa. Even Antonio hadn't seemed sure.

"Honesty and trust, Antonio," I said, echoing the most significant words I'd said to him back home. "Why did you think your family would be implicated in the Chagall fraud?"

His thumb stroked absently along the side of my held hand. "Strange turn of subject, bella."

"Within the last two and a half weeks, you've been present at an auction where a stolen painting was recovered, were involved with a million-dollar fraudulent painting, and now these two thefts and your missing equipment." My gaze fell away from him. I was stepping over a line, but I had to know. There were too many coincidences. I'd had more art crimes to investigate over the last month than I had since abandoning the FBI Art Crimes team.

But after talking to the officer... were his implications the reason why Antonio didn't want me to dig deeper? Was there something behind them?

His head pulled back slightly. "You're not accusing me, surely?"

My eyes shot wide and I shook my head. "No, that's not it. I mean..." It was about his family, but when he said it out loud like that... that is what it sounded like. "I don't know what I mean."

"This is about the questions the officer asked me, sì?"

I let go of his hand and rubbed at my face.

"You still don't trust me, do you?" He pulled my hands down and leaned in so I couldn't avoid his face or the sadness in his pulled-down brows.

"It's a learning process."

His head tilted and he smiled. "That was surprisingly honest, bella."

"I should let this theft thing go, shouldn't I?"

"Sì, I may have suggested this."

"It's just..." I wanted to rub at my face, put up a barrier between us, but he wrapped my hands around his waist. "It all rolls off you, like it doesn't matter. Like nothing phases you. I can't stop thinking about it, and you're busy giving tourist advice to little girls."

"Is my big girl not getting enough attention?" He leaned close to my ear, blowing lightly.

"Stop." I stepped away, frowning at him. The room was full of people, and he was flirting shamelessly. "Can you be serious for five minutes?"

"Two is my record, but I can try." He winked and took a step forward, pulling my hands around him again, which made my frown almost impossible to maintain.

I stepped back, narrowly avoiding running into an older couple discussing the Pompeii ruins model. I put up a hand to stop him before he continued the silly dance and I tripped over someone. "The pigment pots are famous and taken from the lab itself. Please tell me they'll be easy to find?"

"Sì, they already found one. The others will be easy to find as well."

"And the fresco—"

"I hate to say it, but it's likely long gone already."

"Not famous and not easy to find."

"Bella, when we found the stolen painting at the auction, we reported it and moved on. We've finished doing that for the fresco and Bianca already did that for the pigments." He leaned forward and kissed the hand, which was supposed to be my shield. "I want to get back to helping my girlfriend tick off bucket list items before she has to leave Napoli."

I sighed, my irritation evaporating. He was right about all of it. "Damn you and your logic."

"I believe you mean—" He snatched my hand and pulled me into his arms. "—prego, you dashingly handsome man."

"Prego," I chuckled.

He was tall, broad, and strong. I was four inches shorter than him and strong in my own right, but surrounded by those shoulders and biceps, it was like we were in our own world. The smell of his cologne. The soft hair at the nape of his neck. The gentle thrum of his heart under those solid pecs. His warmth. No one and nothing else mattered.

"May your boyfriend kiss you in public, Ms. Caine?" He was right, and I was just being stubborn.

I pushed up on my tiptoes, meeting his lips with mine.

He sucked on my bottom lip and pressed his groin against

me, making his desire clear. "Can we go back to the villa now?"

"Will you make it that far?" I said with a laugh. "You're like a thirteen-year-old with that thing."

"It's a curious effect you have on me." His fingers snaked up to the base of my bun. He wouldn't pull it out, would he? "One we should explore..." His voice dropped in pitch and volume. "More deeply."

The sound shot directly to my core, and heat flashed through me, making me squirm. "Yeah, maybe we should go back to the—"

"You are going to love this!" Mario appeared out of thin air next to us, clapping his hands, causing us both to startle.

The room and all the other people snapped back into focus. What was I doing? Public displays of affection were off the table for me. And while Antonio's gaze held promises that were thoroughly inappropriate in a national museum, I welcomed every one.

Mario continued. "They're preparing a new exhibit. It's off limits for another couple of weeks, but they're letting us in to preview and see several pieces which won't be included. Want to know what it is?"

"Who's letting us in?" Antonio asked, arms still around me, the hardness which had pushed against my hip easing.

Mario waggled his eyebrows. "The curator I'm taking to dinner on Saturday night."

I stifled a laugh, attempting a step back, but failing to separate from Antonio's grip. "What's the display?"

"Some looted items which were recently returned during confession at a nearby church. The tombarolo who took them —although he claimed at first they were in his family for generations—said he'd been suffering horrible luck for years and needed to give them back."

Tombaroli—the Italian term given to grave, tomb, and ancient site thieves—were a big part of the cultural heritage crime problem in Italy. The country was so rich in buried antiquities it was near impossible to police.

"Where were they looted from?" I asked.

"You have one guess," said Mario, holding up his index finger. "And it must be related to a lecture you gave me."

My hand flew to my chest to hold my heart in. "Civita Giuliana?"

Mario winked at me.

I looked back and forth between my sex-god boyfriend and the archaeologist promising me the chance of a lifetime. The choice was obvious, at least for me. And I knew Antonio knew it, too. "I'll make it up to you, Antonio."

CHAPTER 16
SAMANTHA

Thursday was for touring Sorrento. Antonio and I stood waiting for gelato—the best in the world, according to him—on a narrow pedestrian street. Tall buildings, shops, and cafés shaded by awnings lined each side. Two stories above us, laundry dried on lines spanning the gaps between metal balconies. The gelateria was small, and the line was thirty people deep. Although in perfect Italian style, it was more a mass of people who instinctively knew when it would be their turn.

"Lemon?" Antonio wore a black silk V-neck, white linen pants, and boat shoes. Ravishing, as always. He'd begged for me to wear a pale yellow dress, which fell almost to my ankles, and a wide-brimmed hat. His request for high heels was rejected. There was no way I was going on a walking tour in anything but well-cushioned sandals.

I shook my head. "I've had more than enough lemons at the villa to last a lifetime. Mario's obsessed."

"Vanilla?"

"Boring!"

He tsked at me. "Vanilla gelato is the ultimate of craftsmanship. Creating a simple flavor requires a better recipe, finer ingredients, and takes more effort to master." He folded our joined hands behind my back to pull me closer. I had to tilt my head so the giant hat brim didn't poke his eye out. It left me at the perfect angle for him to kiss my cheek.

He smiled broadly, while I craned my neck to check if the staff was still working inside; it was taking so long.

"Bella, patience. The gelato here is worth a small wait."

I frowned, but he leaned in for another kiss. Something I'd never tire of.

The exhibit preview yesterday had been fascinating. And the decision to drop the investigation to just be in the moment with my sexy Latin lover was the right one. We'd made love when we got back to the villa, curled up to watch a movie Mario picked, ate takeout, and made love again. And again.

The idea of chasing down the fresco and pigments was exhilarating—the sort of thing I'd wanted to do since I was a kid. But something changed inside me over the last month. After my divorce, I did everything on my own, moving from town to town for my job and living out of my little RV. Choosing Antonio meant putting an end to that lifestyle.

He'd been by my side for the auction painting and the burned Chagall investigation, and somehow that made them both more satisfying. That was new for me. Scary. And as terrifying as that realization was a few days ago, it already felt almost comfortable.

I sighed and squeezed his hand. It was a glorious day. On the streets of Sorrento with my adoring and ridiculously amazing boyfriend. Touring, chatting, being in... whatever this was.

"How about gianduja?"

My mouth watered at the word. "Now you're speaking my language!"

"No, bella, that's my language. If I'd said chocolate hazelnut, that would have been yours."

I rolled my eyes, unable to stifle the laughter. I lifted on my toes to give him a peck on the lips. "You're so cheesy."

"Anything to hear you laugh, amore."

The group behind us jostled me, and one of them apologized in French.

I turned to smile. "Pas de problème." The young woman who'd knocked into me said something else, but my attention fell past her, to a familiar face at a café down the street.

"Are you alright, bella?"

I spun back to Antonio and hooked a thumb over my shoulder. "I think I see someone I know down there. Get me half vanilla, half gianduja and come over. If I'm right, he'll want to meet you."

"Who is it?"

"Would you believe me if I said another old boss?"

He frowned. Was he still unhappy over my chat with Thomas? Focusing on 'us' over the stolen fresco was supposed to get us past those minor hiccups. I puckered up and he kissed me before I made my way down the street.

I strode toward the café, with its line of small tables tucked under its awning, avoiding running children and strolling tourists. The closer I got, the surer I was that I was right.

Special Agent Elliot Skinner sat with another man. His email had said he was headed to Rome. They each wore a white polo shirt, providing a sharp contrast to Elliot's deep brown skin and short black hair.

I stopped next to the table. Before I could say hello, I froze. What if he was undercover? Instead of starting with his name, I said simply "Buongiorno" and let him lead.

"Samantha! What a surprise!" He took the napkin from his lap, tapped his lips, and placed it beside his pizza. Standing with a grin, he shook my hand. "Changed your mind and tracked me down, did you?"

I smiled at the serious man with him, rich olive skin and gray-streaked black hair. He had a shifty look to him, cracking a cultivated smile which didn't reach his eyes. I returned my focus to Elliot. "We good?"

He nodded and sat back down, gesturing across the small table. "Sam, this is Bruno Gallo, with the Carabinieri TPC."

Shifty look be damned, I held out a hand to shake. The Carabinieri were one of Italy's three primary police forces and it was further divided into several branches. The TPC—Tutela Patrimonio Culturale, or the branch responsible for the Protection of Cultural Heritage—were the preeminent art crimes squad in the world, and I had an unending amount of respect for them.

"Bruno, this is Samantha Caine from America. I mentioned her to you."

A flutter burst through my stomach. He what? Mentioned me to a member of the TPC? That was well beyond asking me to come back to the Bureau.

"It's a pleasure, in that case." Bruno took my hand, the smile finally reaching his eyes. Maybe guarded was more appropriate than shifty. His English was smooth, with the barest hint of an accent to it.

"Your gelato, bella." Antonio arrived next to me, cup held out in offering.

I accepted it, unsure how to react to Elliot's comment. I'd last seen him a week ago in Brenton, Michigan. He'd come to town after Antonio and I discovered the stolen painting at the auction, and then he got involved with the Scott case when the woman behind the Chagall fraud skipped town. That day, he'd asked for the umpteenth time when I was coming back to the FBI and invited me to join his team in Rome. He'd even followed up with an email making the request more formal.

What was he doing in Sorrento?

Both men at the table looked at Antonio, a faint glance between them, then back at me. Right. Too in my head. Introductions.

"Antonio, this is Elliot Skinner, FBI Art Crimes, and Bruno Gallo, Carabinieri TPC." They shook hands all around as I continued. "And Dr. Antonio Ferraro. He's working temporarily at the Pompeii Archaeological Park as a conservator."

Elliot returned his focus to me. "I thought you two weren't in touch." He'd asked me about Antonio before the press conference last week, before I'd hopped on the plane to beg for a second chance. What was his intention with that comment? Was he curious? Accusatory? Conversational? He'd always been a hard man to read.

"We weren't," I said.

"Are you here for anything in particular?" Antonio took a spoonful of his gelato, sounding more suspicious than usual. There was an energy pinging between the trio, which unsettled me. Possibly related to Carabiniere De Rosa yesterday? He wasn't with the TPC branch, but still a member of the force.

A serious mask fell across Bruno's face.

Elliot continued to smile. "We're working a case in Rome,

but came down here after recovering a small pot of pigment taken from Pompeii. As I understand it, there are two additional pots still missing, not to mention a wall painting." He arched an eyebrow. "Know anything about that?"

Antonio put the small plastic spoon back in his cup, the movement reminding me about my gelato, which was melting. "That was fast. We only reported the fresco yesterday. Any leads?"

The two seated men shared another look, which made me sure the answer was yes—did they recover only the one pigment pot or did they have someone in custody—but Elliot shook his head. At least they weren't accusing Antonio of anything.

"Allora..." said Antonio. "Samantha worked for one of you, I understand?"

Elliot sat back in his chair. "That would be me."

"Just an internship," I interjected. Something was off about this conversation, and I wanted it to end. Everyone's guard was up, as though a sub-conversation was going on that I couldn't decode.

Antonio turned to me, blinking rapidly. "With the FBI?"

Before I could respond, Elliot chimed in. "And I've been trying to convince her to come back. I've followed behind her on four cases within the last month alone. Or should I say both of you, Dr. Ferraro?"

"Mi scusi?"

Elliot clasped his hands in front of him. "The auction at the hospital gala, the fake Chagall, now this fresco and the pigments in Pompeii. You two make a good team."

"The best," said Antonio, adjusting his feet so he was closer to me.

"So, Dr. Ferraro, Sam tells me you'll be here until Christmas?"

Antonio looked askance at me, finally taking a bite of his gelato again.

I shrugged. "Elliot wanted to meet you."

"Sì, I remember you now." Antonio pointed his spoon at Elliot. "You were in the press conference about the Scotts. Why did you want to speak with *me*?"

"Yeah. He was—"

Elliot interrupted me. "What I read about you in the files on the auction and the fake Chagall impressed me. I wanted to meet you and express the Bureau's appreciation for your role. That's all."

"Prego. It was the least I could do."

"No," said Elliot. "The least you can do is convince Sam to stop playing insurance adjuster and join my team here in Italy."

Antonio's eyes hit me again, and a pressure built in my chest. He wasn't the only one who'd been keeping secrets.

We'd shared so much of who we were, but not even close to everything. Like my brief FBI past. We hadn't known each other long enough for that. Why on Earth had I thought introducing him to Elliot would be a good idea? Time to head in the opposite direction. "I think that's our cue to leave."

"If I've learned anything—" Elliot stood to shake our hands again. "—it's that you never argue with Samantha Caine. Just keep paying attention and asking questions. Eventually, you'll catch a break."

Antonio grinned at that. "You have no idea, Special Agent Skinner."

"Dr. Ferraro, I'm on the road a lot, but the Detroit office is home." Elliot handed Antonio a business card. "Feel free to call anytime something pops up which may be of interest. I'd like to cultivate a relationship with one of the best art conservation companies in the world."

Elliot turned to me. "And you're more than welcome to join me and Bruno while we follow up on the fresco and the pigments."

Oh my god.

Goosebumps shot up my arms and not from the gelato. This was my in. I could work the case with people who had resources. And the law backing them up. And maybe even beyond that, onto the smuggling case. I could find the stolen flowers for Antonio while staying in the same city as him.

I... I...

The investigation would mean less time with Antonio. And I had to get back to Brenton and my sister for her chemo in less than a week.

All three pairs of eyes bored into me.

"Thanks, Elliot." I flicked a glance at Antonio from the corner of my eye. As much as I would have screamed 'yes' if I were by myself and didn't have responsibilities, I wasn't. And the other reality that was even clearer now that I had this offer? I didn't want to do anything without Antonio Ferraro. "But no. I have higher priorities right now."

Antonio's face broke into a wide smile and my heart swelled at the sight.

Bruno stood to join us and handed Antonio a business card as well. "In case you spot anything else while you're in Napoli, Dr. Ferraro. Or if you get any hints on who took the items from the Park."

We all nodded and said our goodbyes. Antonio and I headed back along the narrow street, enjoying our gelato.

"Intern with the FBI?" he asked once we were out of earshot. "Don't tell me this is another long and uninteresting story?"

I shrugged. "Pretty much."

"Any other internships I should know about?"

"Nope, just the two."

"And he wants you to work with him?"

Every time I saw Elliot, it was the same thing. And I wasn't ready to talk about it with anyone. I pointed my spoon at his gelato. "Is that pistachio?"

He took the hint, stopping to scoop some out for me. I joined him in the middle of the street, grinning when he wouldn't let me take the spoon. He fed it to me, the rich creaminess overpowering my taste buds. It was sweeter than mine, with a subtle nuttiness to it. Kind of like Antonio.

I licked my lips once it was gone. "That tastes almost as good as you do."

"Almost?" He raised an eyebrow.

"Try mine." Scooping up half-and-half gianduja and vanilla, I shared with him, wanting to get back to the moment before I'd seen Elliot.

"They do make the best vanilla." He nodded thoughtfully and winked at me. "But it doesn't taste anywhere near as good as you do."

Shoving my spoon into my gelato, I grabbed his shirt in my fist and pulled him in for a kiss. People detoured around us on the packed little street. My tongue slid over his and swept across his mouth, his hand sliding up my arm to my face. My hat fell off in the process, but who cared.

As we separated, I sighed. "All three together, plus you, makes the best combo."

He stared at me, cupping my jaw with his hand, running his thumb across my cheek. That look said it all. Dropping the investigation was the right decision for both of us. He really didn't care about that fresco as much as he cared about being with me. And that meant more than I would have expected.

CHAPTER 17

ANTONIO

Samantha, Mario, and I rounded the corner from the piazza into the small pedestrian street Friday night, arriving at the end of a long line of bodies in their club-going finest. Button-front shirts, short dresses, laughter, and loud voices. We walked past the crowd as the muffled bass thundered out through the walls, peaking every time the door at the front of the line opened. Above us, the curtains covering the windows flashed with color.

Samantha said she preferred a quiet bar where we could chat. I would normally, as well, but this nightclub was Mario's second home and I loved to dance. She'd agreed to wear the short black dress with a draped neckline, golden medusa medallions on the straps, and crystal-studded sandals. I scanned the women in line as we walked past. None were even a quarter as stunning as she was.

I slung my arm around her shoulders, making our status clear to the men in line who eyed her. To be clearer, I pulled her close for a moment to kiss her temple, and she smiled up at me.

"We won't be able to hear each other in there, will we?" she asked.

Mario slipped his arm around her waist from her other side. "You two've spent too much time talking already."

I winked at him. "Not much talking going on."

She pinched me, a sign to be quiet. I kissed her temple again and grinned at her. She should know me better than that by now.

Mario released her and stepped toward the line, to a pretty young woman. Bronzed skin, jet black hair, curvaceous, in a short red dress. "Buonasera, bellissima."

"Does he say that to everyone?" Samantha said, louder than needed for me to hear, and I laughed.

"Want to skip the line?" Mario had his hand out for her, knowing the answer before she spoke.

She looked at the three women she was with. "Can my friends come?"

Mario shook his head slightly. If I knew him, he'd pursed his lips, following it up with a smirk. He'd taught me many of my best moves, after all.

The woman shrugged her shoulders at her friends and took his hand. "See you girls inside!"

The entrance was small, with a crimson awning and the club's name on the wall next to it in a flaming script: La Fiamma. Mario walked directly to one of the two bouncers. Letting go of the nameless woman, he embraced the man who ushered us in.

"Well, this is a first," said Samantha.

I kissed her again. "Wait until you see the inside."

"You've been here before?"

"Mario always brings me here." Glancing at her, I winked. "I believe we'll finally have that tango tonight."

She rolled her eyes at me with a mock frown. "We've been tangoing quite a bit lately."

"But for the first time, amore, I mean on the dance floor."

Inside the narrow hallway, the music gradually increased in clarity until we climbed the stairs at the end and the room opened. Tiers of seating alcoves with large red couches and chairs surrounded a massive central dance floor, with a long bar to one side. Strobe lights in myriad colors blinked to the music. A wide staircase at the back led to the second floor with more dancers and a view of the main floor from balconies along the edge.

Mario's hands flicked this way and that, signaling hello to the DJ, for drinks from the bar, and to a few of the bouncers. This was his element.

As the four of us sat on one of the large red couches away from the dance floor, a server placed a tray with shot glasses on our low table. Mario and his date spoke into each other's ears, yelling over the music.

"What's this?" Samantha held up the glass closest to her, a bright blue shade.

I shrugged and held up a matching one to toast. "To Napoli!"

She did the same. We clinked and downed them. It was almost violently sugary, tasting of children's drinks and cotton candy.

She shook her head quickly and stuck out her tongue, leaning in to yell in my direction. "Too sweet!"

We both grabbed red glasses and tried again. Tequila,

tabasco, and likely chili peppers. She coughed and spluttered after that one.

"Too spicy?" I asked, and she nodded.

"Third time's the charm?" She selected two creamy brown shot glasses and handed one to me. Taking a cautious sniff first, she nodded. Before she drank it, I twined my arm around hers and we enjoyed them together. Chocolate and cinnamon, like Nutella on a cinnamon roll. She licked her lips when we finished that one and reached for another.

I pulled her shoulder closer. "You've already had three. Slow down!"

She raised her eyebrows at me and gave me a peck on the cheek. Handing me a creamy brown one, she wrapped her arm around mine. "To spontaneous vacations!"

After adding these shots to the wine we enjoyed before leaving the villa, a pleasant buzz prodded at my brain already. But how could I resist her? We polished those off and slammed them down on the table together, laughing.

Samantha's face had softened since Wednesday, since leaving the investigation behind. There was a hint of longing to pursue it still, but she didn't bring it up.

She fingered my shirt collar and trailed the back of her knuckles down the placket where I'd left the top buttons undone. "Are you going to ask me to dance, Dr. Ferraro?" She slipped a hand under the fabric, brushing my bare chest, her eyes never leaving mine.

"There is little in the world I want more than to dance with you." I withdrew her hand and pulled the palm to my lips, savoring her, eyes easing shut to inhale her natural perfume. Intoxicating. I signaled to Mario we were heading to the dance floor, but he was deep in conversation.

As we stood, Samantha handed me a blue shot glass, saying, "One more for the road!"

We threw the drinks back and I returned the glasses to their tray. Still not as good as the chocolate. But when she came close, I could smell the combination on her breath, and it was remarkably improved.

She undid another button on my shirt so it was half-undone. "That's better."

I threaded my fingers over the top of one of her hands, guiding it to the skin she'd exposed. "Is this to be a battle of seduction tonight?"

She rolled her eyes, still shy after almost a week in constant contact.

"You seem to be the competitive type." I released her hand inside my shirt, but hers remained in place. "We could put a wager on it?"

One slow blink and a sly smile. Not the blink of difficult words, nor of uncertainty. No, this blink meant the game was already on.

"I warn you." I inched closer, bringing my mouth close enough to her ear I could lower my voice. "You won't win."

She chuckled low in her throat. "That kinda means I win anyway, doesn't it, Dr. Ferraro?"

I pulled back from her and shook my head. "Touché, Ms. Caine."

As we walked past other couches and seats, down the steps to the dance floor, she grabbed my ass more than once. That stopped when I snatched her hands in mine. There was not enough room for a formal position, but plenty of space to hold her next to me and feel the thudding bass together. Our bodies locked tight, legs bracketing each other, and I rolled my hips to the rhythm, while she echoed every movement.

I snaked my left hand across the small of her back, all the way to her side, and held her tight against me. As her arms rose above her head, my other hand slid up her neck and into her hair. The heat was as all-consuming as when we'd snuck behind the building in Pompeii.

Her arms fell slowly around my neck, and she moved even closer to talk into my ear. "Not many couples dancing together."

"Would you like to stop?" I took advantage of being so close and sucked her earlobe into my mouth.

"Not a chance." She pulled away enough for a kiss, her hips continuing to grind against me. Perhaps she would be the one to win, and who was I to complain?

The combination of shots tasted wonderful on her tongue, despite the sweetness and spiciness. I broke from the kiss and returned to her ear. "Should we just go back to the villa?"

She shook her head, long hair swaying around her face, and pressed against me harder. "You surrender so easily?"

"Not a chance!" I spun her slowly, then let go, so I could watch her dance on her own. She closed her eyes, hands exploring her exquisite body, as she circled her hips and bit her bottom lip. How did tough-as-nails-Samantha, the rock climber and adrenaline junkie, move like this? Like a serpent unleashed by a charmer. And how was this woman all mine?

Perhaps five shots and two glasses of wine was the magic number.

But then I noticed the eyes on her. At least five pairs with as much lust in them as mine surely had. I snatched her hand

and spun her to me, so she danced with her back against my chest. The eyes had followed her, some frowning, others appearing to think they could still approach her. As she writhed to the music, I glared at each of them until they left her alone.

She pivoted to face me and pulled my ear to her mouth. "What's with you, Mr. Serious?"

I held her close to me and scanned the crowd.

Then I saw the worst one. The one who was there for me.

My cousin Cristian—dressed in black suit pants and shirt, with the same dark hair and olive skin as me—stood at the edge of the dance floor and beckoned me with a finger, but I shook my head. I neither wanted to speak to him nor leave her alone in this crowd of alcohol-fueled predators. He pointed to the rear doors, then walked out, confident I'd follow. He wouldn't leave until I spoke with him, otherwise he wouldn't have tracked me down here.

The thrill of having my girlfriend's body against mine faded faster than I would have thought possible. "Sorry, bella, but I need a moment."

"So do I." She wrapped her arms around my neck and kissed it.

Regrettably, I broke her grip. "There's someone I must speak with. You can sit with Mario until I'm done."

"No way! I'm enjoying this game!" She shimmied her hips at me, working very hard to keep me there.

"Would you be happier if Mario dances with you?" I couldn't leave her alone in the throng. "I'll be ten minutes at the most. I promise."

She stopped moving and pouted. Too-much-alcohol-Samantha was an even larger handful than normal Samantha.

Perhaps shy-about-her-body-Samantha would have been a better date for the club. But seeing her in that dress—the way it hugged her subtle curves and draped low across her chest—it was no wonder so many men were looking at her.

"This is only a pause. I'll return to claim my victory soon."

"In your dreams, Ferraro." Her body resumed its movement, causing every cell in my being to protest my choice. All the same, I took her hand and we returned to the couch.

Mario was still engaged in conversation with the pretty woman from the line and paid no attention to us when we arrived.

I leaned down to talk in the ear she was not occupying. "I need you to dance with Samantha."

"No!" He gestured to the woman.

Samantha dropped my hand and started swaying her hips next to me. For a woman who never went to clubs, she was enjoying this one too much.

"Mario, did you see him?"

He frowned and turned away from the woman. We were close enough we only had to raise our voices. "I did. Why's he here?"

"He wants to talk to me. And Samantha was getting a lot of unwelcome attention." We both turned to look at her, her eyes closed as she moved with the music. "I just need you to dance with her while I speak with him."

He pursed his lips but nodded.

I yelled to the woman next to Mario. "I need him to chaperone my girlfriend. Ten minutes and he'll be back. Wait for him."

She, at least, had some sense and gave me a thumbs up.

Mario kissed the woman's hand and stood. He leaned to Samantha. "Will you dance with me, bellissima?"

"Don't be long, hot stuff." Samantha kissed my cheek quickly and, with a grin, downed another shot before grabbing Mario's hand to haul him into the crowd.

Mario was one of the few I trusted completely, without hesitation. He went through women as quickly as I went through socks, but Samantha would be safe with him.

CHAPTER 18

ANTONIO

I PICKED up one of the shot glasses still sitting on the table but thought better of it. I'd need a clear head for this. On the wall opposite the entrance and the bar, double doors led out to a walled-off courtyard where more drinks and food could be had. The music was loud enough to keep conversations private, but at least out here yelling wasn't necessary.

Pausing ten feet outside the doorway, I scanned the area and found him quickly. He sat off in a corner, at a small round table against the far wall, and waved to the chair next to him. As I approached, he stood and held out his arms in greeting.

"Cugino!" He wrapped me in a tight embrace.

I patted his back while we hugged and gave him the respect of determining its length. As we broke apart, I smiled. "Cristian, long time."

Shorter than me by several inches, my cousin carried himself as a man much larger than he was. Perhaps the two men who hovered close enough to be obvious had something to do with it. Cristian had far more wisdom in his eyes than his thirty-five years should have earned him.

He gestured to a glass at the table, at my place. "You've been in Italia a week and a half and haven't visited us in Roma yet."

I leaned back in my chair, waving off his offer of a drink. I didn't trust him as far as I could throw him, but I kept the smile on my face and my voice light. "There's too much work for me here to go running about the country. I already told your father I don't have time to visit." Nor the inclination.

"But your project's been delayed." He crossed his legs and picked up his drink. "Something about a piece held up in transit, I believe?"

"How do you know about that?" A question I knew the answer to before it finished forming on my lips.

"You know me. I do two things well. I hear things and I make things happen." He shrugged as he took a sip. "And right now, Papa wants me to convince you to come and see him. There will be time before your project starts, I guarantee."

"Sì, but my girlfriend is visiting." I looked over my shoulder toward the door. "I should get back to her."

"This is something else I heard." He leaned forward. "She's the one in the Versace dress you were dancing with?"

My muscles tensed, but I did my best not to move and confirm his guess. They might see her as a liability or as leverage if they wanted something I was unable to give. "She's none of your concern."

"American?"

"She is."

He uncrossed his legs and rested his elbows on the table. His eyes narrowed. "She was the one you were working with at the auction last month?"

Goings-on here, I would expect him to know. But that? This

was the same auction Special Agent Skinner had brought up when we saw him yesterday. Most of the work was Samantha's, but everyone seemed to want to give me credit for it. There was something deeper going on. Cristian was on the offensive.

"Tell me you were not involved, Cristian?"

"Interested, but not involved." He waved a dismissive hand. "Papa was proud to hear you were the one who uncovered that art theft."

"Interested?" Proud? When Samantha brought the burned Chagall to me, my father had said something bigger than one forged painting was going on. Something he refused to speak to me about until he returned from Napoli, and then shipped me off here before I could ask.

Samantha's FBI Art Crimes boss in town. With the TPC. A missing piece of the Mars wall and the pigment pots. The Carabinieri knowing of my family. Were they all related like Samantha thought—and claimed she didn't?

Cristian leaned back. "So you're not coming to visit?"

"Sorry, but you can't make everything happen." I pushed back the chair, scraping it across the stone floor, and stood. "My work's important, and we need to get started. If I can recoup the lost time, I'll visit later."

If he was behind the delay in shipment, my message would be clear. If not, it would sound innocent.

He stood with me. "Hopefully, the missing equipment will arrive soon. As soon as... Monday?"

I embraced him when he put his arms out. "My girlfriend's leaving Wednesday morning. I hope it arrives after that."

He nodded as we let go, as clear as he would be. He had

arranged the delay. No doubt at my uncle's orders. It left me with too many questions. How did he know what to delay? How would he know what would have been an inconvenience versus what would put the project on pause? Did he have someone spying on me? Someone on my team?

I stalked back to the door, hauled out my phone, and called my father. I needed answers.

"Antonio!" Papa knew two volumes. Loud and louder. Fortunate, given my proximity to the doors into the club. "How's Napoli treating you?"

"Ask how he's feeling." My sister's voice was barely audible in the background. It was late in Napoli, but they were likely at the office together in Michigan.

"Papa, I'll be brief." I ducked against the wall by the door, out of Cristian's view, and with some privacy. The pounding bass inside would make a call impossible. "What was going on when you were here?"

There was silence on the other end until my sister's voice sounded again. "Put it on—"

The sound changed in the background as she switched the call to speaker.

"Antonio! How are you? Is everything alright? Is Mario looking after you?" Sofia was the best big sister I could've had, and yet stifling at times. "We're in Papa's office, so you don't have to put on the brave face."

This was not what I wanted to speak of, but she wouldn't listen to anything until she heard it. A smile tugged at my lips, all the same. "Thank you for giving Samantha Mario's contact information."

"Did she call you?"

"She said you gave her the address and drove immediately to the airport."

"Oddio! No!" Sofia squealed, an excited sound which was almost enough to nudge me past the original reason for the call. "She's there?"

"She is, and it's wonderful." I leaned my back against the wall, clapping a hand over my right ear to drown out the party goers, which made Sofia's cheer of triumph hurt my ear. "However, I just saw Cristian."

Two gasps on the other end of the call.

"He says he's in town to convince me to come visit, but I don't believe that. He also knows about the stolen painting Samantha and I discovered at the auction two weeks ago."

A woman swayed in my direction, eyes full of intent, but my glower stopped her ten feet away. I had to get back to Samantha before some man did that to her.

"Papa, he or your brother are also responsible for a delay in some of my equipment, putting the project behind."

"Marone!"

"You told us you would explain when you got home, but I heard nothing." The door opened and the music grew louder, so I had to turn away and speak up. "There was something going on when you were here."

"You're right," he sighed. "We came across a stolen painting at the Rome studio. We reported it, but the TPC accused your Uncle Andrea of working with the painting's owners. They said he was trafficking in stolen goods."

"What? With everything we've done to combat—" Sofia paused, likely at a motion from my father.

"They were wrong and cleared him, but things were

touch-and-go in Rome while you were dealing with the copied Chagall here."

"What do those two things have to do with each other?" I asked. Two separate studios. Two different continents, let alone countries. Different paintings, conservators, and owners.

Papa sighed again. "I can't talk about it over the phone. You know that."

Sì, I knew that. Because there was one thing in common with all of it: Ferraros.

Those two paintings and the delay in my project. The accusations from the young pup handling the stolen fresco investigation. I looked to the corner of the building, which hid Cristian from my view, the anger bubbling up again.

Three Ferraro brothers. Two on the right side of the law, one not. My uncle Giovanni was a stain on our family, on the legacy of my grandfather, who'd crossed enemy lines during World War II to save Napoli's cultural heritage. And my cousin Cristian followed in his father's footsteps, doing his bidding. Influencing my work, my life, my time with Samantha.

There was no way I would visit them. Sooner, later, or ever.

"Grazie mille, Papa." I shook my head, wanting to speak of so much more that would have to wait until I was home. "I need to go get Samantha. Ciao."

I finally had the reason Papa was afraid about the Chagall. Why he'd forced me to lie to Samantha all those weeks ago. Forced me to pretend with her. At least we found those responsible for the fraud.

Uncle Giovanni and his crew may not have been behind that stolen painting in the Roma studio, but they were most certainly the reason the Carabinieri TPC blamed my Uncle Andrea. And likely why Carabiniere De Rosa knew my family. He must have been involved in that case, if not something broader with my Uncle Giovanni.

And what could I tell Samantha? What secrets did I have to continue keeping from her? I wanted to build a future with that woman. But how could anything like that happen between me—a Ferraro, with Giovanni's blood in me—and a woman who wanted so desperately to investigate cultural heritage crimes?

I slammed my hand against the wall and marched inside for a drink at the bar. Thoughts rattled through my brain and blood pounded in my ears. I had to relax my jaw and let the rage go before I sought Samantha out. How dare my uncle interfere with this project? Putting me behind schedule by two weeks, delaying my return to Brenton. And my return to her.

Sliding onto a barstool, I ordered a Scotch. Something neither sweet nor spicy, but smooth. I turned to watch the mass of bodies and immediately spotted Samantha and Mario. They laughed and yelled over the music, while he kept a firm hold of her on the dance floor. There were enough people they couldn't move far, but few enough I could admire her from my seat.

And no man's eyes on her body while Mario danced with her.

CHAPTER 19
SAMANTHA

" So, Mario," I yelled over the thudding music, my brain foggy. "Antonio was pretty pissed after I talked to Thomas at the lab. I'm guessing he ordered you to watch me because he's got a jealous streak. On a scale of one to one million, how bad is it?"

He rocked his head back in laughter before dipping me and hollering in return, "Five million!"

"Don't dip me! This dress isn't designed for that."

He dipped me again, and I laughed harder. "But he's okay with you dancing with me?"

"That depends." He smirked at me, the same way Antonio regularly did. "Do you find me sexier than him?"

He spun me and I stumbled slightly as he finished. "Not even close!"

"That hurts, Samantha."

I squeezed his lead hand playfully. "No, it doesn't."

"His trust is hard to earn. I take it seriously."

"You're a good guy, Mario."

"I know!" He grinned again and spun me one more time.

I stopped at the end, while the room continued to spin around me.

He held my hands as the room slowed. "Are you alright?"

"Gimme a sec."

"Stay here." He patted my hands and walked through the crowd toward the bar. *Please, no more alcohol.* I shouldn't have taken those extra shots. I swayed to the music, watching him walk away. When he reached the bar, he stepped aside to reveal Antonio sitting on a bar stool. Not the playful and turned-on man I'd danced with earlier, but dark and intense.

He'd chosen black dress pants and a crisp white shirt. As always, the sleeves were rolled up, and I'd undone the buttons halfway down. Sexiest man I'd ever met, without even trying. At least, it didn't seem like he was trying. When his eyes caught mine, they lightened. Mario slipped something into Antonio's hand and headed toward the alcove where his date might still be sitting.

I began walking to the bar, but Antonio put up a hand to stop me. Tucking whatever Mario had given him into a pocket, he gestured with his fingers for me to dance. I didn't want to anymore. I wanted to kiss those delicious lips and rub my body against his muscled flesh. After wiggling my hips, I took another step forward.

He shook his head and turned slightly to accept a tumbler from the bartender. Bringing it to his nose, his eyes closed as he inhaled the amber liquid. He sipped, slowly, deliberately, licking his lips when he finished. As I stilled, tilting my head at his elegant movements, the crowd moved so I couldn't see him for a moment. When it parted, he was still sitting there, watching me, the exasperatingly sexy smirk firmly in place. He made the gesture with his finger again.

Dance for me, he mouthed.

Christ, I wanted him.

But I was not about to give up. I could win this game.

I started to dance, letting the thudding bass fill me. The lyrics vanished and the crowd became a blur. My entire existence was the rhythm, my body, and his eyes. And the fantasy of his hands exploring underneath my dress.

I latched my legs closed, rocking my hips from side to side. The friction burned, heightening the throbbing in my core, while the dress caressed my skin like the gentle drag of his tongue. My eyes locked with his as my hands slid down my sides, along my hips, and down my thighs. They brushed lightly across my groin and between my legs, taking his gaze with them. That was his map for later. I brought them back up, pulling the hem of my dress dangerously high, then releasing it. They continued along the sides of my breasts, pushing them together and up into my hair.

I kept moving, gyrating for him, making love to his eyes. His wicked smirk remained as he took another sip from his glass. He needed to get off that damn barstool and come dance with me.

Wrapping my fingers in my hair, I pulled it on top of my head and let it fall in a cascade, my hands sliding back to my breasts. But he didn't budge.

He leaned against the bar, one casual elbow resting on it. His shirt gaped open where the undone buttons revealed his chest, showcasing the slope between his rock-hard pecs. He bit his lip as I moved and a jolt ran through me.

The trip to Naples was bringing out a side of me I'd never known before. Somehow, with the ridiculous clothes, the lingerie, the hand-holding, and all the time between the sheets, I'd become more confident in my sexuality than ever before.

His hand resting on the bar pointed to my midsection and flicked downward. What was that supposed to mean? I continued dancing, and he made the motion again. This time, accompanied by an eyebrow raise. Underwear. He wanted them off.

Was he kidding? I laughed, but his face remained steady.

Take them off, he mouthed, teeth bared, as though threatening me.

I rolled my eyes, which caused the corner of his lips to ratchet up higher.

He wanted to raise the stakes? Fine. Time to double down.

I found the edge of the lacy wisp that passed for panties through the dress fabric and inched them down far enough I could do the rest by moving my legs. I coaxed them to my feet, where they caught on my sandals and I nearly fell over as I snatched them.

Great. I'd had too much alcohol for doubling down on anything. But no one was looking at the floor. No one saw me.

Except for him, and he was all that mattered. His lips parted and he ran his tongue along his teeth, head tilting toward me. He'd charge in any second.

I was definitely going to win.

The crowd closed in and I lost sight of him. Running my hands over my torso, longing for his forceful grip on my thighs, I waited for the sea of bodies to part again so I could see him. I could pull at the neckline of my dress. Maybe that would work. Would it be cheating if I beckoned him with a finger? We hadn't exactly set any rules for the game.

Once the crowd shifted, I couldn't see him. A woman in a

sparkling silver dress—even shorter than mine—was directly in front of him, moving her hips between his legs propped on the barstool. All the air rushed out of my lungs. I could see his broad shoulders on either side of her, the top of his head, and his arm on the bar.

She knew how to use her curves. I tensed and my hands dropped to my sides. Her long, dark hair obscured his face as she leaned to him, head angling to kiss him or whisper in his ear or something else equally inappropriate. A pit opened in my stomach.

Was she why he'd pawned me off on Mario? He abandoned his drink and placed a hand on her bare arm. I'd been warned he was a serial womanizer. I was so stupid, thinking I was enough for him.

One week. I'd only been there a week, and he already had someone else.

Or was she from before I got there? The room began swimming again, and I looked to where Mario had been sitting. Or the exit. Which direction should I go?

But I didn't go anywhere. My stupid feet just stuck to the floor as the crowd pulsed, and I lost sight of them. I ran my empty hand over my face and stared at the ground to center myself. *Calm down, Sam. Breathe. The alcohol's making you see things.*

Suddenly there were hands on my waist and hot breath on my neck. I squeezed my eyes shut, willing the room to stand still. The scent was all wrong—cigarettes and sweat. Not vanilla and amber.

"Keep dancing, you sexy thing," he whispered, pulling my hips backward against his body. Wait. Backward? And a New York accent?

My eyes shot open. Antonio launched from his seat, the woman in the silver dress nowhere to be seen. His eyes were lit with a very different fire than before. I put up a hand to stop him and spun out of the stranger's grasp. As I turned, the man who'd pawed me grabbed my hips and pulled me close, reaching around to squeeze my ass.

Holy shit! It was the guy from the Casa. The rude one who dumped his chips and said the place sucked.

Pushing him away, I yelled over the music, "Back off, jackass!"

Before he could respond, there was a hand at his throat and Antonio was between us, towering over him. I couldn't hear a word they said, but Antonio's shoulders broadened and the other guy's hands flew up in surrender.

With a shove from Antonio, the kid—man, technically—stumbled and he and his buddies left.

Antonio turned to me, a wild look in his eyes. He retrieved the underwear I clutched in my hand and stashed them in his pocket. Before I could process what had happened, he grabbed my upper arms, pulling close enough to yell over the music. "Are you alright?"

I shook my head to jostle a coherent thought free, but all I could come up with was "What the fuck?"

"He touched you!" His grip on my arms was too tight.

"Like that woman in the silver dress was touching you?" I wrenched one arm from him, although the jerking motion set my balance off again.

I should have known better.

No, wait. I did know better. Men couldn't be trusted. They were always looking for the next piece of ass.

"Bella." He normally said it with endearment—teasing,

loving. But this time, it was sharp, and his features clouded over.

"Don't 'bella' me, you asshole!"

He flexed his jaw and took my hand, dragging me from the dance floor toward the wide staircase at the back of the room. I yanked for him to let go or stop, but the alcohol threw my coordination off just enough I couldn't.

I pulled closer to him. "What are you doing?"

He stormed up the stairs to the second floor without a word, where I had a full view of the mass of writhing bodies on the main dance floor from the edge of the balcony. We passed people watching over the railing, groups at more alcoves, and pockets of dancers. He stopped at the far end, at an inconspicuous door.

Producing a key, he unlocked it.

He opened the door and ushered me inside with more care than he'd used to drag me up here. Red wallpapered bathroom with soft lights, marble-countered sink with a vase of irises, and one stall. Small black wooden tables stacked with folded white towels. He slammed the door shut, muffling the music outside.

I spun to see him engage a slide lock and stalk toward me.

"VIP bathroom. Mario gave me the key."

"What the hell?"

He blew out a long breath as he ran his fingers through his hair. "You and I need to talk."

"In a bathroom?"

"You may not have noticed this, but I'm having a difficult time with you." His hands settled on his hips.

My head was still swimming. I hated how sexy he looked, how powerful he seemed in that moment, and how weak I was in comparison. He was confidence and control, and there I was, yet again, unable to measure up. I shot back. "What's that supposed to mean?"

"It means you keep constructing walls. Every time I think you're letting me in, you introduce another hurdle."

"What the fuck does that have to do with everything that just happened downstairs?"

His eyes hardened. "Samantha, I am a man—"

"Gee, hadn't noticed." I rolled my eyes dramatically.

"That!" He pointed at my face. "Right there! Pushing me away again."

"You're one to talk. Skulking off with god knows who while you get Mario to distract me? Then that woman at the bar?" I shouldn't have said that. "I guess you need a new flavor for September, don't you?" And I really shouldn't have said that.

His nostrils flared, and the pointing finger transformed into a clenched fist, which dropped to his side. He snarled through gritted teeth, "I won't dignify that with a response. You've had too much to drink."

"I saw you checking out all the women in the line and sucking face with that woman in the silver dress. I agreed to stop doing what *I* wanted to do and play your stupid little dress-up game all week—" I flicked the gold medallion on my dress's strap at him, digging my hole deeper by the second. "—and I'm still not enough for you, am I? What you want is a good little girl who does what she's told. Well, guess what? I'm not that girl."

His face dropped, and he took a step back, mouth gaping open. He looked as though I'd slapped him. Good.

My stomach churned, and bile rose in my throat, burning

with acid. Antonio was exactly the same as Vincenzo. Fucking Italian men! A woman was nothing but a conquest. "I knew I shouldn't have come here! I should have just left Brenton and never looked back!"

I marched around him toward the door, but he caught my arm, spinning me to face him. The adrenaline must have counter-acted some of the alcohol because I didn't stumble that time.

"Samantha," he whispered, so quietly I could barely hear him above the muffled music. "Is this what your ex-husband did to you?"

I rubbed at my face. "Matt has nothing to do with this."

"Neither does that woman in the silver dress. She wanted me to buy her a drink and I told her—very politely—I was here with my girlfriend." He pulled my hand away from my face.

"What? I saw you kissing—"

"She was insistent, rubbed up against me, but I pushed her away gently and told her no."

He wasn't making out with her? My breathing slowed as a little more sobriety eked its way into my brain. Everything he said made sense. I squeezed my eyes shut, focusing on what I'd seen. His hand on her arm. Dammit! Pushing her away, not pulling her closer. And he'd moved his head away from hers when she leaned in.

"And the skulking was with my cousin Cristian. A man I cannot stand, whom I hope you never meet." He squeezed my hand. "You're very quiet. Tell me you believe me?"

"You make me soft and weak, and I hate that." I stared down at his chest. At the undone buttons and the taut skin they exposed. I didn't need people. Most of all, not some man who treated me... so... I sighed. Who treated me like I was the center of his universe. "I'm strong, dammit."

He held my hand against his heart. "Bella, you're as soft as sandpaper."

I choked down the laugh that threatened to betray me. I jerked my hand, without the effort it needed. He was right. I'd had too much to drink and had to get control of myself. And stop imagining the worst of him.

We were both carrying secrets. That didn't mean we were bad people, just that we weren't ready to talk about some things.

"For the record," he said. "Outside, I was thinking how none of the other women in the line were a fraction as beautiful as you. Inside, my eyes were on the men staring at you."

"Why does that even matter?" I clenched his shirt and stepped closer, into the sphere of heat radiating off him. Into his air.

His brows gathered together, and his hand lifted to my cheek. "I don't want another man to think he can—"

"I can take care of myself." Someday, I'd show him just how well I could. But this wasn't the right moment.

"Me standing up for you does not mean you can't do it yourself. It's a way for me to show how much I love you." Why did he keep using that word? Was it even real? His hand slid into my hair, to the back of my head. "That's what I was trying to say earlier. I am a man and I feel a need to protect my woman. You have to understand it's a reflection of my feelings for you, not of my impression of you or any doubts about your abilities."

I was stupid. Blind to all the signs, probably drunk, and stupid. I'd missed the whole point. We were about to start a long-distance relationship, him in Naples and me in the States. Just like when his fiancée cheated on him. "You're scared, aren't you?"

"Out of my mind." He let go of my hand and pulled me against him, stretching his broad fingers to span the small of my back.

"Do you think we can make this work?" My breath picked up, the desire from the dance floor igniting inside me. I had an all-consuming need to dance with him again. Or to tear his clothes off.

He touched his lips to my forehead, feather soft. "Can we live with ourselves if we don't?"

I stretched up on my tiptoes and his mouth caught mine, our lips pressing together until they parted and our tongues slid along each other. My whole body sighed in relief. His question didn't need an answer. The answer was obviously *no*, and that's what terrified me. I couldn't go back to a life without him. Without *us*.

My hand gripped his neck, brushing against the short hair at his nape, damp from sweat. I pulled away, breathless.

"And to be completely honest—" My voice fell to a husky whisper. "Your hand around that guy's throat was the sexiest fucking thing I've ever seen."

His eyes shot open and he shifted his grip. One arm circled my waist and the other went to my ass. He lifted me, taking the few steps to the counter, and dropped me on it. He was on his knees in front of me in a flash, lifting my dress. His tongue licked the length of my seam, sealing over my clit with strong suction.

I sucked in air, flailing for balance. I knocked the flower

vase over with a thud, spilling the water. "Oh, my—what the—"

His eyes snapped up to meet mine for an instant, narrowed and hungry, the mischief sparkling in them. "You win." As he teased and flicked, two fingers thrust into me, working me into a feverish pitch. He found the soft spot just inside and stroked it in a rhythm matching the music.

My hands hit the mirror, the sink, the tap, searching for something to ground me. Between the alcohol, the dancing, and the intimacy, my orgasm built rapidly.

I pulled my knees over his shoulders and slid my wet fingers into his luxurious hair. Bucking into his face, I held his head firm against me. "Oh, god, Antonio! Don't stop!"

But he stopped. Right at that second. He pushed against my grip and stood, lips swollen and glistening with my arousal.

Clenching my inner muscles to fend off the screaming need, I shoved him with a foot. "I said—"

"Shut it, Caine." With a smirk, he wiped the lower half of his face. He undid his belt and lowered his pants and underwear to his hips, releasing his fully erect cock.

I began sliding off the counter to repay the favor, but he stopped me with a hand in the middle of my chest.

"You won, remember?" He withdrew a condom from his pocket and had it on in a heartbeat, plunging inside me without hesitation. I gasped, the fire rekindled before he'd finished the second stroke.

Reaching under his dress shirt, my fingers traveled over his sharp hipbones, to his waist, and to the muscle edging his spine.

I rocked my head back and closed my eyes, but he fisted his hand in my hair and tilted my head back to face him. My eyes shot open and locked with his, deepening our connection.

God, I loved him.

Don't go there, Sam.

"You can scream in here, Samantha." He guided my head to the side and ran his tongue around my earlobe. His free hand slid under my ass, pulling me into him harder, throwing me against the edge of climax. "No one will hear you with all that music outside."

"Really don't stop this time." I leaned forward to kiss him, tasting my own flavor mixed with his Scotch.

Someone pounded on the door. He continued driving into me, not reacting to the noise. I'd never done anything like this. Sex in a public place? In a bathroom? Never. And with someone on the other side of the door?

Pounding on the door again.

"Look at me," he said through fevered breaths, and my eyes flashed back to him.

I locked my legs around his waist, reaching behind me. He found the spot he'd been stroking with his fingers, and heat poured through my veins. The noise at the door came one more time, but weaker, more distant. The lights dazzled as he squeezed my ass, and I let go. I yelled as the peak coursed through my entire body. My legs tightened around him as I trembled with the orgasm.

Mine subsided, and his rolled through us, a ripple effect smashing into me like an aftershock. I bore down on his cock as it pulsed inside me, hitting me with a second climax.

He groaned, louder than he had any time at the villa, a primal noise that almost prepared me for another round. As the euphoria passed, he released my hair and exhaled, meeting me for a slow, deep kiss. I wrapped my arms around him and held tight, our hearts slowing together.

"I love you, bella." He leaned back to look at me. "There will never be another woman. No one. I swear."

I reached for his neck and pulled him in for a kiss. How did this remarkable man choose me? Did it even matter? Because he had.

Brushing the side of his face, I stared up into his big brown eyes with their golden flecks. How did I doubt the sincerity in those eyes? Doubt his words? Doubt anytime the L-word raced through my brain? He kept saying it to me, and I had to start believing it.

Eventually.

"Don't wake me from the dream yet," I whispered.

He leaned his forehead against mine. "Me either."

I closed my eyes, continuing to stroke his cheek, which sported the barest hint of stubble. The most amazing man I'd ever met. Brilliant, talented, handsome, charming. And somehow in love with me. It was real, wasn't it?

When the pounding on the door came again, we both startled.

He chuckled. "We should probably let them in."

My legs unlocked and dangled limply at the side. "VIP bathroom, huh?"

"I was only looking for a private place to talk." He withdrew from me and threw the condom in the trash.

"Quite the talk." The buzz from the alcohol was wearing off, but the buzz from him would likely continue a long time. A very long time. "Can I have my underwear back now?"

As he washed his hands and the lower half of his face, he said, "No. I think I'll keep them."

"Then I'm not dancing with you for the rest of the evening."

He patted his face dry with a small towel, eyes on me in the mirror. "Oh, I think you will, Ms. Caine."

I folded my arms and narrowed my eyes at him.

He leaned a hip on the counter and looked at me straight on. Folded his arms right back at me and raised an eyebrow.

"Yeah, okay, fine."

He held my waist as I hopped down.

Pounding on the door again.

"What do we do now? They'll know what we—"

He waved the dismissive hand. "Anyone who saw us on the dance floor would assume we're sleeping together. So what if we did it here?"

"Not much sleeping going on."

"This embarrasses you, sì?" He unfolded my arms and wrapped them around him.

I couldn't meet his eyes. 'Embarrassed' was an understatement.

"I'll make you a deal. You walk out with your head held high and I'll stop being the stubborn and selfish boyfriend. We'll go back to Pompeii tomorrow and dig for information." He leaned his chest far enough away from mine to extend his hand in the tiny space for me to shake. "Partners."

First, I won the battle of seduction. Then he conceded about Pompeii. What was going on?

Looking up at him, at his smirk, his bedroom eyes, I melted a little. And shook his hand. We did make a good team, just like Elliot had said. "It would appear you know my weakness, Dr. Ferraro."

CHAPTER 20
ANTONIO

SATURDAY MORNING, the crowds were thick in Pompeii. A glorious late summer day, tour groups followed their guides, families and couples consulted maps, while others simply wandered about the ruins. Samantha and I dodged between them, at her brisk pace, toward Casa di Marte. It was a surprise she was up so early and with such energy, given our late and intoxicating evening the night before. It just went to show how strongly she felt about this.

I couldn't shake the feeling Cristian was involved somehow. He knew exactly the piece to prevent my team from starting work, which meant the Casa would be empty and prime for theft. What if convincing me to visit was not his goal with the delay? What if he was merely attempting to keep the site unoccupied?

If I was right, perhaps the flowers were not the only target. He suggested the equipment would be returned Monday, so today would be the last day he might try to take something from the walls. Surely he wouldn't get his hands dirty. There would be at least one other person involved. Not the thugs with him, though. Someone who knew what they were doing, who knew how to liberate an ancient fresco from the wall without destroying it.

It was a leap. One I didn't want to take, but I'd made it before I'd said goodbye to him last night at the club. I was now preoccupied with tracking the stolen flowers, yet terrified what I would find. The offer to return to the site was about Samantha, but part of me wanted to know as well.

"What are you thinking?" Samantha was back to her shorts and T-shirt. She was not the security consultant in her pretty blouse and pants, nor the girlfriend. Today, she was the investigator, and the excitement radiated off her.

Resisting her search for the stolen fresco was a selfish desire to have her all to myself. But this lively creature was the one I'd fallen for. The one who was passionate about matters of import, who saw a need to put things right in the world.

Her steps were more like bounds. "Double-check the Casa? See if anything else is missing? Inspect the cut marks? See what type of tool was used? Not interviews today, though."

"I don't know, bella. This is apparently your specialty, not mine."

She wore her visitor's badge and carried a backpack I had approved by security. Measuring tape, notepads, plastic bags, tweezers, and Mario's camera with a few lenses and a tripod. Samantha had planned it all, gathering items like a child in a candy store from about the villa. And she refused to let me carry the pack.

"We'll start with photographs, especially of the cut marks on the wall, to help identify what they used to remove it. Measure the missing area. Do a tracing of the shape. It may be far-fetched, but we can always check for things like hair samples or... Bianca narrowed it down to last Saturday afternoon or Sunday morning, right?"

"Sì, she did."

She walked faster with each breath. This was the passion I'd seen from her at the gala auction, as she tracked down the stolen painting. Back when I was lying to her about the Chagall's truth. And here I was, not telling her about Cristian. But it was only a suspicion, so not a lie. Not yet.

I said, "The site would be heavily contaminated. The kids on Wednesday, De Rosa and the other carabiniere, Umberto. Plus, there was a team of paleobotanists working there a couple of weeks ago, not to mention the team erecting the temporary roof."

"Good point. And I don't suppose DNA evidence would really help us. Unless they have something at the lab that can analyze that?"

We approached the turn onto Via di Nola and the site, the crowds thinning as we neared the off-limits area.

"Ooh, and what about that other woman on your team? What was her name? River?"

"Océane," I chuckled. "She's French. Mario texted her, but she only said she'd return soon."

"She's still not back?" Her eyes gleamed with excitement. "What if she's the thief and she—"

She cut off, flinging an arm across my chest. We both stopped short.

The sound of a drill.

Our eyes met, each widening as though we stared into a mirror.

She lowered her voice. "You don't think..."

I nodded slowly, the same thought in my brain as hers. "Someone's there."

"Should someone be working today?"

"Bianca had a floor mosaic collected. Perhaps she also requested—"

"With an ongoing theft investigation?"

We both shook our heads, knowing better.

"Quiet," she whispered.

We moved from the center of the road into the ruins of the buildings across from the Casa di Marte, making our way slowly. Through doorways and over low points in the walls.

The drilling continued.

She took the lead, as I would expect, but I shifted in front of her as we got closer.

What would I do if it was Cristian? Or if he was there overseeing the work? My stomach dropped. I wouldn't report him. Not him. There'd be significant consequences from that. And I couldn't let Samantha see me let him go. My heart thundered in my chest, echoing in my ears so loudly I didn't hear the words from Samantha.

She tapped my shoulder, and I stilled, turning to her.

"I said we should take the camera out. We can get a photo of whoever's in there. Just need to switch the lens."

We knelt behind the remains of a wall, only three feet high. I quickly switched to the telescopic lens so we could take a photo without being seen.

"And maybe we should split up, go in two different entrances, so they can't just get out?" The twinkle in her eye inspired more questions, but we had a task to focus on.

"Alright."

She held her watch next to mine, setting timers on each.

"You take the photos and go through the storage room entrance. I'll call Elliot. He can get in touch with the Carabinieri or whoever he needs to. Then I'll sneak down the side street to the atrium entrance. Ten minutes and we converge."

"What about the east entrance?"

She bit down on her lip, eyes flicking back and forth. "I'll think of something. Just get those photos."

I nodded, an electric charge shooting through me. This must be the energy she lived off of. She kissed me quickly and headed for the side street. Her head stayed up, watching her surroundings, steps careful and silent. She moved like a predator, like a character from a movie sneaking up on an evil-doer. I couldn't control my smile as I watched after her.

The sound of the drill pressed into my brain, reminding me of our mission. It was not to admire Samantha's graceful movements or her tactics. The camera was still in my hands, and I slung the backpack over my shoulder.

The walls of the southern entryway into the Casa were mostly intact, save a portion which hadn't survived the excavation and stood only four feet high. Standing, adjusting position, climbing atop the wall across the street—which I should have had more respect for—I angled myself until I had a clear view through the storage room door, past the garden and into the triclinium.

An icy shard stabbed into my spine. The person's face and body were covered against the dust spraying up from where they were drilling into the Minerva wall, above her head. My hands shook as I clenched the camera. The Minerva wall. That was Samantha's wall. The ice on my spine thawed quickly, replaced by bubbling rage, and I lurched forward.

Photos.

First, photos.

I lifted the camera, finding it difficult to take a good shot, as my hands continued to tremble. I took five, launched myself over the wall, and ran across the street. They wouldn't hear me over the drill. There, I could hop the gate and dash forward into the storage room. Keeping my head low, I propped the camera on the crumbled wall separating the storage room from the garden and got clear shots.

My watch showed nine minutes had passed. I put the camera away and studied the figure. Full body covered in white coveralls, which included a hood and facial gear. Male, but not Cristian's body type. No other parties. A small black case sat by his feet, no doubt for transporting the piece once he'd removed it.

I checked my watch again as the seconds counted down to the ten-minute mark. Were we to run in or walk? Say anything? We should have discussed this in more detail. Adrenaline coursed through my body, and I tried breathing through it, but he was cutting out Minerva's face.

Five seconds.

I moved to the edge of the doorway leading into the garden.

As my watch finished counting down, I prepared to run at the man.

"Hi! I'm lost. Can you help me?" Samantha approached from the atrium before I was two steps into the garden.

I paused. Her eyes flicked to me and she made a subtle movement, which was unmistakably telling me to get back into the storage room.

The man stopped his drill and turned to face her. In perfect English, he said, "This building is off limits."

He hadn't noticed me, so I snuck to my hiding spot, peeking out to watch. How would this play out? She smiled politely, speaking in English, in a softer tone than she normally did. With her badge tucked away, she looked like the consummate tourist.

"Is it?" She pouted, putting her hands on her hips. "I got separated from my tour group. We just finished at the Central Baths and were going to the Vettii house next. I was taking some pictures on my phone and didn't notice they'd left."

He pulled down his hood and mask, moving his goggles to his forehead.

Cazzo!

It was Umberto.

Get out of there, Samantha!

Her naïve expression faltered for the briefest moment. And she giggled. She never giggled.

He apparently didn't recognize her. She was putting on a performance, playing up the difference between her appearance and demeanor Wednesday and today. Umberto had barely glanced at her that day, focusing all his attention on me.

I ducked behind the wall separating me from the garden and took a deep breath, fumbling for the camera to take more pictures. I captured him smiling at her, her ruse working. Brilliant.

Umberto raised an arm to the western entrance. "Go back out the way you came, along Via di Nola, and turn right onto Vicolo dei Vetti. There will be signs."

"What are you doing there? Do you work here?" She pulled out her phone and turned away from the wall to snap a selfie. She smiled and gave a peace sign to the phone, then leaned closer to include him in another photo. Once she was done, she gestured at the wall with her phone and stepped closer to it, her smile growing. And her eyelashes fluttering. "Is this Venus?"

Five minutes had passed. I set the backpack on the ground and returned the camera to it, less delicately than I should have handled such expensive equipment. But I didn't want to take my eyes off her for too long. She hadn't given a signal in my direction or looked worried, so I waited. Perhaps she'd been able to get through to Special Agent Skinner and was stalling until the authorities arrived.

"No," he said, moving close to her. "This is Minerva, goddess of wisdom."

She tilted her head, playing at a coy smile. "Minerva? I've never heard of her." She was toying with him. It must be stalling. This must have been her way of covering both doors.

"Have you heard of Athena?"

"Yeah, isn't she the goddess of war or something?"

I bit down on my bottom lip to suppress the chuckle. Watching them from my hiding spot, I fell a little harder for her again. She used every part of her body while she spoke with him, slow eye movements, the seductive smile, extending a hip, tucking a loose hair which didn't even exist behind her ear.

"Athena's the Greek goddess of wisdom and strategic warfare, yes. Minerva's the Roman version."

"That's fascinating!" She placed a hand on his arm.

Heavy, rapid footfalls caught my attention. I looked out through the fallen section of wall and saw the caps of two Carabinieri officers speeding toward the building. I charged around the corner, through the garden. Umberto's head whipped around to see me, eyes and mouth wide, then back to Samantha.

I hurdled the short wall around the garden, while a grin flashed across Samantha's face. Her hand on his arm slid to his wrist and she slammed her other forearm into the back of his elbow.

He howled and jerked forward, dropping his equipment, one leg flailing out beside him. She followed through her movement, like an action hero, but when she took a step, her foot landed on his case. Samantha's leg crumpled underneath her and she screamed.

"Samantha!" I yelled, trying to cross the distance faster.

He hadn't flailed. He'd kicked the case to trip her. And I was not fast enough. I'd paused too long admiring her.

She went down hard, losing her grip on him, pain contorting her face. Knee, side, hands, then head slammed into the ground.

Umberto tore off for the eastern entrance, the approaching footfalls obviously coming from the west.

I came to a sliding halt next to her, picking up her head. "Are you al—"

One hand shot up and she shoved me as she hollered, "Go get him!"

I caught myself before tumbling over, scanning the length of her. No cuts or scrapes, no evident blood. "But you—"

"Go! I'm fine!"

The officers arrived through the atrium, and I launched to my feet after Umberto. If he turned right out of the exit, he'd be back onto Via di Nola and the thin crowds. No matter how many people were there, it would be difficult to hide, given his full-body protective attire. Not to mention he'd be heading for a gate.

No, he would have taken a left, hoping to get up the embankment at the north of the site. Then out through the fields or the trees. He wouldn't have swiped in through the front gate. What if he had a vehicle parked nearby? A perfect escape?

He was probably already gone.

CHAPTER 21

SAMANTHA

Carabiniere De Rosa and a female officer dashed in as Antonio vanished through the eastern door.

When I tripped on the case, the pain had exploded through my ankle, up my calf, overwhelming every sense, and I didn't see which way Umberto went. If he'd gone north, up through the fields, it would be hard to catch him. But Antonio was in peak physical condition and was a runner. Hopefully that put the odds further into our favor.

The officers came to a halt in front of me and I waved them after Antonio. "Dr. Ferraro went after the thief. That way!"

De Rosa sped off, but his partner stayed put.

I got up slowly on my knees, planted my good foot, and began to rise. But pain ricocheted from the side of my head, through my entire body, and I bit back a cry.

"Stay down." The officer's voice was calm, but firm.

I was now a suspect until I proved otherwise.

More shouting voices and hurried feet came from some direction. We were surrounded by full walls, crumbling half walls, the metal roof over part of the Casa—sound bounced around, stabbing into my brain.

Please, let it be Antonio with Umberto in hand.

I gestured at the black case, the cutting tool discarded next to it. "I don't know if he had more tools in there or if it was for transport. But I suspect—"

Elliot burst through the atrium door, Carabinieri TPC officer Bruno Gallo hot on his heels. "Did you catch them?"

"Antonio and an officer ran after him." I pointed at the door they'd left through. "It was Umberto, one of the men on the conservation team."

The two men shared a look, but didn't pursue.

"And yet..." Elliot offered me a hand while Gallo spoke in Italian with the female officer who was watching me. "You're still here, sitting on the ground?"

I waved the hand off and clenched my jaw, letting out a long exhale. The damn case. How did Umberto, mile a minute talking, Antonio-worshipping little weasel who could barely keep up with us, get the jump on me?

No, it wasn't the jump. It was my shitty luck.

"Don't ask." The walking shoes Chiara bought for me weren't designed for hand-to-hand combat. I ran fingers over my hair, prodding the lump forming above my ear. "Listen, there should be a black backpack over by the garden door by the main road. There's a camera in there that'll have photos of him cutting into the wall. The camera belongs to Mario De Luca. He loaned it to Antonio and me. I also have pictures on my phone."

Elliot knelt next to me. "Cutting into the wall in broad daylight?"

I shrugged and pulled my phone out of my pocket, a thin

crack running through the screen. "It's an active conservation site. Who'd question it except someone on the team?"

He accepted the phone and scrolled through the photos I'd taken of Umberto. "We interviewed him, so I know who he is. Background check was clear."

The female officer walked out of the Mars room, through the atrium and garden area.

I eased my neck from side to side, breathing through the painful movement. "We'll have to check out where else he's worked, see if there's a history of missing items."

Elliot frowned, pulling my hair back to look at my head. "Hurt yourself?"

"It's just a bump. I'll be fine." I rolled my ankle in a circle, testing it at all angles. It was already much better. "Give me a hand up?"

He stood and offered me his hand again, which I took this time.

"And several bruises, I think." I was sore, but slowly twisted and stretched to be sure everything really was alright.

A radio on the female officer's shoulder squawked as she returned to us, and De Rosa's voice came through. "No sign of him out here. Did he circle back?"

She responded in the negative and handed the pack to Elliot. Gallo joined us.

I reached in as he held it open and retrieved the camera. Scanning through the photos with Elliot and Gallo, it was clear. Photos of Umberto cutting into the wall.

Gallo nodded. "We'll cross-reference this with any laboratory plans, but I'm sure if Dr. Ferraro didn't know about it, we'll find it's an attempt at another theft."

"Told you," said Elliot, and the TPC officer nodded.

"Told you what?" I asked. But I didn't really have to ask. Elliot had told Gallo about me, and he *told him*, which meant it was something about Elliot wanting me to work with him.

Like usual, he just smiled, saying no more.

"I tripped on the case, Elliot. I had him, was about to take him down, but I tripped on the fucking case and was too dazed to do anything about it." I snatched the backpack from him and unceremoniously replaced the camera.

Elliot patted my arm. "It happens to the best of us."

"Cazzo Madre di Dio!" came Antonio's voice from beyond the eastern wall. He stormed into the room, face red and breath heavy. He scanned the group of us and took one sharp exhale to center himself. Ran his fingers through his hair to straighten it. Narrowed eyes cutting the other three down. "Tell me someone else went after him and you didn't leave it all to me?"

"De Rosa's still out there somewhere," I said.

Antonio gestured at the backpack in my hands. "Did the pictures come out, at least?"

"Very well," said Gallo. "Exactly what we need."

"No, what we need is a body," growled Antonio. One dramatic heave of his shoulders, and he raised a hand to the side of my head, where it had smashed into the ground. "Are you alright?"

"A bump and a few bruises, but I'm fine." Any flinch would catch his attention and the focus would shift from where it belonged—finding Umberto. "You didn't see De Rosa out there? He ran off in the same direction you did."

He shook his head, running hands through his hair again, the sexy little wave fanning back into place after the fourth correction. Like he could convince even hair to do what he wanted. "Once you're up the embankment, there are fields, but there are also buildings, construction trucks, trees and a park beyond. Not to mention people as you get far enough. There are too many places to hide."

His fist clenched, like he was about to punch something. Agitated gaze flying around the room, up to the metal roof over the space, to the officers just outside the Mars room. But then it settled on me, and everything softened. A smile broke. "What was that maneuver you were attempting on him?"

"It was supposed to be a takedown. Twist the arm and use the momentum to get him on the ground and keep him there." I rolled my eyes, heat flushing my cheeks. "I can't believe you saw my epic failure."

"You realize being in a relationship means sharing both highs and lows, sì?" He winked and came closer, threading an arm around my waist and dropping his voice. "It was sexy as hell."

I leaned toward him and we walked together to the Minerva wall.

"Such a shame." He sighed. "Her beautiful face."

Umberto had used a rotary cutter to outline the piece he was going to remove. Fortunately, he'd started cutting into the plaster above Minerva's head and we'd caught him before he got beyond the trees in the background. It was a small blessing.

"We may be able to repair the seam he created while restoring some of the other cracks." He lifted a hand to Minerva's painted face but didn't touch it. "You know, I spoke to her so many times when I first arrived, she's like an old friend."

Spoken to her as a replacement for me. We'd been back together a week after being broken up. Confronting my failures wasn't one of my strong suits, but admitting I'd made a mistake pushing him away was one of the best things I'd ever done.

"The flower fresco isn't here," said Gallo. We turned to face him and Elliot, who were inspecting the contents of Umberto's case.

De Rosa arrived, sweaty and sucking in breaths. He cast a suspicious look at Antonio and me. "I can't find him anywhere. Are you sure there was really someone else here?"

"Calm down, Fredo," said Gallo. "We have photographic evidence."

Given their familiarity, they knew each other, and not just from this investigation, but before. De Rosa said he'd been stationed in Rome. Gallo was working with Elliot in Rome. What was the link there?

"The flower fresco is probably long gone." Antonio's gaze settled on Minerva again, frustration clouding his face.

"We don't have any way of tracking it, do we?" I asked.

Gallo shook his head. "We'll have it added to all the right databases, but odds are it's gone for good." He approached us, holding out his hand. "Thank you for your efforts. Both of you. Come to the office, transfer the photos, give a statement, and then you can be on your way."

"Unless..." Elliot joined him, that familiar smile on his face. That *when are you coming to work with me* smile.

Maybe now was the right time. Join them at the Carabinieri office, upload the files, discuss some leads. Maybe take on some research. An interview or two. Gallo—and definitely De Rosa—may not be happy with it, but maybe Elliot could pull some strings. I'd chosen Antonio over Elliot and the investigation on Thursday, but that was when it was a dead end. Now we had something concrete, a lead to follow.

"We still have that hike this afternoon." Antonio squeezed my waist. "We talked about it Wednesday?"

"But we don't have hiking gear. At least, I don't."

Antonio grinned. "I know you hate shopping, but perhaps a quick trip to Napoli to pick up some basics? There's an old Minervan temple ruin at the tip of the Sorrentine Peninsula I thought you might like. Four and a half miles."

"Oh, I know that place!" piped up the female officer. "There's a grotto near there that's worth the climb, if you're up for it?"

"That sounds perfect for my rock climber." Antonio released me and took the backpack, a broad smile on his gorgeous face.

I could come up with an excuse. Tell him I hurt my ankle when I fell and join Elliot. But if I chose Elliot, Antonio wouldn't have any reason to stay except to watch me. He'd go to the office, or maybe the villa.

The alternative was to buy new hiking gear. I'd need a new GPS. New backpack. My hiking boots needed to be replaced, anyway. It couldn't hurt. And I'd be with him.

Antonio hefted the pack onto his shoulder and kissed my temple. He didn't seem to consider for a second the possibility I'd ditch him. Of course not. He probably figured the investigation in the morning and the hike in the afternoon were just him doing things I loved all day. And it was.

I smiled at him. "You're a good boyfriend."

He held out a hand. "That's what happens when I have such a good girlfriend."

Instead of bothering with the professional appearances, I slid my hand into his and gave him a kiss on the cheek. "You're a lucky man."

CHAPTER 22
SAMANTHA

AN HOUR and a half after leaving the Carabinieri office in Pompeii, Antonio and I were walking out of the outdoor equipment shop. Like so many stores in Italy's crowded city centers, it was long and narrow, but packed to the brim with everything we needed.

I had a new backpack loaded with day hiking gear and Antonio had stuffed some items into the pack we'd brought to Pompeii. Plus, we'd received advice about the Punta Campanella hike from Termini to the tip of the Sorrentine Peninsula. They'd even given us better directions to the grotto the female officer had recommended.

We both wore our new hiking boots and carried our street shoes in our packs. I'd told Antonio I needed to wear mine in, and he did the same, citing that I was the expert.

"You think Chiara will like all this?" I asked.

"Sì, she will." He'd insisted on paying, I'd argued, but he explained he'd keep all the gear and introduce Chiara to his new favorite hobby. Despite this being only the second hike he'd ever been on. I'd conceded, he'd winked at me, and I was sure it was all game. But I agreed to accept him for who he was, money and generosity included, so I didn't press the issue.

The pedestrian street was thick with people, like everywhere else in the city. It was so different from sleepy little Brenton, Michigan. Close enough to Lansing and Detroit to have access to everything you needed, but far enough away from the crowds, you had room to move.

The walkway and roadway were dull gray with long rectangular bricks for the sidewalk, small paving stones in arched patterns for the street.

At the next intersection, we'd hire a car to the trailhead. It would take over an hour to drive from Naples, past Sorrento, and eventually to Termini, but the train could take double that. The buildings were four and five stories high, all stonework and stucco with metal balconies. We passed a leather-goods store with bright pastel handbags in the front window, a tiny alley with a pharmacy and tables set up with tourist knickknacks, and, across the street, posters for exhibits covered the twelve-foot-high windows of a museum.

Tall tables and chairs lined the sidewalk in front of a café, under a red awning. Patrons sat while others hovered at the tables, enjoying their coffees and pastries. We had to walk single-file to get through the throng.

"Smells delicious—" Antonio squeezed my hand and chuckled. "—but our freeze-dried ice cream, trail mix, and granola bars will be far better."

I snorted a laugh. The first time we'd gone hiking together, those were the foods I'd brought, while he'd surprised me with red wine and a small feast. Today would be more hardcore. More my style. "And no fooling around at the end of the trail."

"Opportunities to fool around are everywhere." He veered

closer, kissing my temple without a stutter in his step. "You just need to know where to look."

We slowed as the trio in front of us stopped to admire the display of a gallery at the corner. The gallery building was covered in yellow stucco with gray marble outlining the tall windows at the front. It blended with the sidewalk but stood out with an understated elegance.

One of the three paintings in the window caught my eye. An abstract piece, bright reds and oranges at its center, swirling and radiating out to azure at the corners. A sunset or maybe fire.

"You like this one, bella?" Antonio asked.

I startled, barely registering that I'd stopped to stare. Modern art made you part of it, bringing a lifetime of your own experiences and emotions into the art to find your interpretation. And this one conjured up such a vivid memory, I couldn't rip my eyes from it. "It makes me think of the sun. The day we went for our hike and I was looking up at the sky."

"While I was..." He lowered his voice. "Fooling around?"

I nudged him with a hip and feigned a scowl.

He arched an eyebrow. "Practicing my linguistic skills?"

My thighs clenched, realizing on their own where his joke was headed, and I breathed through a sudden need to take him back to the villa or find a hotel. But I wasn't about to miss Punta Campanella. The staff at the store said it was the best hike in the area.

"I believe I was very..." He came closer, hot breath hitting my ear, creating an energy that curled around in my stomach. "Cunning?"

Heat flushed through my cheeks at the memory of the two

of us on the beach at the end of the trail that day. My fingers clutched in his hair while he—

"Wait a second," I said, pointing at the gallery name stenciled on the window. "Riccardo Emanuele."

Antonio sighed. "You're kidding me?"

"Isn't that where Umberto said his girlfriend works?"

He straightened, stepping in front of me to block my view of the painting. His face pinched, lips tightening until he sucked in a breath and opened his mouth. But no words came out.

We'd been having a moment, hadn't we? A relationship moment.

But maybe this was a moment, too. Instead of telling me to drop it, he held his tongue. Not something Antonio Ferraro was likely used to.

"You wish to go in and speak with her?" His voice was strained but didn't hold the disapproval I'd expected.

I checked my watch. "Twenty minutes, no more. Then we hike."

FOOTWEAR SHOULD CLICK on the marble floor in an art gallery. My thick-soled and bulky hiking boots put me off-balance mentally, but I'd feel equally silly taking the time to switch into my other shoes just to come inside for a quick visit.

Antonio, on the other hand? Maybe it was the way the slate cargo shorts and heather gray T-shirt fit him, or maybe it was just from growing up wealthy, but even in his clunky brown boots, he looked expensive.

The gallery was sparse, a large open building two stories

high with marble columns rising to the ceiling. Unlike the tight display in the front window, inside, the paintings had a great deal of space around them. Ten feet between each, displayed on plain white walls with simple cards listing title and artist. A couple of older tourists—with tour stickers on their shirts—wandered a few paces ahead of us. A middle-aged man stood in front of another painting, head tilting this way and that.

A woman in a short, flowing dress of brilliant emerald with a spray of pink approached us. Late twenties, with a warm smile, pale skin, and stick straight blond hair. An overpowering perfume of lilies washed over me. Her gaze lingered on Antonio. "Good morning. Can I help you with anything?"

Her Italian was accented, with shorter vowels than a native speaker.

I took an educated guess. "Do you speak English?"

"I do." Her eyes drifted to me as she switched languages, then back to Antonio. That happened far too often. What did she think? I was his assistant or something?

He wound his arm around my waist. "My girlfriend was admiring the crimson and cobalt piece in the window."

My head snapped to him. "I don't want it. I just thought it was pretty."

He winked. "Who said I was asking for you?"

"Oh, sorry." My gaze faltered. It seemed the obvious assumption after Chiara's shopping spree for me and the hiking gear store.

"But I was." Antonio chuckled, squeezing me tighter, and returning his attention to the other woman. "It would appear I was incorrect about her selection. Perhaps we shall have a look around in case there's something else which catches her eye."

"Of course," the woman said. "If that piece spoke to you, I can show you some others."

"I don't need more stuff." I needed to talk to Umberto's girlfriend. It had been two hours since we'd caught him trying to steal a fresco in the Park. If we were lucky, he hadn't contacted her yet and she might give us a clue on where to find him.

Correction: Where the Carabinieri could find him.

She continued, despite my weak protest. The accent in her English placed her in the United States somewhere. Not the South, not the Northeast, definitely not Midwest. "We have an excellent selection of pieces by Mr. Emanuele. I can show you some with similar themes or colorways. There are also some works by other artists if you'd prefer?"

"I think theme is what we're looking for, sì, bella?" The corner of his mouth was twitching so much he practically looked like a rabbit. He was incorrigible.

Working hard not to roll my eyes at him, I said, "A co-worker of his recommended the gallery."

The front door opened and a man walked in. The woman speaking with us smiled at him as he strode through the middle of the room. His hair was gray, face lined, and he wore a loose white shirt with a green paint splatter at the hem. Her boss, maybe?

"Eva," the man said with a nod.

Eva. That was the girlfriend's name. I opened my mouth, but Antonio spoke first.

"Riccardo?"

The man paused two steps past us and turned. No flicker of recognition.

"Antonio Ferraro." Antonio let go of me and held out a hand to the man. "You may know my uncle Andrea Ferraro? Or our family business?"

The man's eyes widened. "Of the conservation Ferraros?"

"One and the same." Antonio clasped his hand. "I believe I repaired of one of your paintings eight years ago or so, while I worked at the studio in Roma."

Riccardo nodded absently. "Is Eva taking good care of you?"

"She's trying to. My girlfriend doesn't seem to want me to buy anything today."

Your girlfriend wants to talk to Eva. So why bring Riccardo into the conversation? Distract me? Use up the twenty minutes I promised?

"That's a shame," said Riccardo.

"I told her we are going to spend an obscene amount of money—" Antonio swept a hand through the air, expressing the vastness. "—on something special for our dining room."

Our dining room? Wait, we hadn't discussed buying anything. Oh, shit. He was working *with* me, not against me. Made sure Riccardo knew who his family was, waved his Bulgari watch in front of them both to emphasize his words. Subtle. But highly effective.

"Honey," I said, placing a hand on his arm. "Umberto said we shouldn't talk price here."

Eva's face tightened for a moment before opening back up into the broad and welcoming smile. She was definitely the right one.

"Of course, bella. You're right, as always."

"If you'll excuse me." Riccardo clasped Antonio's hand again and then mine. "I leave you in capable hands."

As Riccardo disappeared through a door next to a sculpture display, Eva ushered us to a painting similar to the one in the window. Larger, with more radiance around the outer edge. But it lacked the window painting's spirit.

She whispered, "Dr. Antonio Ferraro, did you say?"

"Sì, I did."

"I worked for your uncle earlier this year." Her professional smile shifted to a more genuine one. "I've heard quite a lot about you."

I let out a little fake gasp. "Umberto mentioned his girlfriend worked at a gallery and had worked at the studio in Rome. That's not you, is it?"

"It is. And I'm so..." She chuckled. "Surprised he'd recommend you come here."

"Why?" I asked. "The artwork is stunning."

She blushed. "Umberto isn't a big fan of modern art. It makes sense, given his background, but I'm a bit more open."

"His background?"

"Ancient sites, ancient art, ancient everything. If it was made after 1900, it's too new." She gestured to Antonio. "And the way he speaks of Dr. Ferraro, as an ancient fresco expert, I can't imagine he would have recommended anything so modern."

"You're American, aren't you?" I asked.

"I am. Miami, originally."

"And what led you to Italy?"

Eva's eyes flicked over my shoulder and back to me. She pointed at the painting we stood in front of. "This piece is one of Riccardo's more recent ones."

Antonio leaned in to kiss my cheek, turning his face at an odd angle. His lips brushed my ear and he whispered, "Her boss is watching."

I pulled away from him enough to look straight at him. He'd taken me to Pompeii first thing in the morning. Shopped for hiking gear. Helped with this conversation instead of shutting it down. Then he was going to take me hiking.

All his pretty words weren't just words. This wasn't just a man I was sleeping with. Not just a boyfriend. He was a partner. Just like he'd suggested at the club last night.

Had I ever really had that? Even with my husband?

The smile broke in my stomach first, before radiating out through my entire body.

Eva was still talking, something about where Riccardo had painted the piece, but all I could see was Antonio.

Staring, he mouthed.

I know, I mouthed back. But I had to focus on the task at hand, not fall any harder for this amazing man. "Eva, do you have anything by lesser known artists?"

"I do, but they're further toward the back." She waved a hand in that direction, then turned to lead us. Movement would keep Riccardo's attention off her. As long as we appeared to be shopping, I could grill her.

"You were saying," I said. "What brought you from Miami?"

"I met Umberto while I was in Paris three years ago on a plein air painting retreat." Eva glanced over her shoulder, the blond hair swinging gracefully, green dress fluttering about her figure. She was like another piece of art. "I was in a café with some other students and, well, it was love at first sight."

"Sounds familiar," said Antonio, weaving his fingers

around mine. "Samantha and I fell in love in college but were separated for a decade by other adventures."

I frowned at him. Not even close to true. We'd *met* in college, but I turned him down the one time he spoke to me.

Too serious, he mouthed to me.

"He spent four months in Miami with me, then we moved to Rome two years ago so he could finish his studies." Eva slowed as we reached a space in the gallery where the paintings were much closer together. We were out of the natural light, under spotlights. These pieces were more akin to Dali surrealism, with elements melting off the canvas. Far more muted tones than Riccardo's works near the front.

The card next to the painting listed the artist as 'Eva Zabelle.' Was that her surname?

"I like this." Antonio leaned back to take it all in, then stepped closer, releasing my hand. "I need to thank Umberto for recommending the gallery. Is he still in town, given the delay with our project? I haven't seen him since Wednesday."

"He talked about heading up to Rome for the weekend but changed his mind last night." She shrugged, staring at the painting, a gloom falling over her features. "And he was supposed to stop in this morning, but he didn't show."

Could he have been traveling to Rome to meet a buyer and that fell through? Maybe the recovery of the blue pigment pot scared him? Or were his questions about the delayed equipment on Wednesday a fact-finding mission? Maybe he discovered he had more time and opportunity, so he postponed his sale until he had more to sell?

I touched her arm. "You're worried about him?"

She cleared her throat and moved to the next painting,

which none of us really looked at. "I called him a half dozen times, but he hasn't responded."

"No history of disappearing? Taking off without telling you?"

"None." She clasped a hand over the bracelet on her left wrist. "We've only been together a couple of years, so you never know. But we've been pretty much inseparable that whole time."

I pointed at an element on the painting, a distraction in case her boss was still watching. "Is there anything we can do? Anywhere you two normally go or somewhere he's talked about that he may have gone on his own?"

She furrowed her brows. "Why are you asking all these questions?"

"Maybe we can help?"

"I'm sorry, but I haven't had this job long." Her gaze went over my shoulder again. "It's a huge opportunity for me to showcase my paintings here, so if you're not actually interested in any of the pieces, I need to move on to someone else."

None of the art would be under five figures, so buying one just to keep talking was out of the question. Antonio probably could have, but that was hardly a good use of his funds.

"No ideas at all?" I asked. "Maybe where you're staying?"

She shook her head and ushered us toward the entrance. She kept step beside me, her voice low. "He was joking around last night about the project in Pompeii, like he'd be so absorbed in that once it got going that I might not see him again. I laughed it off, knowing the way he got focused about his work."

Antonio said, "But the project has not started yet."

"I know. There was just..." She slowed before we reached

the door. "The way he was talking last night, it seemed like there was something else going on. But I don't know what."

Eva and Antonio exchanged contact information.

I said, "If you think of anything else, let us know. Antonio has contacts in town that may be able to help."

"I will." She shook my hand, then held Antonio's. "It was an honor to meet you, Dr. Ferraro."

We emerged from the gallery, back into the sunshine and jam-packed road.

"Did you get what you wanted, bella?"

"Yes and no. I'd say it satisfied my curiosity." I pulled out my phone and texted Elliot. Eva's worries about Umberto might be important.

"And the no?"

"We didn't miraculously stumble upon him. That would have been nice," I chuckled.

CHAPTER 23

ANTONIO

SAMANTHA and I sat together on the scrubby dirt at the end of the peninsula, a strong wind whipping errant hairs out of her ponytail. The ancient remains of the Minervan temple behind us, gray stone steps and worn red brick lining the edge of the cliff in front of us. Three miles away, across the deep blue water, the rocky cliffs of Capri jutted out of the sea.

I leaned back, propping myself on my hands, with Samantha sitting between my outstretched legs. She tucked a granola bar wrapper into her backpack, put her black ball cap on, and settled against my chest, the extra weight pressing my palms into the fine gravel. One leg folded up, her other straight in front of her.

A family and two other couples milled about the area, relaxing after the short hike to the temple. The start of the trail was easy, little more than a sidewalk for a woman so accustomed to braving the wilds. From here, it was a quick stop into the grotto, then a steep climb up to the top of the peaks before winding back to Termini. If we'd arrived earlier, we could have detoured even farther, to the Bay of Ieranto and its small beach.

"This view is definitely worth the hike." She sighed, tilting her head to let it rest against my shoulder, giving me full access to kiss the side of her hat.

We'd made our way slowly, abnormal for Samantha. My heart warmed with her against me, my fiery girlfriend finally relaxing after being with me for a week.

I drew my knees up and straightened my back, folding my arms around her. "It's hard to imagine my first hike was just over two weeks ago."

She laughed against my chest, wrapping her arms over mine. "You won't need your survival instructor much longer at this rate."

"Perhaps another hike or two and I'll be done with her." I squeezed her tight. "Or two hundred, perhaps? Two thousand?"

Her laughter continued and her eyes slid closed, face drifting toward the sun hanging over the island in the distance.

A couple stopped next to us, chatting in French about the scenery, taking photographs of Capri. A speed boat raced through the channel, a sailboat floated past, and the couple left.

"There's a longer option to the trail, but I think, given the hour, we should take the more direct route. Unless you want to skip the grotto?"

"Did you really work at your uncle's Rome studio eight years ago?" she asked.

That mind. It never stopped churning. "Sì, while I was in school, just as I worked with Papa while I was at MSU."

"And you remember working on one of Riccardo's paintings?"

I rubbed my cheek against hers, letting out a small sigh. "Bella, he's very successful. He sells artwork around the world and wouldn't know if a painting ended up in our hands."

She sat up enough to turn and look at me but didn't release my arms. "It was all a ruse?"

"I thought if I had his attention, we would get more cooperation from Eva."

She smiled and turned back to the water, leaning toward me. "Thanks for that."

Touring the gallery had not been a hardship. The artwork was beautiful, and Samantha was satisfied. It meant something to her.

And after she went back to Michigan, I'd return and buy that colorful abstract painting from the window. She may not want *stuff*, as she liked to say, but hanging a painting that reminded her of that day—of the pleasure I gave her—in my condo? She wouldn't see it until I was home in January, but the look on her face when she saw it would be worth every penny.

Her phone buzzed in her pack, and she released me to retrieve it. She flashed the cracked screen at me. Lucy Chapman. Samantha's former protégé at Foster Mutual.

"This should be entertaining." Samantha put the phone on speaker and before she had time to say hello, Lucy's stream of consciousness began.

"Oh my god, Sam! I was just out at lunch with Sofia and I was telling her that you and I were gonna do some rock climbing and how excited I was and maybe we'd go this weekend and she told me that you were out of town and I said

'How do you know that?'" Lucy took the barest breath, her excitement infectious. "Sofia had this big smile on her face and I was all like 'What's going on Sofia?' Then she told me! Oh my god, Sam! Oh. My. God! You' re in Naples? With Dr. Ferraro?"

Samantha's shoulders shook and she half-turned to me, curling her bent leg. "Yes, Lucy. I'm torn between staring at Capri and Antonio at the moment."

"I would totally pick that jawline over Capri any day!" Lucy said.

I kissed Samantha's cheek audibly, for Lucy's benefit. "Ciao, Lucy."

She squealed on the other end of the call. "Antonio, I tried so many times to change her mind about you. How did you do it?"

"I made my own choice." Samantha sat up straighter and gave me a mock frown. "Sometimes I can be a little stubborn."

"Understatement!" Lucy laughed. "So, when are you going to come home? I really want to—"

"Scusami, Lucy..." I pulled Samantha's hand with the phone closer.

"That's ok—"

"I couldn't make that out... You're breaking... Bad recep... But..." I ended the call.

Samantha grinned at me. "What was that?"

"Today is about you and me. Not Lucy Chapman's excitement over that horrible 'us' word."

"Yeah, it's pretty terrifying," she chuckled. "And what's with her having lunch with your sister?"

"I'm not surprised those two social butterflies might

spend time together." I tilted her hand with the phone. "When did you crack the screen?"

She sagged against me, face shielded by her cap, but the disappointment was thick in her voice. "During my little dance with Umberto."

"We can have that fixed tomorrow."

"I had him, Antonio." She huffed. "I had a good grip on him, but I couldn't keep hold. I let him get away. I can't believe I tripped over the stupid case."

I pulled back from her and shifted my seat to see under her brim. "You didn't trip."

"I did. My foot went right down on it because I was too cocky and didn't pay attention to my surroundings."

"No, I mean, he kicked it under you. I saw it while I was busy being too slow to help. Don't take this all on yourself."

"But you did everything right." Her gaze fell away from mine. "Got the photos, came for me, ran after him. And then you were awesome at the gallery. Me? I failed everything today."

For how short a time we'd known each other, I could recognize this. The doubts she had in herself. She could fly between unsurpassed confidence and crushing self-doubt in the blink of an eye. Surely, she had to understand how amazing she truly was?

I pulled her chin up to look at me, lifting it high enough she couldn't hide behind the brim of her cap. "Bella, were it not for your insistence we follow up, your determination to find out *anything*, we wouldn't know Umberto was the thief. It could have been anyone in Napoli that day. The authorities have gone from a suspect list of millions to just one. That sounds like a success to me."

"He didn't really kick the toolbox under me."

"Sì, he did." It was my turn to feign the scowl. "Now stop feeling sorry for yourself so we can go back to enjoying the day."

She turned to face me and threaded her legs over my hips, wrapping her arms around my neck. Her jaw clenched as she moved, the emotions likely unsettling her. "Let's just sit here a bit longer."

I pulled her closer, scooping her up onto my lap so I had to look up at her. One of the tourists nearby cleared their throat.

"We probably shouldn't sit like this in a public place." She attempted to ease off my lap, but I locked my hands behind the small of her back.

"The first time I kissed these lips..." I pursed my lips in invitation, but she leaned her upper body away.

Sadly, she was uncomfortable with public displays of affection.

No matter. Words would suffice. "You were wearing a ball cap like this one. And a dirty pink work shirt."

"Yeah, super sexy."

"You're the sexiest thing I've ever seen. Regardless of what you are or are not wearing." I stirred underneath her, certainly inappropriate for where we were. "Because your brain is always on. Always at full throttle."

Unlike other women I'd dated, Samantha had no guile about her. No fakeness, no deceit, no shallow desire for superficial things.

I thought I'd loved before, but the need deep inside me to be with her was different. Touching her, being there with her, sharing her space in the universe—it all made me better.

"I love you, Samantha." It came out as a long sigh, floating away with the wind. I slid a hand up to her neck, brushing along the jawline with my thumb.

She stared and she blinked. The words didn't come, but the kiss did. Like in Capri. Tender. Paradise.

"Excuse me," came a female voice nearby. Very nearby. "Can you find somewhere else to do that?"

Samantha separated enough to look at me, edging off my lap with a grin. "That's what I told him."

I shot her a smirk back, not looking at the woman who disapproved of our behavior or the man standing next to her. "Bella, we're in Italia. The polizia would surely arrest me if I didn't kiss those lips at least a thousand times a day."

The man with the interrupting woman whispered, "He's good."

The woman huffed, the man laughed, and they left with their two young teenagers.

Samantha laughed as well. "Can you bank those kisses? Because I'm pretty sure we've kissed enough for a month."

"But we'll be apart for three." I stood, brushing dust off my shorts, and offered her a hand. "I need to bank far more."

She took my hand, grimacing as she stood.

I shouldn't have mentioned that. Time to lighten the mood. "However, today, there is a grotto to be seen and more trail. Shall we be off?"

"We shall."

When she leaned over to pick up her pack, I took the opportunity to smack her luscious, round ass. "Or we could head back the way we came, return to the villa, and do everything that woman was afraid we might do right here."

She rolled her eyes, slinging the pack on her shoulders. With a growl, she said, "Grotto, Ferraro."

~

HAD we not been told about the grotto, I would have missed it. My adventure-minded girlfriend may have gravitated to it, but not me. The entrance was little more than a gash in the rocks, dropping toward the water. An ancient stone wall topped one side, long grasses and bushes obscuring what could almost pass for stairs cut into the cliffside.

The gap between the rocks was only wide enough for two people to squeeze past each other, and it was precarious. In some places, we had to sit on the ground and inch our way along. In others, ancient, knotted ropes hung to help in the descent.

Samantha's smile grew larger by the moment. "It's not quite rock climbing, but pretty close."

I helped a couple lift their son from one rock to another in a spot with a ladder too tall for the child. Samantha pointed out places to grip the wall as we progressed, explaining crimps, pinches, and slopes. With her guidance, the process was far smoother than it would have been otherwise.

She sucked in a deep breath as the space opened up around us to reveal the base of the cliff. She paused with one hand braced on a boulder next to her. "Antonio, it's beautiful."

Water rushed in over the low rocks, a few feet below the bottom stairs and entrance to the small caves. A huge limestone sea stack erupted from the water. Tiny compared to the Faraglioni rock formations in Capri but looming over us ominously. The rocks were uneven, pools of water dotting the edge of the grotto.

When she failed to move, I took the lead, ushering her with me. There was only so far you could walk without getting your feet wet. "Come, let's explore."

It was nearing five o'clock. The hike had been slow going and we'd cuddled far longer than I'd expected. In the distance, more speedboats and a small ferry motored between the peninsula and Capri. We'd passed a half-dozen people leaving as we came down, no doubt because of the time. It was at least a two-hour hike back. We were racing the sunset and had not purchased flashlights. A couple sat on a blanket at the entrance to a cave, packing up the remains of a meal. They waved and smiled at us.

"Let's sit," she said, lowering herself onto the stone stairs near the water's edge. From the bottom step, it was a two- or three-foot drop to the exposed rocky sea floor.

I joined her, waggling my eyebrows as we both removed our backpacks. "We could strip down and go for a swim."

She laughed and nudged me with a shoulder. "Maybe if we were alone, but this isn't exactly a private spot."

As if on cue, the couple stood and folded their blanket. They passed us on their way to the crevice which led to the top of the cliffs, the man winking at me. In stilted Italian, he said, "Enjoy."

I reached to my back and pulled my shirt off with practiced speed. "You were saying?"

Samantha shook her head. "You go ahead. I'll watch."

"No, no." I stood and unbuttoned my shorts, grabbing her hands and pulling lightly.

She resisted but wouldn't win this game of tug-of-war.

"You have three choices, bella." I planted my feet, ready to haul her up. "Naked, underwear, or fully clothed."

I wouldn't actually throw her in, but the threat would make her laugh. The protest barely escaped her lips before I yanked her hands, prepared to catch her against my body.

Instead, the moment her foot hit the ground at the base of the stairs, she crumpled, crying out.

"Samantha!" I dropped onto the rock next to her, the rocky surface jagged against my bare knees. "Are you alright?"

She clutched at her left leg, head buried against her knee. She whimpered, "Ow, fuck."

I gripped her shoulders. What else could I do? "Let me help you up."

Her breaths were slow and ragged, whistling through clenched teeth. "I just need a sec."

"Mi dispiace." I was playing a silly game and hurt her. Taking hold under her armpits, I lifted her up to sit on the steps. "What happened?"

She leaned her face back, staring up at the cloudless sky, blinking rapidly, her breaths coming faster.

"Stay calm." I placed my hands over hers at the base of her calf. "I may need my survival instructor's advice."

A smile mingled with the mask of pain. How high was her threshold? Samantha Caine hardly seemed like the type to overreact to a scratch. No, she seemed more the type to refer to a lost limb as a flesh wound. Her reaction to this, the way she rocked back and forth, focusing on her breathing—this was likely bad.

"Is it your ankle?"

She nodded furiously, sniffling.

"Mi dispiace, bella. I'm so sorry."

The nodding switched to rapid shaking of her head. "I landed funny. It's not your fault."

I stuffed our packs behind her, encouraging her to lean back. "Let me look at it."

She slowly released her grip on the calf, and I took over.

"I need to take the boot off."

"No." Clenching the top of her pack in one hand, she used the other to cover her face. "We should leave it on. It's—" She huffed. "—It's just twisted. The boot will help support it until we get back."

"You think you can walk on it?" I held her leg slightly elevated from the ground. There was no one else down there. No one to help. It was getting late and the sun had just passed the top of the cliffs, sinking us into shadow.

She waved me off, breathing out slowly. "I'm sure I can."

"But then you'll hurt it more, won't you?" My voice rose in volume. That was not helping.

"I've done it before." She swatted the hand in my direction, knocking my arm and jostling her foot. "Ow, shit!"

Marone, no. I did this to her. "Oh, bella, I'm so sorry."

"Stop saying that." She leaned on the bags, both hands scrubbing at her face, pushing her hat off. "I'll need your help to climb up to the grotto and hike back to Termini."

I pulled my backpack out from under her, so she lay further back. I tucked her hat into the pack and withdrew my phone before propping the pack under her ankle. "Is it alright like that?"

She nodded, adjusting against her pack. Snatching my discarded shirt, she held it over her face, breathing deeply. "And I thought tripping on that case was an epic fail."

"Stop that." I sat next to her with a sigh and turned on

my phone. There had to be some sort of emergency pickup we could arrange either by boat or to pick us up at the top of the grotto. But the phone had no signal. "Where's your phone?"

"Underneath me. Top pouch."

I pulled out her phone, which she unlocked, but the same result. No signal. "We had a signal up top. Why not down here?"

She shrugged. "The cliffs?"

"No idea." I stood, holding the phone up like it would make some difference. Walked along the edge of the water, everywhere, even into the cave as if that would improve reception.

Samantha sat up, watching me. Her pinched cheeks and glistening eyes betrayed her true feelings. She was in a great deal of pain and was worried. There was no chance she was walking all the way back. "Just go up top and make the call."

I returned to her and she reclined again, obviously more comfortable in that position. Climbing the dangerous path in the shadows by myself was a bad idea. What if I slipped and fell, then no one was up top to hear me? We'd be stranded until tomorrow. Not even together.

How high did the tide rise here? "Is the water higher now than when we came down here?"

She rolled to her side, peering along the shore. "No idea."

I ran a hand through my hair. What were we going to do?

"We bought hiking poles." Her voice was calming, despite the circumstances. "They're collapsed inside my bag. I can use them like crutches."

A motor sounded nearby in the bay. Loud, rough, but not moving fast. I launched from my position next to her to spot it. Small speedboat, sleek, dark gray with a roll bar at the back. A driver and perhaps one seated passenger.

Our saviors.

I stepped into the shallow water at the edge, slipping enough to remind me to be careful.

"They won't be able to hear you," she said through gritted teeth.

I waved my arms, yelled, but nothing. She was right, plus we were in shadow. I flipped on the flashlight of my phone and waved again. Still nothing.

"Antonio!"

I spun to Samantha, who tossed her phone to me, with its light on, as well. One in each hand, I waved frantically.

The boat slowed.

Per favore. Per favore.

It came to a stop, the motor barely a purr.

"Over here!" I yelled, in Italian and English.

The passenger pointed at me, the man at the helm turned, and the motor resumed. The boat headed toward us. As it neared, two passengers stood, lifting hands in greeting.

"Thank god," whispered Samantha behind me.

They hailed me in Italian, with an almost, but not quite, Tuscan accent. "What's wrong?"

"My girlfriend twisted her ankle, and I don't think we can get her back to Termini before sunset. Can you take us to any town nearby? I can pay."

The speaking man was mid-60s with gray hair. Refined. The boat was twenty feet away, but he was clearly in charge. His helmsman and another passenger were in black T-shirts and pants, well-muscled, likely bodyguards.

If I were not worried for Samantha's safety, I would have

suggested this was not the crew to help us. But the other options were worse.

"Our yacht is moored in Capri. We can take you to Marina Piccola?"

"Sì! Grazie mille!" I waded out of the water, back to Samantha.

"I can't put any weight on my left foot," she whispered, sitting up straight. "I tried."

The motor churned behind me as they moved closer.

"I have you, bella." I slung one pack onto my back, then eased the second pack out from under her leg slowly. After extending its straps, I put it on as well and slid my arms underneath her. "Just warn me if I move too fast."

"This is officially the most humiliating thing I've ever done." She covered her face with my shirt again.

Behind me, one of the men splashed into the water.

"Come now, surely you've done worse." I lifted her, not as effortless as the other times I'd picked her up. Sprinting after Umberto followed by hours of walking and hiking. Not to mention the uneven and potentially slippery ground I was on. And I was transporting the most precious cargo. "What about that time at Caruther's when I was hitting on you?"

Behind my shirt, she chuckled.

The man in the water held the edge of the boat close as I approached with her in my arms.

"You were so nervous, you were shaking." I waded cautiously through the water, steadied by the stranger. "Do you remember that?"

"Yeah, that was pretty bad, too." She moved the shirt as we reached the side of the boat. The helmsman stretched down for her, and she slung an arm around his shoulder as he eased her up.

The bodyguard holding the boat helped me in, then followed.

It was utilitarian, not a leisure craft. There was a seat at the helm, one next to it, and two directly behind. The man carrying Samantha placed her sideways on the cushioned back row seat—which would have held three abreast—and she tucked one arm over the chair back.

I took my shirt from her and donned it, then held out a hand to the older man who sat next to the controls. "Antonio Ferraro. I appreciate your help."

"Pasquale Fiori." His shake was firm, conveying a level of power and control which reminded me of my Uncle Giovanni. "Do you have any family in Rome?"

"Sì." I lifted Samantha's leg to sit next to her and prop it on my lap. Running a hand along her shin, I maintained focus on Pasquale as the engine roared back to life. "I grew up there and have aunts and uncles in town."

The boat started slowly, heading away from the peninsula.

"I know several Ferraros in and around Rome. But I see a slight resemblance to Andrea Ferraro, the art conservator. Any relation?"

Unexpected. Three men recognizing my family name in the same week. First Carabiniere De Rosa, then Riccardo at the gallery, now Pasquale. My family was well known in certain circles, but how did this man fit into that circle? "He's my uncle. I work for the family business in the States."

The motor revved higher, and the boat sliced through the channel. At the first bump, Samantha latched onto my arm, biting back a wail.

Pasquale instructed the helmsman to slow to a more even speed and a fraction of her tension released. "I have a doctor onboard my yacht. I think we should take her to see him before you head to the island."

Samantha grimaced when the helmsman radioed ahead, no doubt focused on how embarrassing all the attention was. "I'm fine."

"Stop saying that, bella. No arguments." I reached back to loosen the death grip she had on the frame of her chair. Perhaps the contact would help relax her. I returned my focus to Pasquale. "We'll take you up on that offer."

CHAPTER 24
SAMANTHA

IT WASN'T JUST A YACHT. It was a small destroyer masquerading as a superyacht. All it needed was guns mounted to the sides and maybe a missile launcher. There was a helicopter parked near the bow and probably torpedo bays under the waterline.

I didn't like this guy. This Pasquale Fiori, who knew Antonio's family and didn't bother to introduce the two meatheads accompanying him. Unnamed beefy guys with military-short hair and aviator sunglasses weren't the type I wanted to hang out with.

At least, not while I was injured and at a disadvantage.

Antonio spoke with the guy in charge the whole way, chatting about his project in Pompeii, about Pasquale's current trip around the Italian coastline, and the last time each of them was in Paris.

We crested a wave and the rib boat lifted, then slammed down onto the surface. I squeezed Antonio's hand as pain ricocheted up my leg.

Antonio shifted back and forth the whole ride, between

the calm confidence that was his default and concern for me, mixed with more than a little guilt. Playing around at the grotto should have been perfect. Relaxing, like the rest of the hike had been. And if no one else had come down the path, maybe we could have made love in the cave and just walked carefully to Termini in the moonlight.

But, no. Pathetic me lands wrong and we both end up— another bump and I swallowed a cry—suffering the consequences. He hauled me all of two feet down and I twist my ankle? After all the crazy stunts I'd pulled in my life?

The motor slowed as we got closer to the yacht. Balconies dotted the upper half of the black hull, three decks painted white above that. Building dimensions or anything interior, I could estimate with fair accuracy, but coming up on the ship from the rear made it difficult. Two hundred feet long, roughly.

Wide teakwood stairs fed out of the lower deck to a platform resting on the water. The helmsman expertly navigated the rib, swinging its stern so we were alongside.

Bodyguard One—boots squelching from wading into the water to help load us in—hopped onto the platform and held the boat in place. Antonio donned our packs and picked me up.

"I can walk," I said, as Bodyguard Two, the helmsman, took me from Antonio. He smelled fresh, like sea air and coconuts, and was exceptionally firm.

Antonio climbed out of the boat and accepted me into his arms. "I'd rather carry you a few more minutes, bella."

His eyes were soft, shutting down any argument. I wrapped my arm around his shoulders and resisted tucking my head against his neck. One more failure. He kissed my temple and I closed my eyes. At least I had him with me.

Find your center, Sam. Calm. Relax. Breathe. The ankle will be fine. You'll never see these guys again. Don't worry if they think you're weak.

Pasquale gestured to curving pale wood stairs leading up to the main deck. "The sick bay is up this way."

There was a matching staircase on the port side. Between the two staircases hung the ship's name in large golden letters, *Five Sunflowers*, and its port of registration below, Valetta. The name didn't match the menace of the ship's appearance.

Bodyguards One and Two followed closely behind us along the deck, between the railing and tall windows, which provided a view into a lounge area. Ornate rugs, long couches, chairs, a piano. And artwork on every wall. That room matched the name.

I inclined my head toward the windows so Antonio could catch a glimpse.

He asked, "Are you an art collector, Signor Fiori?"

"I am." Pasquale glanced over his shoulder as he opened a heavy metal door and stepped inside the ship. "Once your girlfriend's in the sick bay, I can give you a tour."

My arm clenched around Antonio and I gave him a warning look. My gut told me there was something menacing about this place. Separating was another poor choice.

"Don't worry, bella," Antonio said, turning sideways to move through the door slowly, my feet going first. "I'm sure you won't be long."

"Dr. Ivan's the best," said Bodyguard Two, weighed down on one side by a heavy duffel in his hand. "He stitched me back up after—"

Bodyguard One nudged him, imperceptible if I hadn't been looking right at them over Antonio's shoulder.

The interior was opulent. Beige linen walls, dark wood framing, and pot lights lining the edge of the hallway into a library. One wall was all window, the other all books. And more artwork. A woman in shorts and a short-sleeve shirt was dusting the bookshelf. At our approach, she stopped what she was doing and came to ease, nodding at us.

Pasquale opened a wood-paneled door into a small room that looked almost like a bedroom. Twin bed at the center of the room, desk and chair to one side, cabinets all around. Only one small window.

The man sitting at the desk stood. He was tall and fit, not like the creepy guys following us, but lean with broad shoulders, as though he swam a lot. He wore similar navy shorts and light blue shirt as the cleaning woman. Dark blond hair cropped short with kind hazel eyes which settled on me.

Pasquale said, "This is Dr. Ivan Hayle, our physician."

Antonio stiffened. What was that about?

"My patient?" the doctor asked in heavily accented Italian.

"Maybe I should stay with her." Antonio stood just inside the doorway to the sick bay, unmoving.

"She'll be fine with Dr. Ivan." Pasquale gestured to the bed. "I'd like to discuss some of my artwork with a Ferraro, to be honest."

Dr. Ivan put a hand on Antonio's arm. "I promise I'll return her in better condition than you're leaving her."

Antonio lowered me onto the bed slowly, whispering, "Do you want me to stay?"

I looked from him to the doctor, to Pasquale and the bodyguards. Was I overreacting? What was I worried about?

That they were going to kidnap us? Kill us? I was being ridiculous. There was no fear in the cleaning woman's eyes. Despite the bodyguards' near silence, one of them attempted to calm my worries. And the doctor's face seemed kind.

It was my injury, the lack of control and strength. The inability to run, if needed, always threw me off.

I cupped Antonio's cheek, still so close to mine. "Don't worry. The doctor will confirm my ankle's perfectly alright and we'll be on our way in no time."

He pressed his lips to my forehead, then took my hand to kiss it, as well. "I love you, bella."

"Good," I whispered with a smile.

Antonio left with Pasquale and Bodyguard One. Number Two remained inside the door.

Dr. Ivan frowned at him. "I can't work on someone with you right there. Wait outside."

The bodyguard nodded and did as he was told.

The doctor sat on a wheeled stool next to the bed. "You're favoring your left ankle. That's why you're here?"

"You don't have an Italian accent." I switched to English. "Would English be easier?"

"Perceptive," he said in English, spinning on the stool to withdraw a pair of gloves from the drawer behind him. The room was pristine, all white and gleaming stainless steel. He flicked on a rolling light and pulled it to the end of the bed. "But that doesn't answer my question."

"Yes, my ankle. I twisted it on some rocks while we were hiking."

He nodded, standing to open one of the upper cabinets, and swung out an x-ray machine. "If it's not broken or fractured, we'll check for a sprain."

"Definitely not broken." I'd finished a climb once with a broken ankle. It was more a tingling sensation than the intense pain I felt at the grotto.

"I'll check anyway." His hand hovered over the boot. "Can I take this off?"

I nodded, leaning back and gripping the rail on the side of the bed. "So, where are you from?"

"Need a distraction?"

"Yup."

"Originally Detroit, in the United States."

I snapped up. "Really? I'm from Brenton."

He paused with one lace undone. "The Brenton near Lansing?"

"Yeah, small world." I lay back down, the last of my worries fading. "Where'd you go to school?"

"Med school in Ann Arbor."

The unlacing was audible, but I stared at the ceiling instead of watching. Breathing. "One of my best friends studied law there."

"When did she graduate?"

"He." I sucked in a breath as he pulled the boot open, my ankle pulsing again. "Pretty elaborate sick bay you have here."

"It's a cushy job." He eased the boot off, my grip tightening on the rail. "Do you want me to pull the sock off or just cut it?"

A small laugh choked out of me. "I'm assuming you'll be replacing it with a bandage, so please cut it. I don't think I can handle anything else."

"Wise choice."

I gritted my teeth as he worked, until he produced an ice

pack from somewhere, and the pain became more bearable. "So it's cushy, even with the muscle hovering over you?"

He chuckled as he set up for the x-ray. "They're paid to act intimidating, but they're great guys once you've lost a few hands of cards to them."

"Good to know." Reminder: When they kidnap you, play poker for your freedom.

"I'm going to step out for a moment while I take an x-ray." He left, some clicking noises sounded, and he returned almost immediately. "Jason asked if you were alright."

"Jason?"

"The muscle outside." He put the ice back on and I could breathe again. "The image will take a couple of minutes, but from the looks of the ankle and how much pain you're in, I'm guessing it's a sprain."

"Rice." I ran both hands over my face, the soft bed and his easy-going nature lulling me into a comfort I didn't have when we arrived. "Rest, Ice, Compression, Elevation. Got it."

He laughed. "Hurt it before?"

"Call me accident-prone." Not the truth, not even close. I climbed rocks and mountains, jumped out of planes, free dove shipwrecks. But let him believe what he wanted.

He was quiet a moment, then placed a gentle hand on my shin. "Did your boyfriend do this to you?"

"No!" My eyes snapped to him. "I mean yes, but we were playing around on some rocks, having fun. I just slipped."

Antonio had been flirting. His usual charming self. The panic in his eyes when I got hurt was a hot knife in my gut. Not just for how awful he felt over it, but for how it hammered home how much he genuinely cared about me.

Dr. Ivan stood and folded the x-ray machine back into its

cabinet, hitting a few keys on the panel at its base. My x-ray flashed up on the screen. "Not broken, no fracture."

"Good news." I still had four days in Naples. The last thing I needed was a cast or surgery.

The doctor crossed the room and opened a drawer. "Any problem if I give you lidocaine? Allergies or reactions you've had in the past?"

"No problem. And probably a good idea."

He filled a needle from a small ampule, capped it, and returned to my bedside. "This may hurt for a moment, but it'll numb the pain."

"Distraction time again. How long have you been on this boat?" I looked up to the ceiling, preparing to breathe through the injection.

He placed the needle on the bed next to me and removed the ice pack. "Two years now."

"Coolest place you've been?"

"We go to Rome and Corsica a lot." He ripped open a small packet and wiped antiseptic across my ankle. "Mr. Fiori is Corsican."

"Explains the accent." I hissed out a breath, his touch light but so painful. Despite Corsica's primary language being French, the Corsican language was more like northern Italian. "More distraction, please?"

"We mostly sail around the Med. Algiers, Tunis, Malta, Marseille." He pulled the cap from the needle and inserted it. "Last summer, we traveled the US east coast. New York, Atlantic City, down to Miami and the Caribbean."

This was far from my first injection into an injured joint, but he was good. *Close eyes. Deep breath. Don't grit your teeth.* "South America?"

"No. But they're talking about the St. Lawrence next year." He pulled out the needle and covered it with cotton gauze. "Maybe the Great Lakes."

The pressure of the gauze stung, but it wasn't excruciating. That was progress. "Will you visit home?"

"Maybe." He checked under the gauze, pushed it back down, and re-checked.

The pain diminished quickly. "That's better."

"Remember, the ankle's still injured. Treat it that way."

"Is having a doctor and x-ray machine normal on a boat like this?"

"Yes and no." He topped the gauze with medical tape, cleaned up his supplies, and walked them to the disposal on the opposite wall. "Many yachts this size have a nurse, if nothing else. Mr. Fiori employs some men who... tend to get hurt."

"Paramilitary?"

Dr. Ivan barked a laugh. Bodyguard Two—Jason— whipped the door open but was waved away. "Risk-takers. Not sure how your experience on the rib was, but they never do anything at an appropriate speed."

Sounded like me on a better day. "Yeah, the ride wasn't pleasant."

"I think Mr. Fiori originally wanted a doctor onboard for him and his family, but soon discovered the younger staff were the ones who needed me." He returned to his stool next to me with a tensor bandage. "He's a good man, all things being equal."

My worries had been foolish. Dr. Ivan and Bodyguard Jason were looking out for me, not to mention Antonio.

"Has the lidocaine kicked in yet? Can I put the bandage

on?" He pressed his palm against my ankle, the pain muted. "I can give you some crutches, as well."

Crutches. Great. At least I wouldn't need to be carried everywhere. "Go for it."

~

I SWUNG into the lounge area we'd seen on the way in, balanced on the crutches. Dr. Ivan's hand rested on my back, pointing out rug edges, door frames, and anything I could trip over, as though I'd never been injured before. Bodyguard Jason followed us.

Floor to ceiling windows decorated two sides of the room, which likely folded open to expose the entire space to the outside. A short bar obscured a portion of the glass wall. Behind it, a man in the crew uniform mixed a drink in a stainless shaker.

"Samantha!" Antonio rushed to my side, one hand out like he didn't know where to touch me, the other carrying a cut-crystal glass of some amber liquid. He and Pasquale had been standing in front of a painting with a white field and broad swipe of black paint through the middle. "You look far better. The color's returned to your lovely cheeks."

"She's a strong woman," said Dr. Ivan, everyone reverting to Italian.

Antonio glared, evaluating him from head to toe and back up again. Antonio's chest puffed up, his lip curled. With a clearer head, I recognized the five-million scale of his jealousy Mario told me about at the club. Antonio inserted himself between the doctor and me. "We were discussing this painting which was damaged recently."

"Champagne cork," chuckled Pasquale, gesturing with his glass to the black and white piece they'd been in front of.

I made my way over on the crutches, inspecting the damage.

"Samantha's an insurance adjuster," said Antonio, the pride audible in his voice. "With a remarkable eye for art claims."

"Colors are straightforward, tear is jagged, impasto to match..." I glanced at Antonio. "Doesn't look difficult. Few days to fix?"

He nodded. "There's another piece in the salon showing some distortion from the sea air. We discussed repairs, plus moving it to the library, which has better climate controls."

Pasquale shook his head. "I had the yacht designed for the collections, but it appears some rooms were missed."

Despite seeing the paintings through the windows earlier, I hadn't expected an actual art lover. "Did you choose the boat's name, Mr. Fiori? *Five Sunflowers?*"

He put up a hand. "Pasquale, please. And I did. It's named after Van Gogh's lost sunflower painting."

"Destroyed during the Second World War," said Antonio, before I could. Van Gogh had painted many in his Sunflowers series—starting with single loose flowers on a table and moving to vases with a dozen and more flowers—and that was the only one lost.

I stifled a gasp.

Like the lost yellow flowers from the Casa di Marte.

No matter how comfortable I'd been with the doctor, the twisting in my stomach returned.

The sun setting behind the island caught my attention, beams of oranges and pinks filling the sky. It was getting late, and we were due back hours ago. "Have you called Mario? He's probably worried."

Antonio nodded. "I let him know we'll be later than expected."

"We should still get home, though." I didn't want to be there anymore.

Pasquale gestured to the bartender. "My wife will be here any moment, and I'd be honored if you stayed to eat. Antipasti, if not a full meal?"

"A generous offer, but Samantha's correct. We should go." He placed his tumbler on a nearby table and rubbed a hand along my upper arm. "You're feeling better?"

Dr. Ivan piped up. "It's a sprain or just a twist. Keep it elevated with ice."

Antonio's gaze fell to my foot. "This is not elevated. Nor does it have ice."

I forced a smile at the doctor. "He gave me a shot. It helped with the pain, but yes, I should get off it for the evening."

"More than the evening," scolded Antonio.

Pasquale pointed to Jason. "Fly them to the mainland."

Jason nodded and left without a word.

Fly?

"How much do I owe you?" Antonio retrieved our backpacks from a sofa nearby. Money hadn't even crossed my mind, given the pain I'd been in.

"Nothing. Helping was my pleasure. Although..." Pasquale gestured to his black and white painting. "Perhaps you can handle the repair for me?"

"I'd love to." Antonio slung both packs over one shoulder.

"However, as I told you, I'm working in Pompeii until the new year."

"Then we'll hold the favor for later."

"No, no." Antonio put up a hand. "I'll call my Uncle Andrea and cover the repair. He or one of my cousins will work on it. Trust me, they're all excellent."

"I'll call that even." Pasquale shook our hands. "It's been a pleasure, Mr. Ferraro. I look forward to our paths crossing again sometime."

CHAPTER 25

ANTONIO

THE NEXT AFTERNOON, I strolled along the Lungomare—the Neapolitan waterfront promenade—with Samantha on her crutches at my side. To our right, low concrete barriers topped with metal railings separated us from the small Mappatella Beach below. The beach was clogged with people under umbrellas and on towels, some children playing in the protected water. On the far side of the short beach, children climbed the sea break of stacked limestone boulders. And beyond that, the bay.

A mile away, the Castel d'Ovo rose from the water, its sharp squared castle walls our goal for the walk. Past it, Vesuvio towered over the city, as it did from every vantage point. Motorboats, yachts, cargo ships, and tankers flowed through the water.

The pedestrian roadway was a favorite among tourists and locals alike. In the rotunda next to the beach, a group of young men played basketball where two nets had been erected. The referee's whistle was difficult to distinguish from those of the youngsters running around the monument across the street.

The basketball crowd cheered and applauded with each basket, while thudding R&B music streamed from a stereo system, which competed with the squeals of excited children and the myriad of languages.

Behind us, a marina with several yachts which almost rivaled Pasquale Fiori's. What a visit that had been. I didn't like leaving favors on the table, so had already called my Uncle Andrea, who promised to get in touch. Favors were the currency Cristian and his father used. It could have been an innocent comment, but given the size of his ship, the odds were good Fiori shared more than a love of artwork with my Uncle Giovanni.

For once, the crowds dodged around us, as Samantha swung herself on the crutches provided by the too-attractive Dr. Ivan. She wore a long sundress of pale pink with cap sleeves and tiny blue-green flowers the color of her beautiful eyes.

I'd managed to keep her in bed with her foot in various states of elevation, occasionally resting with ice on it, but she grew stir-crazy quickly. Lazing around was not her style, and she only had a few days left in town.

"Do you think you'll make it all the way to the Castel, bella?" I placed a hand on the small of her back as she moved. It was selfish, but the worst part about the crutches was that I couldn't drape my arm about her shoulders or hold her as we walked. The lack of contact felt wrong.

"Did it occur to you that Pasquale's boat was named *Five Sunflowers* and our missing fresco was of yellow flowers?"

It had. And it was almost enough of a coincidence for me to forget that I feared my cousin and uncle were behind Umberto's actions. "It did."

"Do you think there's a link there?"

"Bella…" I shoved my hands into my pockets. "He seemed genuine about his love of art. But even if that would extend to theft, consider the size of his yacht and the men around him. Do you think it's wise to ask such questions about a man with those resources?"

We continued in silence for a moment, her eyes fixed on the Castel in the distance. When she finally spoke, her voice was flat. "Questions are what I do."

How many people in the city could she accuse? Umberto, of course, but we knew his guilt. She'd accused Bianca and even me. She hadn't come out and said it, but I could tell she was suspicious of De Rosa for not catching Umberto, likely had questions about Mario and Eva. No one was beyond her suspicions.

And now a man who was far too dangerous for her to question.

I shook my head. "Then call Special Agent Skinner, tell him your theory and leave it at that. You can't go after a man with Fiori's resources with empty accusations."

Her jaw clenched and she slowed, continuing to stare into the distance, although her gaze didn't seem focused on anything anymore. Something was warring inside her head and I was losing her to it.

"Why did the painting go to jail?"

She halted and turned to me. "What?"

"I said…" I moved in front of her, running my fingers along the backs of her hands. "Why did the painting go to jail?"

"Because it was guilty," she said, the frown battling to remain in control.

I held my smile down as best I could, in case the joke didn't fix her mood. "Because it was framed."

Her lips tightened, but the bouncing shoulders gave her away. "Oh my god."

"But in all seriousness, amore, snooping around a man like Fiori will only bring trouble, whether he was somehow involved or not."

Her eyes darkened for a fraction of a second—the need to challenge everything likely battling against the logical side of her brain. I stood my ground, waiting to see which side won out.

After what felt like an hour, her shoulders relaxed and she let out a long breath. "You're right. I'll text Elliot later."

Every cell in my body rejoiced. For fear a kiss on the cheek would seem condescending, I simply nodded.

She gestured to the side with her head and I moved out of the way. Putting her left foot down on the ground, she took one tentative step. "And my ankle's doing a lot better today."

I frowned and cocked a mock-lecturing eyebrow at her. "What happened to the woman who professed honesty and trust were the two most important qualities in a relationship?"

"Very funny." Her weight returned to the crutches, and she pulled the injured leg up behind her as we continued. "I'm serious. I heal fast."

"I once sprained an ankle playing football and—"

Another whistle sounded, a different pitch from the children and the basketball game. More urgent, repeating over and over. Accompanied by yelps and cries, and the distinct sound of a man's voice shouting "Arresto!"

As one, Samantha and I spun to see a man running in our direction with a purse swinging from his hand, two polizia in pursuit. People launched out of his way, he shoved others, but he was still too fast for the officers.

"Samantha!" I reached for her arm to propel her to safety but met empty air.

She'd reacted faster than me, pivoting toward the running man. Dropping one crutch, she choked up on the other like a baseball player and took the man's legs out from under him. His feet tangled in the crutch as he slammed into the ground, taking her down with him.

I fell to her side, just as the polizia arrived. One put a knee on the thief's back and placed handcuffs on him, speaking in his ear the whole time. The other knelt next to Samantha and me, asking if she was alright.

Samantha sat on the pavement, still holding her crutch, a ridiculous smile on her face. "That kinda hurt."

"Foolish woman," I said, performing a quick inspection. Abrasions on her elbows and knee, but she appeared otherwise fine.

"I know." She laughed through a grimace. "But at least we caught *someone* today."

Fierce and stubborn. This woman did not let things go.

Two women jogged up next to us, one of them speaking excitedly in English. "Thank you! Thank you! I mean, grazie! Grazie!"

The first officer dragged the thief to standing and handed the woman her handbag. She smiled briefly, but her attention remained on Samantha, offering more thanks.

"Don't worry about it." Samantha waved the women's proficient thank-yous and offers of compensation off until the police pulled them aside for questions.

People continued to stare as I helped her up, one polite

gentleman handing her the second crutch. I gestured to the concrete barrier at the edge of the sidewalk which was low enough for her to lean on. I had to be certain she was alright.

"We still need to get to the Castel." Her eyes twinkled like they had yesterday morning at the Casa just before she slammed her arm into Umberto's.

"Bella, I want to check your ankle."

She shook her head. "I'm fine."

After the grotto experience, it was clear this was an argument I shouldn't bother with. A different tack, then. "I know you'll be fine, but I need a breather after all that excitement."

"Wimp." She grinned but walked with me to the barrier and sat atop it, tucking the dress between her thighs like a pair of shorts and propping the crutches up. I knelt in front of her to take a closer look. Her right knee was fine, the left scratched, but not even a drop of blood.

I looked up at her, her eyes cast down on me, and a smile creased her beautiful face.

"It would appear you're right." I kissed the barely scratched knee, and she ran a hand along the side of my face. "Nothing for me to do here."

The day I met the grown-up Samantha Caine, I called my sister, Sofia, and told her I'd met my future wife. Kneeling in front of her, the tenderness flowing between us... it was clear I'd been right all along. It was a good thing I didn't have anything resembling a ring on me at that moment. Samantha would have rolled her eyes and said I was being ridiculous.

"Antonio." She paused, caressing my cheek with her thumb. The smile faded slowly, giving way to a tight mouth. She swallowed hard, holding something deep inside. Maybe it wouldn't have been an eye roll. "You're too good to me."

"Honestly, I may have to go to medical school if you keep this up."

She threw her head back with a laugh. "My own personal physician? Imagine all the trouble I could get into if I had one of those!"

I stood and kissed her. "Why did you get involved?"

"Instinct." She shrugged, looking away from me.

"Between your ankle already being hurt and the way that man was shoving people..." I leaned between her legs, against the wall, and wrapped my arms around her. "If that ever happens again, let me take care of it."

She hugged me back, but her shoulders shrugged again. My reaction was to protect her. Hers was to protect everyone else, at her own peril. "You'll have to be faster next time."

As I separated from her, I looked her square in the eyes. "I think it's time you told me your long and uninteresting story."

"Which one?" She leaned forward to kiss me, but I moved out of her reach. She was not getting away with it this time. "I have a lot of them."

"You just took out a man for the Polizia, despite a sprained ankle—"

"I think it's just twisted." She was like an insolent child at times.

"After talking to a man who says you revised the security models at the British Museum? Oh, and after meeting your *boss* from an internship with the FBI. *And* after watching you handle Umberto yesterday. And you ask me this silly question?"

She looked down the walkway toward the Castel, silent for a few moments. Over and over, she stressed how important honesty and trust were, yet she was terrible at both.

I placed a hand under her chin and lifted her face to me. "No gelato until you tell me."

She shot me the Samantha glare, her trademark look, at the midpoint between exasperation and mischief. It may have been a look she reserved for me. "You play dirty."

"Sì, I do."

"It's not that interesting. I was sort of in the FBI. Not just as an intern." At that, she stopped with another shrug.

I closed my eyes and tilted my head, biting back a chuckle. I knelt again and removed the sandal from her left foot to fuss with the compression bandage on her ankle, attempting to regain some of my earlier irritation. There was nothing wrong with it, but for once, I didn't want her to see me laugh. Otherwise, I'd never get the truth out of her. "So, bella, if *that*'s not interesting, what exactly is?"

"Gelato? I'm thinking caramel?"

"Did you fly all this way to spend time with me and make this relationship work?" I undid the clips on the bandage and tightened the last few wraps as gently as I could. "Or for food?"

She leaned back on the concrete partition and looked up at the sky, closing her eyes in that way she did, as though she gained peace and strength from the sun.

CHAPTER 26
SAMANTHA

HE WAS RIGHT. If I wanted a future with him, I had to let some of the bad stuff out. I had to share with him. Sharing had been easy so far on the trip. Our time had mostly been sex and smiles and lots of touristy stuff. Except for the injured ankle yesterday. The fury inside me at Umberto getting away. And Friday at the nightclub. That argument had taken us to a new level. We'd been more honest that night than I was comfortable with him yet.

When I'd shown up on his doorstep last week, I told him I was running toward him. I couldn't say it and not do anything about it.

"When I was twelve, we took a summer vacation to Boston. Me, Cass, and my mom." I opened my eyes and he was still kneeling, fixing the bandage on my ankle. He looked up at me with a smile and my heart fluttered, like it did every time I saw the love in his eyes. I could do this. I could tell him. It was just a stupid story.

"I'd been obsessed with fine art for a couple of years." Since I'd first seen *Les amoureux dans le ciel*. Pointing that out was a very different conversation, so I skipped it. "But it changed when we went to the Isabella Stewart Gardner Museum."

He stood again, hands sliding up my legs to my waist. "And you learned about the heist?"

The man understood me on a level that didn't make sense. Like he was in my brain.

"Exactly. The heist, the investigation, and..." My fingers grew numb, so I rubbed my palms against the concrete barrier I was sitting on. "That was the day I decided I was going to join the FBI's Art Crimes Team."

He raised an eyebrow. "Very specific for a twelve-year-old."

I cocked my eyebrow right back at him. "Did you know what you wanted to do when you were twelve?"

"I was already working in my father's studio at the time."

"Seriously?"

"Cleaning brushes and sweeping floors. Very glamorous work." He chuckled, poking a gentle finger into my chest when my mouth opened. "But no changing the subject. You're supposed to be boring me with your life story."

I laughed at the wink he gave me. That was exactly what I'd needed. I stopped rubbing my hands on the concrete barrier and flexed them. Surprisingly, they were alright. "So, you know I have an Art History degree. I also have a second bachelors and a master's in Criminal Justice. My thesis was on museum security systems."

"That's what Thomas Grange was speaking of?"

"Yeah, I focused my entire education on art crimes, including the time I worked for him in London. After I finished school, my mom pulled some strings and got me the FBI internship in Detroit."

"How did she arrange that?"

"Damned if I know. She was a state prosecutor then, so it didn't surprise me she had ties with the Detroit office. I asked and she just said she worked with Elliot Skinner on a case. Sometimes, she was as enigmatic as you are."

His face lit up with laughter. "Me? Enigmatic? What is it you say all the time?" He paused, nodding. "Hardly."

I chuckled at him, at his stupid, twitchy lip. He was right. I was the one always holding back. "Can I kiss you now?"

"That depends." The smirk ratcheted up. "Will you continue with the story after?"

Sliding a hand to the nape of his neck, I pulled him close. His mouth met mine, and I sank into him. Eyes closed, the sound of voices buzzing around us, the water, the ships going by, the basketball game. It all faded into the background. My world was him. His vanilla scent, his soft hand on my cheek, and his strong one circling my waist.

How had I survived thirty years without him?

He separated from me, continuing to brush his thumb across my cheek. I nestled into it with a sigh. I could do this. He wouldn't judge me for it. He wouldn't leave me for my failures. After my epic ones yesterday, all he had were reassurances.

A few breaths later, he withdrew the hand, raising his eyebrows, prompting for more.

"I worked with Elliot after I finished my master's degree. My postgraduate training in cultural heritage crimes came in handy, and it went well. Provenance research, tracking down leads, sitting in on interviews... He even took me on an undercover op, which he probably wasn't supposed to do, but it was low-risk."

"He was your mentor?"

"Yeah." I nodded slowly, never having applied that word to him. I was an insurance adjuster, not an FBI agent. "And he helped make sure I was accepted into the Academy right away after my twenty-third birthday."

"Wait. You had all those degrees plus your postgrad at ARCA before you were twenty-three?"

My gaze drifted to the Castel. It was probably too late for me to change his mind about this conversation and just resume our walk. "Plus work experience."

He urged my face back to him. "You're not proud of these facts?"

I rubbed my palms across the concrete barrier. "I missed out on a lot of life between twelve and—"

"Today?" He laughed, and I joined him, my stress evaporating. Again, one right word from him and the pins and needles vanished. How did he do that?

"Oh my god, yes." I shoved him playfully. "Or should I say between twelve and meeting you?"

His face softened, and he kissed me. "My life began for real when I met you."

"Anyway," I said, rolling my eyes dramatically. "Cass' husband, Kevin, had gotten me a short-term job at Foster Mutual until I could start at Quantico. That's when I met Matt Foster."

"Your ex-husband?"

"Exactly. We started dating before I went to the Academy. I graduated, moved back, married Matt, and went to work at Foster instead of the FBI."

His brow creased. I'd skipped the big decision, and my life

made no sense without it. "You didn't actually want to be in the FBI?"

I chewed on my bottom lip, scanning the hundreds of people strolling the Lungomare. Friends, couples, families. Mothers. So many mothers with their kids.

"Matthew made you leave?"

I shook my head, watching a trio of women who looked like three generations. "No, it was my choice."

When I didn't continue, he prodded. "But the excitement in your eyes at the auction and then with Umberto. Your passion is so clear. Why would you turn away from that?"

"It was my mom," I said through a clenched jaw, the stinging behind my eyes growing.

He spoke slowly, quietly. "Your mother told you to leave the FBI?"

"She came to Virginia for my graduation. We had breakfast together that morning. Before I left, she hugged me. Told me she was proud of me. And the last thing she said was—" I clamped my eyes shut, trying desperately to keep the tears from starting. How could I tell him and not think about it at the same time? "She said, 'Next time I see you, I'll be calling you Special Agent Caine.'"

I shuddered, a lump wedging itself in the middle of my throat. As my head fell into my hands, he wrapped both of his strong arms around me.

"I'm here, Samantha." He stroked my hair, giving me exactly what I needed.

Why was I telling him all this? I'd never even told Cass the toll Mom's death had taken on me. But he was so warm and solid. His heart beat slow and steady. I held onto him like the rock he was. He was my shelter. Already. After only five weeks.

He pressed his cheek against my face, and I nuzzled into the side of his neck. Here I was, weak and soft again with him. But this time I didn't hate myself for it. All I wanted was to stay in his arms for the rest of my life. To hold him.

And above it all, not finish my story.

But I had to.

The whole point of this trip was to see if we could have a future together. To see if we could last the months apart and if he was worth changing the entire trajectory of my life. If I couldn't tell him this thing, we didn't stand a chance.

I pulled out of the embrace and he wiped my tears away with his thumbs.

"She didn't make it to the ceremony. Car accident—" My breath hitched and goosebumps crept up my arms.

He rubbed his hands up and down them, nodding.

"I took a week off, then I went to Boston for my assignment."

"For the Gardner Museum?"

"Yeah. I'd landed my dream job right out of the Academy." I focused on the little golden flecks in his eyes, sparkling in the sun. "But every time someone called me Special Agent Caine, I broke down."

He tilted his head toward me as I paused, his brows drawing down. He kept his gaze locked on me, not flinching for a second. As though he were lending me his strength to get through this. How lucky was I to have found him?

"Couldn't hack it. I lasted one week before I quit. Moved back home and told everyone I missed Matt too much. We got married less than a month later."

"Did you ever tell him that?"

"Nope." I fingered the loose neckline of his shirt, tapping him gently on the chest. "You're the first."

"Thank you for trusting me with this." He kissed my forehead. "And what about now? Elliot still wants to work with you."

"I told him I'd call him after Cass's treatments are done."

He froze, eyes widening. Likely worried about me leaving Brenton. Perfectly justified, considering how I'd been obsessing over the stolen fresco.

"Antonio, that was before the press conference."

He pulled away and dropped back to his knees, fussing with the bandage around my ankle.

"Leave that alone. It doesn't need to be tightened." My turn to tilt his face up to me. "I told Elliot that before *us*."

"Bella, I'd never stop you from doing something that means so much to you." He stood and took me in his arms again.

'I know' was the polite response, but it wasn't what the conversation needed. "From age twelve until the day Mom died, I'd been running toward the FBI. Then, I started running away from things. Quitting the FBI, marrying Matt to cover it up, leaving town after we divorced." I grimaced. "From my feelings for you."

"But you stopped. You ran *to* me, Samantha."

What if *he* was where I was really supposed to be, and it wasn't the FBI after all?

That was a conversation for much farther down the road. For spring, when Cass was done her treatments and I had to decide what to do. When he and I had lived in the same town and had figured out if there was something deeper than this intense moment.

"You're embarrassed, sì? About this story?"

I ran the back of my knuckles along his sharp jawline, catching on the stubble he'd let grow. "Quitting the Bureau was the biggest failure of my life. I was worried—afraid—you'd think less of me for it."

"After I found out my former fiancée, Faith, was cheating on me, I moved back to Napoli for a year."

My hand paused. "Really?"

He barely shrugged a shoulder, like her betrayal didn't have any power over him anymore—when I knew it did. "I'd never think less of you for being human. What you need to do is forgive yourself for poor choices in your past and start making good ones."

Chuckling, I stroked his jaw. "It's that simple, is it?"

His mouth touched mine without warning, soft lips and gentle tongue. One powerful hand wrapped around my waist to hold me up as I leaned into him.

"How about that?" He waggled his eyebrows. "Good choice, sì?"

I sighed, losing myself in that adoring face. "You know, Antonio Ferraro, you are exactly the sort of man I swore I'd never date again."

His head tilted back to scrutinize me. "Scusa?"

"Men with big personalities. Full of themselves." I held up a hand when his mouth opened to protest. I'd always been on the intense side, more focused on my studies and future than relationships, and it took a confident man to get past that. An overly confident one, usually. "Matt was the opposite of all of that and he wasn't right, either. You're my Goldilocks. All those things on the surface, but inside, you're kind and compassionate. You care more about my brain than anyone I've ever met."

"It's a very sexy brain," he said with a wink.

I smacked his chest. "Following you to Italy was the first of a lot of really good choices."

"One might even say an excellent choice."

He knelt one last time to put my left sandal back on. Such a gentleman. Once he was done, he backed away from me, holding out a hand. I grabbed the crutches and shoved off the wall.

"Next good choice." He ran a hand down my back, settling it just above my tailbone. "What flavor gelato would you like?"

CHAPTER 27
ANTONIO

MONDAY MORNING, Thomas and I met at the main office for the restoration project in Pompeii. Three of the original top ten candidates for Umberto's position were still available and with things hopefully kicking off this week, we wanted to wrap up interviews as quickly as possible.

I closed the lid of my laptop. "So, what do you think?"

Thomas reviewed his notes, tapping his pen slowly. "Number two's education is more impressive, but I prefer the energy from three."

I nodded, sliding the laptop into my bag. With a clear standout from the interviews, we could finish earlier than expected. This was the first time I was away from Samantha for more than a half hour since she arrived, and I missed her already. But she needed to stay off her ankle. She would have hobbled around Pompeii if she'd come with me. "I agree. I'll speak with Mario and he'll extend the offer."

"I heard Samantha Caine was with you when you found Umberto. Did she head up the investigation?"

"It was coincidence. She'd asked to see the site again to take some photographs and we stumbled upon him."

He leaned back in his chair, a smile creeping up his face. "Does she live here now?"

Hefting the bag onto my shoulder, I did my best to remain calm. This line of questioning was not about to go in a positive direction. "No, she lives in the States."

"But she's still here?"

"She's leaving Wednesday."

"You left so quickly with her last week, I didn't have a chance to ask for her contact information. I don't suppose you have her number or email, do you?"

"If you were thinking about asking her out, don't bother."

He laughed as he shuffled his papers and threw them into his bag. "You tried, too, didn't you? She's still a tough nut to crack, isn't she?"

"Still?"

"She and I spent quite a bit of time together when she worked in London. I took her to the museums and galleries over and over, out sailing a few times, and even to a few plays. She's a big fan of Shakespeare. Did you know that?"

He shook his head as I calculated the fallout of punching him. The Board would cancel the contract, no doubt. Never welcome me back. My father would be displeased. Samantha would find out and be furious with me. Not a good way to finish her visit.

He chuckled as he pulled his bag onto his shoulder. "But in London she was so excited about everything, talking a mile a minute, asking an unending series of questions. Her brain was constantly buzzing, leaving no room for anything else."

"Samantha? Talking a mile a minute?"

Thomas and I walked out together, into the sunshine and stifling heat. The crowds were as thick as the air, typical for a weekday morning. There was a never-ending stream of people coming to see the glory of Pompeii.

"As long as she wasn't speaking about herself. Always. A vibrating energy pulsed off that woman at all times. It was intoxicating."

That was the Samantha from the auction, from the Chagall investigation, from our tour of the archaeological site and the museums during her visit. Thomas didn't know the quiet side of her. The side which required an understanding of what each pause and flick of her eyes meant. The side I knew.

But that had also been Samantha before her mother's death, before her divorce. Before she'd sworn to spend her life on the road with as few connections as possible.

"So, I hate to nag, but do you have her phone number?"

"She's seeing someone."

"A smart man would have a ring on her finger by now." He nudged me with a grin. "Before someone like one of us can snatch her away. A man who can engage a brain like that." A low, guttural noise erupted from his throat, which I considered closing off for him. "Not to mention that body, am I right?"

My chest tightened, and I shoved my hands into my pockets to ball them into fists. Men like this were the problem with relationships. Men who didn't respect boundaries and loyalty. I unintentionally growled, "A smart man will have a ring on her finger soon enough."

As soon as she would agree to it. If only she were not so stubborn and afraid of commitment. I knew how she felt deep inside. Marone, what would happen when she went home?

Nathan Miller would just be the start of it. Then there were men like Thomas Grange and Dr. Ivan Hayle. At least they were half a world away. If only I were not.

I could not lose that woman again.

We took off our staff identification as we left through the main gate, heading for the train.

"Alright, Dr. Ferraro, I tried to do this the easy way." He stopped, narrowing his eyes. "Are you dating her?"

She wanted to keep it quiet around my office, but she was leaving in two days. What did it matter if he knew? "Sì, I am."

"Ha! I was right!" He laughed and clapped his hands. "Bianca owes me twenty euros!"

"Scusi?"

He leaned in, winking. "It would have been forty if I didn't have to ask you outright."

It was a bet. Was anything he said true? He'd been flirting with her at the office last week. Had he not? Or was I overreacting to everything?

"Antonio, I don't know you well yet, but what I've seen and heard has impressed me. I'm happy to hear she's found someone worthy of her." He placed a hand on my shoulder. "Is she working as a security consultant? It sounds perfect for her."

"She's an insurance adjuster."

"Really?" He scratched the stubble on his chin. "Gallery insurance? Historic sites? Museums?"

"Cugino!" came a voice from across the small street. It caught my attention and I turned to spot Cristian walking toward us, his two thugs a conspicuous distance away.

I thrust a hand in Thomas's direction. "See you Wednesday afternoon."

He nodded, taking the hint, and headed off on his own.

Cristian marched straight up to me, arms and smile wide. I clenched while we hugged, scanning the area to see if there was a third man following him. Sure enough, I spotted him further down the street, eyes on us.

"How dare you show your face here," I whispered.

Breaking from the hug, he tilted his head, the smile still in place. "I came to offer congratulations. And this is how you greet me?"

"Congratulations?"

He continued holding me by the upper arms as he spoke. "I hear you and your girlfriend caught someone stealing from your site."

"We found him—" I'd suspected Cristian was behind it all based on our conversation at the nightclub, but the look on his face had me doubting myself. "—but he got away."

"I'm leaving for Roma today. Since you refuse to come visit, we must talk now." He kept one hand on me, guiding me toward the wall by the gate. His men's heads swiveled back and forth, sweeping the area. His voice remained low. "I did interrupt your delivery—"

"Cazzo! Are you kidding?" I slammed my hand against the stone wall next to us. "That put me behind by two weeks!"

He raised a hand, and his thugs stopped their movement toward us. "I apologize. It will arrive Wednesday morning, as you requested."

My stomach churned, and I flexed my jaw, trying not to bare my teeth. "Two additional weeks I have to be here. You don't understand how difficult you've made things for me." Two extra weeks I'd be away from Samantha. More time for her to change her mind about me or find someone else.

"Antonio, listen to me."

"No, you listen to me." I raised a finger to his face, and he kept his hand up for his guards. "This contract is important to my father. Tell *your* father that. Tell him to leave it alone. No more thieves, no more delays, no more distractions. I'm tired—"

"Stop." He glared, with the look of a man used to having people obey him. "I was trying to flush them out."

"What do you—"

"I heard rumors someone would try to steal from your site. That was all I knew. So I delayed your equipment, hoping they would make a move with the time I bought them."

"And they did." Some of the tightness in my chest eased. Was he on my side, after all? Was this related to what Papa had told me of the stolen painting in Roma and the other details he couldn't speak of? Was this part of a larger game? And was I a pawn or a rook?

He nodded slowly. "Papa's shifting business models."

"What do those things have to do with each other?"

He turned my body and did the same, so we were speaking toward the wall, heads together for additional privacy. "When a vacuum exists, something will always move in to take up the space. They think they can mess with our family, but they're mistaken."

"I don't understand, Cristian."

"They were testing the waters. Can they take something from Papa's nephew and get away with it? I was here to ensure they didn't." He grinned. "However, you are apparently too clever for them and found the man responsible before I could. Which provided me with a lead."

Again, everyone congratulating me for her work. "Mostly my girlfriend."

"The auction was her as well?"

"Sì, it was."

Cristian's eyes fell away from me, a fist covering his mouth. "Tell me she does not work for the authorities."

"She's not your concern."

"Stupido! Are you blind?" His fist tapped against the wall, his face tight. "The TPC are on this case. That gives them an in with you, which means an in with my father. I hear there's also an FBI Art Crimes agent in town. Is that your girlfriend?"

"She's an insurance adjuster and trust me, she didn't instigate my relationship with her. She's not using me to get to you." As soon as the words were out of my mouth, I questioned them. Samantha had worked very hard to keep me at arm's length. But what about her sudden change of heart? What about her flying all the way here? And winding up on my doorstep when her FBI mentor was in Italia?

Surely not. That was ridiculous.

I was disgusted the thought even passed through my brain.

"Cugino, keep an eye on her. I swear, keep both eyes open at all times. This is the long game. They may try you again while you're here or once you're back in the States."

"Try me? How?"

"I've no idea. Steal from you, enlist you, get information from you. Just watch your back." He looked up at me again. "I'll find out what I can about the theft here. If I learn anything, I'll let you know."

"Am I in danger?"

He grimaced, shaking his head. "I'm not sure, but I doubt it. You haven't worked with us in a long time."

"You think—"

He held out his arms, signaling the conversation was over.

I hugged him. "Thank you, Cristian. I'll call if anything suspicious happens."

"And you'll eventually visit?" He clasped me by the forearms as he broke the embrace, the public smile back in place.

"I will, but I need to make up the lost time here first. I'll be in touch."

He kissed my cheeks and left, his men moving with him. I ran a hand through my hair, releasing a long exhale. The next four months were going to be even longer than I'd expected.

CHAPTER 28
SAMANTHA

THE VIEW from the terrace on Mario's roof was awe inspiring. Situated atop a hill, it had a full panorama of Naples, Vesuvius, the bay, peninsula, and the islands. As wonderful as the view was, I was still stuck. Plopped on a lounge chair, resting my left leg.

So here I sat, alone with my ice pack. Antonio had headed to Pompeii without me for some interviews. *Relax*, he'd said with a grin, knowing I was terrible at it. *We need that leg at full strength.*

The patio umbrella shaded me from the intense Mediterranean sun, while the light, salty breeze from the bay cooled my barely clad body. The little white bikini didn't cover much. I stretched out in the lounge chair, intentionally not checking the clock on my phone.

The thick copy of *Research and Discoveries in Pompeii* wasn't enough to hold my interest. It was time to move.

I tapped my phone on the small table next to me. Antonio would be back in two hours. Visions of how we'd spend the afternoon and evening together clouded my senses. I closed my eyes and sighed, fingers running across my chest, remembering his soft touch, his lips.

"Samantha!" Mario crested the top of the steps to the rooftop terrace. Carrying two glasses of yellow liquid, he raised one in my direction. He wore nothing more than low-slung shorts, showcasing a body almost as perfectly sculpted as Antonio's.

And I was practically naked in the bikini. I'd worn a beach cover-up on my way out and it was within reach. That would be conspicuous, not to mention rude. And his eyes were staying on my face. I was overreacting. But the hairs on my neck told me I wasn't. I rested the open book on my chest, covering up part of me, at least.

"Would you like some limoncello, bellissima?" Lemons again. It was a large, very full glass.

"No, thanks. It's a bit early for alcohol."

"Perfetto! Because I brought you lemonade!" He grinned and sat on the edge of my lounge chair, reaching over me to place the glass on the small table by my phone. His hand landed on the far side of the chair, so he bracketed my legs.

"Mario—" I moved the book so it covered more of my breasts and inched up the chair. "You're obsessed with lemons."

He waved a dismissive hand, just like Antonio did all the time. "My family grows them. We're farmers, you know."

A thirty-three-year-old archaeologist from a family of farmers. Who lived in a three-story villa outside Sorrento worth a small fortune. Not just farmers.

"The olive grove is ours." He inclined his head to the east. "We also have production facilities for lemons and grapes. We ship our products all over the world. Limoncello, wine, balsamic vinegar, and a great deal of olive oil."

"That explains a lot."

He took a sip from his glass and leaned over me again to put it down, his body coming closer than before. I held my breath, trying to sink through the chair. His eyes left my face, scanning the length of my torso, and he moved back so my legs were trapped against him. "So, what shall we do while we're alone?"

The hairs on my neck stood up straighter. If he hadn't been my boyfriend's cousin, I would have pushed him. Antonio trusted him completely, so I should, too. He wouldn't actually hit on me. Would he? "Mario, you're in my space."

"You know, Antonio and I are very close."

I gestured toward the other lounge chair a couple of feet away from mine. "I know."

He didn't take the hint. "He shares *everything* with me."

I shoved gently against him with a leg, acting like I was simply stretching.

"And do you want to hear something I've learned?" He leaned toward me, his eyes falling to my mouth, his lips pursing. "He has wonderful taste in women."

My heart rate kicked up. There was enough room between us to connect my palm with his nose or an elbow to his midsection. If I slipped down the chair, I could negotiate a knee into his spine. "Mario, stop that."

His eyes raked down to where the book covered my breasts, and he placed a hand on mine to move it. "Antonio won't be back for hours. He'll never know."

"I'm warning you..." I clenched my jaw and a fist.

"I taught him everything he knows about women." He moved the book, leaning closer to my face. "Let me show you."

I cocked my arm back, ready to strike. Definitely the nose. "If you come one inch closer, you'll regret it."

A hint of a smile creased his face as he sat up straight and smacked my leg. "Molto bene, bellissima!" With a wink, he retrieved his lemonade and bounced off the lounge chair to sit on the other one.

"What the hell?" I grabbed my cover-up and held it against me, still ready to hit him if needed.

He held up a hand. "I like you, Samantha."

Apparently.

"And so does my cousin. But I've known many women he's liked whose interests were not pure."

"Yours don't appear to be, either."

He frowned, shaking his head. "He told you about Faith?"

"Yes."

"She came here once while he was working on his doctorate. He bought her things—not as much as he bought you— and she complained it was not enough. As soon as he was out the door, she came on to me. I told him she was trouble, but he didn't believe me." The constantly joking face had hardened. "Three months later, he caught her in bed with another man and moved back here. For a year."

"What does that have to do with me?"

He placed his glass at his feet and leaned forward on his knees, within arm's reach of my fist. "Samantha, he falls in love with his whole heart, but not his brain. That seems to escape him. Her betrayal destroyed him and I'll do anything in my power to be sure it never happens again."

"You could have talked to me about it. You know, like adults."

He waved the hand. "This is the first time he's left your side and you're leaving in two days. No time for finesse."

"Or for being polite." I swung my good leg over the far edge of the chair and dropped my book, pulling on the cover-up. "I really liked you Mario. But this was not cool."

"Do you love him?"

I pushed against the chair arms to help get vertical, biting back the discomfort from not moving my bad ankle for the last hour. "I'm not having this conversation with you. Our relationship is none of your business."

"Scusami." He put his hands up in surrender. "Per favore, I apologize. We will speak like adults."

This was Antonio's favorite cousin. Confidante. And they looked so similar it was difficult to stay angry with him. He had Antonio's best interests at heart.

I folded my arms. "Okay, talk."

"Sofia called before he arrived to warn me about how he was feeling. I'd helped him through it before, so I planned to do it again."

"Through what?"

"Heartbreak."

I glowered at the lounge chair. Heartbreak. Hardly. Our relationship wasn't that serious. We barely knew each other at the time. But then again, the emotions were strong enough I'd flown all this way. And he claimed he loved me.

"So I did the same thing I did after his breakup with Faith." His gaze drilled into the side of my head, but I didn't look up. He had the same brown eyes with little golden flecks Antonio did.

If I looked at him, I'd have to let go of my irritation. "And what was that?"

"Took him to the club and introduced him to several beautiful and willing women."

All the breath in my lungs rushed out. No. He didn't. He didn't sleep with another woman between the Monday I said goodbye and the Saturday I asked for his forgiveness. Or several women? Oh my god, he did, didn't he?

"Samantha?" Mario stood, easing me down.

I bristled at the touch, but stretched the bad leg out and rested my weight on the chair. This wasn't possible. Antonio wasn't Vincenzo with his pretty promises. Or Matt, with his perpetual concern. Antonio said his heart was mine. He said he wanted a future with me.

"We were broken up." My voice trembled as the words poured out. "I don't need to hear this."

"No, no, you don't understand. Nothing happened." He spoke quickly, an arm hovering between us like he was about to hug me. "He bored every one of them to tears. Five of them."

I caught my breath and looked at him. I wouldn't have thought Antonio was capable of boring anyone.

Mario was too close again, but the hairs on my neck didn't react. This was the real him. The friend. The man Antonio had entrusted me to at the club.

"All he talked about was you. How beautiful you were. How brilliant you were. Your passion. Your skill." He sighed and moved back to his own chair when I sat up straighter.

"He what?"

"I saw him through his toughest times, his whole life. Moving to Roma after he graduated, his days with Cristian—"

"His cousin from Rome?"

He held up the hand again, shaking his head. There was still so much I didn't know about Antonio, but Mario knew it all. "How things changed after he lost the weight. After Faith. But I never saw him like after you."

"Do I want to know?"

"He's a man of intense emotions—"

I snorted and quickly covered my mouth to keep it at bay. "Sorry."

Mario chuckled. "He hides much of it behind the charming and joking exterior. After Faith, he was full of anger and sadness. He lashed out. But after you, he was still full of hope and love. All he wanted was to return to the States to win you back. I had to take his phone from him several times after he arrived so he wouldn't call you and beg for your forgiveness."

If I'd heard all this before Antonio and I had spent this visit together, I would've laughed it off. A man like him didn't really want a woman like me. He was just trying to get me into bed, and moving to Naples gave him ample opportunity to seduce other women. Like the ones Mario introduced him to.

But he still wanted me.

Mario continued. "It will take hard work between the two of you to silence the voices in his head. The ones warning him you'll leave him for someone else. Someone you like more, who's more attractive, more interesting."

Our time in Naples had been amazing, and he told me he loved me over and over. But I had a voice in the back of my head, too. Mine told me the relationship wasn't real. That he'd forget me the moment I left, like Vin had done after the summer I spent in Amelia with him. It kept reminding me the more people you let into your heart, the more who'll leave you in the end.

"Perhaps I shouldn't be telling you all this, but Sofia said you were a good match for him. I can see that, but still had to make sure." He ran a hand through his hair, just like Antonio did. Was he upset by what he'd done? "I hope you can forgive me, but if you can't, please understand that he means a great deal to me. I simply don't want to see him suffer. Don't take it out on him."

I eased my legs over the side of the chair closest to him. "Promise you'll never pull anything like that again?"

"Cross my heart."

We shared a smile and I held out my arms to hug him. He was a great hugger, just like his cousin. Antonio had so many people who cared deeply for him, such a strong support system. Only good people had that.

I squeezed my eyes shut. Maybe Antonio did genuinely love me. Everything else he'd said was true, not just words. I relaxed into Mario's embrace.

Maybe I did love Antonio back. But it was hard to trust myself on that and I couldn't say something so important until I was sure.

"Two of my favorite people," came Antonio's voice.

My eyes flashed open as he stepped onto the patio from the stairs, one hand tucked behind his back. Navy linen pants and a white short-sleeved button up. So gorgeous.

I sat bolt upright in my seat, and an uncontrollable smile broke. "You're home early!"

"Stay there," he laughed, coming closer. "We need that leg to heal."

"Then hurry up and get over here. You're always so slow."

Mario got up with his lemonade and headed for the stairs, patting Antonio on the shoulder as he passed him. "You have a good woman here."

Antonio smiled and looked slowly from Mario to me. "I know."

Antonio stopped just shy of my open arms and produced a bouquet of red roses and white lilies from behind his back. "Forgive me?"

"For what?" I dropped my arms when it was evident he wasn't moving any closer. But the devilish look on his face told me there was a joke coming, an innuendo, or a tease of some sort. There was no actual apology.

"For not taking you out for a fancy dinner yet."

I lowered myself onto the lounge chair. "When you say fancy, what does that mean to you?"

He extended the bouquet further, tilting his head. "You don't like flowers, do you?"

Busted. I took the bouquet from him and pulled it to my nose, inhaling the sweetness of the lilies. "Dinner?"

"What *do* you like, bella?"

"Italian." I raised my eyebrows, reaching for his hand.

His eyes narrowed, and he waved for me to lie back on the chair. "I meant instead of flowers."

"That's exactly what I meant. Italian food. Italian coffee." I inched back as I talked, dropping the bouquet onto the small table, almost knocking the glass of lemonade over. "My Italian boyfriend."

One knee planted between my legs, and he put his hands on the armrests, hovering over me. "Good thing I have that one nearby."

"Very good thing."

His chest and hips lowered to meet mine, lips dropping to my ear. "Cocktail dress."

"You're going to look funny in that."

He struggled to hold back his chuckle as he ground his hardness between my legs. "The one you wore to the club is too short."

"True." I dragged a hand along his triceps, my thumb tracing the edge of the muscle. "It wouldn't cover your butt."

"I have something more appropriate—" His tongue traced the shell of my ear, all hint of the joke gone. "—being delivered."

"Hold up." I pushed him back so I could see his face. "Being delivered?"

He leaned in and sucked my bottom lip between his. "Chiara has picked something out and it's on its way."

I shook my head. "No more stuff."

"Oh, bella." He played at a pout. "First you reject the flowers, then a dress you haven't even seen yet?"

My gaze fell to the side, to the pretty bouquet. "I didn't reject the flowers."

He slid a hand around the back of my neck, into my hair, and urged my gaze back to his. "There's a restaurant in town I wish to share with you. But you need something nicer than one of your sundresses or shorts."

I ran a shaky hand over my mouth while he paused there above me. Hope in his eyes. *Be honest with yourself, Sam.* I always spent way more on my niece and nephew for birthdays and Christmas than my sister wanted me to. I'd bought Cass a ton of little trinkets and scrapbooking materials after she got sick.

If I had as much money as Antonio Ferraro did, I'd probably spend it just as freely on the people in my life.

I wrinkled my nose, more at myself than anything. "Is it a good restaurant?"

"It has a Michelin star, if you put stock in that." A broad smile broke across his face. "And the view is spectacular." He kissed me quickly on the nose. "And I booked a night at a hotel in town, so we don't have to worry about the hour-and-a-half drive home."

"Are you going to force me to use the crutches?"

"Do you still need them?"

I lifted my left leg on top of him, hooking it around his thighs. With only a hint of a grimace. "Let's test it out."

He leaned down, lips meeting mine, the hand in my hair traveling down my side. "Just don't complain if I think you need to be carried somewhere."

"I'll always complain."

He broke away from me, laughing. "And you say I'm the incorrigible one?"

"You're rubbing off on me."

"Not yet, Ms. Caine." He shot up and scooped me into his arms. "Let's head down to my room and pack for the hotel."

CHAPTER 29
SAMANTHA

HE'D BOOKED another giant suite, no less extravagant than the one in Capri. The purpose of such large rooms escaped me, since we saw little beyond the bedroom. Although the common room and couches were... also quite comfortable. The balcony overlooked the bay, close enough to the water and high up so nothing impeded the view.

The hotel was a short walk from the restaurant, so we strolled in the warm, dark night. It was a narrow street with a constant stream of compact cars, vans, and scooters. Buildings in white and pale pink stucco lined the north side, a well-graffitied low stone wall on the south. The tops of more buildings peeked over the wall, built further down the hill.

It was slow-going and I was tentative off the crutches, but Antonio kept an arm around my waist to help take some weight off the bad leg. A glass of red before we left the hotel room helped.

My chest swelled, full of a peace and ease I hadn't felt in forever. Relaxed.

Maybe it was the wine. Maybe it was the ornate globe

street lamps, the lights of the city edging the horseshoe-shaped bay, the stars twinkling high above. More likely the man next to me, his intoxicating scent and the soft fabric of his jacket sleeve against my bare back. His strength, the way he slowed to ensure I was as comfortable as possible. The growing intimacy from learning more about each other.

The way he'd accepted my desire to investigate the stolen wall painting in the end. And helped me.

"You sure we need to go for dinner?" I asked.

He glanced over at me, a knowing look. The corner of his mouth rose into that delicious smirk. "And waste that stunning dress?"

It was simple black silk jersey, falling to my knees. The thin straps were edged in sequins, with more scattered over the fabric. Understated. "More I want to keep your handsome self all to... myself."

He squeezed my waist as I shook my head at the silly words. It had been a large glass of wine.

"And here I want to show you off to the world." He kissed my temple. "It would seem we're at odds tonight."

"I suppose we'll have to just stick with momentum and keep moving forward."

"Onward and upward, amore."

The sidewalk widened to accommodate a low hedge along the front of a hotel. Concrete steps led up to automatic glass doors, which opened as we approached. A stunning Black woman with warm brown skin and natural hair piled atop her head like a mohawk strode out. She wore a short one-piece in coral, nose ring, and five earrings on one side.

Antonio's step stuttered.

"Antonio!" Her full lips—painted the same eye-catching

color as her jumpsuit—spread into a broad smile. She floated down the hotel steps on her platform heels, standing as tall as me once she was on the sidewalk. Six inches taller with the hair. They exchanged kisses at each cheek, the second one lingering longer than it should have.

Antonio gestured to her. "Samantha, this is Océane Monet. She's—"

I finished for him, offering my hand in greeting. "The microbiology PhD candidate."

"I've never been summarized quite so succinctly." Her eyes traversed my body slowly, a sly smile emerging. "And you are?"

"Samantha Caine." He stroked my waist with his thumb. "My girlfriend. She's visiting during our delay."

"Lucky man." She spoke English with a thick French accent. Antonio had told me about her, the last member of his conservation team. She was from Paris, but was pursuing her PhD in the States at MIT. This woman was a far cry from what I'd expected based on her dissertation about the reproduction of various bacterial strains. She looked more like a runway model than a microbiologist. "And what do you do, Samantha, to have snagged our Dr. Ferraro?"

Antonio chuckled. "I would love to explain, but the story is rather long and she would say it's boring."

Océane merely hummed in response. Something between *I see* and *Oh, really?* or maybe even *That was avoiding the question.*

"Where have you been the last week?" I asked. We knew Umberto removed the wall painting. But that didn't mean he was the one shipping it from Naples, selling it, or whatever was happening.

His arm around my waist tightened. *Stop that*, his squeeze communicated.

"I went to Rome for a few days. I'd never been. Thought about heading further north, but there was too much to see."

Ignoring Antonio's warning, I pressed. "Did you hear about Umberto?"

"No." She folded her arms, an armband tattoo peeking out from under the short sleeve of her outfit. "Did his girlfriend tire of him and head back home?"

Strange answer. "Sorry?"

"Have you met her? She's a talented artist and he's…" She unfolded her arms only long enough to scratch her brow with one immaculate purple fingernail, looking at Antonio as she replied. "I trust your decision to hire him. My issue is strictly personal."

"How do you know his girlfriend?"

Océane returned her focus to me. "He brought her to Pompeii for a meet-and-greet once we all arrived. Two women new to the city discussing our reasons for being here, and we hit it off. We went for coffee and she complained about him incessantly."

Eva seemed worried about Umberto when we spoke to her. That didn't match up with someone who disliked her boyfriend. "Complained about what?"

"His disrespect of her art, his lack of desire for children, his lack of romance… and his obsession with Dr. Ferraro." She scanned Antonio this time, a small rumble in her throat. "Although who can blame him for that?"

"Not an obsession." Antonio's hand slid down to my hip and back up. "Just sucking up to the boss."

"Peut être." She shrugged one shoulder, as if to say her

maybe was a *no, I'm right.* "Either way, I told her to dump his ass and join me in Rome. But she said she had more important things going on here."

"Did she say what?" I asked.

Her eyes flicked down my body again. "You're a curious little bird. Do you always ask so many questions?"

Antonio chuckled, like he thought our conversation was cute.

I straightened, a twinge in my ankle when I put more weight on it than I should have. "We caught him cutting into the Minerva wall after we discovered part of the Mars wall was missing."

Océane's eyebrow twitched and she made another humming noise.

"Hmm?" I replied in kind.

Her grin remained firmly in place. "I never would have thought him capable of something like that. Perhaps he's more than he seems?"

"More than he seems?" I spluttered.

She was steadily cementing her spot as suspect number two. He could have removed the flowers, given them to her, then she took them to Rome to a broker. Made sure she bonded with the girlfriend about what dead weight he was, so no one would figure out they were working together.

I took a deep breath when Antonio squeezed me again. "When did you leave for Rome?"

"Saturday." She leaned closer to me, a heavy and dark fragrance of cinnamon, wood, and flowers wafting off her. "Is that before or after the timing of the event for which you're going to accuse me of helping him?"

Antonio put up a hand. "No one is accusing anyone."

"Oh, I think she is." Océane bit her bottom lip. "Go ahead. Would you like to come up to my room so I can show you my train tickets?"

Someone had taken the flower painting sometime between Saturday morning and early Sunday afternoon. The blue pigment pot was recovered just before noon on Saturday. Her trip was in our window for the pots, too. She could have gone to Rome and delivered those, then come back for the fresco. "What time Saturday?"

"Oh, Dr. Ferraro, I like her. She has spirit." A car pulled up and she waved to the driver. "But I must apologize. My ride is here."

Antonio kissed the air at her cheeks. "I'll see you Wednesday onsite."

"I look forward to it." She opened the car door and slipped into the backseat. "And it was two in the afternoon, little detective. Does that make me innocent or guilty?"

As the car drove off, I said, "I don't like her, Antonio."

He chuckled, an annoying sound at that moment. "I didn't notice."

I glowered at him. "And I really didn't like how you laughed at my questions and kept squeezing me to tell me to stop."

He shook his head and looked heavenward. "Oh, come now, bella. I was squeezing you because I was proud of your passion."

"And the laughter?"

"She was flirting with you, and you just kept grilling her." He urged me forward along the sidewalk. "I think it turned her on."

"She was not. She was being evasive. And trying to rattle

me." She reminded me of Victoria Meyers, Miss July in Antonio's Calendar Club—the name the group of women he used to date gave themselves. Victoria had tried to instill doubts in me about him and his ability to remain faithful to a single woman.

Doubts I was still wrestling with, despite how amazing my visit had been.

"She left Napoli after the first pot was found in Roma, so she didn't take that. And even so, what are the odds—" He let go of me to pull open the door of the next building and usher me through. "—that two members of my team were in on the theft?"

I limped into the small white marble lobby of a hotel until he caught up and took some of my weight. "That they'd be involved in some criminal plan before you hired them? Slim. But if someone approached them after? Much higher."

He directed us to an elevator, tone serious, not condescending like I'd expected from his earlier responses. "How many pieces could be physically removed before they were caught? Particularly from the Casa di Marte? It would become obvious after two—plus the missing pigment pots—that someone on a conservation team was involved."

"Good point." I leaned against the back of the elevator car, resting my left foot lightly on the floor. When I folded my arms, he unfolded them and draped them around his neck. "Maybe we're just dealing with dumb criminals?"

He laughed, placing his hands on the wall behind me. "Océane was right about two things."

I cocked an eyebrow.

"You're a very suspicious one." He dipped closer to kiss my cheek. "And sexy as hell."

I did my best to control my smile and pulled my arms down to shove him gently. "None of that changes the fact that she was in town when the flower fresco was taken, then out of town for a week after. And Umberto told Eva he was thinking about going up to Rome. Maybe he was going to see Océane? Or maybe... We should talk to Eva again and find out if there was an opportunity for Umberto to have passed the items off to Océane, and that's why he didn't have to go."

"Why Océane? What about Thomas?" He kissed each of my hands, which held him at bay. "He was also involved with a looted krater in London."

"I knew you didn't like him." I grinned, tugging the lapels of his jacket to bring him closer. "Maybe we should invite him to dinner tonight and chat about it."

Antonio pushed my arms against the wall and closed the small distance between us, pressing his hard body against mine. "I'm not sharing you with anyone tonight."

He was right. There was nothing to do about the investigation at that hour.

But we were staying in Naples overnight.

We could pop by Riccardo Emanuele's gallery in the morning before heading back to Sorrento. And find out what Eva knew.

CHAPTER 30
ANTONIO

THE VISTA dell'Ovo restaurant balcony overlooked the Lungomare, the Castel, and the bay beyond. A view made even more spectacular by the woman next to me. We sat at an intimate table for two, one of only five outside. The wrought-iron railing was topped by four small statues of women bearing water pitchers on their shoulders, out of which emerged dim frosted-glass lights.

Samantha took a sip of red wine, her eyes fluttering closed as she sighed. "I'm stuffed."

I ran my fingers along her jaw, up to her ear. The long, drop earrings highlighted her elegant neck, teasing my mouth, which wanted nothing more than to savor that space. "Is this more the type of *stuff* you appreciate?"

"Experiences over things." She placed a hand on mine, pulling it to her lips.

The crackled glass globe at the far side of our table flickered with candlelight, catching the sequins adorning her dress. She looked almost as beautiful as the night we attended the charity gala together, when I'd seen her in action for the first time, tracking down the stolen painting at the auction. The night I almost kissed her.

It was hard to say when I'd fallen in love with her. That evening was one of the many candidates.

"Mario brought the National Archaeological Museum curator here for dinner and recommended the place."

Her eyes snapped open with her laugh. "The one who let us into the tombaroli display?"

"Sì, the exact one."

Our clasped hands moved to the table, thumbs and fingers exploring in their own private dance of seduction.

"Any room left for dessert?" I inched my chair closer to hers and leaned in to keep my voice low. "Or shall we head back to the hotel? I believe there's a spot behind your ear I missed earlier and my tongue is begging to explore it."

Her leg slipped around mine, and she canted her face toward me. "That also sounds like a worthwhile experience."

"So, finish the wine and leave?"

"Let me think..." She inhaled deeply, cheek pressing against mine. "If we leave now, we'll have mind-blowing sex at the hotel?"

"We will."

"And if we have dessert first..." She pulled back with an uncharacteristic giggle. Three glasses of wine was a more magic number than all the alcohol at the club had been. "Then we'll go back to the hotel and have mind-blowing sex?"

I laughed and straightened. "Sì, the end result is the same. One route includes sugar, the other is simply sooner."

"Then I choose dessert." She planted a peck on my nose and stood. "But I need to hit the little girls' room first."

"Shall I wait or order for you?"

"Surprise me." She took one step, then spun back to me, pointing her finger. "Just nothing lemon. I've overdosed. And no gelato."

She walked away, that playful swing to her hips, no hint of a limp. Either the leg was better or the wine was masking her discomfort.

I signaled to our server who brought a dessert menu with six selections. One with limoncello and one with sorbet, so I ordered the other four plus two sweet wines. It would be a surprise, exactly what she asked for.

As the server left, I stared off into the distance, to the lights of the city, to the vague outline of Vesuvio. It had been two weeks since our argument at the studio in Brenton. I thought I'd lost her for good.

She was such a blessing.

Her chair drew back sooner than expected and I looked up, but it was not her.

A man with broad shoulders in a black suit, which strained at his biceps. He had short, dark hair and a serious expression, reminding me of Cristian's thugs or Pasquale's bodyguards. As he sat, he said simply, "Dr. Antonio Ferraro?"

I cocked an eyebrow in response.

"I'm here with a message."

My jaw clenched. These were words I'd not heard in some time.

"I understand you were at Riccardo Emanuele's gallery a couple of days ago." He spoke in English, with a slight accent I couldn't place.

And there was no need for me to respond. This was not a question.

"I represent certain interests who would appreciate if you

did not return there. And who would further appreciate if you did not contact Umberto Longhi or Eva Zabelle again."

"Umberto and Eva who?" I knew who he meant, and my attempt to sound as though we hadn't visited the studio specifically to see her was nothing more than petulant. Men like this rarely delivered messages they were unsure of. I'd known too many of them during my days in Roma with Cristian.

He smiled, a tight-lipped, near-polite movement which didn't reach his eyes. "I'm sure you wouldn't want your pretty American girlfriend hurt."

Bile rose in my throat, and my stomach twisted in knots. I leaned forward, my words coming out as a growl. "You touch one hair on her head and I will—"

He slid the chair back before I could finish, undisturbed by the fury about to be released. If I hit him, the threat would become real. He would not be alone and I wouldn't be able to protect her.

Smoothing his jacket, surveying the view, he said "No, you won't." He left.

My mind raced, every breath burning. I ripped the phone out of my pocket and dialed Cristian. Before he could greet me, the words poured out. "I need to talk to you. Now."

"What—"

"Someone threatened to hurt Samantha."

"Slow down, cugino. Who's Samantha?"

"My girlfriend!" I launched from my chair and stepped to the railing, trying to calm the stutter in my breath. "I swear, if your people are behind this—"

"They're not," he snapped. "And you know I can't talk over—"

"Cazzo! You told me to call if anything suspicious happened and now it has. Send me a phone!" I jabbed the End button, wanting nothing more than to throw the phone at the wall. Threatening me like that. Threatening her!

I texted Cristian the hotel information, ensuring he would contact me in the morning.

A gentle hand ran up my back to my shoulder. "Buonasera, bello."

The sound of Samantha's voice simultaneously sent excited shivers and fits of rage through me. *Deep breath, Antonio. Smile.* I turned slowly, words lodging in my throat. How had she grown more beautiful since she left the table?

She gestured to the phone still in my hand. "Don't tell me someone else has your attention?"

"Of course not." I slipped it into my pocket and pulled her against me at the railing, the lights above the statue casting a soft glow across her face. "Nothing can compete with you."

Behind her, the server arrived, his tray filled with desserts.

"I ordered one of everything, except the lemon and gelato."

She didn't turn around to follow my gaze, just stared deep into my eyes. "Thank you."

"Thank me later." I winked, which prompted a small laugh.

"Seriously. Despite—or maybe in part because of—all the chaos, this has been the best vacation of my life." Her lips sought mine, slow, passionate, loving. She sighed in the kiss, one hand cupping my cheek. No nervous fingers, no hesitation, no complaints about public displays of affection.

When we parted, my smile was again genuine, despite the gnawing deep inside me. "Mine, as well."

It was Monday evening. She was leaving early Wednesday. We didn't know where Umberto was, so I had no concern she'd try to find him. But keeping her away from the gallery after our chat with Océane? I could take her back to the villa and beg her not to leave the bedroom until I was satisfied. She would laugh, tease, and hopefully, she would stay.

I could send Chiara or Mario to buy the colorful abstract painting for me later. And I never had to see that place again.

CHAPTER 31

ANTONIO

I CLOSED the hotel suite door, breakfast delivery bag in-hand. Detoured to the bathroom to grab a plush white bathrobe to match the one I wore and proceeded to the bedroom. In the enormous bed with its dark wood four-poster frame, rumpled sheets pooled all around Samantha. She lay on her stomach near the middle of the mattress, glorious hair spread out across the pillows, the lean muscles of her back and arms on full display above the low-slung blanket.

We had, indeed, had mind-blowing sex after the restaurant. She fell into a deep slumber while mine was fractured. Horrible dreams, unable to forget the man who sat next to me. I'd stared at the clock all night until it was morning. At least I'd held her in my arms as I fretted.

Did they know where we were staying? Know where I lived? He'd known where I would be for dinner and that was a last-minute plan. And who was he? One of Cristian's men? Was Fiori with his giant yacht and staff involved? Or did Umberto simply have muscle I wouldn't have expected him to employ?

I dropped the bag next to the coffeemaker on a chest of drawers, then settled on the edge of the bed.

She groaned, but didn't move.

"Wake up, bella. Breakfast is here."

"Still stuffed from dinner," she murmured. "Come cuddle with me."

"We have to check out eventually." I ran a light touch along her arm before leaning in to kiss it.

"Book another night. This bed is divine."

"What?" I added sarcasm to my voice, thick enough her half-asleep ears would hear it. "You want me to spend *more* money on you?"

She yawned, shoulders shaking with quiet laughter. "You suck, Ferraro."

"If you're lucky."

One eye cracked open. "Walked into that one, didn't I?"

"You did. Now get up and go shower."

Her eye closed again. "You said breakfast was here."

"No food until you're clean." I smacked her ass lightly, which was greeted with more quiet laughter. The temptation to bite it was strong, but that would lead somewhere other than her going for a shower.

She rolled onto her side, pulling the sheet up to cover her chest. "Coffee first."

"Your breath stinks."

"Jerk." She covered her mouth with the sheet. "You joining me?"

"I've already showered."

"And you didn't get me up?" Her eyes widened, then narrowed to playful slits. "That shower's too big for one person."

"The shampoo smells like rosemary and mint. It will help you wake up." I stood when she grabbed for me. As much as I wanted to climb into the shower with her, I had other priorities.

She flopped onto her back, arms flying wide. "I'm not normally a snoozing kinda gal. You're a bad influence on me."

"You don't strike me as a procrastinator, either." I rounded the bed, returning to the breakfast takeout bag to pull out my coffee. Removing the lid, I made an exaggerated show of inhaling the intense scent. "Yours is getting cold, bella."

She threw a pillow in my direction—which was thankfully not actually aimed at me, so I didn't spill scalding coffee all over myself—and grabbed the bathrobe, practically leaping from the bed toward the bathroom, still favoring her left leg. "Five minutes!"

"You can't wash that much hair in five minutes."

"Time me!"

The door swung shut and I ripped an old-fashioned flip phone from the bag. Opened, it displayed a small sticky note reading, *Dial 1*. I hit the eight. One was in case the phone was intercepted or if I was compromised. I had enough years' experience with Cristian to know this.

"Cugino!"

"I have five minutes."

"Talk fast. Tell me what happened."

I did as requested and provided a high-level summary of the last three days. Catching Umberto, the visit to his girlfriend at Riccardo Emanuele's gallery, and the warning at the restaurant. Cristian made small noises of assent as I spoke, not interrupting even though he knew some of it already.

"English speaker?" he said when I finished. "What kind? American, Canadian, British, Austral—"

"I didn't recognize an accent." My head sank into my free hand. There was so little information to go on.

"And they warned you off the artist, as well? Eva Zabelle, in addition to the tombaroli you found at your site?"

"Sì, both of them."

"Alright. I'll find out what I can. But Antonio, take this seriously. Not just for your girlfriend's sake, but for yours. And keep the phone on you. I'll call when I have news."

With that, he hung up and I tucked the phone deep inside my overnight bag. When this was done, the phone and SIM card would be separated and snapped, destined for the shredder at the office.

Cristian was charming, charismatic, and patient. It all served him well in his career, as did his ability to turn it all off in a moment. His fury was not something to trifle with. When he said to take something seriously, there was weight behind it. Years of experience.

And, no doubt, some level of knowledge about what was going on.

What had Samantha and I fallen into?

The bathroom door flung open, and a sopping-wet, robed Samantha appeared. "Coffee me!"

She was in excellent spirits, and I had to play off that.

"Ankle all better?"

"A little sore when I move the wrong way, but—" Her step stuttered as she balanced for a moment on her left leg to demonstrate it was alright.

I settled on the firm cream-colored sofa, swinging the white bag to entice her.

Her fingers combed through her hair as she approached, deftly braiding the long strands. "Is it just coffee or anything else?"

I patted the seat next to me and placed the bag on the low table in front of me. "You have to ask this silly question?"

"Cornetti?" She sat sideways to stretch her legs over my lap.

"Chocolate hazelnut."

She bit her bottom lip and accepted the cup of cappuccino I pulled out of the bag. Sliding down against the arm of the sofa, she was in the perfect position for me to caress her shin and up to her thigh. "Definitely the best vacation ever."

"With the best boyfriend ever?"

"I'll reserve judgment on that just yet." She took a sip, then straightened to grab the bag from the table. With a gleam in her eyes, she exchanged coffee for cornetto, and sank her teeth in. The bite was ambitious and as much of the filling dribbled onto her chin as went in her mouth. She moaned, clearing the mess with her fingers. "So. Good."

"Let me help with that." I slid her legs off me and crawled along the couch.

But she pushed me away, laughing. "No way, this is my filling!"

I swiped at the corner of her mouth and smeared it on my bottom lip. "Then come and get it."

"Ooh, you're in trouble now!" She dropped her food onto the bag and tackled me.

"Looks like you didn't need the coffee."

She sucked the filling off my mouth, licking her lips as she separated from me. "It was the rosemary and mint shampoo.

Once I woke up enough to remember how excited I was to go see Umberto's girlfriend again, I *really* woke up."

My heart lurched. *Distract her.* "Oh, no you don't." Before she was a foot away from me, I grabbed her, spinning us so she was underneath me on the couch. "You're mine this morning."

Her eyebrows flew up, but before she could protest, my mouth was on hers. Teasing out the moans. Her legs spread to grant my hips access, pulling me closer with the bad ankle wrapped around my back. "Maybe a quickie before we go."

"When have I ever been fast at anything, bella?"

She groaned, arching her back as I undid the tie on her bathrobe. "They open at ten. You've got thirty minutes. If we get in before any crowd, we should have more time to talk to Eva."

"Océane isn't behind this. You don't need to talk to Eva to find that out." My lips trailed down her neck, nudging one side of the bathrobe aside to take a nipple in my mouth.

"You're probably right—" She whimpered when I reached the hollow of her hip. "—but we should still go."

I dragged my tongue along the inside of her thigh, and she grabbed a throw pillow from behind her, clenching it in her fists. Pausing, I said, "I have barely twenty-four hours to finish making love to you properly."

"What time's checkout?"

"I'm paying for another night."

She covered her face with the pillow when I blew lightly on the sensitive spot where her inner thigh met her sex. "We can't stay here forever. We have to go back to the villa before I leave, anyway."

I blew across her skin again and her hips lifted toward my

mouth. "Mario can pack your things and bring them to town."

She dropped her hips and laughed, lifting the pillow. "Please tell me that was a joke. I don't want him packing my underwear."

"Oh, bella." I stood and crossed to my overnight bag, retrieving some condoms to drop on the table by the sofa.

She propped herself up on her elbows, eyes widening. "That's going to take a while to go through."

"Exactly my plan. We can stay here all day, order room service, then go to the villa in the morning before you have to leave."

"If I have to," she sighed, rolling her eyes before grabbing the hem of my bathrobe.

"Here, hold this." I snatched the pillow she'd released and plopped it over her face. "You're going to need it."

This was perhaps not one of my smarter ideas. Samantha craved action, movement, exploration. And not just in bed. Nor in one hotel room. Keeping her away from the gallery might be more difficult than expected.

But what else could I do? Tell her about the threat? No, that would convince her she was getting close, encouraging her to take more risks. Instead of keeping her away from Riccardo Emanuele and Eva Zabelle, it would draw her closer. More excited.

And then what? If there had been any doubt about the man who'd threatened Samantha the night before, Cristian erased it all. *Take this seriously*, he'd said. Cristian was not someone who gave warnings lightly.

But how many secrets did I have to keep from her? One lie

in Brenton had snowballed into a deception that had torn us apart. Honesty and trust were paramount to her.

I could do it, because it might save her life. Whether she knew it or not.

The pillow hit me in the chest. "Is that what I was going to need it for?"

I grinned at her, pushing it back down on the sofa above her head. "Oh, bella, you are going to pay dearly for that."

CHAPTER 32
SAMANTHA

I LAY NAKED AND WARM—FROM the inside out—on a bed of blankets and pillows on the hotel floor. Antonio stretched out next to me on his side, dangling a chocolate-covered strawberry over my mouth.

I shook my head. "I guess the answer's nine days."

"Scusa?" He settled back and bit into the strawberry when I didn't reach for it.

My eyes fluttered closed and I exhaled, long and slow, hands clasped over my midsection. "Because if that's not being made love to properly, I don't think I care to know what is."

"You're quite limber. That helps."

I chuckled. "I'll have to start yoga."

Something hit the metal platter near his head, barely audible over the music playing from a small portable speaker; likely the uneaten portion of the strawberry. "So you concede? Spending an entire day in bed is now your idea of a perfect day, as well?"

I tilted my head and creaked one eye open enough to wink at him. "I still say nature hike."

He gasped theatrically and rolled up onto his side, latching a leg over me, pulling my hip to him. "Then we're not done. We have oysters left. And caviar. And so many hours before sunset."

I put up a hand to stop him, but just threaded it into the soft hair at the nape of his neck. We'd abandoned the furniture when the food and champagne arrived around noon. He'd thrown the table onto the bed, so we had as much floor space as possible.

Light poured in through the balcony door, lighting him from behind, so the golden flecks in his eyes were hidden in shadow. But the playful look in them was ever constant.

How had I gotten so lucky?

"You're staring, bella."

I sighed, "I know."

That look came over him again. The one that sometimes ended with a whispered 'I love you' and other times just ended with a knowledge deep in my soul that he was thinking it.

If he was thinking it without saying it, that meant it was real, didn't it? Words were so easy, but feelings were tough. Unpredictable.

Unreliable.

A knock came at the door, and Antonio's eyes danced with mischief.

"What now?"

"Stay there!" He grabbed a bathrobe, barely knotting it about his waist before padding to the door. He opened it, said a quiet "Grazie," and closed the door.

I craned my neck around to see him come down the hallway with another bag. "Not more food?"

"Oh, no." From within, he pulled a small bottle filled with

a pale yellow liquid. "The finest bath oil in the city. Neroli and lavender to relax and remove any remaining stress. If it's possible you have any stress left."

"I feel like I barely even have any bones left, I'm so relaxed."

"First time in your life?"

I eased my position and closed my eyes again. "Pretty close."

"Then you lie here and I'll run the bath." His air filled the space around me and his lips met my forehead. "I'll come back and carry you once it's ready."

"Sounds good."

"Perhaps we shall find some of those *bones* in there?"

I spluttered a laugh and looked up after his retreating form. "Ridiculous."

"Anything to hear you laugh, amore."

That was why I was here. Us. Laughing, chatting, hanging out in an open-top blanket fort. Not chasing after Umberto and Océane.

But what time was it? When did the gallery close?

No, put that aside.

I was leaving tomorrow. It would have been nice to solve the mystery, make Antonio proud, and return home a conquering hero—and maybe with a revised offer from Elliot and the FBI that would keep me in Brenton. But the police could handle the case. I could handle the bathtub. And Antonio. With those shoulders and those lips and those hands.

The tightness started between my thighs again. Something I wouldn't have expected possible after the morning we'd had.

He closed the door but not all the way. Before turning on the water, he muttered, "Should have gotten bubbles."

"No bubbles in a jacuzzi tub!" I raised my voice, but he probably couldn't hear me over the tap. Housekeeping was going to be pissed enough with the spilled champagne and chocolate in the rug.

I'll pay for it, he'd said, waving that silly hand of his.

A buzzing started from somewhere by the bed. "Antonio, your phone!"

No response. He still couldn't hear me over the noise of the water filling the bathtub.

I rolled over and peered around to figure out where the noise was coming from. It was coming from his bag, which was tucked neatly under the bed. On all fours, I crawled over and unzipped it, my hand landing on the buzzing phone.

But it wasn't his phone. It was an old-style clamshell. He used a touchscreen smartphone.

It buzzed again, and I flipped it open. "This is Antonio's phone. He's not here right now, can I take a—"

Click.

The hairs on my neck rose.

Why did he have a second phone? A man with his money didn't need a cheap drug store phone like this. Especially not one with a small note taped to the screen on the inside, *Dial 1*.

And why would whoever called him hang up as soon as I answered?

Antonio's shadow fell across the sliver of light from the bathroom. I snapped the phone shut, hiding it behind my back.

Phones like this were only used for secrets. Illegal activities. Other women.

He kept moving, humming some song to himself. Throat

dry, unsure what I'd say to whoever was on the other end, I dialed one.

"Pizza di Russo," came a woman's voice. It was a disinterested voice, with no hesitation. Like she really was working at a pizzeria.

My heart thundered in my chest, breaking into a thousand pieces. That wasn't who'd called.

I tried the second speed dial. Nothing. Three. Nothing. All the way to eight.

One ring and someone answered. Silence on the other end.

"Hello?" I said.

Click.

"Samantha?" Antonio's voice was surprisingly close.

My gaze shot up from the phone to see him standing in front of me. All I could do was stare and blink. Hold the phone up. I should have known. No, I'd known all along.

He reached for it, but I pulled it back to me.

I clenched my jaw. "Two hang-ups."

His mouth opened and closed like a damn fish.

"Who is calling you on a burner phone?" I stepped closer, the temperature dropping in the room. It was so cold. I was so naked.

One hand drove through his hair. That was his tell. Something was going on. But the man with all the words was silent in response.

I slammed the phone into his chest as I passed him to grab my clothes. "Nothing changed at the nightclub, did it? Except you realized you could get away with your bullshit if you used your pretty little words and fucked me senseless! You goddamn Italian men! You're all the same!"

"Allora, bella. It's…" He huffed and ground out, "Family business."

"Family business? Even better!" I found the discarded underwear I tried putting on before I'd given up on Eva and the gallery. "Like when your father told you to lie about the Chagall and you just went along with it? What are you hiding from me this time? Covering for another family member I might think was involved in something? Ooh, maybe stealing the fresco? Is that who you were sneaking a call to last night at the restaurant?"

"Stop that." His gaze flew around the room, touching every surface we'd been on. Then the ceiling. Then finally me. "Someone threatened you last night."

I hauled on the foolish sundress I'd worn into town yesterday.

"When you stepped away from the table last night."

"Right." I rolled my eyes, waving one strappy little sandal in the air. "Some random person shows up in an exclusive restaurant with a warning and a phone. You should sell that to Hollywood."

"I'm serious. You can't go. It's dangerous."

I stood, snatching my clutch from the bedside table. Black with crystals to match the dress from the night before. "This is the lamest cover I've ever heard."

"Cover?" He shook his head. "You still distrust me so much?"

"I don't know, Antonio. You disappear all morning yesterday for—" I made air quotes. "—*work* that I couldn't be there for. Then you show up with those stupid flowers."

"I wanted to surprise you because I missed you."

"Men send flowers when they're trying to hide the truth."

How many bouquets did I get from Vin when I got back to Michigan the first time? I kicked at a pillow on the floor as I stomped toward the door. "It's all distractions."

He gripped my upper arm, not letting it slip when I tried to pull free. "I'm serious. Someone told me you're not to see Eva again."

"If that was true..." I closed the distance between us, focused on patience over showing him how easily I could break his grip. Twist his arm. Shatter his nose. Knee his groin. "You would have remembered what I said about honesty and trust. And you would have told me."

"Trust?" His lip curled. "Like the way your first instinct is to accuse me? Say I'm just like all Italian men, whatever that means?"

"Honesty's expected, Antonio." I swallowed hard against the acid bubbling in my throat. "Trust is earned."

"Marone! I am in love with you, woman." He leaned closer to me, his robe brushing my dress, the scent of lavender strong on him. We should have been in that tub together. "I have been trying to rebuild your trust in me since you got here. What else do I have to do?"

I grabbed his free hand at the wrist, lifting it to remind him of the phone he was carrying. "Not sneak around."

"Come get in the tub with me." He inclined his head toward the bathroom, thinking that Ferraro charm was all he needed. "Let's go back to where we were fifteen minutes ago. Another reset. I can explain."

We both turned at the sound of water on tile. An overflowing tub was my out.

"You better go turn that off before it leaks through the floor."

He took a half-step, but hesitated, eyes locked on mine, grip just as tight on my arm.

"Too much water leads to mold and you really don't want to pay for a hotel like this one to rip out more than one floor to remediate."

Antonio squeezed his eyes shut and whispered, "Don't leave."

He dashed into the bathroom to turn off the tap, and I was out the door at as close to a run as my ankle would allow.

Skipped the elevator. Too slow. Down the stairs, out the front door, and flagged a taxi before he could catch up. But barely. He came barreling outside in bare feet and a robe just as my cab pulled away.

My phone rang and I almost threw it out the window. It was an unknown number. Probably still that burner.

Flowers and hang-ups. And lies.

But still, that look in his eyes earlier. The *I love you* look. Surely that wasn't a lie.

I accepted the call and lifted the phone to my ear.

"Don't go to the gallery!" Panic poured through the phone, his words and breath fast. "Whatever you do! Please, bella. Just promise me that!"

"This your new tactic? Instead of telling me to let the police deal with it?" My eyes stung and I blinked away the tears that clung to my lids. I'd had to let Matt go six years ago so he could be who he truly was. Maybe Antonio and I needed to do the same. "Stop trying to turn me into someone I'm not."

"I just want you safe."

"Fine. I'm going back to the villa. You can pack my stuff at the hotel." Blinking didn't work, so I rubbed a rough hand across my face. "No wait. Your stuff. The only things I actually own are in my clutch."

"Bene." He let out a shaky breath, ignoring the sarcasm in my voice. "Molto bene. I'll be at the villa as soon as I can and we can sort all this out. I'll give you every detail possible."

The way he talked. Could there be a shred of truth to all of this? Or just more games?

Being in that hotel room with him hadn't felt like a lie. It had felt warm and peaceful and good. Like I was the only thing that mattered to him in the entire world.

But the sound on that cheap phone. The breath and the click.

"I love you, bella," he said with a tremor in his voice.

"Good," I whispered.

Why would he be trying to steer me away from the gallery? Secrets. Family business. What was he hiding?

I had to find out for myself. Could I trust Antonio Ferraro?

After ending the call, I patted the driver's seat. "Do you know Riccardo Emanuele's art gallery near the Piazza Municipio?"

He nodded.

"Take me there."

CHAPTER 33
SAMANTHA

THE TAXI WOUND its way through narrow streets, cutting off and being cut off by reckless scooters. The driver went too fast, but it hardly mattered.

I needed perspective. Help. Who could I call? My sister?

Cass would start off by yelling at me for flying to Naples. She thought I was still in New York with no risk of missing her chemo on Friday. Then she'd yell even louder about me being with Antonio.

She'd call him every name in the book, then spout off all the things Nathan had said about him. Stalker. Not trustworthy. She'd probably get Nathan on the line to tell me again that Antonio was dangerous.

Just what I'd need. A lecture telling me they were right all along.

If they were right.

The taxi stopped, I paid, and got out at the piazza. The gallery was close by, and I walked fast.

Maybe Eva was the person Antonio was meeting with yesterday morning when he said he was in Pompeii. She was pretty. From what Océane said, she wasn't happy with her thieving boyfriend. What better revenge for her than to take up with the boss Umberto was so obsessed with? And it would explain why he didn't want me to go visit her.

I blew out a deep breath.

That was ridiculous.

If I couldn't call Cass, who did I have? I'd pushed so many people away in my life, I had few left. That was how I liked it, though. Wasn't it?

Tourists clogged the street and I had to dodge my way around several of them. No one was walking fast enough. They were all relaxed.

My shoulders fell. All these people were boneless.

I wanted to be in love. Have Antonio continue looking at me the way he did. But to be able to trust it. Trust that it was honest and pure.

My phone buzzed for what must have been the tenth time. Antonio again. So much of my trip to Naples had seemed easy. Being with him, exploring the ruins, touring the city and Capri. Just being present with him lit up my soul.

So why did it have to be so hard? He was right for me in so many ways. But what if... always what if? Why did Vincenzo's promises of *I'll be there next month* and Matt's *I do* keep drowning out Antonio's voice? Why did their false *I love yous* weigh so much more than his?

I was going to be sick.

My body fell into auto-pilot mode and I almost called Cass. Almost accepted Antonio's next call. Almost called Janelle, my best friend growing up, who I'd barely spoken to in a decade.

The smarter call would have been to Eva, if Antonio

weren't the one with her contact information. I could have arranged a meeting when she had spare time to talk. Surely, she would have heard about Umberto's attempted theft. The police would have questioned her. If he'd gotten in touch with her, would she know I was the one who caught him red-handed? How would she react to seeing me?

What if he'd gone missing, like she'd said, and was tying up loose ends? What if the threat was real? What if it was against Eva, not me? Or in addition to me? What if Océane and Umberto were working together and my accusations to Océane last night prompted the threat?

What if Antonio gave up on me after my outburst at the hotel?

Before reaching the front door of the gallery, I paused. There were too many unknowns, and I had to focus on what I did know.

We caught Umberto trying to steal a piece of the Minerva wall. Odds were that he stole the flower fresco, too. When we'd talked to his girlfriend three days ago, she was worried because she hadn't seen him. Océane went to Rome inside our time-frame for the flowers being stolen. She said she'd met with Eva, who'd complained vehemently about Umberto.

And Antonio didn't want me to return to the gallery. He was hiding something on that phone.

Everything else was conjecture.

I heaved on the thick glass door, plastering a smile on my face. At least my dress was appropriate for a high-end art gallery, despite being a little rumpled and the clutch not matching.

A young man met me barely ten feet inside the entrance, all polish and professional.

"Buongiorno. I was in the other day with my boyfriend, looking at some paintings with Eva Zabelle. I'd like to speak with her about them."

"Sorry, but she's not here."

Dammit. That put a damper on my plans. "What time will she be back?"

"She's out for the day." He smiled politely. "But I'm sure I can be of service."

"I really want to deal with her." I folded my arms, doing my best impression of a woman with more money than courtesy. I'd worked with plenty of upscale galleries as an insurance adjuster and had witnessed displays like this. They usually got results. "You can talk to Riccardo. My boyfriend wants to buy me something *very* expensive."

Sure enough, the young man nodded vigorously and headed for Riccardo's office. Moments later, the owner joined me.

"I want Eva," I said. "Today. Call her in."

"You were in with Mr. Ferraro, yes?" Riccardo, in his white shirt with blue paint splatter at the hem today, placed a gentle hand to my back, the other ushering me further into the gallery. "Eva's not available, but I'll show you around my—"

I inched out of his grasp and stayed put. "I need to talk to her specifically. She made a recommendation I want to follow up on."

"I can't do that," said Riccardo. "If you'd—"

Of course he couldn't. I spun on my heel, waving a hand over my head. "I'm taking our money elsewhere."

Outside, my pace was even more rapid than on my way in. Heaven forbid something go right for me. Time to skulk back to the villa like I'd told Antonio I was doing in the first place.

He wouldn't have to know I'd failed again. The girl with the sore ankle who let the thief get away. Who almost got them stranded in a grotto.

No wonder he was looking for something more.

I stopped in my tracks, a giant of a man in a gray T-shirt who'd been walking too close collided with me, and I stumbled, a jolt of pain running up my left leg. He gripped my shoulders, steadying me, and asked in a deep English voice, "You okay?"

"Fine, fine." I waved him off without looking up. Instead of standing there, I detoured to the building next to me and leaned my back against the wall. Rubbing my hands over my face. Breathing.

What was I doing?

Who was I mad at?

Why was I lashing out?

I pulled my phone out. There *was* someone I could call. Someone who wouldn't judge me for going off half-cocked and, if nothing else, would cheer me up.

" SAM!" came Lucy's excited voice. "How's your trip? You never did answer: Can we go rock climbing this weekend? Although I guess I should ask first: When are you coming home?"

"Hi."

Lucy Chapman had worked with me at Foster Mutual for a month. But what a month it had been. I'd met Antonio, taken on the claim that proved to be an arson and murder case, and made up with my former best friend, Janelle. Lucy was a rock through all of it. Always by my side, my sarcasm and attitude rolling right off her.

My circle of friends was small intentionally. But she'd inserted herself without having to try.

"Your reception sounds so much better. I looked it up after we talked the other day, and Naples has really good coverage. But you said you were near Capri. Who did you go with for your provider while you're over there?"

"Lucy, I need some perspective."

She laughed so suddenly and so loud I had to pull the phone from my ear. "That is *not* why people call me."

A hint of a smile tugged at my lips. "You're the only one who was with me through the whole Chagall claim. I used to have reliable instincts, but I'm doubting myself now. I missed major clues, missed Antonio lying about the—"

"Wait, what?"

I'd shut her out from so much to protect her. At the end of her internship, she'd needed a recommendation to be guaranteed a position after she graduated. I'd made sure she got that just before the president of the company was arrested.

But it meant she didn't know about Antonio's lie or why we'd broken up originally. Let alone this time. If we were broken up. Were we? I hoped not.

"Antonio knew the Chagall was a fake the whole time."

"Seriously?" She sucked in a breath, sounding almost impressed. "That's why you decked him?"

"That wasn't me." I groaned, rubbing a hand over my face.

"What's bugging you?"

"A fresco was stolen from the place where Antonio's working. Then we found the guy who stole it, but he got away. I suspect someone who may have helped him, but need to confirm something they said."

"And how does this lead to you calling me?"

"I don't know." I scanned the faces of people walking by. Couples, individuals, families, friends. All with their own lives and concerns, oblivious to everything I was dealing with. "I went to talk to someone who might have answers but she's not at work."

Clicking noises, like tapping on a keyboard, came through the phone. Was she having a separate online conversation? Updating her blog? "Anyone interesting?"

"Just some artist."

"Want me to track her down?"

"Track her how?"

"Gimme her name." There was a popping noise, which, knowing Lucy, was a gum bubble.

"I thought you kicked the gum habit?"

She chuckled, "Around you, maybe."

"Eva Zabelle. She's an artist from Miami originally, normally lives in Rome, and she's staying in Naples for the short-term. She works at the Riccardo Emanuele Gallery here in town."

"I'm on it." The keyboard noises continued, just as rapidly as she always typed.

"Call me back?"

"Nah." Another bubble popped. "I saw this guy on TikTok explaining about how easy it was to find some people through their social media. Followed him over to a series he's done on YouTube—with willing participants—showing all the clues people drop with stuff they post where you can see their house, zoom in to see their street number, then— How long's she been in Naples?"

"Not sure. Maybe a couple of weeks?"

"Then this is her."

"Already?"

"Got her photo from the gallery website, which helped me confirm her profile on a photo-sharing app. A week and a half ago, she shared an outdoor photo with a hashtag *temporary home*, location data turned on. That put her in Naples. But it also included the sign at the front of the building behind her, so I have an address. She's holding the keys in front of herself, but her sunglasses are so reflective, you can totally make out that there's an etched number on the backside of one of the keys."

She texted me the address and I pushed off the wall, heading to the piazza to find a car.

"That's impressive, Lucy. When I get back, you'll have to show me some of those tricks. I imagine they'll come in handy."

"Absolutely! You feeling any better?"

I rounded a corner and nearly knocked into a petite woman in a too-tight black T-shirt. With a smile of apology, I was on my way. "A little bit. It's been a wild week and a half."

"Heart not weeping anymore?"

My sandal scuffed on the sidewalk, jarring my bad ankle. Since the day we'd met, Lucy's lack of social boundaries confounded me. Sometimes it was for the best, other times not. "I haven't quite figured that out yet."

"This Eva woman going to sort it out for you?"

"Hopefully."

Lucy navigated her way through three tangents and a story

about her last trip to Naples with her travel-blogging parents before I arrived at the piazza.

We said goodbye and I stopped before reaching the road. I had Eva's home address. Visiting would mean I'd have body language to work with and more control of the situation.

I probably would have gotten even better information if Antonio were with me. But how could I trust him? Or was he thinking he was protecting me, the way I kept things from Lucy to protect her?

But a burner phone hiding more family business? Carabiniere De Rosa implied Antonio was involved in the wall painting theft. Nathan had warned me Antonio's family might be connected. What did it all mean? And how much was he hiding from me?

Regardless, I had my decision. Surprise visit to Eva Zabelle —on my own—it was.

CHAPTER 34
ANTONIO

I TORE along the narrow pedestrian street, attempting to nudge, not shove, people out of my way. It was a risk. A calculated risk I couldn't afford to not take. Samantha had accepted my call from her cab, but not even one after that. Said she was going to the villa, but she was stubborn. Infuriating. Overconfident. Foolhardy.

Wouldn't let the investigation go. Taped up an injured ankle and insisted we wander around town. Tackled a purse snatcher with her crutch.

I dodged a large woman swinging a shopping bag. A child lagging behind his father. A gaggle of young women staring at some man across the street.

When Samantha had discovered my deception about the Chagall two and a half weeks ago, I'd given her space. She said she never wanted to see me again. But she didn't say that this time. Said *good* when I told her I loved her. I'd hold on to that until I found her and ensured she was safe.

She'd insisted on returning to the gallery. I'd distracted her for hours. But now?

Samantha was too angry with me to retire peacefully to the villa. Either she would be stomping around the streets in a rage or doing the one thing I told her she couldn't do. Going to the gallery.

And I knew that woman well enough to know her choice. If I was wrong, I would incur the wrath of whoever had joined me at our table the night before. But Samantha likely already had.

I rounded the last corner, came to a near-skidding halt at the front door to Riccardo Emanuele's and threw open the doors.

A polite young woman greeted me.

Before one syllable was out of her mouth, I ripped my phone from my pocket and pointed the lock screen at her, showing a photo of Samantha and me from the night before, a selfie with the volcano behind us.

"Have you seen my girlfriend?"

She took a step back, likely from my raised voice. "Are you sure you're in the right place?"

I clenched and released a fist, taking a deep breath so I was less confrontational. "Per favore. I think she may have come here."

The woman peered at the photo, but shook her head.

"Mr. Ferraro!" Riccardo appeared from the rear of the gallery, hands out in greeting. "I understand from your girlfriend you're looking to buy—"

"She was here?" I surely sounded crazed, but didn't care what he thought.

He looked from me to the woman who'd greeted me.

My hands flew out when he didn't respond. "When?"

"Fifteen minutes ago?"

"Where's Eva? Did they speak?"

"No." Riccardo fidgeted. "Your girlfriend came in asking to see Eva, but we haven't heard from Eva all day. We left her a message after your girlfriend left."

Samantha had only left the hotel ten minutes before I had, yet somehow had gained a further lead on me. I hurried out the door without another word to Riccardo, rushing to a cross-street where I'd find a taxi.

Where was I even going, though? Where would she go next? Back to the villa because Eva was not at work?

My stomach lurched. He hadn't said Eva was off or out sick, but rather he hadn't heard from her all day. What did that mean? Worse yet, what did it mean for Samantha and the threat against her life if she returned while Eva was not here? Did that mean she was safe?

I slowed enough to call Samantha with the same result. Niente. I texted Mario again, but he had no update. Texted her, asking where she was and if she was safe. Niente.

What other options did I have? Would she confide in Special Agent Skinner? Tell him about the threat from the man in the restaurant and her suspicions about Océane?

That was it. Océane's hotel, close to where Samantha and I stayed. Perhaps she chose a different confrontation.

I flagged a cab and hopped in providing our hotel's address. The driver pulled out too slowly until I urged him on with the promise of extra money. A lot of extra money. We had to catch up with her, or at least not lose more time.

The burner phone rang and I hauled it out, nearly dropping it to the floor in my haste to answer. "Cristian!"

"What happened?" His tone was serious, unlike our typical conversations.

"My girlfriend found the phone. She accused me of—" I dragged a hand through my hair, staring at my feet. It felt like that dinner at my parents' place all over again. The hurt in her eyes. "She ran off to the gallery after I told her about the man who threatened us at Vista dell'Ovo last night, exactly as I feared she would. Tell me you have news."

"I have a lead on the man who approached you and it's not good."

My heart came to an immediate and irreparable stop. "How not good?"

"If my sources are correct, he's American. Trained in a private camp with some sort of former special forces agents."

I gripped the seat in front of me. "Where can I find him?"

"It's not that simple, cugino. He's likely already following her, so finding her is your best option."

We sped by buildings and vehicles, past people wandering down the sidewalks. Happy, peaceful people floating through their ordinary lives. While I raced through a city of three million searching for one headstrong woman who didn't want to be found with a potential killer on her heels.

"Did she find her answers from the woman at the gallery?" Cristian's voice had softened, an almost unnatural sound coming from him.

"No, the owner said Eva was out." I exhaled a long breath. "They don't know where she is, either."

"How badly does your girlfriend want to talk to this woman? Is it possible she went to the woman's home?"

"Sì, possible." That made more sense than going to Océane's. But Samantha didn't know where to go. Riccardo wouldn't have told her where Eva lived. "But I got her phone number and email, not her address. Mario might be able to get it from the Pompeii office, but—"

"Give me the number. I can track her down faster."

I did as he asked and he became muffled, speaking with someone else on his end.

"How resourceful is your girlfriend?"

"Very, I expect." She trained at the FBI Academy, so perhaps she could hold her own for a short time against the behemoth who might be hunting her.

"And you're certain she's not working for the authorities?"

"This again?"

The driver came to an abrupt halt, so I had to brace my hand against the seat in front of me. My focus snapped up to see a construction crew had shut down one lane of the narrow two-lane road. Had Samantha hit this slowdown? Was she even headed in this direction?

"You know our business. I need to be sure."

If there'd been any doubt before our stroll along the Lungomare, our talk that day had cemented it for me. A portion of her soul remained dedicated to solving art crimes— evident from her handling of the Chagall claim, the stolen painting at the auction, and now our experience in Pompeii— but it was not part of her professional life. Although, did she want it as part of her future? "Trust me. She doesn't work for the authorities."

"Bene. Then we have an address."

I passed the details to the driver, despite being stuck in place, the road so narrow we couldn't get around the construction while the oncoming traffic crawled by. What I'd give at that moment for a wide Michigan highway with passing lanes and shoulders. "Grazie mille, Cristian. I don't know what I'll do if something happens to her."

"If I can help, I will."

I nodded and hung up, then called Eva. Perhaps Samantha was already there.

No answer.

The map on my phone told me Eva's place was closer than Océane's. Ten minutes by car, plus whatever extra time for construction. It also told me it was a forty-minute walk. I could run that in fifteen or less.

Throwing a wad of cash at the driver, I dashed out of the car and down the street. Praying the whole way that I was right and she'd be at Eva's. And safe.

CHAPTER 35

SAMANTHA

UMBERTO AND EVA'S apartment sat on the edge of a large piazza ringed by century-old buildings. Stores and restaurants dominated the main floors, plus a bank and a couple of hotels. Hawkers and street food vendors—talking to everyone and no one—competed for space with the tables and chairs spilling out from the restaurants. Graffiti decorated the walls anywhere the company owning the frontage didn't cover it.

Above the ground level, narrow metal balconies and portable air conditioning units dotted the buildings.

There must have been a train station nearby, as dozens of people wheeled small luggage bags behind themselves. Scattered through the crowd were members of the municipal police in summer dress; navy blue short-sleeved shirts and cargo pants, with white duty belts.

Their building served as a combination hotel and apartment, its double-doors almost swallowed by the patio umbrellas of the restaurants on either side.

I slipped through the door into the narrow lobby, head down, focused on my phone. In my periphery, I scanned the space. As long as I didn't draw attention to myself, it was unlikely anyone would stop me.

The front desk ran along the right side of the room with dim lamps and pigeon-holes on the back wall. One man in a black uniform clicked at a computer. He looked up, but meeting no request for information, returned to his business.

To the left, a small library with cushioned chairs.

I passed the end of the desk and an elevator when the sign for the stairs caught my attention. Thirty-eight was etched on Eva's key, so I made my way to the third floor.

The stairs led to the middle of a long gray hallway, the hotel obviously extending above the restaurants on either side of the lobby. Small photos hung at regular intervals along the wall and artful room numbers in large white script adorned the black doors. Everything was clean, no lights were out.

A tall, broad man with short hair and a black T-shirt stood at a door in the direction I was heading. But on the odd number side, facing the back of the building. Was he going in? Coming out? His hand rested on the door handle, not actually doing anything. He turned slowly toward me and his eyes narrowed, causing my pace to slow.

I looked down only long enough to dial 1-1-3 on my phone and settle my finger over the send button. But when I squared my shoulders and leveled him with my most confident glare, his face spread into a smile.

"Samantha?" He straightened, releasing the door.

Bodyguard number two from the yacht? The one who stood guard while the doctor worked on my ankle then flew Antonio and me to Sorrento? "Jason?"

"Yes." He spoke in English, not leaving the doorway. "This is a surprise."

My heart thumped in my chest, and my eyes flicked around the space. What would a bodyguard working on an international yacht moored in Capri be doing here? Was he coming in or out of that room, or was it a cover?

Oh, no. Was Antonio's story true? Had this guy threatened me at the restaurant and now was here to hurt me? No, Antonio would have recognized him last night.

"Surely you and Mr. Ferraro aren't staying here?" He glanced at my feet. "How's your ankle?"

I'd stopped one door away from Eva's, two away from him. If I turned and ran for the stairwell, he'd catch me. My ankle was up for a lot of activity, but not a race. "What are you doing here?"

"Visiting a friend." He gestured to the door.

"Who's your friend? We might be visiting the same person." I fished for information.

His smile faded. "I liked you better when you were in pain."

Words like that were designed to make you uncomfortable, make you want to acquiesce. Surprisingly, I'd dealt with so many emotional reactions as an insurance adjuster, I was nearly immune to them. "Not surprising."

The smile returned with a laugh. "I see why Dr. Ivan liked you. You're funny."

Funny wasn't what I was aiming for.

Jason pulled a card from his pocket and waved it for me before placing it in front of the door lock. It clicked, and he pushed down on the handle. "Close friend."

With a nod, he ducked into the room, and I was alone in the hallway again. Just me, the photos on the walls, and the hairs standing up on my neck.

I MUST HAVE STOOD FROZEN in the hallway for five minutes, waiting to see if Jason came right back out. If he did, would he be armed?

With every passing second, my gut yelled louder and louder that I should have listened to Antonio. Trusted him. Left my emotional baggage behind and let the man into my heart.

Deep breath, Sam. I canceled the call on my phone and rubbed a hand over my face. What was Jason doing there? Should I turn around and go back to the villa like I'd told Antonio?

Despite it all, my logical brain was still telling me to move forward to the next door. Talk to Eva. Find out more about Océane and any possible link between her and Umberto.

But what was Jason doing here?

If he was sent to hurt me, surely he would have done something already, likely before he'd gone into the room. He wouldn't have smiled and laughed while standing there. He would have done it while moving toward me.

My instincts never used to fail me, but since meeting Antonio, my entire world had tipped on its side. People lied and I didn't notice. I'd been schemed and manipulated too many times over the last month.

It was time to put an end to that. Take control again.

I marched up to Eva's door and knocked, casting a backward glance at the room Jason was in. No noise in that direction, but the sound of footsteps and a quiet voice inside Eva's. She creaked open the door, a phone plastered to her ear. She smiled politely and ushered me in.

"Sorry, I have to go." She took a half-step into the hallway, looking to the left and right, then snapped the door shut. "I have company. Talk to you later."

The apartment was small, its origin as a hotel room evident. Beyond the tight entryway with wall-mounted coat rack, there was a queen-sized bed with deep blue sheets against the left wall. In the narrow space between the foot of the bed and the opposite wall, a desk with a laptop and shelving above.

A four-foot square painting hung above the bed, a pastoral scene reminiscent of a John Constable.

Next to the bed, a small table, then kitchenette, then a door leading to a tiny bathroom.

The whole place could have fit inside the bedroom of our suite.

"Eva, I'm not sure if you remember me, but—"

"Samantha, right?" She swallowed hard and crossed to the fridge, pulled out two plastic bottles with sparkling water and held one up to me. "You and your boyfriend had concerns about Umberto."

I took the offered bottle but didn't open it. My plan hadn't included her letting me in so easily. The intention was to be professional, express my continued concern, provide some empathy. This was almost too easy. "Did you ever hear from him?"

She leaned against the sink and let out an ironic laugh. "I heard from the police, that's for sure."

"So you know what he did?"

"Yeah, I do." She nodded slowly, opening her bottle, the fizz hissing out. "Some jackass officer came by my office. Almost got me fired."

"Not Carabiniere Fredo De Rosa, by any chance?"

She pointed at me and nodded. "I imagine he grilled Dr. Ferraro, didn't he?"

"He did."

"The officer used to work in Rome. I guess there was some fuss about the Ferraro studio and a stolen painting after my time there." She took a sip. "He suggested my being tied to people at the sites of two thefts was incriminating."

That sounded like De Rosa. Even more suspicious than me. But what was that about a stolen painting at the Rome studio?

"Were you able to give him any information? Ideas on where Umberto might have gone or anyone who might have been working with him?"

"You know, moving here with him isn't turning out quite the way I planned." She stared at her bottle, fiddling with the label. There was more she wanted to say but seemed to be battling with herself. Should I wait and see if it came out or urge her forward with my own theories?

My phone buzzed in my pocket, the distinctive pattern I'd set for calls from Antonio. Then the buzz of a text from him. It was like the night of our fallout at his parents' house all over again. He'd called over and over that night and I declined every one. At least today, I'd answered the call from the cab. And then completely ignored his warning.

"Everything alright?" Eva asked.

"I talked to Océane Monet last night. She was—"

Her lips tightened. "Obsessed with my boyfriend?"

"She said you two went out for coffee one time?"

"Yes, and all she talked about was Umberto." She sighed, her shoulders falling. "Since the project in Pompeii was delayed, she suggested the three of us go to Rome. She wanted to see the sights and thought we'd be good tour guides since we live there."

Océane had told us she'd invited Eva. Told her to dump Umberto and go to Rome, just the two of them. Miscommunication or... one of them was lying.

Eva returned to picking at the label on her bottle. "I think they might have had something going on. I know we haven't been here long, but he brought me to a get-together with his new team and it was like Umberto and Océane already knew each other."

"Knew each other how?"

She shook her head and turned toward the sink, wiping at her cheeks. This was going in an unexpected direction and she was rapidly shutting down.

Back to step one I'd learned in my insurance job: Build rapport. Get your interviewee comfortable, then navigate to the harder questions. I pointed at the painting over the bed. "Did that come with the room, or did you do it?"

She swiped at her cheek again and turned to see what I was pointing at. "That's mine, actually. There was another one there when we moved in—a very quote-unquote *hotel* landscape. They put it into storage for us."

I opened my bottle, the cap cracking just as the carbonation escaped the top. There was a painting on the wall next to the patio door and a couple of small ones on the shelves. "These, too?"

"All mine. Um..." She crossed the room, squeezing between me and the bed, to angle one of the paintings on the shelf toward me. Books and knickknacks surrounded it. "I got a call from the gallery that you'd come in looking to talk to me. I figured it was probably about Umberto, but part of me was hoping your boyfriend was interested in one of my paintings."

The piece she moved was only a foot wide, eight inches high, sitting on a small easel stand. A conceptual landscape with meandering river and rich jewel tones with loose, easy brush strokes.

"This is beautiful." I reached for it, but she didn't let go. Odd.

"Thank you." She inclined her head toward another painting on the shelves, closer to me. It was just as stunning, but the fact that she continued to hold the other one inspired more interest.

A television turned on in the next apartment, its volume loud enough to highlight how thin the walls must be. An action movie, by the sounds of gunfire and explosions.

We both startled, laughing. In the process, she nudged the painting she'd been holding. Revealing a sliver of terracotta behind it. A rounded shape.

Like a little pot.

She wasn't highlighting the painting. She was hiding something.

Change the topic before she realizes, Sam. "Do your neighbors always listen to things so loud?"

"Always!" She rolled her eyes dramatically, adjusting the painting again and finally letting go of it. "But it was hard to find somewhere big enough for just four months in our price range."

I placed my water on the desk and pulled out my phone. "Can I take a picture of these two paintings? Antonio's been looking for a few smaller pieces to decorate his place while he's here."

She straightened, brows raising. "Really?"

"Absolutely." Not at all. I needed a photo of that pot to see if it was one of the ones removed from the Pompeii lab. And if it was, was she intentionally moving that painting to hide it from me? Because that would mean she knew what it was.

"Do you want me in the photo?"

"With the first one, yes, so I don't forget." I took one shot, then stepped back, knocking into the corner of the bed and falling onto it. "Tight fit in here."

"I imagine Dr. Ferraro lives in a huge villa outside the city, doesn't he?" She offered me a hand to help me up.

"Thanks." The fall had gotten me closer to the painting, at a better angle to photograph the terracotta pot. I followed it up with several pictures of the second painting. Despite my ulterior motives, her paintings were quite lovely.

"Can I see?" she asked.

I scrolled through to find the best one and zoomed in before flipping the phone for her. If she was hiding the pot intentionally, I couldn't let her see that most of the photos contained at least part of it. "This one's the best."

"You think he'll like it?"

"I'm sure he'll..." I placed a hand on my belly and grimaced. "Can I use your..." I pointed at the bathroom door and dashed in before she could respond. Not graceful, but it worked.

With the door closed, I zoomed in on the pigment pot, able to inspect the lump of pink inside it more closely. It was either an excellent reproduction or the real thing. Considering it was in the apartment of the fresco thief whose girlfriend was trying to conceal it from me, this had to be it.

Hands shaking, I texted Elliot, *Not sure how they missed*

this. Did no one search Umberto's place? Because his girlfriend was hiding it from me!

Then texted him the photo which highlighted the pigment pot, the one with Eva, and her address.

The three dots of a response started dancing right away, and his reply came through. *You there legally?*

I bit on my lip to control the chuckle. *Yes*

I'll call Bruno. We'll be there soon.

We didn't have the fresco—or from what I could see, both missing pigment pots—but this was something. An art crimes team's priority was recovery, not prosecution. We'd have one piece back and maybe Eva knew where the rest was.

Had there actually been any tears in her eyes? Or was she playing me the whole time?

My mouth slowly fell open. The way she'd played Océane. That coffee meeting was Eva's cover, not Océane's. Tell someone else how unhappy she was in the relationship so no one would think she was in on it if he got caught.

I flushed the toilet and ran the bidet, then the sink.

Should I text Antonio while the water ran? I wanted to share this victory with him, but what would he say? He'd probably just tell me to get out of there. The Carabinieri were on their way. I probably should cut my losses and go instead of risking her figuring things out.

The door to the apartment opened, and a man's excited voice began before it was closed. "I did it! The fresco's sold."

"Shh!" came the immediate response.

I froze, facing the inside of the bathroom door, water still running. Every inch of my body clenched, fending off the desire to do a cartwheel. Instead, I placed an ear to the door.

The man asked, "You don't want to hear—"

Eva's response was too quiet for me to make out anything other than "told you," and "in there."

It was Umberto. Had to be. Her sad girlfriend routine was all an act. From his tone, it was clear she knew about the sale.

The sale of the flowers fresco.

Oh, shit. He'd just sold it. Where? When? Did we have enough time to track down his buyer?

I texted Antonio and included the same photos I'd sent Elliot. He'd sent me a barrage of texts since I'd left him at the hotel. Part of me wanted to apologize, but what I really wanted to say was, *I knew it.*

As a concession, I followed it up with, *Umberto's here, he just sold the flowers. I'm going to find out where they are.*

The police were on their way. My only goal was to keep Umberto there until they arrived. Unless I could also find out who he'd sold the fresco to.

He wasn't getting away this time.

Water still running, I flung the door open and charged out. Dodged Eva—who let out a scream—and slammed Umberto into the wall. The worm crumpled and I fell to the floor on top of him between the desk and the bed, pulling one of his arms behind him and twisting it until he yelled.

"You budge and I snap this arm like a twig," I growled in his ear, then turned to Eva. "The police are on their way."

"I wasn't involved," she cried, throwing her hands up in surrender. "I'm innocent! It was all him!"

Umberto swiped a foot in Eva's direction. "She put me up to it!"

"Asshole!" She kicked at him but hit my bad ankle.

Pain seared up my leg and I bit back a wail. My grip on

Umberto faltered, but I leaned into it, bracing my good foot against the desk and my shoulder against the bed.

The front door burst open. The police had arrived. The day wasn't such a loss after all.

I swiveled to see a man coming through the doorway. Big, broad, gray T-shirt that was a size too small.

Recognition flashed through my brain. This wasn't the police. This was the man who collided with me on the sidewalk outside the gallery.

Fuck.

The threat.

It was real all along.

And it followed me to Eva's.

There wasn't enough time to release Umberto and get up before the man had a fistful of my hair, hauling me through the air. Both of my hands flew back to grab his wrist. I stumbled, trying not to put any more weight on my left ankle than necessary, but managed to lock my elbows in front of my head before he slammed me against the wall. Agony coursed up my arms, through my shoulders, and all down my torso. Dammit, he was strong.

Not letting go of my hair, he dragged me backward again. I sidestepped, pivoting my body to twist his arm. But my ankle gave out and I tripped, giving him the chance to hurl me to the floor.

The air flew out of me when the man's knee landed on the small of my back. Fire licked through my body, an agonizing blanket spreading out from where he pinned me.

My phone buzzed. Another call from Antonio. I should have listened to him. *I'm sorry, Antonio.* This was going to kill him. *Please let the police get here soon.*

The man dug into my pocket and pulled the phone out. He lifted my head and smashed it down onto the fl—

CHAPTER 36

ANTONIO

I INHALED ON THREE STEPS, exhaled on three, blisters already forming. Running in sockless oxfords was a horrible idea, but she was at Eva's. Fool woman. She'd found one of the pigment pots and sent me a photo.

I told you so, her text had said.

After those messages, I'd paused enough to call Special Agent Skinner, who informed me she'd texted him the same information. He and Gallo were coordinating officers to descend on the building. When he learned about the threat delivered last night, he cut me off with a simple, "We'll hurry."

I slowed to a jog, dialing her number again. The phone rang three times. She'd declined each of the others after one ring, so this was either an improvement or she was too busy to even reject my call.

But this time, she finally answered. An impossible weight lifted from my shoulders. My words came thick through heavy breaths. "Samantha! I was so—"

"I warned you." The deep voice on the other end of the

phone sent a shock wave through me, bringing me to a dead stop.

I blurted out, "Whatever you're being paid, I'll double it."

Silence.

"Triple it! I don't care, just don't hurt her!" I pressed a hand on the wall of the building next to me, scraping my fingers on the brick, trying to steady the rage. "Or I swear upon all that is holy, we will come for you."

"You'll never find us."

He clicked off and I ran. Faster than I'd ever run before.

I was not losing this woman again.

I'd been such a fool. If I'd told her about the threat right away, she would have been more likely to believe me. We could have talked about it. Made a plan. As much as she would have wanted to pursue the investigation, I could've convinced her to call Skinner and at least get his opinion. Go with him.

Marone, *I* could have gone with her if she persisted in investigating. She wouldn't be alone with those criminals.

Samantha Caine was strong and capable, but I treated her like a fragile doll. A woman like that needed a partner, not a boss or a manager.

That was it. Everything.

After she ran *to* me, I acted like I was in charge.

The piazza came into view minutes later, and I checked the map on my phone. Eva's building was on the opposite side and I dashed through the center, past a fountain, sending tourists, children, and angry pigeons scattering. The hotel was straight ahead, surrounded by a throng of people, talking and pointing.

My stomach clenched.

Something had already happened. Was I too late?

I tore through the crowd, ordering people out of the way as I went instead of apologizing.

An officer guarding the front door was distracted with answering questions, so I slipped past him and ran inside. The man at the front desk snapped his attention to me, eyes wide.

"Are the police upstairs?" I demanded.

He continued staring, most likely in some level of shock, and nodded once.

I slammed a fist on the desk and ran past him. Past a library and an elevator. When I finally hit the stairs, I took them two at a time.

The police were there. That was something. But was Samantha safe? Was she alright?

Was she even alive?

Hand on the railing to maintain as much speed as possible, I rounded the landing midway between the second and third floors, colliding into a man huddled on the stairs. I careened into the wall, clutching onto him for balance.

I didn't have time for this.

But as I pushed off him, I grabbed him again, spinning him up to slam him against the wall. My forearm at his throat. "You!"

Umberto's eyes grew wide. He clawed at my arm until my fist connected with his midsection. His face contorted and he wheezed, "Help me."

"Where is Samantha?"

"Room thirty-eight."

I hauled him off the wall and wrapped a fist in his shirt. "Did your man hurt her?"

"She's okay."

Baring my teeth, I closed in on him. "If you're lying, I swear to you—"

"I'm serious." His eyes flicked from side to side, and he whimpered, "The other guy got there and he…"

I continued up the stairs, dragging Umberto each step. She wanted to catch the thief. Even put her life on the line for it. And she would have him.

He pulled at my hand, beat at my arm, but he was no match for my strength and adrenaline. "Eva made me do it!"

"You stole the fresco." Two more steps to the top. "And you're not getting away with it."

"I was liberating it, not stealing." He tripped over the last step, falling to his knees.

Tightening my grip, I heaved on his upper arm until he was standing again.

"The government puts it all on display for people who don't appreciate it. Like those kids. It belongs in the hands of someone who recognizes its significance."

I pulled open the door and shoved him through, knocking him against the far wall.

"Your master's thesis talked about the effects of the weather and how Pompeii is fighting a losing battle. We should do what the museums do. Put the best pieces into controlled spaces so they'll be safe," Umberto pleaded with me.

I grabbed his shirt with both hands and pushed him in front of me. "And for that, my girlfriend's life is at stake?"

"I told you! That was Eva's idea." His head craned around to see the activity behind us, the blue-shirted polizia coming in and out of a room down the hallway. He stumbled, landing on his knees again. "Please, just let me go."

Leaning down, I grabbed him and threw him over my shoulder, rushing the rest of the way.

"No!" He beat at my back, flailed his legs, but I wouldn't let Samantha down. Her fugitive would go to prison.

A female officer with long blond hair hollered at me to stop, but I continued to her, close enough to see the activity was in room thirty-eight.

I looked over her shoulder, hoping to spot Samantha or an officer I recognized. "My girlfriend was in there. I'm afraid they hurt her. Can I—"

"One, unless you're a resident of one of these rooms, I can't let you pass." She rested her hands on her duty belt. "And two, you need to put the man down."

"Fine." I dropped Umberto at her feet, and he yelped. "He must have gotten out of there before you showed up. He's involved in all of this mess."

Umberto crawled to the wall, but knew better than to attempt an escape.

The officer eyed me. "You want to tell me again why—"

Carabiniere Gallo came out of the room and waved to me. "Let Dr. Ferraro by."

I hurried to meet him, feeling as though I couldn't move fast enough. All the same, not wanting to see what would be in room thirty-eight. "Is she alright?"

He stopped me before I reached the door. "We have ambulances en route, but she won't be the first one to go."

"What do you mean?"

Special Agent Skinner joined us, casting a glance at Gallo. "Sam has a head injury. It looks bad, but she'll likely be fine."

"Likely?" I barely resisted shoving them both aside. "Can I see her?"

Elliot nodded and waved me into the small apartment.

Everything was a haze except for her, sitting on the floor by the door, leaned against the wall by a desk. A female officer sat next to her, chatting quietly.

Samantha held a small cloth to her forehead, her eyes closed.

The space was so miniscule, there was barely room to kneel in front of her. "Bella?"

Her eyes fluttered open and she grimaced. "They wanted me to stay lying on the floor where they found me, but I was like, I've had head injuries before. My neck's fine. I wanna sit up."

I spluttered a laugh, reaching for her cheek, but unsure where to touch. "So Samantha."

"That guy, though..." She gestured with the washcloth to the space next to the bed behind me. A gash at her hairline sprouted fresh blood, and the officer eased the washcloth back. "Not so much."

"Oddio, your head..."

Her left leg was stretched out, propped on a pillow.

"And your ankle?"

She gestured with the washcloth again, and I ripped my eyes from her. Finally seeing the room around us. The blood splatter on the wall. The stain on the floor at the foot of the bed. Eva in handcuffs, crying next to a hulk of a man lying face-up by a kitchenette.

He looked asleep. Unconscious? An officer sat next to them, bracing rolled up towels beside his head. The giant's arm lay at an unnatural angle.

"Just to confirm, Antonio..." Samantha's voice shook.

The female officer stood so I could take her spot on the floor beside Samantha.

"Is that the guy from the restaurant last night?"

"It's hard to tell. His face is..." I took hold of the washcloth against her head. "Did you do that to him?"

She slid her now-free hand onto my lap and, with a groan, shifted position so she was leaning against me. "He knocked me out. I came to when the police arrived and he was like that."

I placed a hand over hers, wanting to squeeze it. Wanting to pick her up in my arms and take her far away from the chaos. From the three officers milling about the room, the others outside, and all the noise.

"I should have listened to you," she whispered.

"No, bella." I brought her hand to my heart and kept my voice down, finding whatever privacy we could in the crowded room. "Honesty and trust. If I'd been honest about him from the beginning, trusted that you would discuss it with me, none of this would have happened."

"Your heart's beating so fast." Her arm was heavy and speech slow, as though she were near sleep.

"When I heard his voice on the phone..." The words lodged in my throat. In the moment, the rage had pushed aside my panic. I'd felt an overwhelming need to get to her and protect her. I pulled the hand to my lips, avoiding the blood on her knuckles.

"I'm so sorry, Antonio."

"You're amazing, Samantha." And so fortunate for whatever happened to the man. "You caught them."

She blew out a long breath, wincing as she did. "Umberto got away again."

"I found him in the stairwell and literally dropped him at an officer's feet."

She laughed quietly and it cut off into a groan of pain. "Guess I can go home now that the mystery's solved."

I chuckled at her weak attempt at a joke. "Hopefully it was just the three of them and they weren't part of a larger organization."

"Umberto said it was all Eva's idea..." She inched closer, laying her head more heavily on my shoulder. "But she said the same thing about him, so who knows?"

"I have someone checking into it." A complete honesty I couldn't share with her just yet, no matter how close we were becoming. There were still secrets we needed to keep a while longer.

"The burner guy?"

"Sì, the burner guy." I tensed, running my fingers over her injured hand, maintaining the cloth on her forehead.

But she didn't ask any further questions, frown, or sigh. Not a single sign she didn't trust me, which probably took every shred of energy she had.

"I love you, bella."

"Good," she said with a shaky breath. "I was really afraid I screwed that up."

I pressed my lips to the side of her head, gently, in case there were injuries I couldn't see. "You'll have to work a lot harder than that to push me away."

"I'm a lucky girl."

"Sì, very lucky."

Her shoulders shook and she sucked in a breath. "No more jokes, Ferraro. They hurt my head."

There was a hint of laughter in her voice, but she needed a doctor and some rest.

"Shh." I peeked under the washcloth, but the blood sprouted again. Which blood was hers? The wall? The floor? The bed? Somewhere unseen?

The man on the floor should have been thanking his lucky stars for whatever knocked him out. Because I would have done far worse if I'd arrived when he was hurting Samantha.

I KISSED Samantha's hand one last time before they loaded her stretcher into the ambulance. "I'll see you at the hospital as soon as they let me."

"Thanks," she whispered and lay back, closing her eyes. She looked so tired.

They closed the back doors and the engines started up. I stepped away from the vehicle, finally letting out a breath. The EMTs said the wound on her forehead would need stitches but would heal just fine. She joked it would make a great scar to add to her collection.

The primary concern would be a concussion since she lost consciousness when the thug smashed her head against the floor.

He—the muscle, whoever he was—was in far worse condition. A broken arm, three broken ribs, and a potential neck injury. Broken nose, broken orbital bone. Good. All of it.

The ambulance drove slowly through the pedestrian area, police clearing the way.

"She'll be alright?" came a voice next to me.

I startled, turning to see Pasquale's helicopter pilot. The

bodyguard who'd followed Samantha while we were on the yacht. What was he doing here?

"They expect she will."

His aviator sunglasses hid his eyes, but a cut at the top of one cheek was visible. Fresh. Also a scrape along his jaw.

"Did you—"

He held up a hand, then slung his messenger bag across his chest. "I'm not sure how much I'm supposed to tell you but based on the favors you were able to call in over this, I expect quite a bit. You understand my words go no further than this moment?"

I nodded slowly. "Sì."

"The man who came after your girlfriend is Eva's brother." He tilted his head toward me and raised a hand to cover his mouth. "Fiori wanted the flower fresco and one yellow pigment pot."

I sucked in a breath. Samantha was right about the connection between the yellow flowers and Fiori's *Five Sunflowers* yacht.

"We had some dealings with Eva in Rome earlier this year—"

The stolen painting at Uncle Andrea's studio?

"—so when we heard her boyfriend was working with you, we reached out. But Umberto got greedy. Took three pots but we only accepted two of them. The blue one ended up in the Carabinieri TPC's hands in Rome, along with our courier. The pink pigment is in their apartment." He tightened his grip on his messenger bag's strap, moving it slightly in my direction. "The fresco and the yellow pigment won't be seen again except in Fiori's private collection. If you value your girlfriend's life the way I think you do, you won't pursue it."

"I understand." But I didn't like it, knowing that I couldn't share any of this with Samantha. The secrets between us were supposed to be decreasing, but this was not up for discussion.

"Tell your cousin I won't be in touch for at least two months after this. It's brought too much attention to me." He flicked the hand away from his mouth like a wave and strolled off through the piazza before I could get in another word, disappearing into the crowd as much as a six-foot-three muscle-bound man could.

Samantha's savior was Cristian's employee? Working on Pasquale's yacht? Was Fiori in business with my Uncle Giovanni? Or was this some sort of undercover role? He provided answers, but so many more questions.

Was he right about Umberto and Eva—and her brother?—contracting for Pasquale Fiori? Was this the threat to my family Cristian had spoken of?

My head hurt. Feet hurt. And my heart ached.

I made my way to the nearest street and found a cab to take me to the hospital. Samantha would be fine. They would stitch her forehead, likely order her to use crutches again, and I'd watch her for the night to be sure there were no signs of further injury.

And we would have at least one morning together without the mystery of the missing fresco and pigment pots hanging over our heads.

CHAPTER 37
ANTONIO

THE NEXT DAY, I carried Samantha up the stairs at Mario's villa, careful of her head and ankle. The elevator would have been easier, but it was not wide enough to be certain I wouldn't jostle her against either side.

"I can walk," she huffed, as though it were some great hardship. "I was walking yesterday."

"And then someone nearly killed you." We crested the third floor and continued to my room. "I saw you wavering when you stood up at the hospital. You're not winning this battle today."

They'd kept her overnight for observation because of the head injury and I slept in the chair next to her. Mario had brought us clean clothes—white T-shirt with navy shorts for her, pink striped shirt with black pants for me.

And today, she was not leaving my sight.

"I have to pack. My flight leaves in a few hours."

I nudged the door open with a foot and brushed my back against the frame to ensure she had the bulk of the space. "You're leaving tomorrow. We'll call the airline."

"I have to get home for Cass's chemo. This isn't up for debate."

Once I'd set her down on the bed, she twisted as though to get onto her hands and knees and crawl off.

"Samantha, stop right there."

"I'm serious."

I sat on the edge of the bed, putting out a hand to stop her. "When's her treatment?"

She rolled her eyes and sat back. "You know exactly when it is. Friday morning at ten."

"That's two days away."

"I need buffer time in case I miss a connection or something."

I pulled out my phone and selected a contact. "My travel agent will handle everything. Trust me, if anything goes wrong with your flights, she'll have you taken care of. If you're flexible enough—" I cocked an eyebrow, which was met with a feigned scowl. "She can work miracles. And besides, the stitches on your forehead and bandaged ankle will get you sympathy and help from everyone at the airport."

She lay back on the pillow, staring at the ceiling while I spoke with the agent, and gestured vaguely to her backpack when I asked for her flight details. It was a testament to her injuries that she didn't argue further.

A knock came at the door as I hung up, and I crossed the room to let Mario in. He carried a tray with cappuccino and laden with cornetti. "How's the patient feeling?"

"Like a prisoner." She pouted, but gave him a private smile when she thought I was not paying attention. "He canceled my flight home."

"It's being changed, not canceled," I said.

Mario sat on the side of the bed, placing the tray next to her. He was uncharacteristically serious. "That's the smart plan. We were worried about you yesterday."

She eased up and grabbed a cup. "Yeah."

"And don't tell anyone I made you cappuccino at noon." He patted her knee and stood, heading for the door. "I'd be thrown out of the country."

I finished with a few additional texts with my agent and sat back down next to Samantha. "A service will pick you up at the airport in Lansing and—"

"My motorcycle's at the airport in Detroit. I'm good."

"Seriously?" I looked pointedly along the leg she had stretched out in front of her. "I know you're a risk taker, but that's too much."

She dropped her cup onto the tray, some of it spilling over the edge. Angry with me. But no, she leaned back slowly and closed her eyes, clasping her hands over her stomach. "You're right. Every time I move too fast, I get the spins."

I crawled the few feet across the bed and lay down next to her, wrapping an arm around her waist. "If it continues tomorrow—"

"I really can't stay another day."

"—then I'll fly back with you and be sure you're alright."

The eyes fluttered open and she rolled her head slowly toward me. "You can't leave your project."

"Bella..." I kissed her cheek. "If you were shipping a priceless piece of art across the ocean, who would you entrust it to?"

Her eyes narrowed, but quickly released, no doubt pulling at the stitches on her forehead. They would cause a stir once she got home, not to mention the bruises covering her arms and legs. She attempted to brush the gash off, but it was nothing more than stubbornness.

"Exactly," I said. "You would entrust it to no one but yourself. And I would do the same—"

"Don't compare me to a piece of art."

"Shall I instead compare thee to a—"

One hand flipped up to smack me gently. "Don't go there, Ferraro."

"Thou art more lovely and yet significantly less temperate than a summer's day."

She closed her eyes and chuckled, then grimaced.

"Head hurts?"

"Only when I laugh."

"Mi dispiace, amore." I interlaced my fingers with hers and held them tight to me.

"Never apologize for that." She squeezed my hand. "It's one of my favorite things about you."

"One of? So there are more?"

She chuckled once and sucked in a breath, bringing her free hand to her head by the stitches.

My heart ached each time she made that face. I needed to be more serious. "Do you want to nap?"

"No. Since you're forcing me to stay another day—" She smirked and flicked her eyes toward me, then back up to the ceiling. "I think I'd like to spend the day talking."

"About what?"

"Everything. Do you remember living in Brenton when you were little? What was it like growing up in Rome? Who was your best friend in fifth grade? Favorite holiday memory?"

"So literally everything?"

She removed her fingers from my grasp and rolled onto her

side facing me, tucking one arm under her pillow. Her left leg, injured ankle and all, rose to rest on my hip. She was still for a moment, eyes crinkled, mouth pursed. Likely fighting through a wave of nausea or pain. "Maybe it's not *just* when I move fast."

"Believe it or not..." I ran my fingers along her arm, unsure what else to do but what I did best. Talk. "I would say Mario was my best friend in grade five. There was also a boy who lived close to us named... allora... I can't remember his name. But he moved to Roma from Berlin that year and he taught me my first German."

Her eyes remained closed. "You speak German?"

"Sì, not as proficiently as English, of course, but well enough."

"This is going to take a long time, isn't it?"

"What is?"

"Getting to know each other."

"We have all the time in the world." My hand skimmed along her side, down her narrow waist and hips, along the strong thigh. "Is there anything else big you have yet to tell me?"

"Like that I was in the FBI?" Her eyes finally opened again, those beautiful pale green eyes.

"More along the lines of you not liking flowers. What woman doesn't like flowers?"

She stilled, breathing deeply through her nose.

"Scusami. No jokes."

"They're beautiful, but they die too fast."

I brought my hand up to brush her cheek. "And you prefer things that last?"

"Experiences over things."

"I love this idea." I leaned in to kiss her nose. "The last ten days have certainly been an experience."

"No kidding." She rolled onto her back again, groaning quietly.

"You need a nap."

"I think so."

I moved the tray to my desk, pulled back the covers and picked her up, placing her on the sheets.

"I can do this myself," she said while stifling a yawn.

"Let me help." I undid the buttons at her waist and eased down her shorts and underwear, kissing her abdomen before stripping them off. "You'll be more comfortable like this and I'll feel like I've accomplished something."

She didn't argue when I pulled her shirt and bra off, nor when I kissed her neck as I did.

Once she was fully naked and tucked in, I locked the door, removed my own clothes, and snuck into the bed behind her. I pushed one arm under her head and wrapped the other tight around her waist.

Lips pressed against the back of her head, I whispered, "Mario was right, you know. We were very worried about you."

Her hand stroked along the length of my arm at her waist, finding my hand and interlacing our fingers. "I know."

"I don't know what I'd do if—" A lump lodged in my throat and I pulled her closer.

A shiver wracked her.

I shot up enough to look down on her face without letting go. "Are you cold?"

Her face was tight, chin trembling. "I was so scared, Antonio."

"It's alright." I lay back down and tightened my grip. "You're safe."

"I really thought I was going to die." She clenched her fingers around mine. "And for what?"

"For your life's passion."

She sucked in breaths through her nose and blew them out slowly, the shake easing until only her voice trembled. "All they recovered yesterday at Eva and Umberto's apartment was one pigment pot."

What was I to do? Jason was clear that telling her the truth —that he'd saved her life *and* taken the fresco—was out of the question. No reassurances would fix this. I was so tired of secrets. "Umberto, Eva, and her brother are in custo—"

"Brother?" Her muscles finally relaxed. "No one told me that."

That was a careless slip. "I overheard one of the polizia talking about it."

"Of course. And you're right. They're in custody." She let out a long yawn. "That's something, at least."

"More importantly, you're alright." I pressed my lips to the back of her head. "And you're here with me."

"I think I need that nap now. Would you... um..."

I kissed her again. "Anything."

"Would you stay here with me? It feels... I mean, I..." She sniffled and wrapped my arm tighter around her. "Just don't leave me. Please."

That she would ask that—show a shred of vulnerability— meant the world to me. And likely to her.

"I would stay until the end of time, if you asked me, bella."

CHAPTER 38
SAMANTHA

A LIGHT PRESSURE on the top of my head. The sound of a kiss. A salty sea breeze brushing my bare shoulder. Warm, taunt skin—Antonio's chest—under my cheek.

"Time to wake up, bella."

I felt the words under me as strongly as I heard them. "Mm-mmm."

He chuckled, bouncing me slightly. "How's your head?"

"All better." I extended an arm around him and tightened my grip. "Let's stay here all day."

"Three days in a row in bed?"

"You're habit forming." I nestled closer.

"You'll miss your flight if we do that." He traced his fingertips along my arm.

"I don't wanna leave." As much as I'd protested delaying my flight a day, it had been a wise decision. I'd barely been able to sit up until last night, let alone trek through airports. And spending a quiet day wrapped in Antonio's arms had been magnificent.

He kissed my head again and squeezed back. "I don't want

you to leave, either, but you have to get back to Cassandra. And your work would likely want you to return eventually."

"I hate my job." Not entirely true. I was good at investigating insurance claims, which brought me some pleasure, but unless I was working on a fraud or art case, it was just a way to pass the time.

"Then quit."

I laughed and lifted my head to look at him. The sun was up, but hadn't reached his corner of the villa yet, so the golden flecks in his eyes weren't on full display. My time in Naples had seen some success on the art crime side, but not enough to leverage the FBI to let me work from Brenton. "Hardly. And live on what?"

"I have more than enough money for both of us." He brushed back the hair which fell over my face.

I crawled on top of him, his naked body warm where I'd been in contact with him all night and rested my chin on his chest.

He sighed deeply, scanning my face, eyes lingering on the stitches at my hairline longer than they should have. I'd never had a man try to protect me like that before. Not a single boyfriend or my ex-husband would have run into a potentially deadly situation like Antonio attempted. He didn't make me soft and weak. He made me safe.

All the same, who'd gotten there first? Who really saved my life?

"We have two hours until we must leave for the airport." He leaned up to me and I met him. We kissed slowly, tenderly, and I moved my hips from side to side, eliciting a small moan from him.

He lay back on the pillow, running his fingers through my hair. "Did you see enough of Napoli, bella?"

"Yeah."

"And of Pompeii?"

"Yeah."

"Anything else you want to see this morning?"

My heart grew at his soft smile. "Just you."

"So, what comes next, amore?"

"I go home and we move on with our lives?" I tried to be playful, to look serious, but from his grin, it was clear I'd failed.

"You've been spending too much time with someone who tells bad jokes."

My body shook with a laugh. "Alright, then how about video chats every weekend?"

He feigned offence. "Only on the weekends?"

I smacked his chest. "Six-hour time difference!"

"Fair enough. Texts every day?"

"That I can do." I kissed the spot on his chest, moving down a few inches so I could feel him hardening underneath me.

He latched his hands under my arms and pulled me back to where I'd been. "You promise not to move away from Brenton while I'm gone?"

I froze. How could he ask that? It was a major reason I was staying in Brenton. Every time I chose him over the investigation... of course he was asking the question. I'd chosen the fresco over him too many times.

"I want you, Samantha. Only you."

What was the truth? That giving up so much of my lifestyle to be with him still scared me? That the prospect of losing him scared me even more?

"You said something at the hotel yesterday. It was in anger, but between that and what you said at the nightclub, I suspect there's truth behind it. You said I'm just like all Italian men." He caught my hand when it moved toward my face, to rub, to put a barrier between us, to think. "Matthew's not the only one who hurt you, is he?"

My eyes and jaw clamped shut. This was why I didn't talk about things. Because talking about one thing turned into another and another and eventually you were sharing everything. Of course, that was also the point of this visit, wasn't it?

His thumbs brushed my cheeks, and he waited. He was so good at that.

"Yeah, there was someone else." I opened my eyes and stared at the spot on his chest I'd kissed. "The summer I studied in Amelia."

"So, you *did* learn Italian customs from a man?" He winked, breaking my tension. That was one of the earliest things he'd teased me about during our first meeting. When I'd been so shy around him, I blushed every time I looked at him. Palms sweating, words twisting on my tongue. Barely a month ago.

I couldn't help but smile. We'd come so far in such a short time. "You don't actually want to hear this."

He slid his hands back from my cheeks to hold the sides of my head. Forcing me to nod.

"Alright. It was a guy in the art crimes program. His name was Vincenzo and he was local, planning to join the TPC. But we met and..." I pivoted my face so one cheek was in his palm, and my lips moved against his skin. "He said he wanted to move to the States to be with me."

"But he didn't, I assume?"

I shook my head and kissed his hand. "One delay after another until it was just..." One shoulder barely shrugged, trying to tamp down the memory of walking into Vin's apartment, seeing nothing was packed. "Over."

Antonio wouldn't do that to me. There was more to us than there was with me and Vincenzo. Vin was always up for everything, never argued with me, never told me I was wrong. Just went along for the ride, promising the world, but not backing it up with anything.

"Look at me, bella."

A pricking started at the backs of my eyes. I loved it when he called me 'bella.' I'd never tire of that. It was special. Just for me.

"And so here we find ourselves," he said. "On opposite sides of the same coin."

"What?" One tear escaped my eye.

He brushed it aside and whispered, "You, heading back to the States to wait for your man to come home from Italia. And me, here, waiting to go home to my woman. And both hoping the result will be different from the last time."

My jaw clenched and I gave a tiny nod. How did he understand me so well?

"It will be different, I swear."

"I hope so."

"Which brings us to..." He craned his neck toward his bedside table, which was out of his reach.

Taking the hint, I slid off him so he could retrieve something from a drawer. I pulled the sheet over myself—naked was easier when it was against him, rather than on full display —and propped my head up on a hand.

He rolled back over to face me, the rare nervous smile making an appearance.

My stomach dropped and I clenched the sheets tighter to my chest.

Oh my god.

In his hand, a small white jewelry box.

CHAPTER 39

ANTONIO

MY HEART BEAT HARDER in my chest, my stomach churning. The way to Samantha's heart was to push her gently forward. But she never said she loved me in response to my declarations. Was this a push too far?

Her body tensed with silent panic. I knew she loved me, deep inside, but her scars held more sway than she would admit. All the same, I needed a commitment from her. And I wanted to give her a symbol of mine. Once I had creaked the box open, her face relaxed, confusion replacing terror.

"What's that?"

Inside the jewelry box was a thick black ceramic men's ring. Next to it, a smaller trinity ring of three bands; black ceramic, white gold, and more white gold encasing a channel of diamonds.

"I only ask for a promise that you wait and not make any big decisions without me. That you'll remain in Brenton until I get home. And not date other men." My throat tightened. The last was the hardest request, the most important. After seeing her with Nathan Miller, with Thomas, and the men at the club... I shouldn't have to put it into words, but I did anyway.

"I don't need a ring for that. Saying it out loud is enough."

"Your words at the club, after Umberto got away from us, at the hotel." I took the men's ring out and placed it in her palm. "They didn't escape me. You still don't think you're enough, but you are. And this ring will show every person I meet that there's someone in my life who's more important to me than everyone else."

I held out my left hand, fingers first. When she didn't budge, I inclined my head toward her palm.

"You're serious about this?" Her gaze remained fixed on the trinity ring in the box.

"I've been accused of being a hopeless romantic. Perhaps you've noticed?"

"That's an understatement."

I tapped her nose to bring her attention back to me. "Most of all, Samantha, this ring will be a reminder of you. No matter where I am, I can see it and remember us in this moment."

"That other ring's way too expensive. I can't accept that."

The diamonds sparkled as I swiveled the box. I held my smirk down as much as I could, having expected her to say this, and already having a response planned. "Consider it a loan. I promise when I tire of you, I'll take it back."

She rolled her eyes and shook her head. "Couldn't get through a single serious moment without a bad joke, could you?"

"That's usually your role, bella."

"Fine." She slid the ring indelicately onto my fourth finger, chuckling at me. Someday, she would replace it with a wedding band. That was my unspoken promise, one which was better not shared with her yet.

I withdrew the other ring from the box and arched an eyebrow when her hand balled into a fist around the sheets again.

"Is this what you snuck off for in Capri?"

"Sì, it is."

"And when you were playing around in the jewelry store, having me try on all those fashion rings I swore I didn't want?"

"The jeweler was determining your ring size."

"So, this isn't about the club or any of those other things." She chewed on her bottom lip, eyes flicking down to the ring and back up to me several times. Then to the ring on my left hand. "You bought these rings before all that."

"You don't have to accept this if you don't want to."

She let go of the sheet, but her hand bypassed the ring and rested against my cheek to urge me forward. She kissed me tenderly, like our kisses on the sun beds in Capri. The kiss to show she loved me.

As we broke apart, her hand remained on my face. "I meant everything I said when I got here. I want you and only you. I want to make this work, and I'm willing to do some scary shit to make it happen. Flying here, opening up, deciding to stay in Brenton…" She released my cheek and flopped onto her back with a loud sigh.

"Bella, tell me. What's the matter?"

She stared at the ceiling, then the balcony doors and the curtains billowing in the salty breeze. "Cass is the only one I talk to about important things. And even still, she pretty much has to lead both ends of the conversation. I'm more comfortable on my own."

"Do you truly want to be alone?"

"No." She squeezed her eyes shut, dragging her hands across her face. Her jaw flexed, mouth opening and closing. There were words she wanted to say and they would be significant. And I would wait for every word. "I'm still afraid you'll wake up one day and realize you made a mistake choosing me."

I directed her face to mine and looked her square in the eyes. "Stop pushing me away. Stop running."

"And..." She let out a long breath. "Don't ever lie to me again."

It was a gut punch. Saying it out loud meant my lie about the Chagall was still closer to the front of her mind than I'd thought. This must have been where many of her doubts came from. And all I did by hiding the threat against her was remind her of it, not protect us against it.

No matter how blissful the visit had been, I had much more work to do to regain her trust. "It takes time to learn a person's life."

"Maybe your life, but mine's been pretty boring."

I laughed and pulled her to me. "This from the woman who was in the FBI, has climbed El Capitan more than once, and has jumped out of how many airplanes?"

"I guess it's just as well we have four months of video calls and texts ahead of us."

She smiled, and our lips met. We kissed, slowly, the love pouring from me to her and back again. I lent her all the courage and faith I could muster. When we separated, she held up a shaking hand, and I slid the ring onto her finger.

"Samantha Caine, I promise I will continue to love you,

admire you, be faithful to you, and be proud that you are the woman in my life. And I promise honesty."

"And I promise..." Her voice trembled as much as her hand, her eyes glistening in the early sunlight. "I promise to earn all that, Antonio Ferraro. To wait for you. To talk to you as often as possible and share all the minor details of our lives. And to do my best to stop running."

"Another good choice." Before the emotions overwhelmed her, I lightened the mood and pulled her on top of me. "That was not so hard, was it?"

She chuckled, sitting up. "Not very hard at all." She grinned, inching her hips backward to re-awaken my lower half.

"Do you like the ring?"

She held it up in front of herself, grimacing slightly. "It's gorgeous."

"But simple enough to be Samantha Caine's ring?"

Tight-lipped, she continued staring at it, at me, and back again. Something churned in her brain, but this time, her thoughts were not coming out.

"Enough." Grabbing her by the ribcage, I rolled her to the bed next to me, careful of her injuries, and we tangled in the light sheets. I leaned down to plant a peck on her nose.

Her mischievous grin was the only warning she gave before wedging her good leg under me and using it to shove me off her. She gracefully followed the movement, so she was straddling me once more.

"Be careful! You'll hurt yourself!"

She rubbed her hands across my stomach, saying, "I'm fine."

Always *fine* with this woman. "We only have two hours

left, bella, and you still must pack. Come down here and kiss me."

She didn't move, just stared at me. Her firm breasts heaved with a deep sigh. "Thanks for not giving up on me, Antonio. Right from day one."

"I told you already. I'm stubborn." Taking her hands, I kissed them both, then kissed her ring. "Almost as stubborn as you."

She squeezed me hard with her remarkably strong thighs.

"Ow!" I winked as she let go. "Alright, I'm nowhere near as stubborn as you!"

She squeezed again, but I pulled her forward onto me, my flesh aching for hers. Our mouths met and we kissed, long and slow, savoring our last morning together.

Samantha was my anchor. My miracle. It had taken us eleven years to find each other, but after less than six weeks, she was already my whole heart. My project in Napoli would pass in the blink of an eye. Then I would come home to her.

To the love I'd finally found.

To the woman I was meant to be with.

EPILOGUE
ANTONIO

I smoothed my black suit jacket and tie, inspecting myself in the video preview on my laptop. Perfetto. Three minutes until midnight. A small plate of lamb and roasted vegetables sat between the computer and me. It was a late meal, even by Italian standards, but it was date night. I'd turned off all the lights, other than the one on the bedside table. It was dark, but just bright enough I could be seen.

The screen flickered, and Samantha appeared. I placed a hand on my chest to hold my heart in, it leaped so hard against my rib cage.

She was breathtaking, wearing the ice blue silk dress from the gala in August. Her hair was down in loose cascades, the way I liked it best. And she wore make-up, although not so much that it hid the scar at her hairline.

"Hey, handsome." She smiled broadly, resting her face on her left hand, the diamonds on her ring sparkling. "You look amazing."

I touched the screen, caressing the image of her glorious

cheek and hair. "I am but a reflection of the beauty in front of me."

She laughed, covering her face. "Where do you come up with this stuff? Do you have a handbook or something?"

"Sì, it's called 'How to Woo Samantha Caine' and I own the only copy in existence."

"You're funny." Her smile didn't slip for a moment, and my cheeks were already aching.

"Funny looking, you mean."

Laughing again, she adjusted in her chair. "So, what do you have to eat tonight?"

I held my plate up to the camera for her to see.

"Wow, that looks amazing!"

"And you, bella?"

"Lasagna!" A beeping noise sounded in her room, and she launched out of her seat. The same background view for the last three months—the extended-stay hotel. The microwave door opened and closed. She sat back down, showing me a black container with a clear plastic cover.

"Frozen dinner for date night?" My first night back in Brenton, I'd prepare a home-cooked feast for her. No more microwave meals.

She gave a quick shrug, distracted by something to the side of her computer. I heard a flicking noise. She moved from one side to the other, then winked at me. She was gone again and the overhead light went out. As she took her seat, gentle lights danced against her face.

"Candles?"

"I thought the ambiance, my dress, hair and makeup were more important than the food." She pulled back the plastic cover and picked up a fork.

I did the same, diving into my meal. "Can you believe it? Less than a month before I'm home?"

Covering her mouth, she said, "It's funny. It feels like it's going so fast, but so slow at the same time."

"So, you still have not found the right apartment?"

She swore she'd been looking, but it had been over three months already, and she hadn't moved yet. "Lucy came with me to a horrible basement apartment this morning. It was gross and the floorboards all squeaked. She actually suggested I move in with her!" She pretended to cringe.

"That would be..." How to politely suggest the woman who'd become her best friend over the last few months was not roommate material? At least, not for Samantha.

"A nightmare!" Her face was brilliant, just like every video call we had since she left. There'd been tears on both sides, sadness, but always the smiles. I hadn't needed to give her the ring. Even so far apart, we grew closer every day.

"Are you ready—" Mario whipped my door open and leaned in, his face pinching as he took in the scene. He couldn't see the screen from the doorway. "What are you doing? Are you watching—"

"Vaffanculo!" I waved my hands angrily. "Get out!"

Samantha chuckled. "Hi, Mario!"

"Is that my girlfriend?" He marched over to my desk, wrapping an arm around my shoulders and leaning in to see her. "Buonasera, bellissima! No wonder Antonio's late."

"Late for what?"

"For nothing," I said, pushing him away.

He grabbed my face and kissed my cheek soundly. "We're going to the club. I need my wingman."

Samantha raised an eyebrow. "Your wingman?"

"He's the best I've ever had. The women flock to us, he wiggles that little ring, and I get them all."

I shook my head at him, his vast exaggerations, and turned back to her. "You know it's not like that, sì? Most nights we spend with our friends or Chiara and her group. He's not the Casanova he thinks he is."

Mario shoved me playfully.

"He's mine for the next half hour, Mario, so buzz off." She'd bonded with him over something the day I left them at the villa together. I never asked what, just appreciated they got along so well.

"Don't forget to call me when you're bored of him!" He leaned in and kissed the camera before I could move it out of his way.

Samantha laughed loudly, shielding her face. "My eyes!"

Mario focused on me, unable to contain his grin. "You know she loves me, right?"

"Mario, I'd love you more if you gave us some time alone." She motioned for him to leave.

"Alright, you two lovebirds. You have thirty minutes!" He waved to her and headed out, throwing a wink at me over his shoulder.

"You handle him very well, bella."

She hopped out of her chair again. "Thirty minutes means no time to waste. Guess what I—" She sat in front of the camera. "—got in the mail yesterday?"

"My Christmas present?"

"Did you send something?" Her brows and shoulders dropped. "I thought we were waiting until you got home?"

"No, sorry, that was a joke. What did you get?"

She pushed her lasagna aside and stared at her lap, taking a deep breath. Her arms moved and there was a sound like folding paper. It was difficult to tell in the candlelight, but her cheeks appeared to redden.

"Test results?"

Her lips twitched, and she held the sheet of paper in front of the camera. It trembled slightly, but I could make it out: Her test came back clear. Mine had been completed months ago.

"Why am I so embarrassed by this? It's just a standard STD test." She folded it and placed it to the side.

"Because it represents another step in our relationship, and we both know how much you love speaking about your feelings."

Her eyes flicked up to me and back down at her letter. "Ha, ha."

"So, there's just one more thing we must speak of." I pushed my food aside and leaned forward. "If we'll be skipping the condoms when I get home, you'll be on birth control?"

She nodded, not looking up at me. "Have been for a long time."

"It's not perfect, though."

"What would you do?" Her lovely smile faded. Serious words were never her strong suit.

"If you became pregnant?" My thumb drifted to my lips, and I toyed with my ring. There was an answer I wanted to give, and then there was the right choice. "I'd ask what you wanted."

"If I didn't want to keep it?"

"I'd try to change your mind but would respect your wishes."

"But if I did?"

I lowered my hand to lean on it, smiling at her until she looked back up. Her face was drawn, serious. I blinked slowly, staring into her captivating eyes, which didn't quite settle on me. One of the worst things about a video chat. The eyes were never right.

"Samantha, I would tell every person I know that the most miraculous woman in the world was having my child. I would celebrate every day, go to every class, every doctor's appointment, and do anything you asked. I would be the happiest man on the planet."

Her lips tightened as I spoke, and her gaze snapped to the ceiling. I knew this face. The first time I'd seen it was the night we truly met, when she told me of her sister's illness. This was her *don't cry* expression. Perhaps the answer I wanted to give most was the right one, after all.

She composed herself and her smile slowly re-emerged. "Well, I guess that's settled, isn't it?"

"Would you prefer we talk about the weather?"

"What's the first thing you want to do when you get home?" She pulled her frozen dinner over and resumed eating.

"I'm assuming you mean after I've kissed you, held you, and made love to you for three days straight?"

Covering her mouth, she spluttered, "Three days?"

"You booked two weeks off, sì?"

"I did, but I may need some food before the first three days are up. I was thinking more like we should go to Caruther's."

"Together? Or shall we meet at the bar? And I can try to pick you up again?"

"Maybe I'd even let you introduce yourself this time."

"Would you say yes if I asked you out?"

"I don't know. See, I've got this boyfriend I'm kind of fond of..."

"Kind of fond of?"

"Very fond of?"

"We'll have to work on that."

She scrunched her nose. "Does that mean more talking about our feelings?"

"There will be a great deal of talking about our feelings once I'm home in Michigan."

"Ugh. You sure you don't want to stay in Naples longer?"

"Not a chance. I love this city and this job, but I'd rather be wherever you are."

She stared out from the screen, eyes still not quite on mine. From smile to frown, finally to downcast eyes. I couldn't feel her heart beating against my chest or hear her breath change, but I still understood.

"Samantha, look at me."

Her head shook, but she looked up through her eyelashes, jaw tight.

"I love you. Stop doubting that. I'm a grown man who makes his own choices and my choice is you. In some ways, it's been you for eleven years, and will continue being you for as long as you'll have me."

The jaw relaxed, and her face rose with a soft smile. "I know."

"And it will even be you as long as it takes for you to figure out you love me, too."

She rolled her eyes but didn't deny it.

It was just words. Words I wanted to hear, but patience

was the key to her heart. Her fears were still in the way, but we had a lifetime to work on that together.

Because she loved me as deeply as I loved her.

And eventually, she'd admit it to both of us.

THE END OF BOOK 2

BOOK 3: What happens when Sam and Antonio learn his project's been extended four more months? A last-minute flight home for Christmas sounds perfect, but when they find themselves in the middle of another mystery and with a gunman on their heels, their relationship will be tested like never before.

Continue the story with *Disarming Caine* at
https://janetoppedisano.com/DisarmingCaine

BONUS SHORT STORY: It's the last day before college exams and a nervous Antonio approaches his secret crush (Sam) after her Roman Art and Archaeology presentation.

Get your copy of *Admiring Caine* at
https://bf.janetoppedisano.com/9tje3ykn5t

ACKNOWLEDGMENTS

When I started planning the 'Samantha Caine' series, it was a trilogy and this book didn't exist in the list. The second book was actually supposed to be what's now become the third book. Confused yet? Welcome to the club!

While I was working with my amazing editor, Miranda Darrow, on *Burning Caine*, we played around with adding some epilogues to that story. Sam and Antonio were going to have their big reunion, then... the first epilogue candidate was their first time making love. We chucked that. The second epilogue candidate was their last morning together in Naples (without the ring exchange). We also chucked that.

After writing what's now the third book (*Disarming Caine*), I went back to those two deleted epilogues and started creating a story to fill in the missing days. The entire purpose was to watch Sam's trip to Naples unfold, so I had a firm grasp on the evolution of their relationship.

What started as two chapters became a forty-thousand word novella. But the more I looked at it, the more I knew I was missing some of the story.

So, I dug back in, added subplots, changed characters, and ramped it up to more than double the original length.

If you'd like some more specifics on the original novella story, I invite you to join my newsletter. I love sharing these behind-the-scenes glimpses into my stories.

So many thanks to all my beta readers: Paula and Pat, who are always there to read everything I write; Colin, Melissa, Tara, and the crew from Hidden Gems. Your thoughtful feedback and excitement over the evolution of Sam and Antonio's story is incredibly helpful.

More thanks to my editor, Miranda Darrow, for all her tough love, her keen eye, and the way she knows these characters almost as well as I do!

And finally, I'd like to thank you, my reader. Without you, I'd just be typing in my basement (or at my dining room table or in a hockey rink or in the car) for nothing. Knowing someone out there is going to read my words and find a little bit of enjoyment or an escape for a few hours means the world to me. So yeah, thanks again!

- Janet

About Janet

Janet Oppedisano delivers award-winning romantic suspense with smart, driven women and sexy, protective men that will keep you on the edge of your seat. Her heroines excel in their fields and aren't looking for love—until they meet the charismatic heroes who fall hard and fast for them. Throw in gripping mysteries, heart-pounding danger, and a touch of history or legend, and you've got stories that keep you hooked.

With a Mountie father and a Navy diver husband, Janet's life has been steeped in adventure, inspiring her high-stakes stories. She's lived all over Canada, from the Maritimes to the Prairies, and her books reflect the authenticity and depth of her journey.

When she's not plotting her next twist, Janet is baking, hiking, traveling, or cheering for her hockey goalie son.

And if you're wondering about her last name, it's pronounced oh-ped-ih-SAH-no—just like it looks. Honest!

**You can find Janet and all her social media links at:
https://janetoppedisano.com**